LENORA BELL

What a Difference a Duke Makes

❧ School for Dukes ❧

AVONBOOKS

An Imprint of HarperCollinsPublishers

Excerpt from *For the Duke's Eyes Only* copyright © 2018 by Lenora Bell.

WHAT A DIFFERENCE A DUKE MAKES. Copyright © 2018 by Lenora Bell. All rights reserved. Printed in the United States of America. No part of this book may be used or reproduced in any manner whatsoever without written permission except in the case of brief quotations embodied in critical articles and reviews. For information, address HarperCollins Publishers, 195 Broadway, New York, NY 10007.

First Avon Books mass market printing: April 2018

Print Edition ISBN: 978-0-06-269248-1
Digital Edition ISBN: 978-0-06-269242-9

Cover illustration by Paul Stinson
Cover lettering by David Gatti
Cover photograph by Shirley Green Photography

Avon, Avon & logo, and Avon Books & logo are registered trademarks of HarperCollins Publishers in the United States of America and other countries.
HarperCollins is a registered trademark of HarperCollins Publishers in the United States of America and other countries.

FIRST EDITION

18 19 20 21 22   QGM   10 9 8 7 6 5 4 3 2 1

"Not one in one thousand governesses would lecture me as you do, Miss Perkins."

"As a governess I have a duty to point out misbehavior."

"Impudent minx."

Why was he grinning at her as if he liked impudent minxes more than anything? And why couldn't she stop noticing how nicely shaped his lips were? Firm on top, yet sensually flared below.

"Perhaps I deserve a thorough tongue-lashing," he mused.

Which sounded quite wicked when spoken in such a low, husky voice.

His gaze shifted to her lips. "Are you planning to give me another?"

"Only if you're bad, Your Grace."

He must have taken a step nearer to her. Or had she been the one to move closer? *So close.*

A reckless desire formed in her mind, blotting out her customary good sense. A desire to misbehave. Just this once.

"Or . . ." She rose to her tiptoes, placing her palms against his rock-solid chest. "I could be the bad one . . ."

By Lenora Bell

WHAT A DIFFERENCE A DUKE MAKES
BLAME IT ON THE DUKE
IF I ONLY HAD A DUKE
HOW THE DUKE WAS WON

Coming Soon
FOR THE DUKE'S EYES ONLY

For my parents, with love.
Thanks for the overflowing bookshelves.

Acknowledgments

Writing romance novels is a privilege and a pleasure, and I'm blessed to have so many people in my life to guide me on this grand adventure. Many thanks to my witty and wise agent, Alexandra Machinist, and my wonderful editor, Carrie Feron. I'm indebted to Carolyn Coons and everyone else on the fabulous team at Avon Books. Everlasting gratitude to Neile and Rachel for their careful reads of the manuscript. My family gave me support and love every day. My brilliant brother, Carl, assisted with historical research. Mr. Bell . . . you make me believe in happily-ever-afters. Finally, to all the amazing readers, bloggers, librarians, and booksellers . . . thank you so much for loving and championing romance!

Chapter 1

❧

"**Y**OU'RE LATE," SAID Mrs. Trilby, staring down her long nose at Mari.

"Only f-fifteen minutes," gasped Mari, wiping raindrops from her cheeks, her heart still pounding from running the entire distance from the coaching inn.

"Punctuality, Miss Perkins, is the cornerstone of my agency."

"I'm dreadfully sorry, truly I am. There was a lame girl trying to cross a crowded avenue and I was afraid she'd be crushed. I sprang to her assistance, but while I was helping her several children made off with my trunk. Little ruffians."

"Humph," sniffed Mrs. Trilby. "A common enough scheme to rob country folk. You should have been on your guard against trickery."

"And let the poor girl be trampled to death?"

"Heaven helps those who help themselves, Miss Perkins."

"Well I'm here now," Mari said brightly, "and ready to be a credit to your agency."

"I'm afraid Mrs. Folsom was in no humor to wait. She required a governess immediately and I supplied her with one." Mrs. Trilby's gaze flicked over

Mari's wrinkled, travel-stained pelisse. "I have a registry of presentable, punctilious ladies waiting for situations."

"But I was promised the position. I have your letter right here." She drew it out of her reticule and presented it as evidence that she'd been offered the position as governess to Mr. Folsom, a mill owner with a brood of eight children.

Not too fine a family, nor too genteel.

Mrs. Trilby folded her hands on top of her desk. "The position has been filled."

"But—"

"No buts, Miss Perkins. My Superior Governesses must always be scrupulously ahead of schedule. You might seek more suitable employment, perhaps as a scullery maid."

Mari crumpled the letter in her fist.

She'd spent the last decade studying Latin, geography, and history into the wee hours of the morning, after all her many duties and chores at the Underwood Orphanage and Charity School were finished.

She was not going to become a scullery maid.

A governess would receive a higher salary and precious free days that would allow her to follow the clues she'd recently uncovered about her parentage.

Hope flooded her heart.

To find her kin. To belong somewhere. It was all she'd ever wanted.

She folded her hands together and took a deep breath. "I'm qualified to be a governess to a tradesperson's family. Is there another position, perhaps? I can't afford to be particular. I'll accept anything, no matter how difficult or insalubrious the conditions.

Give me a dozen children and you'll not hear me complain."

"A post for a girl of your circumstances does not simply materialize out of thin air, you understand."

Mari swallowed a sharp retort.

A girl of her circumstances.

An orphan raised in a charity school. Unwanted and burdensome.

She'd learned the hard way that no one wanted a girl like her to exhibit any backbone.

She'd learned to bite her tongue. Bide her time.

Hide her true emotions with a smile and a proverb.

"I'll wait then," she said with a decisive nod. Though she couldn't afford to stay in London very long.

"A waste of your time," said Mrs. Trilby. "I only offered you the Folsom post because you studied under my dear schoolmate, Mrs. Crowley. God rest her soul."

Mrs. Crowley. Even her name made Mari's belly lurch. The headmistress at Underwood had made her childhood a misery.

She could well imagine the two women had been bosom friends, as they shared a similarly glacial and unsympathetic disposition.

"This was your one chance, Miss Perkins," said Mrs. Trilby. "Now good day to you."

Her one chance. The chance to break free from the stifling confines of the charity school. To discover the truth of her birth and make something of her life.

"Mrs. Trilby, I do implore you to reconsider. I've no family or friends in London, and nowhere to go. I've never even left Derbyshire before now. Besides which, all of my possessions were stolen this morn-

ing. I do hope you might find it in your heart to help
me find another family."

"Quite a tale of woe." Mrs. Trilby rose from her
desk, her expression stern and unyielding. "If I had
a shilling for every girl who thought it my duty in
life to rescue her, I'd be a very rich woman indeed."
Gripping Mari by the elbow, she steered her out of
her office, back through the parlor, and toward the
entrance hall.

A maid stood at the ready with Mari's bag and
umbrella.

Dread clutched at Mari's throat. "Please, Mrs.
Trilby. You wouldn't cast me out into—"

"Good day, Miss Perkins."

The door slammed in her face.

Mari's shoulders slumped.

Well this was nothing new. Life had been slam-
ming doors on her since birth. Abandoned at the
orphanage when she was a babe, she'd known only
harsh words and hunger.

*Wicked, ungrateful girl. Plain and unpleasing. You'll
never amount to anything.*

Where could she go now? There were few options
for orphaned girls of no family or fortune.

The pretty charity school girls sometimes married
farmers and left in a one-horse cart, with no further
need of the education they'd received at Underwood.

Freckled and unfortunately red-haired girls like
Mari had to create their own opportunities, or spend
their entire lives within the gray stone walls of Underwood.

She would eat her straw bonnet before she returned to that cold, lonely cage.

Heaven helps those who help themselves.

She'd known that no one would hand her anything on a silver platter.

There was nothing for it but to march back inside and find a way to convince Mrs. Trilby to give her another chance. But before she could move, a stout woman in a tall bonnet trimmed with gold braid swept past her and rang the bell.

The door opened. "Miss Dunkirk? We're not expecting you," said the maid.

"A word with your mistress, if you please," said Miss Dunkirk in a loud voice.

Recognizing her opportunity, Mari snuck in behind Miss Dunkirk.

Mrs. Trilby appeared at the door to her offices. "Why, whatever is the matter, Miss Dunkirk? Why aren't you at Grosvenor Square?"

"I'll never go back to that den of vipers, Mrs. Trilby," barked Miss Dunkirk. "Not if you shower me with all the jewels in Christendom."

"But I had such high hopes for your success." Consternation wrinkled Mrs. Trilby's brow. "If you can't make those children behave, then all is lost."

Something was amiss. Miss Dunkirk had left her post precipitously. Could this be an opportunity for Mari?

"Those little heathens have run away from me for the very last time," huffed Miss Dunkirk.

Mrs. Trilby caught sight of Mari. "I thought I made myself very clear, Miss Perkins," she said coldly. "Good day to you." She motioned Miss Dunkirk to follow her. "Come, Miss Dunkirk, have a spot of tea and tell me all about it."

Determined to learn more, Mari surreptitiously ripped one of the black grosgrain ribbons from her bonnet.

"Oh dear." She waved the torn ribbon at the maid. "Have you a needle and thread?"

The maid gave her a sour look. "One moment, miss."

When she was alone, Mari raced to Mrs. Trilby's door, knelt down, and flattened her ear to the keyhole.

"I've half a mind to retire completely," she heard Miss Dunkirk say. "My nerves have suffered a severe strain."

"Please don't retire, I beseech you!" wailed Mrs. Trilby.

"They don't want an honest, hard-working governess, Mrs. Trilby. What they want is a ruddy clergyman."

"A clergyman?"

"To perform an exorcism of demons. Those are not children, Mrs. Trilby. They are Lucifer's imps in human form! And their father? *Well!*" Miss Dunkirk gusted an enormous sigh. "He's the worst sinner of all."

She lowered her voice so that Mari only caught fragments of her next words.

Stormy . . . changeful . . . Beelzebub himself . . . Babylonish scarlet women.

And something that sounded very much like *damned* and *bastards*, though Mari was certain a superior governess would never speak such words aloud.

"Oh. My," Mrs. Trilby replied faintly. "Sherry in your tea? No? I'll take just a drop." There was the clink of china and the sound of liquid being poured. "That makes four governesses in two months. I'm at my wits' end. I've no idea what to do."

"Do, Mrs. Trilby? *Do?*" Miss Dunkirk's voice rose

shrilly and her *r*'s trilled with indignation. "Why, you mustn't *do* anything. If you care for decency, if you value propriety, if you prize the unsullied reputation of this agency, you will do nothing at all."

"You mean I shouldn't send him a replacement? What a shocking notion."

"That's precisely what I mean. Make him suffer for his transgressions, I say. Somebody ought to."

"There is, of course, the matter of the rather large fee he's already paid me."

"Which he must forfeit. It's not your fault his children are ungovernable."

There was a pause. The chime of a teacup meeting a saucer. "You know, Miss Dunkirk, I've had nothing but trouble from that man and his unholy offspring," said Mrs. Trilby, a note of defiance creeping into her voice. "I've my reputation to consider."

"Quite right, Mrs. Trilby. Quite right. You mustn't send him anyone else. Not even if he crawls here on his hands and knees and begs."

A snort from Mrs. Trilby. "I can't imagine a duke begging for anything. No doubt Banksford believes highly qualified, morally irreproachable governesses grow on trees and may be plucked at whim like ripe cherries."

A *what*? Mari sucked in her breath. A *duke*?

Mrs. Trilby may as well have said *a mysterious sea serpent inhabiting a Scottish highland lake*. Or *a supernatural monster patched together by a mad scientist and animated through electricity*.

The daring plan she'd been forming hadn't included anything as terrifying and mythical as a duke.

The sound of footsteps sent her running back to the parlor.

The maid handed her a mending basket and Mari

refastened her bonnet ribbon with hasty, uneven stitches. She'd heard all she needed to hear.

The Duke of Banksford, of Grosvenor Square, required a governess.

And Mrs. Trilby had washed her hands of him.

She slapped her bonnet over her braids, tied the ribbons tightly, and hoisted her cloth bag and umbrella.

Of course, there was the small problem that she wasn't even remotely qualified to be governess to a duke's privileged offspring. But this was no time for timidity.

As she left the agency, the noise and clamor of Old Bond Street assaulted her senses, reminding her that she was, most definitely, not in Derbyshire any more.

The air smelled of horse dung, coal smoke, and wet woolens.

Carriages lurched past, their occupants briefly visible—a crescent of pale cheek, a child's nose pressed to a window, puffs of breath making a hazy cloud on the glass.

She opened her reticule, squinting at the black silk lining in the vain hope that her funds had multiplied since her last inventory. They had not. She had the grand sum of one pound ten shillings to her name.

A portly gentleman slowed his gait. "Are you, perhaps, in some difficulty, miss?" he asked, with a suggestive look that made her skin crawl.

She closed her reticule and pointedly turned away from him, hoping he would go away.

"Why don't you come and have a nice hot meal with me?" the man persisted.

Did she have naïve country girl stamped across her forehead? Was everyone going to attempt to take advantage of her?

Lifting her umbrella handle, which was cunningly shaped like a parrot's head, she brandished it menacingly. "I'll thank you to move along, sir."

The man eyed the parrot's sharp beak and then shrugged and ambled away.

She waited for him to disappear around a corner before consulting her map and setting off toward Grosvenor Square.

Wind howled in her ears. Horses whinnied, plodding through puddles.

Something is about to begin, the raindrops pattered on the paving stones.

If you are brave enough to chase it, the wind whistled back.

A passing cart splashed muddy water onto her skirts. *Botheration.* Now she was even less superior.

When she reached the square, a maid carrying a market basket informed her that the duke lived at Number Seventeen.

Educating a nobleman's privileged and pampered children shouldn't prove too difficult, given that she was accustomed to instructing orphaned girls with troubled souls and bleak outlooks.

It wasn't the children who worried her—it was the father. He would probably take one look at her shabby coat and muddy boots and slam yet another door in her face.

She'd read about aristocrats in the pages of her favorite novels, borrowed from a circulating library, but she had no practical experience with the nobility. On rare occasions, wealthy patronesses had visited Underwood, lifting their snow-white hems daintily to avoid touching anything to do with orphans.

The matrons had delighted in telling the cautionary tale of a girl who had returned in disgrace from a maid's apprenticeship in a baronet's household, already showing signs of increasing.

With her slight figure and pernicious freckles, Mari rather doubted the same fate might befall her. Only . . . she paused and hugged her traveling bag to her chest. What if the duke was a roving-fingered lecher who fancied anything in skirts?

Would he attempt to besiege her at the earliest opportunity?

Besieged by the devilish duke.

It sounded like the title of a lurid novel. One where the meek, doe-eyed governess shrank from the advances of her elderly employer, who walked with a limp and had a wife, or two, locked in his attic.

Provident that Mari wasn't doe-eyed. Or meek. At least not on the inside.

She may have had to adopt a docile façade, but inside she was a seething pit of rebellion.

But a superior governess would never *seethe*. Oh Heavens, no.

The moment she stepped inside his gate she must be the most prim, proper, and unassailable governess in all of London.

Absolutely no betraying of her true emotions, or her less-than-superior background.

She must remain calm. Impassive. Even if he was the stormiest, most arrogant duke ever to darken the streets of London.

And even if his gate was an immense, glowering wrought iron affair with the motto *mutare vel timere sperno* emblazoned on a gleaming brass placard.

He scorned to change or fear.

Perfect. Even his gate was arrogant.

What was she doing here? Could she deceive a *duke?* Descended from a long line of dukes, no doubt.

All of whom scorned to change, and most likely ate country governesses for breakfast.

Beyond his unyielding gate stretched a daunting mountain of glittering marble stairs.

You don't belong here.

Before she could lose her nerve, a strong gust of wind caught her umbrella and fairly carried her up the steps, depositing her in front of the red-painted door.

It was a desperate gamble. It was also her best hope at the moment.

She closed her umbrella and straightened her spine.

It was time to seize the day. Or the duke, as it were.

He was merely a man. Fortune favored the bold. And no adventure ever began with a bell un-rung.

"KINDLY INFORM OUR mother that I don't need a wife," said Edgar. "I need a governess. The twins chased away another one today."

"Not another one," exclaimed his younger sister, India, from her chair by the fireplace. "How many is that now?"

"Four governesses. Two months. One man at the end of his rope." Edgar scratched a vehement row of crosshatches on the steam engine plans he was drawing, shading the crankshaft to set it apart from the cylinder.

Perhaps somewhere in the intricate linkage system he would find the peace of mind which eluded him.

Fatigue and frustration scratched at his mind like the pen nib scoring the page. Why couldn't he identify the missing piece to the puzzle? The engine was still so heavy and cumbersome. They'd need three horses to draw the blasted thing.

"Maybe Mama is right," said India. "A wife would

oversee your household, including the hiring of governesses."

"You know I could order *you* to stay here and mind the twins for a spell."

"Bollocks," India replied with a smirk. "I haven't a motherly bone in my body. And you know I'm preparing for my next archaeological expedition."

"How could I forget? Since I finance your reckless jaunts around the globe." Although he loved thinking of his fearless sister giving the male antiquities experts hell, from Cairo to Athens. She'd only returned a week ago from her last expedition.

"I'll spend some time with the children before I leave again," India promised. "Are they truly so unruly?"

"Half-wild, really. Arrived on my doorstep without warning two months ago. Wary eyes and shallow breathing. Abandoned by Sophie, raised in poverty in that squalid French seaside village. Why didn't she tell me about them sooner? I would have acknowledged them in a heartbeat. Given them a better life here in England."

The frustration of it hit him square in the gut. Why had she kept the twins a secret from him?

Not good enough for husband. Not good enough for father.

"She wasn't much for family, Sophie, if I remember correctly," said India.

"She didn't like anything hemming her in. Lovers. Children. Walls." He'd been infatuated with the worldly poetess, ten years his senior, with the epic, unheeding love of callow youth.

She'd crushed his heart and left him with nothing but a deep-seated belief that love was a twisted, damning emotion that gave another person far too much power.

Never again.

Now he had the twins, Michel and Adele, the illegitimate product of their affair.

And they didn't seem to want him either.

"I've built this life, India, this useful life that progresses day by day with precision and purpose. My foundry. My steam engines. And now these needful little cogs are stuck in the workings. I don't know the first thing about children. Isn't it enough to feed them, clothe them, and provide them with the most expensive damned governesses in London?"

"One would think."

"Yet they terrorize the governesses and run away at every opportunity. They're off in the park again right now. The coachman will bring them home any moment."

"Give them time," said India with a sympathetic smile. "All of this sudden upheaval must be bewildering to them . . . and to you."

"I'm glad Sophie sent them to me, and I've vowed to give them every advantage in life, but it's rotten timing, India. I'm so close . . ." He stared down at the engine plans. "So close to producing a steam-powered fire engine lightweight enough to be drawn by a single horse."

"A single horse? Why would that be better?"

"Because it will arrive at fires faster, and it will pump water farther and douse even the most aggressive blazes." He traced the troublesome boiler with his pen. "Plus, it won't show up drunk to the fire, like half of the fire brigade do."

"I think it's wonderful what you're achieving with your foundry, but certain other people aren't so thrilled."

"I suppose you mean Mother."

"Let me see, I want to get this right." India lifted her nose in the air and assumed the supercilious tones of the dowager duchess. "'Please tell the duke that his dabbling in trade and commerce is most unseemly, ruinous for his reputation, lowers his station, and will make it more difficult to attract a suitable wife and mother to his heir.'"

"Ruinous?" Edgar sputtered. "How do you like that? It's my foundry that lifted this family from the threat of impoverishment after our father nearly ran it into the ground."

He held out one scarred, burned hand. "Tell her I'm more foundry man than duke now and nothing will ever change that."

"You could visit and tell her in person. It's been nearly a decade. When you disappeared for those seven long years she pretended not to care, but I could tell she was devastated." India's eyes clouded over. "It wasn't easy for any of us. Not knowing where you were, or whether you were safe."

Edgar's quill dug so hard it cut through the paper. "I never meant to cause you pain. I had to leave. Before I left, she told me she never wanted to see me again."

"She's changed since father's death. And she's longing for grandchildren."

"Then you'll have to marry and produce some. I'm too busy at the moment."

India lifted her brow and gave him a quelling stare. "Well that's not going to happen." She drew a banknote from somewhere beneath her mannish coat. "Fifty pounds," she said, waving the note.

He gave her a quizzical look.

"Fifty pounds says you'll marry first and produce a grandchild for our long-suffering Mama."

Edgar threw down his quill and opened the drawer of his desk. "I'll raise you fifty. One hundred pounds says you'll be the first to marry."

"Ha. May as well burn that note, instead of wager it."

Edgar smiled. It would take a special sort of gentleman to match his sister's unconventionality, wits, and fire.

"You'd better be careful," she laughed. "I could ask Mother to draw up a list of suitable debutantes and spread a rumor that you're on the marriage mart."

"You wouldn't."

His sister smiled wickedly.

Oh God. She probably would. He'd better send her back overseas quickly.

"What I need is a list of suitable governesses," said Edgar.

"What are the requirements?"

"Nerves of steel. Stomach of iron. Eyes like a hawk. Brawny as a boxer."

India chuckled. "Why don't you put Robertson in a gown and have him double as the governess?" She grinned at the butler as he entered the room.

Robertson gave her a horrified look.

"For the salary I'm offering," said Edgar, "there ought to be a line of broad-shouldered, steely nerved governesses at my door vying for the position."

Robertson cleared his throat. "There's just the one, Your Grace. And she's not particularly broad of shoulder."

"The one what?" asked Edgar.

"The one governess. At your door."

Edgar squinted at him. "Dunkirk only left a few hours ago."

"Nevertheless, there is a governess here."

Edgar had allowed Mrs. Fairfield to screen the

other governesses and they'd all been less than satisfactory. "Bring her to me, Robertson. I want to interview this one in person. Test her mettle."

"Very good, Your Grace." Robertson bowed and left.

Perhaps Edgar's life could progress as planned, after all. "Maybe this will be the one, India. Maybe she'll be able to calm the children and restore some order to this chaos."

"At least she's punctual," said India. "That's got to count for something."

"COME IN, DEARIE, come in out of this dreadful wind and rain. When will it ever decide to stop raining, do you suppose? Why, it's nearly the middle of May!" A tall, gray-haired woman wearing an elegant black silk gown ushered Mari into a desert of blinding white marble, accented by bloodred carpets and enamel cloisonné vases set on carved wooden stands.

Did children really live here? Mari could see no evidence of them. No scuffmarks on the marble, no stray toys in the corners.

Those precariously perched vases, thin as eggshells, wouldn't be safe around any children of her acquaintance.

"Oh bless me. I haven't introduced myself. I'm Mrs. Fairfield, the duke's housekeeper. Here, give me your bonnet."

As she spoke, she bustled around Mari, untying her bonnet, handing her bag and umbrella to a liveried footman, and removing her gloves. "I can't believe you arrived so swiftly."

"Have the children returned?" asked Mari. "Miss Dunkirk intimated that they had run away."

"I've sent the coachman to fetch them home. They'll be in the park, I expect."

The butler who had greeted Mari upon arrival returned to the entrance hall. "His Grace wishes a personal interview with Miss Perkins."

"He does?" asked Mrs. Fairfield, her eyes questioning.

The butler nodded. "He said he wished to test her mettle."

Tested by the devilish duke. Mari gulped. "Very well," she said bravely. "I'm ready."

"Let me have a look at you." Mrs. Fairfield captured Mari's hands and lifted her arms. "Why, you're as rosy cheeked and fresh as a daisy. But you're just a slip of a thing and your hands are freezing. After your audience with His Grace you'll have a nice hot cup of tea."

Couldn't she have the tea before *the duke?* With an effort, Mari tamped down the rumbling of hunger and fear in her belly.

"Come along, dear." Mrs. Fairfield tugged her toward a staircase bordered by mahogany banisters which gleamed so aggressively they appeared to be made from colored glass.

Mari had to trot to keep up with her. "Ah . . . silly me. I seem to have forgotten the children's names and ages."

"The twins, Michel and Adele, are nine," said Mrs. Fairfield over her shoulder.

She pronounced Michel in the French way, softening the *ch* and elongating the *i* into an *e*, so he must be male.

"And their mother?" Mari asked. "Is she in residence?"

Mrs. Fairfield stopped so abruptly that Mari nearly ran into her and had to grab hold of the banister to keep her balance.

"I thought Mrs. Trilby would have told you about the . . . unusual nature of this post."

"I expect she didn't have time. I was sent over so swiftly, and all."

Mrs. Fairfield searched her face for another moment before answering her question. "The twins were raised on the coast of France by a Moroccan nurse. A most unorthodox upbringing, though they did have an English tutor and their speech is quite correct. Their mother has passed away."

Did their unusual upbringing mean the children were illegitimate? It would explain Miss Dunkirk's whispered censure.

"They only have the duke, and he's very absorbed in his work," said Mrs. Fairfield, resuming her swift ascension.

Did dukes work? Perhaps Mrs. Fairfield meant brandy sipping. Or billiards.

The housekeeper turned at the first landing, walked up another flight of wide stairs, and traversed a hallway at a fast clip, almost as if she didn't wish to field any more questions.

She knocked forcefully on a carved oak door and cracked it open. "I've brought the new governess to meet you, Your Grace," she called into the room.

Before they could enter, a maid in a white apron and cap came flying down the hallway. "It's Laura, Mrs. Fairfield," she gasped. "She's set fire to the biscuits again."

"Well? Did you throw water on them?" asked Mrs. Fairfield.

"She upended a pan of drippings over the range and it flared up and singed her eyelashes clear off. And cook is out and no one knows what to do."

Mrs. Fairfield made an exasperated noise in the back of her throat. "I'm afraid I must leave you, Miss Perkins. Don't be frightened, dearie."

Which of course produced the opposite effect. Was this duke such a terror?

"Lady India is here so you won't be alone with him." Mrs. Fairfield squeezed Mari's hand and left her standing there.

Alone.

Merely a man. Merely a man.

She shook out her skirts, tucked a flyaway curl back into the braids atop her head, and marched purposefully into the room.

Banksford's head was bent over his desk, chestnut hair falling over his brow and obscuring his face as his quill scratched across a large piece of parchment.

He was garbed in a sober black coat and haphazardly tied cravat, quite different from the silk and frills she'd imagined the nobility wore.

"Good afternoon, Your Grace," she said in her most superior tones.

He raised his head.

Merely a larger-than-life monstrosity of a duke, she amended. *Though he'd clearly been assembled from all the best parts of mere mortal men.*

Glittering gray eyes. Shadowy cheekbones. An angular jaw and a commanding slash of a nose. The powerful shoulders and lean frame of a tavern boxer.

He didn't look pliable in the least.

Mari shivered, feeling slightly light-headed confronted by all of this blatant masculinity. She'd spent her whole life in a school for girls, after all.

"And you are . . . ?" he asked.

Name. She knew that one. "Miss Mari Perkins, Your Grace. Mari with an *i*—it rhymes with starry."

Why had she told him that? What a silly thing to say to a duke. He didn't care that she'd changed the spelling and pronunciation of Mary, the name the orphanage had assigned her, in a small, yet soul-sustaining, act of rebellion.

She gave a confident, businesslike nod. "I came from Mrs. Trilby's Agency for Superior Governesses." Which wasn't *entirely* untruthful. She'd walked here directly from the agency. And she *had* been promised a position.

Just not this one.

"It's lovely that you were able to come so swiftly, Miss Perkins," said the lady sitting near the fire. "I'm India. Which doesn't really rhyme with anything, I'm afraid."

Mari curtsied. "Pleased to meet you, my lady."

Lady India was the most beautiful creature Mari had ever seen, with hair the color of ripe blackberries, pale violet eyes, and high slanted cheekbones.

Though her attire was decidedly odd, almost rakish, even. A tailored gentleman's cutaway coat over a draped gown that almost appeared to be split down the center.

Mari dismissed the preposterous idea. The lady couldn't be wearing trousers.

"How old are you, Perkins?" asked the duke.

"Twenty, Your Grace. Though I've had the care and tutelage of young children for many years."

His unsettling gaze pierced through her clothing, skin, and bones to see through to her wildly beating heart. She stood taller under his scrutiny, careful to maintain a half smile on her lips and a calm, efficient tilt to her head.

She could tell he found her lacking by the way the line between his brows deepened.

"Your shoulders—" said the duke, staring in the general direction of her bosom "—are insufficiently brawny."

"Ah . . . I do apologize, Your Grace. I will begin performing strengthening exercises immediately."

Another frown. "And your smile is suspiciously cheerful."

He didn't want cheerful. Mari instantly dropped the smile. "How impertinent of it. I specifically told it to be stern and capable."

She matched the thunderous frown on the duke's face.

His eyes narrowed and he tapped his pen against the blotter. "Flippancy is not a trait I'm looking for in a governess."

"I meant no disrespect, Your Grace," she replied, keeping her expression neutral and humorless.

Her future rested in his hands.

His extremely large, surprisingly rugged hands. The hands of a man who knew hard labor. Rough-padded and crisscrossed with burns and scars.

Where had he acquired those scars?

He watched her closely. She widened her stance and threw back her shoulders in an attempt to appear more substantial. She held her breath, sending a silent prayer heavenward.

"You're too small, Perkins," he said.

"Never judge things by their appearances, Your Grace. I'm stronger than I appear."

Strong enough to survive the typhoid fever that

had taken Helena, her only friend, and left a gaping hole in Mari's heart.

Strong enough to withstand years of punishment, freezing damp, and deprivation.

"Spare me your proverbs, Perkins," said the duke. "I'm not a child."

"Of course you're not, Your Grace. You're definitely all man. That is to say, your shoulders are more than sufficiently brawny, er . . ."

What had come over her? She never dithered.

He was just so very *male*. She hadn't meant to let on that she'd noticed the breadth of his shoulders or the size of his hands, though what girl wouldn't notice?

"You're too small, Perkins." He dipped his quill in his gold filigree inkwell, signaling the end of the interview. "You won't do."

Chapter 2

❦

"WHAT DO YOU mean I'm too small?" Mari advanced on the duke. "I fail to see how that is relevant."

The duke sighed and set down his pen. "I owe you no explanations but since you don't appear to be leaving, I'll further elaborate that my son is afflicted with night terrors. His governess must be able to physically subdue him, which is nigh impossible at times, so heavy are his limbs, so violent his movements, and so profound his sleep."

Mari planted her muddy boots on his expensive carpet. She wasn't going anywhere. She wouldn't relinquish this chance for respectable work with a good salary, and free days, without a fight.

Night terrors were nothing new to her.

"You're making a mistake," she said. "I'm experienced with night terrors. I've cured several children of similar afflictions."

"I never make mistakes. Not anymore. My mistake-making days are over," was the very arrogant, very unyielding response.

Lady India snorted. "Really, Edgar? You sound like an arse right now."

The duke frowned.

Mari barely refrained from smiling at Lady India. "You scorn to change, is that right, Your Grace?"

He cocked his head. "You read my motto?"

"I read Latin, converse in French and I'm far stronger than I appear. Give me one week's trial, Your Grace. I promise you will see an improvement in the children."

Was his gaze softening slightly?

"Nothing ventured, nothing gained," she urged.

He shook his head. "You won't last two days."

"And why not, may I ask?"

"Because not only are you too slight of stature, you've an air of naïvety and optimism about you. My children are bound to dash your spirit and send you running back to your agency."

"I should like to see them try. I may have lived my whole life in the countryside, but I'm hardly naïve."

The weight of his stare turned solid footing to quicksand. Good Lord, but he was handsome.

And not in a foppish, bandbox sort of way.

In a manly, gruff-voiced, and wide-shouldered sort of way.

"Out of the question." He tapped his pen to the paper. "I never engage attractive, unmarried females. Too distracting for the footmen."

He considered her to be attractive? The novelty of the revelation momentarily stunned her to silence. She'd just been contemplating his inordinate beauty and . . . he felt the same way about her?

Impossible. It must be just another reason to dismiss her.

"I'll wear wire-rimmed spectacles," she offered.

"Won't help."

"White lace caps with long flaps over the ears." She mimed pulling the flaps down and tying them under her chin.

He frowned.

"Voluminous smocks," she tried. "Surely your footmen will be able to resist a bespectacled, freckled, cap-wearing spinster in a voluminous smock."

"Do stop badgering the girl, Edgar," chided Lady India. "She's from a reputable agency, is she not? And she can't be any worse than the others. They've all been unqualified disasters."

Mari smiled gratefully and Lady India returned the smile, her violet eyes dancing with humor. Such familiar speech between the lady and the duke. They must be intimates.

Mari cared not a whit if Lady India was one of the scarlet women Miss Dunkirk had whispered about with such disapproval. Right now the lady was her only ally, and Mari could use all the help she could get.

"The children are always running away, Miss Perkins," said Lady India.

"I was told that the coachman has been sent to search the park," said Mari.

"They always find their way home." A sliver of pride crept into the duke's voice.

"I wonder how they occupy themselves when they run away?" mused Lady India.

"I mean to ascertain exactly that," Mari said. "I'll gain their confidence posthaste and report back. Give me one week's trial, Your Grace."

He threw down his quill, rose abruptly, and slapped his hands down on either side of the desk. "Why are you still here, Perkins?"

She took an involuntary step backward and stumbled as her hip encountered an obstruction. Flinging out an arm for support, she encountered a handle and held on tight.

Unfortunately, the handle was attached to a large globe. Which was attached to . . . nothing.

She staggered sideways, the globe crashed to the floor along with several other objects on the table. Her foot crunched down on something which seemed to rise up like a claw to trap her boot. She did an awkward, foot-shaking dance, attempting to keep her balance.

A vicelike grip caught her by the waist and lifted her off the carpet.

"Damnation, Perkins! You've crushed my engine."

The duke's thumbs jabbed into her ribcage, making her breath come in short gasps.

"I'm terribly sorry," she panted. "If you'll just set me down . . ."

"Can't. It's stuck around your boot." He shook her by the waist in an attempt to dislodge whatever she'd stepped upon.

Her boots dangled over the carpet, her right foot still surrounded by a heavy weight.

Mari had to admit that her daring plan was not off to a promising start.

Apparently she'd destroyed something precious to the duke and he might shake her to death in retribution.

"Do you have to . . . agitate me . . . quite so hard?" she asked, through rattling teeth.

He stopped shaking her and did something much, much worse.

He shifted her weight in his arms, slung her over his shoulder, and began to march.

THE WRIGGLING WISP of woman he held over his shoulder couldn't weigh more than seven stone, soaking wet, yet Edgar could hardly fail to notice that her slender body was curved in all the best places.

Soft breasts jounced against his back.

A nicely rounded bottom squirmed beneath his palm.

"Let me go!" squeaked the destructive Miss Perkins, pounding his lower back with her small fists.

"Believe me, I want nothing more than for you to be gone, Perkins."

He already knew she wouldn't do. Too young and inexperienced.

Also, far too pretty.

His late father's appetite for comely servants had nauseated Edgar. He would never misuse his power or position in such a way, but why bring her into his home?

Besides, the children would only chase her away.

He strode to the hearth, clenching his jaw against the twinge of pain in his bad knee.

Lowering his bundle of indignant female into a chair across from India, he sank to his good knee and caught Miss Perkins by the ankle.

"Heavens!" she said, staring with startled eyes, as if transfixed by the sight of his hand up her skirts.

"My, my," said India with a chuckle. "This interview certainly took an unexpected turn." She grinned at Edgar, her shoulders shaking with suppressed merriment.

His sister always had enjoyed a good laugh at his expense.

Miss Perkins attempted to jerk her foot away from his grasp and only succeeded in jabbing him in the thigh with a shattered piece of metal.

"Hold still," he said.

"I hope you're not injured, Miss Perkins?" India asked.

The governess smoothed auburn curls back from her flushed and freckled cheeks.

She certainly wasn't a traditional beauty, but there was something arresting about her.

Thick braided coils of hair the color of sunlight filtering through rubies. Golden brown freckles scattered across her cheeks and the bridge of her small straight nose.

An unmistakably clever and challenging light in her blue eyes.

"I'm unharmed . . . I think." She ran her hands over her slim waist, setting her gown to rights and drawing his gaze to the curve of her small breasts, which had nearly been jostled out of her bodice by her upside-down journey.

"Can't say the same for my model engine." Gripping the thin metal framework, Edgar attempted to ease the engine over the toe of her boot, but it was tangled in her bootlaces.

He didn't want to cut her trim, elegant calf. All of her was slender and elegant.

Too slender.

Had she eaten anything lately? She had a hungry look about her.

He'd dined on meat pies for luncheon. If Miss Perkins had been there, he could have fed her some pastry, and then licked the crumbs from her fingers.

Good God. Why was he thinking about licking the governess? He never had such uncontrolled thoughts.

She must go. This instant.

Free her boot from his ruined handiwork and send her on her way, to destroy someone else's peace of mind.

His sister caught his eye and grinned. She'd always possessed the uncanny ability to read his mind.

"What is that thing, Your Grace? You called it an engine?" Miss Perkins bent her head to have a closer look. "Is it a toy for the children?"

"It's not a toy. It's a small-scale model of one of my steam engines."

India chuckled, confound her. "You might call it a toy, Miss Perkins. He does love to play with his miniature engines. He's planning an invasion, you see."

"Not an invasion," he said. "A railway line that will connect London and Birmingham. I've invested heavily in the London, Coventry, and Birmingham Railway Company, one of two companies vying to build the railroad. My Vulcan Foundry Works will supply the steam-powered engines for the railway, and soon, I hope, for a consolidated fire brigade of London."

"You build engines?" she asked, with a puzzled wrinkle between her brows.

Always the reaction he received. Dukes weren't supposed to engage in trade.

Even a governess knew as much.

"I'm perfecting a design right now with my chief engineer for a new version of a steam-powered fire engine that will be smaller in size and weight, while still generating far more pressure than the hand-pumped variety," he explained.

"Pray, don't encourage him, Miss Perkins," drawled India. "He's quite passionate on the subject and we'll be here until midnight having an exhausting conversation about exhaust pipes, molten metals, and all manner of ever-so-fascinating ramming and smelting techniques."

Molten. Ramming. The words echoed through the chamber.

Miss Perkins's cheeks flushed a deep pink.

His hands were still under her skirts.

End this swiftly.

"The laces must be cut and the boot removed," he said gruffly. "India." He held out his hand and his sister provided the dagger she always kept in a leather holster at her side.

"Oh," squeaked Miss Perkins, at the sight of the knife. "Must you cut them?"

His fingers closed around her calf, steadying her for his blade. The touch sent sparks running up his fingers, and fire licking along his spine.

Their gazes locked. Her lips parted.

He'd been so intent on his work, of late, with no time for female companionship.

No time for soft, slender limbs. Blue eyes like oxidized copper.

Her lower lip trembled when he raised the dagger. He made short work of her frayed bootlaces.

Her corset laces would be much more fun to cut.

Enough.

He clenched his jaw. He was no profligate like the late duke.

He wrenched the boot and the engine free and rose from the floor. Probably irreparably damaged, but he could try to bend it back into shape.

Miss Perkins folded her foot under her skirts, and her hands in her lap. "I trust you'll return my boot with expediency, Your Grace."

"And I trust that when you have both your boots, you'll use them to walk out of my library with expediency, Perkins. Straight back to your agency where you will inform Trilby that I require an older, more experienced, and far less fragile-boned governess."

"Humph." She gave an injured sniff. "I'm hardly fragile."

"Edgar," chided India. "Surely you won't send the

poor thing away with cut bootlaces. You should purchase her new footwear, at the very least."

"They *are* my only remaining shoes," said Miss Perkins. "My trunk was stolen by thieves this morning at the coaching inn."

"That's not my fault, Perkins," he growled. He couldn't keep from growling. These inconvenient urges were making him feel out of sorts. One more thing in his life that he didn't have any control over, it seemed.

"How dreadful." India clucked her tongue. "Well never mind. I'm sure you'll be able to purchase an entire new wardrobe with Edgar's very generous salary."

Now that was helpful.

If his hands hadn't been full of the shattered remains of his model engine, he might have throttled his meddlesome sister.

"About my salary, Your Grace," said Miss Perkins cheekily. "I'll require five pounds over what Miss Dunkirk was to be paid."

She was bold, he'd give her that. "You expect thirty-five pounds per annum?" he asked skeptically.

A momentary flicker of uncertainty crossed her face. "I'm a bargain at any price," she said.

India gave Miss Perkins a delighted smile. "I'm quite sure you are."

"And I'll want every other Thursday off," Miss Perkins continued.

"Only every *other* Thursday?" asked India.

"That's enough, India," said Edgar warningly.

"Oh, don't be such a bear." She turned to Miss Perkins. "He does bluster and growl but he's quite harmless, really."

Miss Perkins nodded crisply. "Then it's all settled. I'll begin my post immediately."

"Nothing is settled, Perkins." Edgar handed her back her boot.

Somehow, the situation had run away from him. They were already in league, India and Miss Perkins. Conspiring to overthrow his dominion over his own household.

Miss Perkins laced up the boot halfway and tied a knot in the shortened string. "I'll just go and fetch the children home, then." She rose from her chair and headed for the door.

"Don't move another inch, Perkins," Edgar commanded. "I haven't given you permission to leave."

She tossed him a sunny smile. "Splendid. Then you agree to keep me on as governess? I shan't disappoint you."

"That's not what I said."

"Then I may go and fetch the children?"

He eyed her warily.

India laughed. "I like you *Mari-rhymes-with-starry*. I think you're precisely what this household requires."

The starry-eyed Miss Perkins was precisely what he did *not* require—a small, yet dangerous, bundle of crackling energy ready to burn through what little remained of his sanity.

He was about to tell her as much when the door swung open and Mrs. Fairfield's kindly face appeared. "Pardon, Your Grace, but the twins have returned and 'tis a constable who escorted them home."

He tensed. "They're not in trouble, are they? Not injured in some way?" He'd have Miss Dunkirk's hide if any mishap had befallen them. They'd always returned none the worse for wear after their little excursions in nearby Hyde Park.

"Not a bit," said Mrs. Fairfield. "Though I do believe the constable might have sustained a minor injury. Something to do with a sling and a stone."

"That sounds about right." India laughed.

"I'd better go and smooth things over." Edgar started for the door.

"Don't move another inch, Your Grace," commanded Miss Perkins. "Leave everything to me."

And she spun on her heel and marched for the door.

Chapter 3

✦

"**D**ID THAT FEMALE just order me to stay?" Edgar asked incredulously.

"Like a foxhound in training." India's throaty chuckle reminded him of the dowager duchess, though he hadn't heard his mother's voice in many years.

"Flame-haired, glib-tongued, peace-destroying baggage."

India's grin widened. "So you noticed the color of her hair?"

"One could hardly fail to notice such a hue." He'd noticed more than her vibrant red locks. He'd been all too aware of her *everything*.

The intelligent spark in her eyes.

The impression she gave of constant movement, as if she were a flickering flame, licking at his library furniture as well as his composure.

"Poor Michel." India rose from her chair. "I didn't know he suffered from night terrors. I'm sure Miss Perkins will set him to rights."

He shook his head. "I can't hire her."

"And why not?"

"You saw what she did to my model engine. Too troublesome."

And tempting. Far too tempting.

"Footmen, eh?" India tilted her head. "I rather

think it would be dukes she'd distract. Give her a chance. What can be the harm? You're gentleman enough to resist a pretty face." She laid her hand on his arm. "You're not like Father."

"Precisely," he said shortly. "I'm nothing like Father." And never would be. Everything he did was done in opposition to that man's cursed memory.

The late duke had been a drunkard—Edgar never imbibed. His father had been a lecher with a taste for serving girls—Edgar would never make advances toward a servant.

His father had believed a nobleman should never dirty his hands with trade, and almost ruined the family in the process. Edgar had rebuilt their fortune with his foundry.

"Shall we see how Miss Perkins is faring with the constable?" asked India.

"More like how the constable is faring with Miss Perkins."

As they descended the stairs, India paused. "Oh I almost forgot to tell you the other reason I visited today. You're hosting an antiquities exhibition for me."

She drew a card from inside her jacket and handed it to him.

> *His Grace the Duke of Banksford is pleased to*
> *extend an invitation to an evening exhibition of*
> *the antiquities discovered by Lady India Rochester*
> *on her recent expedition to the temple complex at*
> *Karnak . . .*

"I can't host a society event here. You know that," said Edgar.

"You're turning into a hermit. All you do is work

on those engines. It might be diverting. Mrs. Fairfield would enjoy planning a party, I'm sure."

"I don't want a herd of inquisitive antiquarians poking about my house."

"Well they've already accepted their invitations, so there's nothing to be done," she said breezily. "Oh look." She pointed toward the entrance where the constable stood with his arms crossed over his leather belt. "Miss Perkins is lecturing the constable."

Indeed, the constable had a chagrined expression on his ruddy face, while Miss Perkins's blue eyes blazed with cold fire. The children stood on either side of her skirts, and Mrs. Fairfield hovered nearby.

"Poaching?" Miss Perkins exclaimed. "I must have misheard you."

"They was poaching, all right, miss," said the constable. "Shooting pigeons in Hyde Park, bold as you please."

Adele jutted out her chin. "We weren't poaching."

"We were hunting snakes," explained Michel.

"You shot a pigeon with your sling, young sir." The constable leaned forward. "And you clipped my ear in the process."

"They are dreadfully sorry about that. Aren't you, children?" asked Miss Perkins, bending to stare at first Michel and then Adele. "Apologize to the constable."

Michel scuffed the carpet with his boot. "I'm sorry for shooting you, sir. I was only trying to rescue our snake from that mean old pigeon. And I did it, too!"

He reached into his pocket and extracted something slender and olive green in color.

Something which proceeded to twine over his wrist and rear a shiny black head.

"Snake!" shrieked Mrs. Fairfield, leaping with surprising alacrity onto one of the carved wooden chairs that decorated the entrance hall.

The constable raised his stick. "'Ere now, what do you mean by waving that about in front of ladies?"

Edgar was poised to intervene when Miss Perkins took matters into her own hands.

Literally.

She grabbed the snake from Michel and stuffed it into her reticule, closing the clasp.

"Thank you ever so much, Michel. This will be very useful for our herpetology lesson tomorrow," she said.

The constable eyed her with exactly the same wary expression Edgar must have used earlier. "You *asked* 'em to bring you a snake?"

"Why, of course." Miss Perkins regarded the constable as if it were the most common request in the world. "And they found me a splendid example of a grass snake, or *natrix natrix*, isn't that right, children?"

Michel nodded, gazing up at Miss Perkins. "Is that his name? Natrix?"

"We'll call him Trix," announced Adele with a toss of her tangled black curls.

"Is he venomous?" asked Mrs. Fairfield in a trembling voice.

"Not in the least," said Miss Perkins. "Grass snakes are a peaceful, water-loving breed, as I informed the children. The only reptile native to England that must be avoided at all costs is the adder, or common viper. But those are usually only found on the moorlands or in bogs."

"We found Trix by the Serpentine," said Michel proudly.

Miss Perkins nodded. "Very appropriate."

"They were all alone," the constable said, scratching his chin. "Two children tearing through Hyde Park. Splashing about in the water."

"Yes," she nodded. "We've already established that they were hunting snakes. Where there's a will, there's a way."

She was always at the ready with a proverb.

The constable frowned. "They said as their father was a duke but, you'll excuse me, miss, I had my doubts."

"Why should you have had doubts?"

"They was all covered in river mud. And they're not exactly fair complexioned to begin with, now are they?"

"True," said Miss Perkins, in her lilting, cheery voice. "But then neither are you, Constable. Fair complexioned, that is. To my eye you're rather a plummy sort of shade, especially about the nose." She peered closer, examining the appendage in question. "Almost as if you overindulged in the tipple of an evening?" She leaned forward and sniffed at his breath. "Or an afternoon. Tut, tut."

"I beg your pardon," sputtered the constable. "I never."

Michel and Adele grinned at Miss Perkins.

India snorted. "She's perfect," she whispered in Edgar's ear.

"Why, because she orders me about and keeps snakes in her purse?"

"Because she stands up for the children."

"Thank you for bringing the children safely home, Constable," said Miss Perkins. "Cook will have something for you in the kitchens. Off you go then," she said with a stern look. "Mrs. Fairfield will show you the way."

The constable knew when he'd been dispatched.

He followed the housekeeper out of the entrance hall with a dazed expression.

"Are you going to be our new governess?" Michel asked Miss Perkins when he was gone.

"That's for your father to decide." She straightened and turned toward Edgar.

The flame in her blue eyes dared him to dismiss her then and there.

"Oh please, sir," Michel said, addressing Edgar. "May we keep Miss Perkins? She's not like the other ones. She's much prettier. With rosy cheeks and interesting freckles."

And that was the bloody problem, now wasn't it?

"Has Miss Dunkirk left?" asked Adele.

"You know very well that you chased her away," said Miss Perkins.

"We called her Miss Dungheap," announced Adele.

Miss Perkins frowned. "Tsk, tsk, tsk. How unkind."

"Well she was quite odiferous," said Michel. "And that means smelly."

"Those who can see the faults of others sometimes cannot discern their own," said Miss Perkins. "To my nose, there are two odiferous children in my near vicinity. Children who need baths in the very worst way."

Again she turned a questioning glance at Edgar.

All eyes were on him, awaiting his decision.

He found he didn't have the heart to send her away.

Not with the children gazing at her with such interest and none of the antipathy they'd shown toward their previous governesses.

Her smile faltered. A crack in her confident façade. He sensed that she wasn't quite as bold as she pretended to be. Somehow he had the feeling that this employment meant the world to her.

She'd said she just arrived from Derbyshire. What if she had nowhere to stay in London? What if she had an ailing father and five sisters to support back in the countryside?

His mind revolted at the thought of Miss Perkins abandoned to the tender mercies of London. A cheerful country girl like her would be swallowed alive.

He cleared his throat. "One week's trial, Perkins."

A smile bowed Miss Perkins's lips, touching her eyes with relief. "I swear you won't regret it, Your Grace."

He already regretted it. The twins might be momentarily disarmed by her, but they'd turn on her soon enough and chase her away.

And then he'd be right back where he started. Governess-less and racing to finish a design that required finesse, focus, and, above all, a clear head.

"I knew you'd make the right choice, darling." India planted a kiss on his cheek. "See you at the exhibition."

She left him standing by the stairs and shook Miss Perkins's hand. "Welcome, *she-who-charms-snakes-and-children*."

"That's a jolly nice dagger you've got there, Lady India," Adele said admiringly.

"Why, thank you, Adele. It's a replica of an Egyptian ceremonial dagger."

"Have you been to Egypt?"

"I returned from there only one week past. Your father is hosting an exhibition of the antiquities I discovered. Should you like to attend?"

"May we?" asked Michel.

"I don't see why not. Unless there's some ducal objection?" India quirked an eyebrow at Edgar.

"I think having something for the children to look forward to would be a wonderful idea," said Miss Perkins.

What she meant was that it would keep the twins from running away if they had a reason to stay.

She had a point.

"We'll see," Edgar said, in an attempt to maintain some control over his household.

But the smile that his sister and Miss Perkins exchanged revealed that the two females knew exactly what had happened.

They'd already won.

"Mind Miss Perkins closely," India said to th twins. "I've a feeling she has much to teach you."

His sister departed in her swaggering fashion, after one last triumphant over-the-shoulder *I-told-you-so* glance.

As Miss Perkins passed him on the way to the stairs, he caught the warm scent of her skin. A lingeringly sweet floral soap. Lilies. Or lilacs.

The fading afternoon sun lit the coronet of her braids and set it aflame.

Those prim, tightly woven braids. He had a sudden image of those braids unbound.

Of his fingers buried in her hair.

Drawing her closer to map her freckles with his lips.

Did she have freckles on her shoulders . . . or sprinkled across her breasts?

This would never work.

"Perkins," he called sternly.

She turned. "Yes, Your Grace?"

Trepidation in her eyes. Desperation. Hope. "Good afternoon to you," he finished, unable and unwilling to disappoint her.

A smile flirted with her lips. "Good afternoon, Your Grace."

She disappeared up the stairs, the children trailing after her like tired little ducklings.

She may be fashioned specifically to tempt him, but Miss Perkins was far too sunny and guileless, she was in his employ, and she must be an example for his children.

Which set her entirely off limits.

Thrice forbidden.

And never to be explored.

SHE'D EVADED THE executioner's block, at least for today.

As the twins led her to the nursery, Mari wondered what had changed the duke's mind.

He'd had such a long list of objections: she was too small and weak, too inexperienced, too hypothetically distracting to footmen.

That last one had been unexpected, to say the least.

She had one week to overcome all of his objections and to prove her indispensability.

That is, if Mrs. Trilby didn't find her out and ruin everything.

A new life in London and the princely sum of thirty-five pounds hung in the balance.

A small fortune, her heart sang.

"Here's the nursery, Miss Perkins," said Adele, leading Mari into a spacious, high-ceilinged room with luxurious silk carpets and an expansive view of the park.

The duke had spared no expense in outfitting the children's nursery.

Framed maps and prints dotted the walls, along with a large blackboard. In a sunny alcove stood an enormous wooden chest filled to the brim with wooden soldiers, balls, hoops, dolls, and a heap of other toys. Handsome oak bookshelves occupied one of the walls, bulging with shiny new leather spines.

Only the best for a duke.

Mari wasn't the best. Not even close. She hadn't been educated in one of the elite private academies, her Latin and French were merely adequate, and her charcoals more enthusiastic than skillful. Her accomplishments may be few, but if there was one thing she knew, it was children.

Though these two would be a challenge, no doubt about it.

They had identical black hair and delicately pointed chins, and the same wariness and mistrust in their dark brown eyes.

What had happened to them during their upbringing in France? Mari had expected the cosseted children of a duke to be plump and petted. These two children were as lean as orphans bred on watery

And no more shooting constables, is that understood?"

"You're not like our other governesses," said Adele. "They couldn't abide snakes. Or spiders."

"Or toads in their beds," added Michel.

Mari sniffed. "I should think not."

"Miss Perkins, allow me to introduce Mrs. Brill, the children's nurse." Mrs. Fairfield entered the room followed by a fair-haired woman with round cheeks who wore a white apron over her blue gown.

"Did you run off again, you naughty things? Why, you're covered in mud." Mrs. Brill gave Mari a sideways glance, as if including her in her disapproval. "You'll never catch a husband crusted in mud." She pinched Adele's cheek.

"Bah! I don't want a husband." Adele gave her a haughty stare. *"Et ne jamais pincer mes joues!"*

"What's that you say?" Mrs. Brill tilted her head.

"She doesn't want you to pinch her cheeks," Mari translated.

"Well," said the nurse. "Might I be allowed to give Her Majesty a bath?"

Michel

Mrs. Fairfield. "What will Mr. Robertson think? He's the butler, dear," she explained to Mari.

"You may tell Mr. Robertson that the snake is an educational specimen."

"If he were a specimen he'd be dead and pinned to velvet, now wouldn't he?" replied Mrs. Fairfield.

Mari's reticule chose that moment to quiver violently.

"You're frightening Trix." Adele's brow furrowed ominously, reminding Mari of the duke.

Mrs. Brill captured Adele by the elbow. "It's time for your bath. I hear you've been splashing about in the Serpentine. Heaven knows what lives in that water besides snakes."

Adele stuck out her lower lip. "Trix needs a home."

"We won't have our baths until he has a home," said Michel.

Battle lines already.

She must win this one for the twins. "He's quite harmless, Mrs. Fairfield. He's not the biting kind of snake. And if he did manage to get free he would simply slither away. He's far more scared of you than you are of him."

"I suppose you may keep him," Mrs. Fairfield said doubtfully. "But only one day, mind you. Wait here and I'll find something to house the reptile."

"His name is Trix," said Adele.

"Naming snakes . . ." Mrs. Fairfield shook her head. "Whatever will you think of next?"

Mari waited until the housekeeper left the nursery before smiling at the twins. "There, you see? Trix shall have his home. And you shall have your baths. Now off you go with Mrs. Brill. No dawdling."

They dragged their feet, but they obeyed.

She must discover the reason they ran away so often. They must be grieving if their mother died so recently and they'd been uprooted from their life in France.

Children felt things so very keenly.

Often they needed someone only to listen to them. When they felt their grievances were heard, when they unburdened their troubled souls, it was sometimes enough to restore their spirits.

In the time she had with these children, whether it was weeks or years, she would show them what it was like to have a stable, patient caregiver, one who respected them and never talked down to them.

"I'm to give you this, miss." A strapping golden-haired footman in smart black-and-gold livery entered the room and handed her a large water jug, a scrap of butter muslin, and some twine.

Mari smiled at him, but he seemed singularly undistracted. Perhaps she was only distracting to dukes? How odd.

"What's your name?" she asked.

"Carl, miss."

"Carl, you aren't frightened of snakes, are you?"

"'Course not," the footman scoffed.

"Hold the jug tilted, just so." She unclasped her reticule, reached inside, and transferred the snake to his temporary home. Clapping the porous muslin over the lid, she directed Carl to hold the fabric while she secured the twine with double knots.

"Farewell for now, Trix," she whispered. "You were a great help today." She set the jug on a low table near the blackboard.

Mrs. Fairfield returned to the nursery. "The children allowed Mrs. Brill to wash them?" she asked with an amiable smile.

"The children are in the bath and the snake is in the jug." Mari tapped the side of Trix's temporary home. "Thank you for allowing them to keep him."

"We must choose our battles, must we not?"

"Indeed." Mari had only known Mrs. Fairfield a few hours but she was fast coming to the conclusion that the older woman was wise, kind, and a potential ally.

"Now how about that hot cup of tea?" the housekeeper asked.

At the mention of sustenance, Mari's stomach rumbled. "That would be lovely," she said gratefully. "I haven't eaten yet today."

"Oh you poor thing. Come with me immediately. I'll show you to your chamber. I'm sure you're tired after your journey and you'll want to refresh your toilet."

Mari glanced ruefully at her dusty black skirts. Until the duke paid her, she'd have to make do with the one gown. It was a good thing she was plain and practical, with no reason for vanity.

Her bedchamber was two doors down from the nursery and Mari was glad of the proximity. If Michel had a night terror, she'd be the first to respond.

Was this really to be her chamber?

It was light-filled and airy, with blue silk on the walls and green trees outside the windows instead of dreary gray stone. There was even an adjoining sitting room furnished with a matching set of scroll-backed walnut furniture.

"Now, my dear, tell me how you find us thus far. Will we do?" the housekeeper asked with a twinkle in her eyes, accepting a tea service from a maid and setting it on the table in the sitting room.

"I shall be very happy here," said Mari, joining her at the table.

As Mrs. Fairfield poured out, Mari settled against the cushioned chair back, easing the tension between her shoulder blades.

"You've certainly a much readier smile than any of the previous governesses, and that's a vast improvement," said the housekeeper.

Mari accepted a delicate teacup patterned with pink cabbage roses.

Mrs. Fairfield proffered a plate heaped with lemon-scented biscuits. Mari longed to swallow one of the delicate biscuits in a single bite, but instead she bit off a small, ladylike morsel.

Everything about her must proclaim refinement.

"Michel and Adele are intelligent, spirited children who only want proper encouragement and guidance," Mari said.

"A very charitable way of framing the picture."

"I try to be an optimist, Mrs. Fairfield."

She'd had a reputation for efficiency and results at Underwood. A colicky baby? A girl who was unable to recall her lessons? Mari Perkins would take care of everything.

She'd made herself indispensable there, and she would do the same here.

"I'm so glad to hear it," said the housekeeper. "I'll have to personally thank Mrs. Trilby for sending us someone so cheerful and capable."

"Please don't! That is, she and I don't always agree on . . . things. She prefers the Miss Dunkirk sort, if you understand my meaning?"

Mrs. Fairfield gave her a conspiratorial smile. "I understand completely."

"Will you tell me more of the children's upbringing?" Mari asked, to channel the conversation away from treacherous waters.

"I'm afraid I'm unaware of the particulars. All I know is that their mother gave not a fig for those children and they were raised by a nurse in a small seaside village in the Riviera of France. Can you imagine?" Mrs. Fairfield set her teacup down with an indignant clink. "A mother abandoning her own children? Though one shouldn't speak ill of the dead, I know."

Mari had spent her whole life imagining a mother who might abandon her child, as Mari had been left at the orphanage. In her dreams her mother was still alive, and she hadn't chosen to give her child away. There had been some mistake. Perhaps Mari had been stolen away.

In her dreams her mother had been searching for her all of these years.

"At least their mother engaged an English tutor," said Mrs. Fairfield. "Otherwise they might only speak French."

"Might I ask you a rather delicate question, Mrs. Fairfield?"

"Of course, dearie."

"Are the twins . . . are they the duke's legitimate issue?"

"The duke never married." Her eyes clouded over. "I do hope you won't think ill of us and leave?"

No chance of that, given her own uncertain origins. "The children had no control over the circumstances of their birth. I shan't hold it against them. And I must say it was good of His Grace to acknowledge them."

"He was fair livid when they arrived. Said if he'd known of them earlier he could have provided them with a proper British upbringing with no expense spared for their comfort."

No expense spared. Yes, that seemed to be his philosophy. Outfit the twins in expensive clothes and fill their nursery with expensive toys.

But affection and loyalty couldn't simply be purchased.

They must be earned.

"Someday the duke will marry and the twins will have half siblings," said Mrs. Fairfield. "Though at the moment he spends far more time at his foundry with his iron horses than with marriageable ladies."

He may shun suitable ladies, but he made no secret of his paramours, for surely that's what Lady India had been. They'd used such a familiar address. And she'd called him darling and kissed him good-bye in front of the children.

Mrs. Fairfield stirred her tea, a pensive expression stealing across her face. "I want a babe in the nursery before I'm too old to dandle the precious thing. And I'm not the only one. The dowager duchess is near to despairing, she wants an heir so badly."

"Does the dowager live here?" Mari certainly hoped not. From everything she'd read of dowager duchesses in novels, they were most definitely to be avoided.

"She and the duke are estranged because of a sordid incident some years past. He walks with a limp now, I'm sure you noticed. But that's a sad tale, and best saved for another time."

She hadn't noticed the limp, but then he'd been dangling her over his shoulder, so her view had been of his buttocks. His taut, rounded buttocks.

It had been rather a nice view, actually.

"I gather he's greatly preoccupied with his foundry?" asked Mari.

"Pray, don't label him unfeeling, Miss Perkins. He cares for the children's welfare. But if you could find a way to maintain an air of tranquility and peace in the household . . . so that while he is here he may work undisturbed . . . ?"

"Leave everything to me, Mrs. Fairfield. I'll soon set things to rights."

"If anyone can achieve such a miracle, I believe it will be you, Miss Perkins. Now I'll leave you to settle in. I'm sure you'll retire early today. Don't worry, you won't be needed until tomorrow morning, when you may begin your lessons with the twins."

"Thank you, Mrs. Fairfield," Mari said gratefully. She was drowsy and filled with tea and biscuits.

The large, comfortable-looking bed was beckoning.

Mari rose with the housekeeper and escorted her to the door.

Had she blustered her way into a duke's household? It hardly seemed believable, and yet here she was.

She opened her cloth bag and drew out her remaining possessions, setting them on the dressing table. A worn hairbrush missing half its bristles; several beloved novels; a Book of Common Prayer with a cracked black leather cover; and a carved wooden rabbit wearing a tattered, green velvet dress.

Last year, Mrs. Crowley, the headmistress at Underwood, had contracted a fever. On her deathbed, stricken by remorse, she'd made an unbelievable confession.

She'd told Mari that, three years past, a lawyer from London, Mr. Arthur Shadwell, had visited Underwood searching for a child who matched Mari's description and circumstances.

In an act of ill will, the headmistress had informed him that Mari was dead of a fever.

The stinging betrayal of it was still raw and fresh in Mari's mind.

If someone had been searching for her, it could mean she had a family, that she wasn't completely alone in life.

It could mean that the stories she'd made up in her mind about a reunion with her mother might prove to be true.

The prayer book and the wooden rabbit had been bundled in her swaddling cloth when she arrived at the orphanage. It wasn't until after Mrs. Crowley made her confession that Mari had realized they might hold some key to her past.

She opened the prayer book and read the inscription as she had a million times before: "Ann Murray, 1808."

Who are you, Ann Murray?

Who am I?

There were sure to be a great many Ann Murrays living in London. But how many lawyers named Arthur Shadwell could there be? She would consult a business directory and find him on her very first off day.

She would search until she found answers.

When she'd lost her friend Helena, she'd channeled all of her energy into her studies, determined to escape the orphanage and not die there, friendless and alone.

Whatever the truth of her past turned out to be, the knowing would be so much better than the not knowing.

To keep this post, she must gain the confidence and trust of the twins and make their lessons diverting enough to keep them from running away again.

And she must continue to deceive the duke into believing she was superior enough to be their governess. She needn't tell any outright lies, only small untruths and omissions.

He wasn't anything like the man she had pictured. He wasn't a monster. He was a man with vision, building engines to fight fires. A man who cared for his illegitimate children.

Which was, perhaps, more dangerous than his broad shoulders and his handsome face.

Kneeling at her feet. Cutting her bootlaces.

Heat rippled through her body as she unbraided her hair and removed her gown. She must be constantly on her guard. She was pretending to be a superior governess, one who would never permit anything as maudlin as sentiment to muddle her thinking.

Feeling anything other than practical and businesslike emotions for her employer was completely forbidden.

She must stay as far from him as possible.

He might have a list of objections, but she had a list of her own.

He was far too abrupt and changeful.

Entirely too gruff and given to growling.

More attentive to his mistresses and engines than his children.

And he had a most alarming way of using his enormous size to intimidate a girl.

Had it been absolutely necessary to lift her clear off the carpet and dangle her about like a kite in the wind before throwing her over his shoulder?

And why did a delicious little thrill ignite in her

mind every time she thought about his large hands gripping her waist?

And that, she reflected, *was the most objectionable trait of all.*

The elicitation of illicit thrills.

Utterly unforgivable.

And most definitely to be avoided.

Chapter 4

❧

HIGH-PITCHED SCREAMING WOKE Mari the next morning: *the children.*

She fumbled into her stays and black dress. There was a new pair of bootlaces laid out on a table. Were they from the duke?

The memory of his roughened fingertips brushing her ankle unwound in her mind as she coiled her braids atop her head. Ruthlessly, she pinned her hair, and her propriety, firmly into place.

She had no time for daydreaming about dukes. It sounded as though his offspring were attempting to murder one another. If she didn't calm them and restore order to the household she'd be out on her ear with only a new pair of bootlaces to show for her troubles.

She followed the screams to the nursery and paused inside the doorway.

Well she certainly had her work cut out for her.

A shirtless Michel was chasing a shrieking Mrs. Brill through the nursery, his skinny arms flailing and one hand clutching the snake.

Adele stood atop the toy chest, hands clasped in front of her, elbows out, proclaiming doggerel at the top of her voice, "I once knew a nursemaid named Brill, who thought fleeing from snakes quite a thrill.

The snake it did slither, the nursemaid did quiver, and—"

Mari placed two fingers between her lips and produced her most earsplitting whistle.

Everyone froze and stared at her.

A superior governess would never resort to anything so vulgar as a street vendor's whistle, but desperate times called for desperate measures.

"Merciful Heavens," huffed Mrs. Brill, her breath coming in puffs. "This is simply the last straw. I'm giving my notice. I leave them with you, Miss Perkins. *You* see if you can control the little heathens."

"Please don't leave—"

"My mind is quite made up." Mrs. Brill hurried out of the room.

Adele and Michel exchanged glances. "We didn't mean for her to leave forever," said Michel.

"Then maybe you shouldn't have chased her with a snake."

Mari knew she must be firm with the children, yet she sensed that scolding them would only make them mistrust her. "Poor Trix." She made a sad face. "He has a terrible case of vertigo."

"What's that?" Michel held the wriggling snake close to his face. "It's not fatal, is it? I don't see any spots."

"He's dizzy," Mari said. "How would you like to be rushed about the room like a spinning top? And what if he has to do the necessary? Poor dear."

She marched to Michel and held out her palm.

He gave her the snake.

She carried him to the water jug.

Michel followed. "Do snakes use the privy?"

Mari hid a smile. Introducing the subject of bodily

functions never failed to capture the interest of children.

"Not in the same way as humans do." Mari retied the muslin. "Snakes can go a whole year without excretions."

"*Bof.*" Michel made a very French noise of astonishment. "A whole year?"

"How do you know?" asked Adele, who had joined them by Trix's jug.

"Because I read encyclopedias," replied Mari. "You may wish to do the same."

"I could write a verse about reptilian excretions," Adele said.

"I'd rather you didn't," replied Mari.

"What rhymes with excretions?"

"Now, what was all of that about?" asked Mari.

"Nurse tried to dress me in this." Michel scooped a frilled shirt with lace at the cuffs from the floor. "I'd be a fribbling milksop."

"I think you'd be bee-yoo-tee-ful," said Adele with a smirk.

"I won't wear it."

"It's not very practical, I'll admit. Let's find you something a little less lordly, shall we?" Mari rummaged through the wardrobe in the adjoining bedchamber and found a plain white lawn shirt for Michel.

She popped his thin arms through the armholes and pulled the shirt down. "You'll have to apologize to Mrs. Fairfield, you know. For chasing away Mrs. Brill. Now I'll have to be your nursemaid as well as your governess."

"Apologize, apologize, apologize. That's all we ever do." Michel kicked at a chair.

"We're bad. That's what we are. We're bad and we're only going to get worse, just you wait and see." Adele crossed her arms over her chest. "We'll run away and join a traveling show. We've got many talents. And people will pay to see them."

"I'm sure you do," said Mari. "You'll have to show me all of them someday. I'd like to know what it is you do when you run away." Perform for money? And why would they need money when they had the expensive toys and clothing the duke showered them with? "But what's all this talk about being bad?"

"Everyone says we're bad," said Michel.

Adele frowned. "Miss Dunkirk rapped our knuckles with a ruler."

Mari's heart squeezed. "I'll never strike you," she promised.

Michel tilted his head. "No matter how bad we are?"

"No matter the sin. We'll reason through things together with our words."

"But we have ever so many sins and vices." Michel pointed at a large blackboard hung on the far wall, covered with writing in blunt chalk letters.

"What are the vices of youth?" Mari read. "Peevishness, Pride, Selfishness, Deceit, Uncleanliness, Heedlessness, Rashness, Fickleness, A tattling humor . . ."

She clenched her fists. She was intimately familiar with the pious, shaming methods of instruction favored by sanctimonious disciplinarians.

She'd been punished for the sins of pride and deceitfulness. Which just meant she hadn't learned to keep her mouth closed, yet.

She'd been made to stand alone in the front of the schoolroom, atop a chair, for hours on end . . . until her legs trembled and she'd nearly fainted.

Until every other girl had gone to supper and the sun had sunk from the sky, leaving her in the cold and the dark.

She shivered.

She couldn't believe the duke had allowed such teachings in his home. Did he not monitor what his children were learning?

Grabbing the rag that hung on a hook nearby, Mari scrubbed away the damaging words.

Next she scooped up the two copies of *Dr. Pritchard's Catechisms for Children*, and dumped them into the dustbin.

Michel's eyes widened. "You can't throw books away."

"I can if they're tiresome rubbish. I'll find better books for you to read."

"You'll learn to hate us, too." Adele's lip quivered. "Because we're bastards."

Mari froze. "Where did you hear that?"

"Miss Dunkirk told the second housemaid that we were sunburnt infidel bastards who didn't deserve an English education," said Michel.

"I found it in the dictionary." Adele raised her finger. "Bastard: a child begotten and born out of wedlock; an illegitimate or spurious child."

"A bad child," said Michel.

Mari's heart cleaved in half like a dry log beneath a sharp blade.

She should have jabbed Miss Dunkirk with a hairpin when she had the chance.

She walked to the bookshelf and found a dictionary, opening it at random.

"Bastard," she proclaimed, running her finger along the text as if reading from the book. "A child simply bursting with potential, promise, and possibilities."

"That's not what it says," said Adele.

"It most certainly does. Are you contradicting me, young lady?"

"No, miss."

"No, Miss Perkins," she corrected. "Now then, children. Coats, hats, boots." She returned the dictionary to the shelf and clapped her hands together. "Well don't stand there staring. Quickly now. We're going for a walk."

"Don't want to go for a walk," said Michel, glowering at her.

"I'll buy you some boiled sweets." She wasn't above a bit of bribery, even if it meant depleting her small store of coins.

She'd hit upon a winning argument.

They scrambled for their coats, which were hanging on pegs by the wardrobe.

The outdoors was the best place for them. They had been curled in on themselves, just surviving, for so long.

What they required was fresh air and freedom.

Today she must be the Pied Piper. Lead them on an adventure.

"Follow me, children. Shipshape and Bristol fashion, if you please."

EDGAR HOPED MISS Perkins was faring better today than Bonny Brindle, the prizefighter he'd wagered his money on.

Brindle was receiving a right drubbing, staggering about the sawdust-covered floor like a drunken sailor on a pitching boat.

"Flatten him!" shouted the Duke of Westbury,

cheering for Brindle's opponent, a hulking pugilist appropriately named Big Ben.

Edgar had reluctantly agreed to meet his childhood friend, whom everyone called West, at the Red Lion public house, because the duke had refused to meet anywhere else.

Attending illegal boxing matches was hardly a priority for Edgar, but he needed to convince West to allow the railway to run through the edge of his pleasure estate, Westbury Abbey, near Watford.

And so here he was. Not where he should be, at his foundry, working on the engine design. But here, in a crowd of bloodthirsty, inebriated men, with the scent of stale ale and sweat filling his nostrils.

There were so many other, less nauseating, odors. Sweet lilac and warm woman, for example.

Mari-rhymes-with-starry.

What a whimsical way to describe oneself.

She may pretend to be strict, no-nonsense, and cut from the same cloth as Miss Dunkirk, but he imagined Miss Perkins had a wildly romantic streak.

There was something about the light flickering in her blue eyes—the glimmer of hope and optimism.

She probably memorized poetry while bathing. With rose petals bobbing in the bathwater.

He'd like to bob in her bathwater.

Good God. He kept having the most inappropriate thoughts about her.

Maybe it would be best for all concerned if the twins sent her running back to her agency.

Though it was unlikely they would wear down her resolve in only one day, but not out of the realm of possibility. They'd rid themselves of Governess Number Three in a matter of hours with some sort of homemade itching powder.

Actually, he'd been rather proud of their ingenuity on that occasion.

Had they put pepper in Miss Perkins's tea? Pebbles in her boots? The toads and spiders wouldn't work. She was hardly squeamish.

He almost believed Miss Perkins would win any battle she undertook.

Still, the children's innovation when it came to dispatching governesses was inspired. Perhaps one of them would grow up to be a famous inventor.

Big Ben struck a thudding blow and Brindle wobbled, his eyes crossing, and finally crashed to the floor with a deafening crack. The crowd surged forward, yelling the count.

"On your feet, Brinny," Edgar shouted, just for show. "I've got twenty on you."

"Bad luck, old friend. He's flopped," said West, with a lopsided grin.

Edgar steered him away from the boxing match and toward a quieter table in the shadowy reaches of the public house. He motioned to a barmaid.

Several other gentlemen eyed them, curious about Edgar's rare appearance in a public house.

When the ale arrived, Edgar sipped, while West pounded back one flagon and received another.

"I think you know why I agreed to meet you here tonight," Edgar began.

"The railway."

"That's right."

"Don't want any damn railway carving up my land," said West.

"Never took you for the stodgy, traditional type."

"'Course not. But I'm not as progress-minded and sober as you."

"The route needs to go through Westbury Abbey."

"Why?" asked West, already working on his third ale.

"Avoiding the estate entirely would be disastrously expensive. We'd have to carve out the hillsides along Chiltern and make our own embankments across the Colne."

"So you'll carve my lands instead."

"It will also cross my estate as well."

"My hedge maze is more intricate than yours."

"Your hedges won't be compromised."

"But my view might. You can't promise me that I won't catch a glimpse of your infernal steam-belching dragon from my parapet."

"Not even from your parapet. I promise you."

"But I'll know it's there. The clanking cacophony of *progress*."

Why was he being so stubborn? Westbury owned several estates and castles, all of them more impressive than the small and decrepit Abbey.

"It's progress that will double the profits of your Birmingham holdings," Edgar said.

"You think about commerce too much for a gentleman."

"You sound like my mother."

"I can see the wheels churning in your mind." West made unsteady swirling motions in the direction of Edgar's head. "*For the love of money is the root of all kinds of evil*, as the good book says."

"It's not all about profit."

"What's it about then?"

"Speed and ease of travel. Lowering prices on coal and commodities. My steam-powered engines will run on the railways, but I'm also developing fire engines. Someone has to stop these fires from sweeping across London every year, killing hundreds and ruining countless livelihoods. The current system isn't adequate. Those dilapidated old hand-pumped engines."

It made him so angry that the parish fire brigades still insisted their way was the best.

He was going to show them. He knew that there was talk of consolidating all of the brigades into a citywide one. And he would be ready with his more efficient fire engine when that happened.

"S'that right? Noble cause, eh?"

"Very noble."

"But profitable."

"Extremely profitable. If you won't let the railway through, why don't you sell me Westbury? It's only a moldering pile of drafty stones with an army of ghosts. I'll pay triple what anyone else would."

West shook his head. "Been in my family too long. I've a sentimental attachment to it. Had my first tup there, with a buxom village maid."

"Sell it to me. No one else will buy it."

"No."

"No?" Edgar hadn't expected so much resistance. This was a former friend. His best friend before Edgar had thrown his old life away.

"You've been back in London for nearly two years and you've never called on me," said West. "Not once. After the . . . incident . . . with your father, you just disappeared. What happened to you? Where have you been all these years?"

Now Edgar understood—West was hurt by him leaving. "I'm sorry, old friend. I'm not the same devil-may-care fellow I was when I left. I didn't think you'd want anything to do with me. I renounced my birth. Went underground. Spent seven years as a foundry worker in Birmingham and wasn't even planning to ever return. I know what they say about me. That I'm not fit to be the duke."

West slammed down his mug of ale. "You're joking. A foundry worker?"

Edgar tugged off one of his kidskin gloves and showed West the scars on his hands. "It wasn't easy, but it was a damned sight more of an honest life than the one I led here."

"Everyone said you'd gone soft in the head. I didn't believe them but now . . ."

"Believe what you want," Edgar sighed. "But let my railway go through your estate. Or sell me the damned estate. What can I do to convince you?"

"I've no need for money. You know what I do need, though?" He stared into his ale morosely. "A husband."

"Er . . ." Maybe West had changed more than Edgar had realized in the decade since their last meeting.

"For Blanche," West amended. "Remember her?"

"This high," Edgar swiped the air at his waist. "Straw-colored hair. A penchant for sweetmeats?"

"That's the one. Only she's nineteen now, and she's got a penchant for marriage. I've got a surfeit of marriage-aged sisters on my hands."

Edgar shook his head. "Not going to happen."

"What's not going to happen? I haven't asked you anything yet."

"While your sisters are lovely girls, I'm not going to take one of them off your hands."

"Who said I want you to marry one of 'em? You don't have the most spotless of reputations at the moment, y'know."

"I suppose you're referring to my children?"

"Twins, are they?"

"A boy and a girl."

"From the Frenchwoman?"

"Yes." Edgar clipped the word. He didn't want to talk about it.

About the scandal that had dogged his days ever since he'd met Sophie. The reason he walked with this damned limp.

"Heard they're troublesome. Chasing away governesses, what?" asked West.

"Word travels quickly."

"Governesses." West shuddered. "Dreary, humorless race. Was petrified of mine as a boy."

"I've a new one. She's quite promising."

"Stern and commanding, is she? More hair on her upper lip than you've got?"

"Not at all. Wavy auburn hair. Slender waist. Clever gaze. Saucy mouth."

"I'll have to meet this governess of yours," said West with a wolfish grin.

"Absolutely not."

"Protective of her, are we?"

"You're not to pursue my governess, West."

If anyone would pursue her, it would be Edgar.

No, no. That was all wrong.

"If you say so." West swallowed the rest of his ale. "Now, about my sisters—"

"I'm not going to marry one of your sisters."

"Told you, don't want you to marry 'em." He waved his hand at a barmaid.

"Haven't you had enough?" asked Edgar.

"Not even close." West reached for more ale and downed half of it in a few hearty swallows. "Now, see here. This is what you'll do."

He drew on the sticky table with a wobbly finger. "Take Blanche riding in an open carriage. Act besotted. Parade her down the Ladies Mile. Stop here at an agreed-upon time." He jabbed his finger against the table. "Greenlea's Flower Shop. Leap out of the carriage, impulsive action, et cetera, and purchase her a big bunch of flowers."

Edgar snorted. "Sounds like courtship to me."

"'Snot." slurred West. "She's trying to bring Laxton up to scratch. You'll drive him mad with jealousy."

"How do I know he'll be watching?"

"Because I'll bring him near Greenlea's at the hour we agree on. It can't fail."

In Edgar's experience, plans made by inebriated lords usually failed.

"D'you want your railway through Westbury Abbey or not?" asked West.

"You drive a hard bargain."

"I have *five* sisters. Laxton will offer for Blanche then and there if he thinks he's competing with a duke." He wiped his palms together. "Problem solved. Sister number one off the shelf. Apparently she must marry before the other ones can tie the knot. Bloody rules of matrimony. Don't understand what all the fuss is about."

"This'd better not be a trap."

West slapped his hand down on the table, making the ale mugs jitter and jump. "It'll be like old times, eh? You used to be such a rakehell before . . ." He glanced at Edgar's lame knee and then closed his mouth abruptly. "Come with me to the opera tonight. Forget about the governess. What you need is a mistress."

"First of all, I'm not thinking about the governess, so I don't need to forget her. Second, I'm far too busy with steam engines for songbirds."

"Suit yourself." West leaned back in his chair. He

gave Edgar's nether regions a significant glance. "But if it withers away and falls off don't say I didn't warn you."

"No chance of that." His anatomy was in exemplary working order.

Far too exemplary when it came to thoughts of redheaded governesses.

Chapter 5

MARI WAS DETERMINED to give the children enough physical exercise to render them quiet and peaceful enough to please even the most demanding of dukes. If the children were walking by her side, they weren't running away.

Armed with a guidebook and a map, she'd marched them across London, stopping at all of the sights. She was tired, but the twins were near exhausted.

Their shoulders were beginning to droop, and their steps to drag.

"Isn't it teatime yet, Miss Perkins?" asked Adele.

"Teatime?" she replied. "Why, we haven't even seen the crown jewels yet, and the guidebook says there are waxworks, and menageries—"

"We're tired, Miss Perkins."

"Tired? But I thought you liked exploring London."

"We do," said Michel. "Only . . ."

"You might like some tea and biscuits in your nice house."

"We'd prefer French bread," said Adele.

"Why, what's wrong with good English bread, if you please?" asked Mari.

"Too soft. No crust to speak of," Adele explained.

"Not long enough either." Michel shaped an elongated loaf with his hands. "You break off a piece and . . . mmm."

"We've one last place to visit before we go home," said Mari, consulting her guidebook. "Westminster Bridge."

"Who wants to see an old bridge?" asked Michel.

"Tut, tut. I'm quite sure the bridge has no wish to see such a sullen fellow, either. But see it we will."

They passed the grounds of Westminster Palace and soon they were standing near the entrance to the bridge, watching the carriages and carts rolling by.

"Ah, the Thames," said Mari, turning her nose up to the late afternoon sun.

"Not very impressive," scoffed Michel. "Not compared to our seashore near Narbonne."

"I've never seen the seashore. What's it like?" asked Mari.

"Never seen the sea?" cried Adele.

"Never. I was raised in Derbyshire which is quite landlocked."

"Well . . ." Adele bit her lower lip. "The seashore is a mixture of smells and sounds. Salt with sunshine mixed into it. And seagull cries. And grass."

"Grass tall as me," said Michel.

"Tall as I," Mari corrected.

"The grass smells sweet and clean," continued Adele. "The cleanest thing you ever smelled. Cleaner than laundry drying on a line. And it whispers to you when the wind moves through it."

"That's a lovely description, Adele. Practically a poem already."

"Amina made baskets out of the grass after she dried it and our house always smelled like the beach."

"Who is Amina?" asked Mari.

"Our nurse. We thought she loved us better than anything in the world but then she sent us to live here."

"Why do you think your nurse sent you here?"

"Because our mother asked her to send us here, before she died."

Adele's thin shoulders tensed. "Amina has probably already forgotten about us."

"She'll never forget you," said Mari. "You're quite unforgettable."

"It's been so long though."

"Months," agreed Michel.

Mari touched Adele's arm. "I have an idea, why don't you write to Amina?"

"Write a letter?" asked Adele.

"Why not? I'm sure your father knows how to reach her."

"We hadn't thought of that," said Adele.

A look passed between the twins. One thing was clear, they were planning to return to France and that's why they'd been running away.

"I know a poem that was written about the view from this very bridge," said Mari. "By a fellow named William Wordsworth. Which is a very good name for a poet, incidentally."

"Why did he write a poem about a silly old bridge?" asked Michel.

"Because he was on the beginning of a journey, traveling from London to Calais, in France. To visit his nine-year-old daughter, Caroline, whom he had never met before. He wrote quite a pretty sonnet about that meeting as well."

"May we hear some of the poem?" asked Adele.

"*Dull would he be of soul who could pass by, a sight so touching in its majesty,*" quoted Mari. "*This City now doth, like a garment, wear the beauty of the morning; silent, bare . . . ships, towers, domes, theaters and temples lie, open unto the fields, and to the sky.*"

She paused. "That's the beginning."

"*Wearing the beauty of the morning*. I like that."
Adele traced circles in the dirt. "It's not as if we can't
appreciate the beauty of England, Miss Perkins, and
our fine new home here. But the duke means to separate us."

"What do you mean, separate you?"

"We overheard Mrs. Fairfield saying that he'll
send Michel to Eton next term."

"Ah . . . I see." Now she really did see. They'd been
running away, rebelling against this new life, because they didn't want to be separated.

"The duke wants to change us into proper, fribbling, milksop prigs," proclaimed Michel, dislodging
some stones from the bank with the toe of his boot.

"You? A fribbling milksop prig? I hardly think it
possible," said Mari.

"He wants to change us, all right."

"Thomas Moore has a lovely poem called 'Come
O'er the Sea' that says 'the true soul burns the same
where'er it goes.'"

"You memorize a lot of poetry," said Michel.

"What do you think Mr. Moore meant?" she asked.

Adele's nose wrinkled as she thought about it.
"Maybe . . . maybe he meant that what's inside us, the
things that make us different from anyone else, those
things don't change when we live somewhere new."

"I think that's precisely what he meant, you clever
girl."

They sat in silence for a few moments, watching
carts and carriages cross the bridge.

"Interesting things, bridges, don't you think?"
asked Mari. "They connect one place with another.
I think perhaps you need a bridge right now."

Michel frowned. "We don't need a bridge. We need a ship."

Adele elbowed him in the side.

"Ow!"

"You're not supposed to tell anyone about the ship, Michel," scolded his sister.

"So there is a ship," said Mari. "I thought as much. And this ship will take you back to France, is that right?"

Another glance passed between them.

"You must miss France, and your life there. And you don't want to be separated. That's why you've been running away, I suppose. So . . . which ship is to be yours?" She pointed into the distance between London Bridge and the Tower where the ships' masts bristled in the Pool of London. "Will you sign on as cabin boys?"

Michel's eyes widened. "How did you know?"

"Adele will have to chop off her hair, to pass as a boy," mused Mari. "Luckily, I've brought some scissors." She reached into her reticule and extracted a glinting pair of sewing scissors.

Adele scooted away. "What, right now?"

"No time like the present, I always say. Oh your father will surely weep for your absence, and I shan't be thought much of a success as a governess, but you'll be on your ship bound for France. You'll swab down the decks, and trap rats, and clean up drunken sailor vomit. It will be ever so much fun."

"You don't make it sound very fun," said Adele.

"Hello there, sir," Mari called to a wizened old man mending a net below them on the bank.

He touched his cap.

"Might you know of a ship sailing for France that's hiring two cabin boys?" called Mari.

His tilted his head. "Can't say as I do. But perhaps my nephew might. He's first mate on *The Fairweather*."

Michel tugged on Mari's sleeve. "Miss Perkins."

"Yes, Michel?"

"We've changed our minds."

"What? Changed your minds. How can that be? This fine fellow will take you to his nephew."

"We want our tea and biscuits," said Michel, his lip wobbling.

"Never mind, sir," called Mari to the fisherman. "They've changed their minds."

The man gave her a confused look and returned to mending his net.

She'd called the children's bluff.

It had been a risky strategy—she couldn't stop them if they were set on running away—but acknowledging it, confronting it head on, might force them to see the danger in their escape plans.

Adele gave her a sheepish look. "I want to see Lady India's daggers."

"How silly of me. I forgot about the antiquities exhibition. You won't want to miss that. Well in that case, shall we go back?"

Adele nodded.

They didn't trust her yet. She was too new to them, and they'd been betrayed before. Abandoned by their mother and, they felt, abandoned by their nurse.

She would have to tread carefully. Find ways of giving them ownership in their education, and a sense of pride in learning. But one step at a time.

The children were tired and, she suspected, disinclined to run away again until after Lady India's exhibition.

Today's victory would simply be a quiet, peaceful

home for the duke to return to. She was determined to give him no reason to dismiss her.

"Come along then," Mari said. "Best foot forward. We'll be home in a trice."

WHEN EDGAR ARRIVED home all was superficially quiet, but he knew chaos must lurk somewhere in the house.

"You're home early, Your Grace," said Robertson as he took his hat and overcoat. "How was your day?"

"Unsatisfactory." Why the devil had he agreed to take Lady Blanche riding? It was a losing proposition. If word got out that he was on the marriage mart it would be disastrous.

Edgar rarely attended social events. And he never, *never* was seen with an eligible young lady. But what choice had he been given? West had resorted to blackmail.

"Will you dine in?" asked Robertson.

"I already dined. Where are the children?"

"In the nursery, I believe."

"And Miss Perkins?"

"With the children, Your Grace."

"Any tears today? Constables? Cannon fire?"

"All has been tranquil since morning. I believe she took the children on an extended outing."

Sound strategy. Tire them out so they couldn't misbehave. Chalk one up for Miss Perkins.

Edgar took the stairs two at a time.

He had to see this purported tranquility with his own eyes.

Chapter 6

❦

EDGAR HEARD THE murmur of voices from inside the nursery. Miss Perkins's musical tones and Adele's questioning ones.

Cautiously, he opened the door and entered the room.

Long shadows fell across the blackboard.

Only a matter of a few steps across the room and he slipped into place just outside of the doorway to the children's adjoining bedchamber.

He had a view of Miss Perkins's back where she sat in a chair between the children's beds, reading to them from a book.

He couldn't see the children over the high railings of their beds, and, surprisingly, he couldn't hear them, either. They appeared to be listening to her.

What witchcraft was this?

He crept closer, to hear what she was reading.

"'It is a beauteous evening, calm and free,'" she read in her joyful, ringing tones. "'The holy time is quiet as a Nun. Breathless with adoration; the broad sun is sinking down in its tranquility . . .'"

The elegant lines of her profile rattled something loose inside Edgar's chest.

"'Dear Child! Dear Girl! That walkest with me here, If thou appear untouched by solemn thought, Thy nature is not therefore less divine . . .'"

The words rang like a muffled bell inside his shuttered heart.

He knew the poem well.

Wordsworth had written it for his daughter by a Frenchwoman. It was a lovely poem, about meeting the illegitimate daughter he'd never met until that day.

He had to admit it was appropriate, though the children could hardly understand the full significance of the choice.

She closed the book.

"Very pretty," said Adele.

"Not enough fighting," scoffed Michel. "I only like poetry with a good battle scene."

"I see you've plenty of toy soldiers to play with," said Miss Perkins. "Tomorrow we'll stage a battle re-enactment, shall we?"

"Pah! The duke thinks we're babes in arms. We're too old for toys," said Michel.

That was news to Edgar. He'd chosen the same toys he liked to play with as a boy. They didn't like them?

"Too old for toys?" exclaimed Miss Perkins. "What a dreadful notion. Why, I believe a person is never too old for toys."

"*You* don't play with toys," said Michel.

"I most certainly do." Miss Perkins pulled something out of a bag at her feet. "I have my rabbit." She held up a carved wooden rabbit with tall ears and jointed limbs that dangled at crooked angles. There was something familiar about the rabbit. Where had he seen one like it before?

"She's been with me since I was a little girl," said Miss Perkins.

"You still play with her?" Michel sounded so incredulous that Edgar smiled.

"I write stories about her. Because she has so many strange and unusual adventures, you see. Don't let this velvet gown fool you." Miss Perkins stroked the tattered green gown the rabbit wore. "She's quite fearsome. She's known throughout the world as P.L. Rabbit, the Scourge of the Seven Seas."

"She's a *pirate* rabbit?" asked Michel.

Edgar clapped a hand over his mouth.

"What does P.L. stand for?" asked Adele.

"Why, Peg Leg, of course. See?" Miss Perkins lifted the rabbit's paw. "She has wooden pegs holding her limbs together. But that doesn't mean she can't carry a sword. Why, just the other night, she set sail on her ship, *The Silver Hind*, with her trusty crew of fearless bunnies. They were hunting for sunken treasure off the coast of Barbados when they were set upon by the dread pirate rat known as Drew the Destroyer . . . oh, but I forgot, you're too old for toys."

A breathless pause. "But what happened?" asked Michel.

"I've no idea. I haven't written the ending yet. Perhaps you can help me think of a good one," said the clever Miss Perkins.

Edgar saw exactly what she was doing. Trying to engage the children, make them participants instead of antagonists.

He had to admit that even though she appeared fragile and defenseless, she had quite a few tricks up her sleeves.

"Here's your ending," said Michel, sitting up so that Edgar could see the tips of his ears sticking out from his head. "They're on the deck, see."

"Yes, I can see it," said Miss Perkins. "The crew of bunnies set upon by the hideous rat with glowing red eyes and razor-sharp teeth."

"That's right," said Michel. "And then P.L. shouts 'slit that rat from his gullet to his boots!' and the bunnies set upon the rat and, because it's four of them to one of him, they gut him and throw him to the sharks and—"

"And then," Adele jumped in, bouncing so that Edgar caught a glimpse of the crown of her head, "an enormous sea serpent swallows all of the rabbits whole, even P.L., and they have to live for years in its belly and they have to poke him from the inside with their swords and tell really bad jokes until he vomits them onto a beach."

There was a pause.

"Well that's one potential outcome," replied Miss Perkins. "Rather bloodthirsty, I must say. But when you write your own stories you can make the characters do whatever you want them to do. If you want them to become sea serpent vomit, well then, you may."

"Did you write a lot of stories when you were a little girl?" Adele asked Miss Perkins.

"Hundreds. And they were all about P.L. Rabbit. I have them all recorded in the pages of my journals. Should you like to write stories in a journal?"

"I guess so," said Michel. "But you'll read them, won't you?"

"Absolutely not," said Miss Perkins. "They will be your private journals. For your eyes only."

Adele yawned and stretched her fists over her head. "It's strange to think about you as a little girl, Miss Perkins."

"Even your tall, formidable father was a child once," said Miss Perkins.

Formidable, eh?

"I can't picture that," said Michel. "He must have

been a proper boring milksop. Spouting off his sums and always knowing the right answers."

Excuse me? Was that what they thought of him? Edgar had to stop himself from joining the conversation.

He'd been cocky, headstrong, full of the devil. Always in the thick of everything, the instigator, the troublemaker.

Quick with his fists. When the lads at Eton had taunted him for being a namby-pamby duke's heir born with a silver spoon in his mouth, he'd shown them.

"Sums do have practical applications, Michel. They're not just a unique form of torture devised by governesses. Your father must have applied himself to learning his sums in order to be able to design steam engines."

At least she was defending his honor.

"Perhaps he will come to the schoolroom someday and help you with our sums," Miss Perkins said.

"Oh no," said Adele. "He would never come to the schoolroom."

Michel nodded. "He doesn't even want us here at all."

Edgar flattened his palm against the wall. *They thought he didn't want them?*

But he'd taken them in and purchased them the best of everything.

"Oh my dears. Of course he wants you." Miss Perkins bent closer to Adele. "He's extremely occupied at the moment, that's all."

"He doesn't want us," insisted Michel. "That's why he's sending me away to Eton. To be rid of me."

"We've never been apart," said Adele with a sad note in her voice. "Not even for one day."

Miss Perkins made a sympathetic noise in the back of her throat. "I hadn't thought of it like that."

Edgar had never thought about how strong their bond must be, having faced so much adversity. It gave him pause.

He was separating them for their own good. Because it was a mark of honor and distinction for the males of the family, legitimate or otherwise, to attend Eton.

"We won't let that happen," said Michel fiercely. "Don't you try to convince us that it's the right thing because we won't listen."

"We'll never leave each other. Never as long as we live," vowed Adele.

Miss Perkins was silent for a moment. "I'll not try to convince you of anything tonight," she said, "except to take a spoonful of this."

She fetched a glass apothecary bottle from a shelf and Edgar had to duck backward for a moment so she didn't catch a glimpse of him.

Miss Perkins held up the bottle and read the label. "One Tea-Spoon to be Taken at Bed-Time in the Event of Homesickness."

"Homesickness?" asked Adele. "That's a funny thing for a label to say."

"Well some children are beset by colds, others with overexcitement. This will help what you're troubled by. Try a small taste. I promise you'll like it."

"Do we have to?" groaned Adele.

"I won't," said Michel.

Miss Perkins poured some liquid into the spoon and held it out to Adele, who took a tiny taste.

"Sweet as strawberries," Adele said with astonishment, finishing the spoonful. "You'll like it, Michel."

Miss Perkins wiped off the spoon with a cloth and

poured some for Michel, who drank his spoonful down in one gulp.

"Not half bad," he admitted.

Miss Perkins smiled at the children. "I told you that you'd like it. Now then, it's past your bedtime. Go to bed late, stay very small. Go to bed early, grow very tall."

"Miss Perkins?"

"Yes, Adele?"

"When we were sitting by the Thames, you said we needed a bridge."

"There's no bridge between England and France," scoffed Michel.

"I've figured out what you meant," said Adele softly.

"Have you now?" asked Miss Perkins.

"*You're* the bridge, aren't you? Crossing from our old lives to our new ones."

Miss Perkins smiled at Adele and swept a lock of hair away from her face. "That's right. I'll be your bridge. If you let me."

A lump rose in Edgar's throat.

He'd built his defenses and written his rules so methodically.

CONTROL YOUR ANGER. DRINK ONLY IN MODERATION.
CONTROL IN ALL THINGS.
GUARD AGAINST THE MISUSE OF POWER.
GUARD AGAINST LOVE, FOR IT MAKES A MAN A FOOL.

What he'd failed to do was build a defense against something like this.

Miss Perkins reading to his children. Telling them stories and giving them remedies for homesickness.

The innocent tenderness of the moment.

Blindly, he backed away, feeling for the edges of the room.

All he knew was that he didn't belong here.

He had to leave.

MARI WAS ON a mission.

The books in the nursery had been sadly lacking. More than lacking. Harmful.

She'd made some small progress with the children today, but she couldn't teach them using *Dr. Pritchard's Catechisms*. There must be something more wholesome for them to read in this enormous marble-and-gilt mausoleum of a house.

Adele loved poetry so Mari would find her poems in French to translate into English.

And they both seemed to like adventure stories.

It had broken her heart when they'd said they would never let the duke separate them. Their bond was so incredibly strong. So unlike anything she'd ever experienced. What would it have been like to grow up with a sibling?

Wiping away a stray tear, she walked resolutely to the duke's library. She must do everything in her power to help the children adjust to their new life and that meant finding the right books to anchor them here.

She knew the exact location of the library—along this corridor, down a narrow flight of stairs, round the landing corner, and three doors down.

What she didn't know was the exact location of the duke.

She didn't want to run into him by accident. Not even a glimpse of him through a window.

And especially never anything to do with him kneeling at her feet, touching her, lifting a knife to cut her bootlaces.

Why couldn't she stop thinking about it? It was only that it had been wholly unexpected.

His powerful grip on her ankle. His hand under her skirts.

She stopped a housemaid carrying a bundle of linens. "Is His Grace in this evening?"

"That's doubtful, miss. He stays late at The Vulcan most nights, working on 'is engines."

"Thank you." How many servants lived in this house? Seemed a fair army.

She hadn't considered that living in the duke's home might feel so isolating. Even though there were people everywhere.

Footmen posted at doorways. Maids scurrying through the corridors.

They mostly avoided her eyes and went about their business.

A governess was an odd sort of creature, living betwixt the upstairs and downstairs worlds.

Mari knew she was more qualified for the position of serving girl than governess, but no one else did. In the servant's eyes, she was above them. And in the duke's, she was far, far below.

About the size of one of his miniature engines.

Mrs. Fairfield had said he spent more time at his foundry than anywhere else. Was he still there working on his steam engines? Or was he somewhere else . . . perhaps out carousing with dissipated friends.

Lolling about on a velvet divan, smoking cigars while voluptuous women fanned him with ostrich feathers.

She couldn't quite picture it. Or maybe she didn't want to think about it. She'd rather picture him in his shirtsleeves, hands stained with oil as he worked with his engineer to construct an engine.

Well wherever he was, he wasn't here, and that was the most important thing. She could plunder his library in peace.

He wouldn't miss a volume or two.

She passed a footman standing sentry outside a room and gave him a confident nod, as if to say: *yes, I have business here, no cause for alarm.*

She peeked into the library. There were lamps burning on the tables and a fire lit in the grate.

How extravagant.

Checking to make certain there were no dukes or model engines in her path, Mari entered the room, leaving the door ajar.

Wouldn't do for the footmen to think she was trying to hide something.

A noise made her jump but it was only the chiming from a clock standing against the wall.

Lamplight flickered over metal tracks and engines on the table that held the model of his proposed railway. Drawn by curiosity, she ventured closer.

Miniature trees flanked the tracks that snaked around the table. He'd even fashioned miniature estates, painted to look like stone, complete with coats of arms over the doorways and pennants flying on the battlements.

The engines were platforms mounted on metal wheels with staffs and barrels bristling out of them. Tiny men in even tinier top hats stood atop the locomotives, feeding their engines with little shovels.

Wouldn't Michel and Adele love to play with these? A whole new world. The world the duke wanted to create. Engines carrying goods and passengers of all social classes across England.

It would change everything.

An image rose in her mind of Banksford painting each figure with longing and precision.

His huge hands performing the most delicate of tasks.

They'd been stained with ink, his hands, and she'd noticed several burn marks.

Working with steam and combustion must be dangerous.

Whenever she thought about his hands, warmth ignited in the pit of her stomach.

He'd lifted her so easily, circling her waist in an iron grip. And when his fingers had brushed her calf, the touch had spread through her whole body like wildfire.

Right here, in this very room, a commanding duke had knelt at her feet.

Not something she'd ever pictured happening to her.

None of this was how she'd thought her life would progress.

She pushed one of the locomotives and it slid along the rail, its wheels somehow staying on the tracks.

Her life in London was supposed to have been a difficult and trying one.

The engine under her fingers ran smoothly along the tracks, passing trees and country estates.

At Mr. Folsom's house she would have been little more than a nursemaid. Her bed would have been tucked into the garret. She would have dined on leftovers.

But here . . . she lifted the model engine off the tracks.

Here, she'd gone off the rails of her prescribed life. Living in luxury, treated with respect.

This was completely new terrain, uncharted and filled with both great potential . . . and even greater pitfalls.

Pretending to be upper class. Letting the duke assume that she'd been educated at an elite private academy.

Sin by omission.

She didn't like telling untruths. Especially ones that could land her in prison for deceiving a duke.

But she had to take the risk. She needed to buy enough time to search for Mr. Shadwell and ask him why he'd come looking for her at Underwood.

Without warning, a hulking shape loomed behind her and large arms hugged her, pinioning her wrists together in front of her navel.

"What are you doing sneaking about my library, Perkins?" a deep, gruff voice asked.

So much for avoiding the duke.

Chapter 7

MARI TWISTED IN his arms, trying to break away, but he held her easily, one of his large hands trapping both her wrists.

"Are you a spy?" he demanded.

"Pardon? Of course not! I'm a governess. I thought we established that yesterday."

"A spy from a rival railway company. Or perhaps from one of the fire brigades." His arms tightened around her, drawing her back against his solid warmth. "Very clever. Send a lady who's just my kind of temptation to steal my secrets."

His kind of temptation?

Her heart fluttered in her ribcage, trying to escape her chest.

"I'm not a spy," she said. "I'm here to instruct your children although I won't be much use in that endeavor if you squeeze me to death."

He dropped her wrists but didn't move away. "My apologies. You're not a spy. You're merely a governess."

She bristled. "That's right. An ordinary, commonplace governess."

He bent closer, his breath fanning her cheek. "I thought you said you would wear voluminous smocks, Perkins."

"My trunk was stolen, Your Grace. If you wish me to wear shapeless smocks, you'll have to provide them. But just so you know, your footmen appear to be singularly undistracted by me."

His low laughter struck a chord somewhere deep inside her. She liked making him laugh.

"How dare they be undistracted?" he asked.

"Well *I* didn't expect them to be. You're the one who had that wrong-headed notion."

Probably she should step away now. But she rather liked the feel of his body behind her. His proximity was somehow more comforting than threatening.

Really, what she wanted to do was lean backward and fit herself more closely against him.

If he wrapped his arms around her, it might feel like the first safe place she'd ever known.

And she who makes a sheep of herself, becomes prey to the wolf.

She stepped away and turned to face him.

If his presence behind her had made her heart race, his front view was even more devastating to a girl's composure.

Rumpled chestnut hair falling over silvery eyes. No coat to speak of. And his cravat was undone, looped loosely over his neck with the ends dangling over a wedge of bare chest.

Bare. Chest.

This was precisely why she must avoid him. This heat that shimmered through her body. The way she couldn't tear her eyes away from that tantalizing glimpse of bare flesh.

A sudden longing to find a dagger and cut off his shirt buttons, as he'd slit through her bootlaces, gripped her mind.

He'd had a good, long look at her ankles. Shouldn't she be allowed to see his chest? She could rip the rest of the shirt. Rend it in two.

The rhythmic pulse visible in the shadow of his throat was proof that he was merely a man. Flesh and blood, sinew and bone. Warm and strong and inviting.

She'd never had such wicked thoughts. At least not about a real, live duke. She may have imagined herself as the heroine of a few romantic novels.

To cover her confusion, she pursed her lips and gave him a disapproving look. "Must you always leap to these drastically inaccurate assumptions about me, Your Grace? I'm neither a temptress with designs on your footmen, nor a spy with designs upon your engineering plans. I'm a plain, unassuming governess."

He grinned. "If you're plain and unassuming, then I'm a ruddy chimney sweep. You must admit the situation could be misconstrued. First you crush my model engine, and now you're sneaking about my private rooms, examining the model of my railway. You looked guilty."

"I'll admit nothing of the sort."

"Then why are you here?" he asked, adjusting the cuffs of his shirt to cover his wrists.

"I found the children's bookshelves to be sadly lacking in scope for the imagination. And filled with moralizing tripe. *Dr. Pritchard's Catechisms*. Really, Your Grace. I expected better of you."

"Uh . . ." His chin ducked toward his neck. "Who is Dr. Pritchard?"

"The most priggish, sanctimonious fool to ever set quill to paper and compose fire-and-brimstone morality lessons for children. I found his teachings written upon the blackboard in the nursery. It is small wonder the twins run away."

"Are you lecturing me, Perkins?"

Good lord. She was lecturing a duke. That would

never do. No one wanted a *governess* to exhibit any backbone.

"I do apologize for my stridency, Your Grace." She cast her gaze demurely to the carpet. "It's only that I hold a strong belief, based on personal experience, that children respond better to encouragement than censure."

He was silent for so long that she raised her head and encountered that steady, unnerving gaze of his.

"Never apologize for stridency, Perkins. You've a valid point to make. I'm ashamed to admit that I had no idea the children were being subjected to the sanctimonious Dr. Pritchard."

A different kind of warmth seeped through her at his words. No one had ever wanted to hear her true opinions before.

He swiped a hand at the library shelves. "Take all the books you want. But leave the model engines alone."

"I thought the children might like to play with them."

"For the love of . . . they're not toys," he said. "The children most certainly cannot play with them. I use the model engines to visualize my designs before they are built on a larger scale."

"But you must admit they do *look* like toys."

He scowled down at her. "I'll admit nothing of the sort. They're models of a very serious and historic undertaking, I'll have you know."

"But they're just so cunning and delicate." She knew she was playing with fire but couldn't seem to stop herself. "And those adorable little gentlemen in their teensy top hats . . ."

She stopped speaking because he appeared about to combust.

"Someday I'll bring you to my foundry, Perkins.

Believe me, the words adorable and teensy will never cross your impertinent lips."

She liked the sound of someday.

It sounded longer than one week.

"I should like that." She gave him a teasing smile. "I'm sure your engines are ever so formidable and impressive."

Like everything else about him.

"Extremely formidable." His gaze dropped to her lips. "And impressive."

Were they still talking about steam locomotives? Something about the mischievous glint in his eyes and the way he was perusing her lips made her think they weren't.

Then what were they discussing . . . ? *Oh.*

Mari had been raised in a school for girls. She'd heard a whispered thing or two about male . . . *engines.*

Was he flirting with her? It was wrong, of course, and should be stopped immediately.

And yet . . . she'd never been flirted with before.

It was exhilarating. As though she were walking along the edge of a cliff.

Danger calling to the pit of her stomach.

Warning her away and daring her to jump at the same time.

"I suppose it would depend on the perspective." She flicked her gaze lower, daringly close to his breeches. "And it would probably require flattering lighting."

His snort of laughter caught her off guard.

"There's more to you than meets the eye, Perkins."

"My name is *Miss* Perkins, if you please. I won't be referred to solely by my surname."

"It's the done thing," he said in a clipped tone.

"It may well be the done thing to reduce your servants to surnames, to view them as necessary items of furniture, meant to support your weight and never bend or break, but I find it demeaning."

"*Miss* Perkins, you're welcome to pillage my bookshelves, but then be so kind as to leave me in peace. I've had a very long and disappointing day."

He stalked to his desk.

She'd been dismissed. Which was better than being besieged, wasn't it?

A dim part of her brain wasn't too sure about that.

EDGAR TURNED UP the lamp at his desk. He'd come to the library to work on his engine design, and his mind had caught fire, not with engineering solutions, but with a blaze of attraction.

He couldn't just reason it away, the tingling at the base of his skull, the itching in his palms. The heightened awareness.

Not just an awareness of her body, though that was pleasing enough—slender, yet curvaceous, garbed in the same black gown but with a white apron over the top.

Not simply her beauty. Her quick tongue and even quicker mind.

The way she spoke to him without flattery or deference.

He liked her intelligence and fearlessness.

Something new. Something worth knowing.

First the tender scene he'd witnessed with the children and then the achingly perfect feel of her slim curves pressed against him.

Can't keep your hands to yourself, can you?

To think about anything other than Miss Perkins's pert backside, he got out his paints and began coloring the wheels of a model engine.

Or at least he attempted to paint them. His brush kept missing the mark whenever his gaze wandered back to Miss Perkins.

She was taking her time choosing books for the children.

When she ran her finger across leather-bound spines, he felt the caress on his own skin.

Touch *me*. Choose *me*.

She bent at the waist, holding the lamp close to view books on a lower shelf.

How could a simple white apron be so seductive? The narrow straps that crossed over her back ended in a big white bow.

The point of uniforms was to make people conform.

Miss Perkins conform to a silent, diffident role? Never.

She was still bending over, presenting him with a splendid view of her gift-wrapped arse.

His brush slipped. "Damn."

She straightened, pursing her lips to puff a curl away from her cheek. "Is anything the matter, Your Grace?"

"Nothing's the matter," he muttered.

Except that he'd painted the inside of his wrist blue instead of the engine wheels, like an addlepated fool. He grabbed a rag and wiped his arm clean.

When he looked at her he heard drums beating in the distance, advancing with the warning of war. The battle for dominion over these forbidden thoughts.

A war against wanting to know her better.

Obviously he wasn't going to accomplish anything this evening. Not with her in the room.

She lifted her small stack of books. "I'll bid you good-night, Your Grace."

She was halfway across the room when the top volume caught his eye. He rose from his desk. "I wouldn't use that particular volume of poetry if I were you."

She glanced at the book. "Why not?"

"Because it was written by the twins' mother. The woman who hid their existence from me for nine years. The woman who abandoned them."

Her cheeks paled. "I'm dreadfully sorry, I had no idea."

"What fiendish, unseen hand directed you to that book, I wonder?" he asked.

"What fiendish hand forced you to keep it on your shelves, I wonder?" she rejoined.

She had a point. He was quickly learning that she usually did.

He'd thought he was in love with Sophie, with the heedless passion only a very naïve, very foolish young pup could feel. It must have been some lingering attachment to the memory of his first, ill-fated love that had kept the book on his shelves.

A passion that had torn his family apart.

A love that had nearly destroyed his life.

"I'm not sure," he finally answered her, shaking himself out of his painful memories. "It was a mistake."

"Perhaps the children would like to read her poetry. It may be their last remaining link to her."

"No," he said unhesitatingly, harshly.

"Well it was merely a suggestion," she replied in an affronted voice.

"Sophie left them with only a hired nurse to care for them. They could have died, and I never would have known."

"I'll return the book to the shelves."

"Please don't. Just . . ." He held out his hand. "I'll dispose of it. It's of no consequence now. It's in the past."

Yet the past wouldn't stay buried.

It stared at him accusingly from Adele's eyes. *Sophie's eyes.*

Not good enough for husband.

Not good enough for father.

She handed him the slim volume and he set it on a table.

"I gather your late wife, er . . ." Realizing she'd made a blunder, Miss Perkins paused. "I mean to say, your late—"

"Mistress," Edgar supplied, though he knew it was unforgivably rude to speak of such sordid topics.

He half expected her to make a hasty retreat, but she remained, standing close enough for him to touch.

"I gather she was French?" she asked.

"Her father was from Paris, and her mother from Casablanca, in Morocco. I attempted to find her parents after Michel and Adele came to live with me. I thought they might want to meet their grandparents, but both of Sophie's parents are now deceased."

"The children do have a grandmother here in London, I hear."

"The dowager and I are estranged."

She waited for him to say more, watching his face. He wasn't going to touch that subject.

"After she bore the twins, Sophie left them in France and traveled first to Morocco, then to India, on a quest for *poetic enlightenment*, whatever that is." He tried to keep the rancor out of his voice and failed.

He waited for her to make some comment, perhaps of censure.

The other governesses had been quietly appalled at the notion of illegitimate children being raised in the manner of heirs and heiresses.

The subject didn't seem distasteful to her. She listened thoughtfully, with a small furrow of concentration between her delicate brows.

"I've said enough." He tugged on his shirt cuff. "I don't normally speak of these subjects. You may leave now, Miss Perkins." He gestured toward the door.

Her smile was quick and playful, and it made him want to smile back. "Haven't you discovered by now that I'm not easily dissuaded or dismissed, Your Grace?"

He wanted to discover so much more about her. For instance, why was such a bright, lovely woman relegated to the role of governess?

And then there was the burning question of whether her apron was tied with a knot . . . or whether the bow would come undone with one tug.

He gave himself a mental shake. Neither one of those questions would ever be answered.

"Take your books and leave me in peace." Leave him to sit in the library alone, beset by ghosts and dark memories.

"I'd like to know more," she said softly. "It will help me to understand the children better, and find ways to ease their minds."

He knew it wasn't a good idea, knew he should insist that she leave, but now that the memories had risen from the dead, he found he didn't want to be alone with them.

A few moments of conversation couldn't harm anything, he told himself. It was only so that she could better understand the children.

Not because he was lonely. Or because the sympathy in her eyes warmed him like coal feeding a furnace.

"Sit with me, then," he said gruffly. "If you dare."

"I dare," she replied.

Chapter 8

❧

MARI TUCKED HER worn boots out of sight under her skirts. The duke settled across from her, propping one of his elbows on the arm of the chair, which did interesting things to the bulging muscles beneath his shirt.

Why had she decided to stay? He'd given her every opportunity to retreat, but then he'd dared her to stay. Her reckless side had responded to the challenge, though she'd rationalized her decision by saying it was because she wanted to know more about the children's past.

Which she did, but she also wanted to know more about Banksford. What had painted all of those shadows in his eyes?

A footman banked the fire. Another fluffed the cushions on the settee and trimmed the lamps. They moved soundlessly, seeing to his every comfort.

What must it be like to have all your desires fulfilled before you even knew what they were?

Yet another footman positioned a silver platter heaped with glistening fruit and sweetmeats on a table between their chairs. Taking up a pair of silver tongs and a small plate, the footman waited expectantly.

"Would you care for some fruit, Miss Perkins?" asked the duke.

Mari recognized a cluster of dark purple grapes

and some strawberries, but the rest of it was a mystery. What were those yellow triangles with pockmarks in them? They looked rather stringy.

"I'll have some grapes, Your Grace," she said, making a safe choice.

The footman served her a cluster of grapes.

She'd never eaten grapes before. She mustn't betray her lack of gustatory experience with a telltale *ooh* of astonishment.

The dark purple fruit burst under the assault of her teeth, flooding her mouth with sweetness. There was almost a hint of violet. The way violets smelled. Something musky and perfumed.

The seeds were slightly bitter, but easily swallowed. She ate another. And then another.

She could become accustomed to being served grapes like the ancient Romans.

Only, if they were ancient Romans, she and the duke would be lounging about on the carpet, half naked.

Good gracious. What manner of thought was that to have?

A forbidden thought, that's what.

She glanced at him from under her lashes. His lips were perfectly shaped for . . . grape eating. Firm and well defined on top, and flared below.

The duke cleared his throat.

She hauled her attention back to modern-day England, where she was a superior governess and he was a duke and they would never, ever roll on the carpet together.

"You said you had a long and disappointing day, Your Grace?" she asked.

"I had an interview with an old friend of mine, the Duke of Westbury, who doesn't want to allow the proposed railway to pass through his estate. Many noblemen oppose the railway. I'm to give a speech at my club on the subject."

"Have you written the speech?"

He drew a sheet of crumpled paper from inside his coat and threw it onto the table. "I've attempted to."

Mari wiped her fingers on a serviette and lifted the ball of his speech, smoothing it out on her lap. "May I?"

"By all means. I've rewritten it three or four times but there's something lacking. Are you an author, Miss Perkins?"

"I, Your Grace? No. I'm a teacher. More skilled at editing others' compositions than writing my own. Everyone can use a good editor."

He waved a hand at the speech. "Be my guest."

His penmanship was bold, commanding and it marched full tilt across the page.

She was aware of him watching her read. Watching intently, as if her opinion of his words mattered greatly.

Again, she was struck by how little he matched the picture she'd painted of him in her mind, before she met him.

An arrogant duke wouldn't care what the governess thought.

She folded the speech and set it back on the table. "It's a very eloquent speech, Your Grace. I can feel how deeply you care for your subject."

"But . . ." he prompted.

"If I offered a friendly criticism, I'd say it lacks a certain . . . passion. Instead of dwelling so heavily upon figures and profits, and the interchange of commerce and manufacturing supplies, you might mention some of the more altruistic and noble benefits of such a system of travel."

"The Whigs won't want to hear about the benefits to commoners. There's always fierce objection to any tidal shift in power." He separated two of the yellow slices to one side of the platter. "The stagecoaches opposed the canal boats." He moved the yellow slices close to what looked like a large slice of melon, though she couldn't be sure because she'd never seen one of such a vibrant red hue.

"They both oppose the railway." He arranged grapes in a row on either side of the melon slice. "And my fellow landowners with pleasure estates don't want their lands carved by the rails or commoners to travel their hallowed ground." He added more grapes. "And the parish fire brigades are mired in the past, married to their old, inadequate methods."

She studied his culinary map, placing several strawberries atop the melon. "Yes, but the railways will provide inexpensive and expeditious travel for people of all classes. And your fire engines will save countless lives."

"And the railway I help finance will provide much needed access to more inexpensive coal and medicines for people living in hard-to-reach areas. Children, especially."

"Couldn't you explain this to the gentlemen, Your Grace? Wouldn't they listen?"

"They don't care about the plight of the common man. They fear the railway as a threat to their way of life. A blow against tradition."

She ate a strawberry, ruminating on his words. She liked that he appeared to be one of the rare noblemen who cared about the plight of the common man. He certainly cared about his illegitimate children.

"I've found that telling a story can sometimes

be more effective than more pontificating, didactic methods of communication," she said.

"My pride will be quite deflated by the end of this day, Miss Perkins. First Michel accuses me of being a boring milksop and now I'm a didactic pontificator?"

She nearly choked on the strawberry. "How do you know what Michel said?"

He gave her a guilty look. "Ah . . . I may have been listening at the door this evening, as you put the children to bed."

He'd been watching? She tried to recall the details of her conversation with the children. Had she said anything incriminating about her childhood? She couldn't risk him learning she'd been raised in a charity school and was unfit by society's standards to be his governess. "It seems *you're* the spy in the household, Your Grace. Lurking about doorways."

He made a slight bow from the waist. "Touché, Miss Perkins. It's true, the gentlemen at my club take pontification to a whole new level," he said. "It's difficult to squeeze a word in edgewise."

"But they still have hearts. And children. What you need to do is hit them square in the chest. Tell them the story of an actual child living in the countryside who died from lack of medicine. I knew such a girl." She blinked her eyes, staving off the sudden tears that always threatened to spill over when she thought of how easily Helena could have been saved.

"Was she your sister?"

"Bosom friend."

"And she could have been saved?"

"She had typhoid fever. The medicine from London didn't reach her in time."

"It's a shame they don't allow females at my club,

Miss Perkins. If you gave the speech, their hearts would be moved."

When he smiled, the ice in his gaze cracked and spread into appealing crinkles at the edges of his eyes.

"I can tell that after only one brief day, the children are beginning to thaw toward you as well," he continued. "It was very clever of you to give them that elixir. I had no idea they are so very homesick for France."

"And for their nurse, a woman named Amina. We wrote a letter to her today. I think it would mean so much to them to receive a reply."

He nodded. "Another excellent idea."

Now there was definitely approval in his eyes. It made her feel warm inside, as if she'd gulped down an entire cupful of hot tea.

"If you were there, outside the door, why didn't you make yourself known?" she asked.

His gray eyes filled with the same hesitation and mistrust she'd seen in Michel and Adele's eyes earlier.

He crossed his ankles and stretched his long legs toward the fire. "I would have ruined the moment. I'm afraid I'm no good with the children." He rubbed his left knee. "They don't want a half-lame giant of a father. I frighten them."

Half-lame giant? That's hardly how she would describe him. Didn't he know how he muddled a girl's thoughts and made her heart race?

"That's funny," she said gently, "because they seem to think that *you* don't want *them*."

"Of course I want them." He made an impatient gesture. "I even wrote them into my will."

"If you were listening then you know that the twins don't want to be separated. They have a very strong bond."

He shook his head. "You'll not convince me that Michel shouldn't attend Eton. Every male child in this family, legitimate or otherwise, attends Eton. It's a mark of distinction and acknowledgement."

"I understand, Your Grace, but they need to be prepared for the separation. Perhaps you could talk to them. Tell Michel some stories from your years at Eton. Give them time to come to terms with the idea."

He chuckled, his shoulders shaking with laughter.

She ducked her chin. "Did I say something humorous, Your Grace?"

"Are you assigning me a task to complete?" He grinned. "Because it seems like maybe you're planting notions in my head."

"The idea." She sniffed. "I would never do such a thing."

"Oh yes you would."

She couldn't help smiling back. "Well perhaps just a few gentle nudges, Your Grace."

"As I surmised."

"It's just that children absorb and reflect their surroundings," Mari said. "We teach them with every expression of our face, every word we speak . . . and don't speak."

He sobered. "I wasn't the recipient of many kind words from my own parents. I've tried, Miss Perkins, truly I have. But everything I say comes out all wrong. Adele, in particular, has such a look of panic when I speak to her."

She didn't want to lecture him, but there was a clear question in his words. He wanted to know how to communicate with the children.

"Well," she said, choosing her words carefully. "Many people think that when they speak to children they should use a different voice, but children don't respond favorably to that. They don't like to be talked down to."

"So I should speak to them as I'm speaking to you."

"Exactly. They are people in their own right."

"I've hardly had time to speak to them at all," he said. "I thought outfitting the nursery with toys from Lumley's shop would be enough. You said you'd never been to London, Miss Perkins, but that wooden rabbit you showed the children is from Lumley's. It's such a magical place."

"My rabbit is from Lumley's Toy Shop? It was given to me as a child and I had no idea of its origin."

Excitement buzzed in her mind. This could be a clue. Now she knew where the rabbit had been purchased. She added Lumley's shop to her list of destinations in London.

"Mr. Lumley is known for his wooden toys. I had a nutcracker with a jaw that moved up and down."

"Perhaps you could bring the children to a toy shop someday. Show them the toys and games you used to love when you were their age."

"Perhaps I will. After my new steam engine design is complete."

"And you could try simply sitting and listening to the twins. They have a lot to say, I've found. I believe that we can learn as much from children, as they learn from us."

"An interesting philosophy."

"I've read widely on the subject of children's education. I support the learned philosophers who argue that children's natural inclinations and interests should guide their studies. Though most of the philosophers are not keen on the education of females, which I think should be a right and not a privilege."

"Bit of a bluestocking, are you?" He regarded her with interest.

"Not particularly. I form my opinions from what I observe. Michel and Adele are equally intelligent and resourceful . . . and resilient."

He didn't deny it, which was more endearing than she was willing to admit.

"What do they miss most about France, do you think? Besides their nurse," he asked.

"They spoke at great lengths about the inferiority of English bread. Apparently it's doughy, crustless, and lacks any kind of flavor at all."

He laughed. "Noted."

"And they miss the seashore."

"I'm learning more about the children from you, than you'll ever learn from me, Miss Perkins."

She shrugged modestly. "It's my job to make these observations. Any governess would do the same."

"No, I don't believe so." When had his eyes lost their shadows? "You're not like other governesses, as far as I can tell. You're witty, confident, highly intelligent . . ." His gaze searched her face. "Why *are* you a governess? A gentleman's daughter with such winning attributes could have her pick of suitors."

Had she told him she was a gentleman's daughter? She didn't think she'd told him such a lie. He must be making assumptions because she'd come from Mrs. Trilby's agency.

This was an extremely dangerous line of questioning.

Say something off-putting.

Leave immediately.

"Marriage is hardly the solution to every female's problems, Your Grace," she said tartly.

"It would surely be preferable to *this.*"

"Caring for other people's children instead of my own, you mean? Perhaps."

"What of your parents? Don't they wish you to marry?"

Stay as close to the truth as possible and leave swiftly.

"I never knew my mother," she said carefully. "And my father was a distant figure. Being a governess is my lot in life." She rose from her chair. "Now, if you'll excuse me, it's growing late and I must be going."

He rose as well. "I didn't mean to anger you."

"You're just being you."

He stepped closer. "And what's that supposed to mean?"

"Nothing."

"No, please tell me. I want to know why you have such a bad opinion of me on such short acquaintance."

"It's not you, in particular. It's dukes, in general."

"I see. It's my rank that bothers you."

"Dukes breathe such rarified air. You've lost the ability to think as a commoner. The eagle never catches flies, as they say."

"It's not every governess who would make such an observation. I daresay you're unique among your tribe, Miss Perkins."

"And you're not at all unique, as far as dukes go."

It was far better to argue with him than field questions about her past.

Mari plunged ahead. "Oh Great Duke. King of your castle. Flinging governesses over your shoulder at will. *Mutare vel timere sperno.* Everyone else must change, not you."

"Careful, Perkins," he said, his gaze gathering storm clouds.

"Life ebbs and flows by your whims. 'And how is

the duke feeling today? Will he thunder and scorch us with lightning or will it be a tranquil day?'"

She expected him to lash out then, to tell her she was wrong and didn't know her place.

That's why his deep, rich laughter startled her. "Not one governess in one thousand would lecture me as you do."

"As a governess I have a duty to point out misbehavior."

"Impudent minx."

Why was he grinning at her as if he liked impudent minxes more than anything?

"Perhaps I deserve a thorough tongue-lashing," he mused.

Which sounded quite wicked when spoken in such a low, husky voice.

His gaze shifted back to her lips. "Are you planning to give me another?"

"Only if you're bad, Your Grace."

He must have taken a step nearer to her.

Or had she been the one to move closer?

So close.

What had come over her? She felt nearly weightless, as if she might float away if he didn't touch her, anchor her to the ground. Of all the ridiculous things to long for . . . a kiss from the finely molded lips of a devilish duke. Lady India would surely disapprove if she were the duke's paramour.

How many ways could she deflect his questions about her past before he became suspicious? Maybe, instead of arguing with him, she should try distracting him by other means.

A reckless desire formed in her mind.

A desire to misbehave. Just this once. To actually experience life, instead of reading about it in books.

He awakened these hidden desires in her. She had no idea where they were coming from. She only knew they made her want to do things like . . . this.

She rose to her tiptoes, placing her palms against his rock-solid chest. "Or . . . I could be the bad one."

HER PALM RESTED on his chest, over his heart.

Edgar could see each individual golden freckle sprinkled across her nose. The freckles continued over her cheeks, lighter there, and even kissed the edges of her lips.

Pale pink lips, slightly parted.

The flare of heat in her eyes. An invitation.

An invitation innocently given. One he could never accept.

Her hair was braided and wound round her head so forcefully it drew her eyebrows up slightly. Her actions didn't match those tightly wound braids.

Braid away the brazen.

Batten up the bold.

It would never work. The true fire of her nature would always flare to life.

He wanted to kiss her more than he'd ever wanted anything in his entire blighted existence.

You can have this, a seductive voice whispered in his mind.

All of this sweetness and exploration. This sensual awakening.

Give the lady her very first kiss. Kiss her so well she'll spend the rest of her life dreaming of you.

Lose yourself in her eyes. No need to think of past guilt, past pain. Live for today. Live through her eyes.

He cupped her cheek with his palm, brushing his thumb over the slender bones of her jaw. "You're not intimidated by me."

She dropped back onto her heels. Her hand stayed on his chest, a slight pressure, a small patch of warmth.

"Should I be?" she asked.

She was the one who intimidated him. She breached his walls. Pitted out handholds in his defenses.

And it was terrifying. She'd accused him of tyranny. Making servants dance to his whims. Everything he'd vowed never to do.

This must end, and never be repeated. He must keep his hands off her.

And hers off him . . .

Gently, reluctantly, he removed her hands from his chest and stepped away, putting distance between them.

"I'm not your typical duke, Miss Perkins. I left London for seven years and lived in disguise as a commoner, working in a foundry. It was because of what happened with the children's mother. I didn't tell you the whole story," he said. "Of Sophie."

She backed away. "Sophie."

Nothing like introducing the topic of an ex-lover to dampen a fire. "Sophie seduced me."

"*She* seduced *you*?"

"When I was only seventeen and she was nearing thirty."

Her eyes widened. "I see."

"She'd had a very brief affair with my father years ago, but he never kept one mistress very long. She seduced me to have her revenge on my father. Flaunted it in his face. She was only using me."

"That must have stung."

"She strung me along on a leash for three years before cutting me loose. She left without warning, without a word of good-bye." Such a heartbreaking, shameful story.

He really should stop talking now, but something compelled him to keep going. It wasn't in his nature to leave something unfinished. "Sophie wrote a letter that she sent with the twins. I only received it after her death. After she returned to London and . . . took her own life. She swore they were mine, and no one else's. The timing was right. They resemble me."

"They do, indeed."

"The whole experience taught me a valuable lesson, Miss Perkins. Love, especially the love experienced in youth, is illusory, elusive, and fleeting at best. A cruel joke at worst."

There. He could see that she had received the message.

Don't long for me to kiss you. Don't fall in love with me.

"I'm glad their mother sent the children to you," she said.

"I'm not sure the children are glad of it," he said. "They run away every chance they have. I'm afraid . . . I'm afraid they'll decide to run away forever."

"Have faith, Your Grace. I believe anything broken may be mended. While we yet breathe, there is hope."

"You're a woman of strong convictions."

At nine and twenty, he'd made far too many mistakes to hope for new beginnings.

Firelight played across her skin, bathing her freckles in golden light.

"I'm beginning to understand now," she said. "The complicated nature of your relationship with your offspring. You think of them as mistakes. If you think of them as regrets, you'll never see them any other way."

"I don't . . ." he began vehemently, and stopped.

Could that be true?

"It's more that I see them as the innocent results of a mistake. Nothing about my interlude with Sophie was pure or innocent, except the results. These two beautiful children, raised in hardship and poverty. I will ensure the rest of their lives are lived in comfort and security."

"Maybe this guilt isn't something you're supposed to carry. Maybe you don't need to wallow in it."

"Wallow? Pigs wallow. Dukes never wallow."

"I chose my wording poorly. Perhaps revel. It's almost an indulgence, isn't it? To repeat one's missteps over and over in one's mind until that's all one can see? If you're not careful, you could become stuck in a continuous loop in your mind, going over and over the dark, bad things and never moving forward, into the light."

How had she become so wise? Her words solidified in his mind like molten metal cooling into a new shape. But it was too late for him to be reshaped. "What light? There's no light to find. Why don't you go and tell the twins a story with a happy ending? Because there is none to find here, do you understand me?"

She took a step backward.

"I understand." Tension played along her jaw. "Because I'm merely the governess. Not fit to give a duke advice."

"Something like that."

She glared at him, and then gathered her pile of books and left the library without a backward glance.

Which should have made him happy. He'd achieved his aim of driving her away.

He sat in the chair she'd been sitting in, remembering the way she'd eaten the grapes with such gusto and pleasure. She was so vibrant and opinionated.

So beautiful and intelligent.

They'd had such a far-ranging discussion.

They'd covered death, lost love, children's education, marriage, rights for women . . . it had felt like a year's worth of conversations fit into one evening. India had been right, he reflected. Miss Perkins was exactly what his children required. The problem was, she was also precisely what he desired . . . and could never have.

The stars shining in her eyes were not for the likes of him. She was filled with light and conviction. Just on the beginning of her luminous path in life.

Any light in his heart had been snuffed out long ago, leaving him in darkness.

Take my books, Mari-rhymes-with-starry.

But leave my heart and my rules intact.

Chapter 9

"Wake up, Miss Perkins. Are you still abed?"

Mari rubbed her eyes.

Five o'clock and time for morning prayers.

Rise and scrub her face, supervise the sleepy masses in face washing and hand scrubbing. Walk with them to the stone chapel.

Kneel on the cold stone floor. Scent of tallow and penitence.

Her eyes flew open.

No Underwood. No lumpy straw ticking. No smell of mildew and mouse droppings.

Soft linens beneath her cheek.

A mattress fashioned of feathers and clouds.

And a beautiful face leaning over her bed, violet eyes dancing, and glossy black hair tumbling forward. The spicy scent of bold perfume.

Lady India?

Mari bolted upright. "I've overslept. Where are the children? What time is it?"

Lady India laughed. "Don't fret, it's still quite early. I wanted to catch you when I knew that Edgar wouldn't see me. The man is nocturnal. Always poring over his engineering plans past midnight."

It had been a week since Mari's encounter with the duke in the library.

Edgar, Lady India called him with such familiarity. The name fit him. Hard-edged and guttural, like his voice had been, telling her to leave.

Or I could be the bad one . . .

She still couldn't believe she'd spoken those words. Placed her hand over his heart. Raised onto her tiptoes.

Oh God.

Her cheeks burned, thinking of their last encounter. Lady India wouldn't be smiling at her if she knew what Mari had done.

"Are you well, Miss Perkins?" asked Lady India, peering down at her. "You look rather flushed."

Mari startled. "Quite well. May I help you with something?"

Lady India nodded. "You may. Hop straight out of bed and put this on." She handed Mari a silk dressing gown of a dusty rose hue. "The footmen are queuing at the door."

Mari rubbed her eyes. Perhaps she was still dreaming. "Footmen?"

"Hurry now." Lady India tugged her out of bed and helped her into the dressing gown, tying the sash tightly. "Enter," she called.

The door swung open and a line of footmen streamed into the room, their arms filled with boxes and parcels of all shapes and sizes.

"What's all this?" Mari asked.

A maid in a white frilled cap arrived carrying several long flat glove boxes. "Where do you want these, my lady?" she asked Lady India.

"On the bed for now, Fern."

More footmen. More boxes.

"I don't understand," said Mari. "What are all of these parcels?"

"Your portmanteau was pilfered. This is the new wardrobe you were promised."

"I can't accept all of this! I don't have the resources to . . ." She knew a proper lady never discussed finances, but she must impress upon this woman that she couldn't afford such clothing. "I can't recompense you, Lady India."

"Piffle. What would I want with recompense? These were all purchased on Edgar's account."

The duke was outfitting her? Out of the question.

"Take it all back." Mari was beginning to have the sinking feeling that the duke might have formed the wrong impression of her.

"Nonsense." Lady India opened a box to reveal a gauzy white muslin gown with puffed sleeves and a scarlet sash.

She lifted the dress, shaking it out and holding it up to Mari. "What do you say, Fern? Will it suit her?"

"Splendidly," the maid replied. "Such a slender figure you have, miss. When Lady India described it to me, I scarcely believed her but now I'm glad I nipped everything in at the waist."

Governesses did not wear filmy white muslin with scarlet sashes.

A woman like Lady India would wear such a stunning gown.

"I fear perhaps the duke may have formed the wrong opinion of me." Could it have been her wanton behavior in the library?

What had come over her? She blamed it on the grapes. They had tempted her to thoughts of kissing. *You're addled, Mari Perkins.*

A freckled, carrot-haired governess kissing a duke.

What utter rubbish.

She didn't want to offend the lady, but she must

say what she had to say. "I'm a respectable governess and I'm not for purchase. These gowns are far too frivolous and dear and therefore I can only assume, lamentably, that they are intended for a lady of the . . . light-heeled persuasion."

"Light-heeled? Heavens!" Lady India dissolved into giggles, throwing the gown across the bed. "You think Edgar is trying to make you his mistress?" Her peals of laughter rang through the room, turning the footmen's heads.

"Er . . ." Why was that so funny?

"Wait a moment." Lady India clutched her hands together. "Do you think . . . do you think *I* am Edgar's mistress?"

The maid made a strangled sound.

"I'm sure I haven't formed any opinion at all on the subject of your relationship with His Grace."

"Yes, you have! Why, Edgar is my brother, you silly goose."

"Your brother . . . ?"

Of course.

If she'd been thinking clearly she would have seen that they had the same sharp cheekbones, the same dark hair and pale eyes, though the lady's were lavender where the duke's were an icy gray.

Because you wanted to believe Banksford was a profligate who casually entertained his paramours in front of his children.

Because it would have made him easier to hate.

"I'm terribly sorry for jumping to conclusions, Lady India."

"I'm not trying to corrupt you, Miss Perkins." Lady India fluffed the delicate white fabric of the dress strewn across the bed. "I only want to clothe you. Besides we've already thrown out your old gown. So you've nothing else to wear."

"It was an honest mistake. These garments aren't exactly . . . governess-ish." Mari stroked the red silk sash. "This one looks as though it should be worn to an elegant ball."

"As it was intended to be. My poor mother. She sends me these girlish, flimsy gowns in the vain hope that I will attend a ball and snare a husband at last." Her eyes lost their laughter. "I'm a lost cause. And so the dresses are now yours. They suit you perfectly. Fern had all the alterations made."

The maid curtsied. "It was a pleasure, milady."

"I'm far too plain and obscure for gowns such as these," Mari said.

"Is that how you see yourself?" Lady India shook her head. "Gracious, but you've a lot to learn about the world."

"I haven't." Mari knew her place in the world. And she wasn't meant for these gowns. "Where would I wear something like this?" she asked.

"Oh I don't know," said Lady India. "Swan about in it any old time. I never follow the dictates of fashion."

Clearly. Mari glanced sideways at the masculine cut of her clothing. Was she wearing a *waistcoat*?

"I've never understood why females must garb themselves in fripperies and furbelows as if to draw the male gaze by sheer volume of ruffles and bows," said Lady India.

It was no wonder she didn't understand. Lady India would draw every gaze in every room, no matter what she wore.

"It's very kind of you to outfit me so lavishly, I'm sure, but I simply can't accept any of it." Mari caught sight of a darling pair of ivory slippers trimmed with scarlet ribbons and rosettes. *Merciful Heavens*. She'd never seen such delicious shoes. They looked almost edible.

"I'm a thoroughly practical person who wears serviceable clothing," she continued. "I'll be knee-deep in mud following those children about. I couldn't possibly . . ."

She tore her gaze away from a box marked with the name Madame Clotilde.

Even she had heard of Madame Clotilde, fabled dressmaker to the nobility.

What was in that box?

Fern caught the direction of her gaze and lifted the lid. "What a shame it would be to return this one," she said, lifting a blue-and-white-striped poplin dress with long sleeves and a high, ruffled neckline. "It's poplin, so it will wear well. And one could wear a nice apron over it. Very practical, aprons."

Mari drifted toward the dress. Traced one of the blue stripes with her finger.

It did have a modest neckline.

"Poplin *is* rather serviceable," she said.

"Ever so serviceable," whispered Lady India in her ear, untying Mari's dressing gown.

Before she could protest, Fern had fastened Mari's stays around her chemise.

Lady India raised Mari's arms while Fern slipped the striped gown over her head.

"I won't . . . accept charity," said Mari, her voice muffled by poplin.

"Stuff and nonsense. You can't wear that old black rag every day for the rest of your life. You must look the part of governess to a duke, mustn't you? It's not your fault your trunk was stolen."

Mari's head emerged from the neckline and Fern began doing up the buttons in back.

What did she mean by *look the part*? Did she know Mari wasn't as superior as she was pretending to be?

But the lady's eyes were earnest and her smile open and friendly.

"I see commanding natures run in the family," Mari grumbled, to mask the sudden wave of gratitude flooding her heart.

It was like all the Christmastides she'd never had, all arriving at once.

Lady India's kindness almost made her feel like crying. But that would be far too sentimental. "Why are you doing all of this?"

Lady India gave her an enigmatic smile. "I have my reasons."

"Thank you," Mari said. "It's very generous of you."

"Please don't mind my brother, Miss Perkins," Lady India continued. "He's brusque and bearish at times, but his heart is the truest I know. Only give him time and you'll see. I'll leave Fern with you for a time, to see you settled and to make any further alterations."

The clothing *would* help her act the part. "Thank you, Lady India."

It was all so seductive. The fine clothing . . . the handsome duke.

She mustn't forget her true purpose in being here and become caught up in an impossible dream.

"Until my antiquities exhibition, then." Lady India kissed her on the cheek. "I look forward to seeing the progress you make with the twins."

Fern drew a silver hairbrush from the vanity.

That wasn't her old hairbrush with the missing bristles. Had they gotten rid of it along with her dress?

"Such hair you have, miss." She tugged the brush

through Mari's hair. "Such a rich auburn and it spirals so easily."

"It certainly has a mind of its own. That's why I always braid it so tightly."

"A less severe style might look well on you."

As Fern dressed her hair, Mari thought that perhaps she could become accustomed to the genteel life. It was certainly easier than struggling into one's clothing and wrestling with one's hair by oneself.

"There, miss. Come and see." Fern gestured Mari toward the standing looking glass.

Her hair was drawn back in a simple knot and Fern had artfully drawn several spiraling curls to softly frame her face. The blue-and-white-striped gown matched her eyes and gave her cheeks a healthful bloom.

For the very first time in her life Mari felt almost elegant.

What an unusual sensation.

She'd always been told by the matrons of Underwood that she was the scrawniest and plainest of girls, with knobby knees and jutting elbows.

"You've worked quite a transformation, Fern."

"Not I, miss. It's all you . . . with a little help from Madame Clotilde."

Mari was about to admit that she'd never worn such a modish gown, when she remembered the role she was playing.

She mustn't thank the servants. Or make up her own bed. Or admit to being anything less than superior.

"That will be all, Fern," she said briskly. "I'd best go to the nursery now."

With one backward glance at her reflection, Mari left, half hoping she might run into the duke today.

Now that Mari looked the part of a superior governess, there was no one to impress.

She hadn't seen the duke since the unfortunate incident in the library.

She was determined to be the very model of propriety at their next meeting. So prim, proper, and superior that he would question whether he'd fabricated the whole sordid episode in his mind. And he'd never even think to question her past again.

Her days were spent instructing the children. She'd composed a schedule of lessons and posted it on the wall of the nursery, so they knew what was expected of them every hour of the day. Their life had been so chaotic of late, that staying with a schedule was important for building their trust.

They'd been moderately well behaved, adhering to the schedule, taking an interest in their studies.

She made their lessons amusing and interesting, playing games to distract them. Today the children were sitting side by side, absorbed in reading _Captain Cook's Voyages Round the World_.

She always watched for Banksford outside the nursery, wondering if he'd be back to monitor her progress, but he never came again.

He was avoiding her. Which was for the best.

The one week anniversary of her employment had come and gone without fanfare, which meant she was able to breathe a little more easily, though the duke would surely dismiss her if he knew she hadn't been sent by Mrs. Trilby. Mari was here under false pretenses. One wrong word, one inquiry from Mrs. Trilby, and she could lose everything.

Sometimes, she took tea with Mrs. Fairfield of an evening.

Always, she researched the clues from her past. Using a copy of *Johnstone's London Commercial Guide* that she'd found in the library, she had located Mr. Shadwell. His offices were listed in Cheapside.

Tomorrow was her first off day. She'd already planned her schedule. First to Mr. Shadwell's office, and then to Lumley's Toy Shop, since Banksford had said P.L. Rabbit came from there.

It was a vague hope, at best, that a toy shop could trace P.L.'s purchaser, but she must try every avenue.

She would leave no stone unturned.

This was the reason she was in London. To find the truth about her birth.

Not dally with dukes.

"What is that smell?" asked Adele, lifting her head from the book.

There was a warm, homey scent wafting through the open windows from the kitchen ovens.

"It smells like . . ." Michel sniffed the air.

"France!" they cried in unison.

"Someone is making French bread," Adele said. "I'm sure of it."

"Amina," cried Michel. "She received our letter and she's come to live with us!" He jumped up from the window seat. "May we go to the kitchens, Miss Perkins? May we?"

"I'm sorry, Michel, but the post to and from France will take a fortnight."

His face fell. "But I still smell French bread."

"I don't suppose there's any keeping you here with the promise of French bread in the air," said Mari. "Walk with decorum, if you please, children," she called as they ran out of the room. "We are not lions scenting gazelles."

In the kitchens, an unfamiliar woman with dark

hair and winged black eyebrows was up to her elbows in flour, kneading bread in a large bowl.

Michel walked straight to the hearth and stared inside the oven. "*Ç'est le vrais!*"

"*Oui, mes petites,*" said the woman, smiling at the children. "Your bread."

"Good afternoon," said Mari. "I'm Miss Perkins, and these are the duke's children, Adele and Michel. Fall in, look lively."

The twins fell in line beside her.

"My, such beautiful children! As you can see, I'm covered in flour at the moment, but my name is Miss Martin and I've been hired to make you the bread."

She had a pronounced French accent that made her *r*'s guttural and her *the*'s sounded like *z*'s. Had Banksford hired her because Mari had told him the children missed the bread in France?

Had he actually been *listening* to her?

"*Merci*, Miss Martin!" The children launched into a rapid stream of French that quickly left Mari behind.

Miss Martin chuckled. "My goodness," she said in English. "I didn't know I would be so very popular."

"The twins have been pining for the taste of their homeland."

"Do you know how to make meringue?" asked Adele.

"And *tarte aux pommes*?" said Michel.

"*Oui, bien sûr.* I am the best French pastry chef in London."

The twins pelted Miss Martin with questions on her culinary repertoire, giving Mari a moment to think.

She was surprised by the duke's gesture. But really, should she be? This was what he knew how to do best: spend money. Hire the most prestigious French cook in London.

Still, it was a very nice thing to do, and it had made the children very happy.

"The bread will bake faster if you're not watching it, Michel," she said. The boy was standing with his head practically in the range.

"Why don't you sit down in the breakfast room?" asked Miss Martin. "I've a loaf very nearly finished."

Mari led them into the breakfast room and soon a tray arrived with a long thin loaf of bread.

The children were silent for a moment, gazing at the bread. Then Michel broke off a piece.

"Don't you want butter and marmalade?" asked Mari.

"Never!" he said, affronted.

Adele turned to Mari. "Did the duke do this for us?"

Mari nodded. "He did."

She'd noticed they never called him father. Only "duke" or "sir."

"I told him you were missing French bread."

"It was very good of him." Michel chewed contentedly. "Perhaps he's beginning to like us."

"I should think engaging a cook especially to make French bread is a good sign," said Mari.

"Where does he go all day? Why do we never see him?" asked Adele.

"I expect he goes to his foundry. And his club."

"Clubs. Pah." Michel reached for more bread. "When I grow up I'll never go to a stupid old club because they wouldn't allow Adele inside the door."

"I agree that it's a very silly rule," said Mari, "but, who knows, perhaps we females wouldn't want to go to those stuffy clubs. The important gentlemen in their important clubs probably just sit around reading the papers and making bad jokes."

"Our jokes are hilarious," said a deep voice from behind them.

THE CHILDREN'S LAUGHTER rose like bread in an oven. Edgar realized that he'd never heard them laugh before Miss Perkins arrived.

He'd been on his way out, to fulfill his bargain with Westbury, when he heard voices in the breakfast room. Drawn by the conversation, and the warm, inviting aromas emanating from the kitchens, he'd drifted closer, meaning only to observe and then escape, unnoticed.

Somehow his feet had carried him closer, and then he hadn't been able to resist joining the conversation.

"Tell us one of your jokes, sir," said Michel.

"Sir?" Edgar asked. "Won't you call me father?"

"Tell us a joke . . . Father." Michel tested the word on his tongue like the bread.

A fissure cracked across Edgar's hardened heart. "Good morning, Miss Perkins. Would you like to hear a joke?"

She gave him a half smile. "I'm at your pleasure, Your Grace."

He closed his eyes for a moment and his belly clenched tight.

Don't. Don't say that.

There was something different about her today. What was it? Ah, the braids were gone, replaced by a simple swirl of auburn with loose curls on either side of her neck.

The plain black gown was gone as well. But it definitely hadn't been replaced with a voluminous smock.

She wore something elegant and simple in a blue-and-white-stripe with a white apron over the top. She looked far more delectable than the bread.

"I'm afraid our jokes aren't suitable for polite company," Edgar teased.

"Are they about breaking wind?" asked Michel with a devious grin. "Because I know a good one about that."

Miss Perkins stared at Michel with mock censure. "You know, Michel, he who says the rhyme did the crime."

Adele giggled. "He who declares it blares it."

Edgar laughed. Ah . . . flatulence. The age-old subject for merriment. "I'm shocked." He laid a hand over his chest. "Is this what you discuss during your lessons, Miss Perkins?"

"We were reading Chaucer's *The Miller's Tale* and the subject may have . . . arisen," she said primly.

Adele giggled.

"I'll endeavor to change the subject," said Edgar, catching Miss Perkins's eye. "Have you changed the style of your hair?"

She touched one of the soft red spirals at her cheek. "Why yes, Your Grace."

"It suits you."

She blushed. She didn't like compliments, he noticed. Wasn't comfortable with them.

"Will you have some bread, Father?" Michel gestured toward the loaf of bread on the table. Edgar hadn't planned to linger. He needed to be on his way to the park, to escort West's sister, Lady Blanche, on a carriage ride in order to make her suitor jealous. Of all the harebrained schemes. He'd rather poke out his own eye with the butter knife. He could put off the dreaded carriage ride for a while longer.

"I might have a piece of bread at that." Edgar removed his hat and sat across from Miss Perkins.

"Thank you for hiring Miss Martin to cook for us," Michel said.

"You're very welcome. Though I was under the mistaken impression that our bread here in England was perfectly adequate."

"This is far superior," said Adele.

"You can't cut it with a knife. It must be torn." Michel tore off a piece and held it out.

"So you approve of the bread?" Edgar asked.

Michel nodded, his mouth too full to speak.

Edgar tried to catch Miss Perkins's eye. Did she approve?

"You were listening to me," she said, with the barest hint of a smile.

"Of course I was listening. You gave me an assignment, and I completed it."

"High marks for listening," she said.

"She gave *you* an assignment?" asked Michel with a puzzled expression.

"That's right."

"Does the bread meet your exacting standards?" he asked the twins.

"The crust is hard." Michel tapped on the bread with his fingernail. "And inside . . . fluffy like clouds. Melts on the tongue."

"I can see that now." He broke off a piece. It was still warm from the oven, fragrant and comforting as only fresh-baked bread could be.

"Next you'll be saying that our beef isn't cooked correctly," he said.

"It's not!" declared Michel. "It's too dry."

"One mustn't look a gift horse in the mouth, Michel," said Miss Perkins.

"And how is the infamous P.L. Rabbit doing? Escaped from Drew the Destroyer, I trust?" asked Edgar.

Michel's jaw dropped. "You know about P.L.?"

"Everyone knows P.L. What adventures has she had lately?"

"Yesterday, she mixed cook's baking powder with some vinegar and made an awful mess trying to make a volcanic eruption," said Adele.

"Sounds like old P.L.'s a better pirate than a chemist," Edgar laughed.

"Today, she's going to voyage round the world with Captain James Cook and meet some penguins," said Michel.

"Miss Perkins says penguins waddle like this." Adele stood up from the table and performed a lurching, sideways walk with her arms glued at her sides.

"Sit down and finish your bread, if you please," said Miss Perkins, but there was a smile on her lips. "The children can hardly contain their excitement about Lady India's antiquities exhibition, Your Grace. She sent a note to say that they will have a role in the historical tableaux she's presenting."

"We're going to wave palm fronds," said Adele.

"Always making a spectacle, my sister," said Edgar. "She loves to set tongues wagging. When we were children she was forever mounting theatricals but she was never interested in playing a supporting role. It was always Cleopatra or Joan of Arc for her."

"I like Lady India," announced Adele, with a nod of her head.

"I'm quite sure you do," said Miss Perkins. "Will there be many guests, Your Grace?"

"Two dozen, I believe. Everyone has accepted.

Antiquarians and nobility. The Duke of Ravenwood will be here. Haven't seen him in years."

"Another duke?" asked Miss Perkins.

The way she said it made it sound like another duke would be the worst possible thing to appear.

"He wouldn't miss it. He's India's sworn enemy." He turned to the children. "Just like P.L. and Drew the Destroyer."

"Why are they enemies?" asked Michel.

"Well that's a long story. We grew up in neighboring houses, and they used to be very good friends, but they had a falling out. They both have a passion for antiquities, but extremely different methods of going about it."

"We'll be learning about Egyptian antiquities in preparation for the exhibition," said Miss Perkins.

"Do you think Lady India will battle the Duke of Ravenwood with her dagger?" asked Adele eagerly.

"I shouldn't be surprised," said Edgar. "There was an incident several years ago with a vase. He thought it was a priceless Ming Dynasty piece, and she proved it was a fraud. By cracking it over his head."

Finally, he'd made Miss Perkins laugh.

"I suppose that wouldn't necessarily endear her to him," she said.

Adele grinned. "That's why I like her."

"Why isn't Lady India married?" asked Michel. "She's ever so pretty."

"That's a good question, but don't, I pray you, ever ask Lady India that," Edgar warned. "Women tend to dislike questions about being unmarried."

"It's a very impertinent question, to my way of thinking," said Miss Perkins primly.

It hit him that her ramrod posture and pursed lips

were an overcompensation for what she must view as the indiscreet conversation they'd shared.

He'd certainly had the opportunity to go over their conversation in his mind word by word. It had been extraordinary, by any measure.

Remembering her whispered words, the way she'd risen on tiptoe, was not something he should be thinking about. "I'll be off then," he said gruffly. "Please excuse me." He donned his hat.

"Must you go, Father?" asked Adele.

"Afraid I must. My foundry needs me."

How he wished he could go to the foundry, but he had a job to do first. A promise was a promise.

West had better keep his end of the bargain though.

Chapter 10

THE CHILDREN HAD been far too restless and excited after the duke left, so Mari was taking them for a walk in the park.

Despite their loud protests, she'd also insisted that it was high time to return Trix to his natural habitat. Michel carried the snake in a basket.

It was the golden hour in Hyde Park. The trees were cloaked in green and the children's eyes were bright as they skipped along beside her. As they walked down the path, Mari was careful to keep a watch out for any tall, stern-looking matrons.

It would be disastrous if she were caught by Mrs. Trilby with the children.

"May we show you our talents today, Miss Perkins?" asked Adele.

"We brought our chalks," said Michel. "For drawing on the paving stones. We used to do that by the seaside and people would put money in my cap."

"Is that what you did when you ran away from the other governesses?"

"Sometimes. Other times Adele made up verses about people and they paid a pence each for a poem. Or she told their fortunes."

"Or sometimes we just came here to hide," said Adele. "There are ever so many hiding places. There's one." She pointed to an oak tree with a hollow trunk.

"There's another." Michel pointed at a hedgerow.

Mari spread a blanket in a shaded, quiet area and lowered Trix's basket.

"I know you're attached to Trix," she said, "but he'll be so much happier in the park. And Mrs. Fairfield won't allow him in the house any longer. She was quite firm on the subject."

"Let's not release him just yet," said Michel. "Please, we need him a little longer."

"Very well. But we're letting him go before we return home."

"Would you like to see one of my drawings?" Michel drew some chalks out of the bag of supplies he'd brought with them. "There are some nice flat paving stones here."

"What will you draw?"

"The seaside."

"That would be lovely."

Not much potential for clipping constables with chalk.

Mari was watching Michel draw when she noticed two tall, stout ladies in the distance.

Mrs. Trilby and Miss Dunkirk.

Her guilty heart raced. She was seeing things. Or was she? One of their bonnets was very military in silhouette.

Botheration. She had to hide. There was nothing else to be done.

"Carry on with your drawing, Michel," she said. "I'll return shortly."

"Where are you going?" asked Adele.

"I need to . . . visit the hedgerow."

Adele wrinkled her nose. "Why?"

"Never mind that, I'll be right back. Quick as a wink."

Mari fled behind the hedgerow.

Moments later, she heard footsteps. Her heart pounded. "Miss Perkins?" whispered Adele. "Are you hiding?"

"Yes," Mari whispered.

Adele drew a few branches down and peered at her. "Oh . . ." She nodded sagely. "I understand now. You have to *visit the hedgerow.*"

"Precisely. Now give me some privacy, if you please."

Adele ran away. Let her think Mari was answering the call of nature. She had to hide. She just couldn't take the risk.

She crouched low, praying that Mrs. Trilby wasn't nearby. That she wouldn't see the children and stop.

All was quiet. When she felt it was safe, she peered over the hedge.

She couldn't see Mrs. Trilby or Miss Dunkirk, but the children had gathered a small audience in her absence.

Mari stepped out from behind the hedge, shaking twigs from her skirts.

The twins weren't drawing anymore.

Michel sat cross-legged on the ground, wearing a white sheet tied over his clothing. He was blowing upon an oboe-like instrument with two reeds, which produced a high, thin melody.

Adele had shed her bonnet and was swathed in what appeared to be one of the red patterned damask curtains from the nursery.

What on earth?

There were letters scrawled across a paving stone next to Michel. Mari drew closer to read them.

SNAKES CHARMED.
PALMS READ.
TUPPENCE FOR THE THRILL OF A LIFETIME.

And next to the lettering, Michel's cap, upended, with several coins inside.

Oh dear. This hadn't been what she'd envisioned when they said they'd be showing her their talents.

Unfortunately, they were also showing them to perfect strangers in Hyde Park.

She had to put a stop to it, but in a way that wouldn't make them feel like they were bad for doing it.

"Who will have their palm read by the all-knowing Lalla?" Adele demanded in a husky, mysterious voice. "Cross my palm with silver, ye who dare."

"Ain't you a little young, Lalla?" a blowsy woman in shortened skirts called.

Adele fixed the woman with a piercing stare exactly like the duke's. "You, madam. You think me too young, but the arts of divination know no age. Hold out your palm. I delight in proving skeptics wrong."

When the woman kept her hand close to her side, Adele shrugged. "Free of charge. Just this once."

Adele lifted the woman's right hand, spreading her fingers out and bending over her palm.

Michel began playing a low, mysterious melody on his pipe, setting the scene for his sister's act.

Their gestures were freer and they looked older. More confident and self-assured.

Mari realized that this must be what they had been like in France.

Adele ran her finger over the woman's palm. "Your name is something that begins with the letter *b* . . .

no, I'm receiving another letter. *D*. Your name is Deborah. But your friends call you Deb."

The woman's face drained of color. "'Ow did you know that?"

How *had* she known that, Mari wondered?

"Lalla knows all," Adele intoned in a low, eerie voice.

The spectators hushed.

"This line here." She traced a line on the woman's palm. "Your heart line. It tells me that you fall in love easily. It ends here, at this fork. Oh . . ." Adele closed her eyes. "How very sad."

"What?" Deborah asked in an urgent voice. "What do you see?"

Adele dropped the woman's hand and held out her own. "If you want to know more, you must cross my palm with silver."

Deb narrowed her eyes. "Where's your mum, eh? Who are you?" She peered at Adele.

Mari stepped closer, to keep the woman from complaining. "Miss Lalla," she said. "I'm prepared to pay the price."

She dropped a coin into the cap.

The pace of Michel's reedy tune increased as Adele made an ostentatious show of tracing the lines on Mari's palm. "You have a fiery temper and you've been unlucky in love. This line shows that you were jilted at the altar, were you not?"

"How could you know that? Bert." She rolled her eyes. "Left me standing at the altar, the blighter. Is there hope for me?"

Adele nodded. "I see a tall, broad-shouldered man in your future. Is he an earl?"

Deb snorted from the sidelines. "Not bloody likely."

The small crowd laughed.

"No," Adele shook her head. "No, he's not an earl."
She paused, closing her eyes tightly.

Her eyes flew open. "He's not an earl. He's a duke."

Mari snatched her hand away, shaken. "You must
be mistaken."

"Only in our dreams, eh?" said Deb. "'Ere now the
sign says snakes charmed. Where's the snake then?"

Michel lifted the lid of Trix's basket and resumed
playing his pipe.

Trix's black head peeked out of the basket, and the
onlookers gasped, but then he ducked back into his
hiding place.

Apparently, English snakes weren't meant to be
charmed.

"THAT'S WHAT THE *ton* considers charming these
days?" Edgar asked incredulously.

A gentleman in a ridiculously high collar with his
hair plastered in waves over his ears and over his
forehead minced along the footpath, waving a lace-
edged handkerchief at every lady he saw.

"Oh yes." Lady Blanche nodded emphatically,
setting her golden ringlets bobbing under her pink
bonnet. "Lord Crewe is an Exquisite and everyone
consults him on matters of taste. He's the arbitrator
of the elegancies."

"Matters of taste?" The man was wearing more
maquillage upon his face than a bawdy house madam.

Crewe raised his quizzing glass to stare at them as
they passed him.

Crewe waved his frilly handkerchief and Lady
Blanche let out the breath she'd been holding in a
loud exhale and happily waggled her fingers at him.

"Did you see that? He waved at me," she said tri-
umphantly.

"Congratulations."

"You don't find him exquisite?" asked Lady Blanche.

"That's not the adjective I would use," said Edgar.

Just as he'd promised West, they were putting in a fashionable appearance in his two-horse curricle, setting tongues wagging and drawing curious stares.

Lady Blanche had been nattering on about the intrigues of the *ton* the entire carriage ride.

She was everything his mother could ever hope for in a match for him. A wellborn English rose with a tidy fortune. But she didn't interest him in the least.

As she prattled on about ladies and lords, balls and bonnets, and all the other tiresome goings-on of the fashionable set, Edgar's thoughts ran toward aprons.

More specifically, apron strings tied with bows.

And the untying thereof.

He gripped the reins tighter. His mind had been in a constant loop, going over and over that moment with Miss Perkins.

The one where she'd stood on tiptoes, placed her hands on his chest, and said she felt like being bad.

There were so many other ways the evening could have progressed.

He could imagine at least twenty.

His imagination had been going down the wrong paths ever since. The ones that began with him kissing her, and ended with her in his bed, moaning his name as she reached her pleasure.

"Your Grace."

"Um, yes?"

"Are you listening to me?"

"Yes. What were you saying?"

She sighed. "You've been away from society too

long. You don't flirt properly. You're supposed to make Lord Laxton jealous with your attentiveness, you know."

"Well I'm not going to wave a frilly handkerchief at you, if that's what you want."

"You're no Exquisite, and that's certain." She turned her head toward him. "Your shoulders are far too broad. Are you a Corinthian, I wonder?" She tapped her pink parasol against his knee. "Do you box, fence, and ride?"

Lady Blanche seemed to want to fit everyone into neat little boxes.

"I lift barrows full of coal and stoke foundry fires," he replied.

Lady Blanche closed her eyes briefly. "I'm just going to pretend you did not say that. Now. Back to the lighthearted conversation, where I say witty things and you laugh loudly."

It wasn't a suggestion, it was an order. "Hahaha." He laughed loudly.

She hit him with her parasol. "I haven't said anything witty yet. But I will. As soon as I determine what you are."

"Do I have to *be* something?"

"Let's see . . . you're certainly not a Rake, because you haven't even winked at me yet. Nor a Puritan, though some do pronounce you monkish." She leaned closer. "What are you, Your Grace?"

"I'm retired."

"Oh no, you mustn't retire. Why, you'll put all the ladies out of countenance. There are so few eligible dukes these days. One wouldn't know it, to read the titles of the boudoir novels. *The Devil Duke's Dark Desires*, and so on and so forth."

"My society days are over, Lady Blanche. When I

decide to take a wife, I'll do so in a manner that will mean I won't have to attend even one more ball."

She pouted. "My friends, not to mention my four lovely sisters, will be most disappointed. My friends all swoon over my brother, because he's a duke, but he's acting most shamefully of late. Do say you'll exert a calming influence upon him? He's been drinking too much lately. He's terribly dissipated. I fear he has become a Rogue."

What would she say if she could read his thoughts about Miss Perkins?

They were definitely of the roguish variety.

"Never say," breathed Edgar. "Not a Rogue."

"Yes." She closed her eyes briefly. "A sister's work is never done. He must be reformed, before it's too late."

"I'm sure he'll settle down eventually, Lady Blanche," Edgar said reassuringly.

"Well he mustn't have too much fun. He has four more sisters to bring out. Do please say you'll exert your influence on him?"

"I'm not sure I'm the right fellow for that."

"Oh Heavens." Lady Blanche waved at a lady in a passing carriage. "There's Lady Philippa. Wasn't she just green with envy, though? Did you see the set of her teeth? That will leave a mark upon her lip, I daresay."

"I can only hope Lord Laxton will be overcome by jealousy, as well," Edgar said, steering the conversation toward her intended and away from him. "Do tell me about him."

"Lord Laxton is my ideal in every way." Her face fell. "Except one . . ."

"He hasn't offered for you yet."

"That is his one and only fault. And I'm so willing to forgive him, if only he would . . ."

"Offer for you."

"Precisely. I don't like trickery, mind you. It can so easily go wrong. One need only read the comedies of Mr. Shakespeare to know how very wrong. However, this is but a small maneuver, designed to win a war with as little show of force as necessary. And I daresay, you don't find the duty too onerous?"

"Hardly." He winked at her. "Your company is delightful."

"Why, Your Grace, perhaps you are a Rake, after all. It's not true what they say, that you've taken vows of monkhood."

The feelings he was having for Miss Perkins were hardly celestial in origin. Firmly rooted in the earthly.

Why couldn't he stop thinking about her? When Lady Blanche giggled in that silly manner, Edgar couldn't help wishing he were still at home with Miss Perkins and the children.

They'd been so contented, eating their French bread. Miss Perkins had smiled at him approvingly.

He wanted to make her smile again.

"There's West's carriage," Edgar said with relief. "It's nearly time."

"So it is. And there's Lord Laxton." Lady Blanche fussed with her hair. "I do hope this works."

"Don't worry, I'll be the rakish, doting swain of your dreams."

"Thank you, Your Grace."

Edgar leapt down in front of the flower shop, handed his reins to a groom, and helped Lady Blanche down.

"Don't forget the violets," Lady Blanche whispered.

The violets must convey some message. Edgar would never understand the intricacies of the *ton*'s mating rituals. He reemerged a few minutes later with a large bunch of pink roses punctuated by purple violets.

West and Laxton had exited their carriage and were chatting with Lady Blanche at the edge of the park.

This would all be over soon.

Edgar approached, flowers in hand, ready to pretend to be courting the lovely, if slightly vapid, Lady Blanche. "My lady," he swept a low bow, holding out the bouquet. "For you."

Lord Laxton frowned. "Banksford?" He turned to Lady Blanche. "I didn't know you were acquainted with His Grace, Lady Blanche."

"Oh yes, he took me for such a nice ride in his curricle just now." She accepted the flowers, sniffing daintily. "Do smell the roses, Lord Laxton. They smell simply heavenly, as do the violets." She giggled. "They're for constancy, you know."

Laxton brushed away the flowers, glaring at Edgar. "Quite extravagant."

"I spare no expense when it comes to beautiful ladies," said Edgar, giving Lady Blanche a smarmy smile.

West gave him a wink.

Could Edgar leave now? Laxton appeared to be insanely jealous.

"Will you be attending the dancing tonight at Vauxhall?" Lady Blanche asked Edgar. "I'm quite unspoken for."

"But," sputtered Laxton. "I assumed, that is, we always dance together, Lady Blanche."

"Do we?" asked Lady Blanche, fluttering her eyelashes. "I hadn't noticed."

Lord, save him from these marital games. How soon could he leave?

"I say, what are those children doing?" asked West, pointing into the distance.

"What children—?" Edgar turned. Froze.

He must be hallucinating, although he'd know that glowing shade of auburn anywhere.

Miss Perkins. And the twins. Who appeared to be draped in curtains?

Michel sat cross-legged on the lawn, playing upon a pipe, while Adele was speaking to a small cluster of onlookers, gesturing dramatically.

And what was Miss Perkins doing? Putting an abrupt end to their antics?

Of course not.

She was playing along. She said something with a toss of her bonnet, and the onlookers laughed.

"Those aren't, by chance, yours, are they?" asked West with a laugh.

Edgar glared. "They are," he said through gritted teeth.

West whistled softly. "They didn't make governesses like that when I was a lad."

Miss Perkins did look fetching in a long coat and bonnet of a rich blue color that teased roses to bloom in her cheeks and found the deeper russet in her hair.

"Pooh. Governesses," said Lady Blanche. "She's quite negligent if you ask me, allowing your children to make such a spectacle."

West peered at the inexplicable tableau. "What are they doing?"

"I've no idea," said Edgar. All he knew was that he needed to stop them from doing it. This was far too public a place for playacting.

"Shall we go and say hello?" asked Lady Blanche, with a desperate edge to her voice.

Laxton hadn't taken the bait yet. What did Edgar have to do, grab the lady and kiss her in front of him?

"While I would love for you to meet my children, Lady Blanche," Edgar said smoothly. "These are not the circumstances I would choose."

Lord Laxton threw Edgar a look that could only be described as murderous. "She's never to meet them, Banksford. Why, the idea, an innocent meeting children such as those."

"Don't be silly. They're just children," said Lady Blanche.

Laxton lowered his voice. "They're not respectable."

"I'd like to meet your governess," said West.

The gossips were openly staring now, waiting to pounce. He never should have agreed to take Lady Blanche riding. But it was too late now, he'd been seen escorting her, and now his children had been seen performing in Hyde Park.

What a disaster.

"No one is meeting anyone," he said stiffly. "If you'll excuse me, Lady Blanche." He bowed over her hand and made his escape.

There was a rogue governess on the loose.

Chapter 11

❧

*D*AMNATION!

Mari had never uttered a profanity before now, but a dark and stormy duke drove her to sin. He loomed suddenly in front of her like a giant cliff emerging from a treacherous mist, waiting to dash governesses to their deaths.

"I can explain, Your Grace," she said.

"I don't think you can." Banksford turned such a ferocious stare on the small crowd of onlookers that they immediately dispersed.

He studied the chalk lettering. *"Tuppence for the thrill of a lifetime?"*

Why, oh why, hadn't she erased the words?

"What exactly is happening here?" he asked, looking at first her, and then the children, whose eyes were wide as saucers.

"It was an experiment," Mari said hastily. "We were conducting an experiment in the charming of snakes . . . and audiences."

He glowered at her.

"Well obviously it doesn't work on dukes," she said.

"Here's an experiment to conduct," he said. "The speed with which all three of you can climb into that carriage." He pointed at a dashing black curricle with gold wheels. "Right. Now."

"I'm not sure we'll all fit," she said.

"We'll fit. It's only a short ride."

The twins had already shed their sheets and packed up the chalks and instruments.

Mari helped Adele retie her bonnet strings.

"It was our idea, Father," said Adele. "You weren't meant to see it."

"Clearly."

"It was badly done of us," said Michel, hanging his head.

The duke's eyes softened and he laid a hand on Michel's cap. "I'm not saying you're bad. But it was a very public display, and my friends . . ." He glanced over his shoulder at the group of two gentlemen and a lady who were watching them. "They wouldn't understand."

Mari understood perfectly. She'd humiliated him in front of his aristocratic friends.

No wonder he was dressed in all the finery of a duke-about-town, from glossy black beaver hat to polished hessians, and everything broad-shouldered and trim-flanked in between. He hadn't been going to his foundry.

He'd been going courting.

The lady, who had golden hair and wore a straw bonnet with pink ribbons, waved and began to walk toward them.

"Carriage. Now," said the duke urgently.

"Too late, I'm afraid," said Mari.

The group was upon them.

The duke drew himself up to his full height.

"Lady Blanche, Westbury, Lord Laxton," he said in a pompous tone. "My children, Adele and Michel, and their governess, Miss Perkins."

"Miss Perkins, you have a twig in your hair," said Lady Blanche. "Just . . . there." She reached out and plucked the twig free.

Mari nodded. "Er . . . yes. I was . . . retrieving a ball that had rolled into the shrubbery."

Mari nudged Adele and she curtsied.

Michel bowed.

"What pretty children," said Lady Blanche. "How old are you, my darlings?"

"We're nine," said Adele.

"And what were you doing?" she asked.

"Telling fortunes and charming snakes, apparently," said the handsome man Edgar had called Westbury. He pointed at the chalk lettering.

"Will you tell my fortune?" asked Lady Blanche.

The parsonlike Lord Laxton pursed his lips. "We really ought to be going, Lady Blanche. Someone might see us."

"Nonsense," said Lady Blanche. "I want to know my fortune. I have many questions about my future."

She held out her hand to Adele. The parasol that was hooked over her arm knocked Trix's basket and the lid came off.

Mari moved closer, intent on replacing the lid, but, sensing his opportunity, Trix seized the day and slithered away.

"Is that a snake?" Lady Blanche turned white, tottered for a moment on her heeled slippers, and fainted dead away, rather suspiciously falling squarely into Lord Laxton's arms.

In Mari's experience, fainting spells were rarely so well aimed.

"Come back, Trix," Michel shouted, diving after the snake. Adele followed.

Lord Laxton lifted Lady Blanche into his arms. "Make way, make way. She's fainted. She needs air."

"She's in a park," said Mari.

Banksford gave her a warning look. He didn't look too pleased about his golden-haired lady falling into another man's arms.

Something like this *would* have to happen. What if he'd been going to propose to Lady Blanche and Mari had ruined his plans? She realized she had no idea whether the duke was marriage-minded.

He should be thanking her, if that were the case. Lady Blanche wasn't a suitable mother for the children at all. She was . . . a fribbling milksop, if ever there was one.

Ruffled skirts. French-heeled boots.

Fainting at the sight of snakes. Her corset was probably laced too tightly.

"I'm escorting her home. Don't try to stop me, Banksford," said Lord Laxton.

"I wouldn't dream of it," said the duke.

Laxton left with the still-limp Lady Blanche in his arms.

Westbury touched the brim of his hat and grinned rakishly. "Very nice to meet you, Miss Perkins. I hope we may become better acquainted." He gave Banksford a military salute. "Well done, you."

He hurried after Lord Laxton and Lady Blanche.

"I'll fetch the children," said the duke.

Mari quickly rubbed away the chalk lettering with one of the curtains.

The duke emerged from the shrubbery with a twin in either hand.

"T-Trix has left us," said Michel.

"Trix," said Adele, starting to cry.

"He didn't like living in a water jug, did he, Miss

Perkins?" The duke turned desperate eyes to her. Obviously, he didn't know what to do with sobbing children.

"B-but we didn't have a chance to say good-bye," wailed Adele.

"Please don't be sad. How about a nice goldfish?" the duke asked with a panicked look. "Or what about a parakeet?"

Mari wasn't going to help him out of this one.

"How about another snake," he said. "I know, I'll buy you a python. They're very rare. And very long. They can swallow a whole goat."

Michel gaped at him. "A whole goat?"

Bravo, Banksford. Gruesome topics as a distraction. She almost felt like clapping.

Adele wiped her eyes. "I d-don't think Mrs. Fairfield would like that very much, do you?"

"A snake that could swallow her whole?" Mari sniffed. "I should think not. Come along, children. Best foot forward. Trix will be much happier in the park. Our experiment is concluded for the day but I shall expect a written report tomorrow morning."

The duke raised both of his eyebrows as if to say *there will be no tomorrow for you, Perkins.*

MARI HELD THE children's hands as they followed the duke up the stairs of Number Seventeen.

The limp in his left knee was very pronounced, she realized. Why didn't he use a walking stick?

Michel and Adele exchanged worried glances.

Adele mimed slitting her throat. *"Vous êtes à la guillotine,"* she whispered to Mari.

"I'm not going to the guillotine, dear."

"You'll be dismissed and that's sure," Michel whispered.

"Dismissed?" replied Mari, bending closer to the boy and putting her hands on his shoulders. "I'm *never* dismissed. You'll see. Don't worry about a thing."

She honestly didn't think the duke would go that far. She trusted him not to throw her out. But he did have an ominous expression on his face.

She'd humiliated him in front of his friends.

Michel's smile fell away. "I hope you're right. We didn't mean to get you into trouble."

Mrs. Fairfield appeared on the steps. "Did you have a nice outing?" she asked.

Then she saw the duke's face.

"Whatever is the matter, my dear?" she whispered to Mari.

"I'll explain everything later."

They followed Banksford into the house. In the entranceway, Michel turned troubled eyes on his father. "Are you cross with us, Father?"

"No, I'm not cross." He ruffled Michel's hair. "Why don't you and Adele see if Miss Martin made any pastries?"

"The most delicious smells have been issuing from the kitchens all day," said Mrs. Fairfield.

The children cast doubtful glances at Mari, but the promise of French pastries was more than they could withstand. They left with Mrs. Fairfield.

Mari began to back slowly out of the room. Perhaps if she just quietly went about her business he'd forget about her and she would live to see another day.

"And just where do you think you're going, Miss Perkins?"

Damnation.

"You and I are going for a ride," he growled.

Chapter 12

✑

"*B*AA," SAID MARI.

"Did you just bleat, Miss Perkins?"

"Yes. Because you're herding me like I was a sheep."

"Get in the carriage."

"Where are you taking me?"

"Just get in." He helped her step up into his curricle, setting her down a little too forcefully on the peach velvet upholstery.

She swished her skirts into place.

He landed beside her with a thud that shook the entire frame of the curricle, and took up the reins from his groom, who had been holding the spirited pair of brown bays at the ready.

They set off from the mews at such a fast clip that Mari had to hold on to her bonnet with one hand, and the edge of the curricle with the other.

"Where are we going?" she shouted over the noise of the wheels and the wind whistling under her bonnet.

"You'll see."

"You can't just kidnap me. It's not civilized."

"What I just witnessed was hardly civilized."

"You gave me permission to ascertain the children's talents and interests and to direct the content of their educational program accordingly."

"In the privacy of the schoolroom, Miss Perkins. Not in Hyde Park."

"Not in front of your friends, you mean to say."

He stared at the horses, gripping the reins in his gloved hands, his profile stern as a granite cliff. "That was the Duke of Westbury, Miss Perkins. And he holds the future of my railway venture in his hands."

"He didn't look too scandalized," said Mari. "I thought he was rather friendly and accommodating."

"That's because he was making eyes at you," the duke said. "Like he was a wolf and you were a little lost lamb."

"How peculiar." So it *was* only dukes that found her distracting.

"Westbury's my friend, but if you chance upon him when you're out, I want you to walk right by, as though you've never been introduced."

"Humph," said Mari. "You can't dictate whom I speak with on my own time."

"He's not a fit companion for a respectable girl."

"I'll wager he's a great favorite with the ladies. He's very handsome."

"Don't let those gilded locks fool you, Miss Perkins. He's a notorious rakehell."

"Wicked as sin?"

"Dangerously depraved. And best avoided."

"Maybe I like wicked," she said archly.

He jerked on the reins and the horses whinnied, slowing their gait. "Stay away from Westbury."

If there was any time to be meek and subservient, it was probably now. But she just couldn't seem to resist goading him.

Some devilsome urge drove her.

It was too much fun watching him lose his sang-froid.

"Why?" she asked. "Are you jealous?"

"Of Westbury? Not a chance. He's sunk low of late. His sister is worried about him. She's asked me to be a steadying influence."

"His sister?"

"Lady Blanche."

"Ah yes, Lady Blanche. The perfect pink-and-golden lady. Tottering on heeled slippers, hanging on your arm, and flapping her eyelashes. She'd make a terrible mother for the children."

His lips quirked and he gave her a sidelong glance. "You're not jealous, are you, Miss Perkins?"

"Of a lady who faints at the mere thought of a snake? Not a chance."

He chuckled. "That actually worked to my advantage, her swooning." He made a clicking sound with his tongue and the horses increased their speed.

"I thought it had ruined your romantic tryst. Sent her into another man's arms," said Mari.

"Ruined it? More like saved it. Lady Blanche falling into Laxton's arms was the plan all along."

So he hadn't been interested in Lady Blanche. Why did that make her heart lift? "So you're not angry with me then?"

"I didn't say that."

The carriage halted in front of a huge brick building on New Road. Several chimneys and one very tall column rose from the roof, belching black smoke into the air.

A groom opened a gate and they rode into a paved courtyard.

He tossed his reins to the groom and helped her

down from the curricle. She tried not to notice the way he lifted her so easily.

He was upset with her, so she was upset with him. Tit for tat.

"We're here," he said.

"We're where?" she asked, though she'd already guessed.

"The Vulcan."

"If you dispose of my body in your place of business, someone's sure to find me. Hadn't you better drown me in the Thames, instead?"

His tall black hat blocked out the sun for a moment as he stepped closer, his eyes narrowing. "What I should do is bundle you right back to your registry and ask for a new governess."

Mari's heart sped. "You wouldn't do that, would you?"

Maybe she'd pushed him too far.

"Didn't I hire you on a trial basis?" he asked.

Hell's bells. She smoothed out her skirts. "One minor wrinkle in an otherwise perfect record of employment—"

"Minor wrinkle, you call it? My offspring were telling fortunes and charming snakes in the middle of Hyde Park during the fashionable hour."

"First of all, the season is finished and so there were few witnesses, and second, we were not in the middle, we had chosen a quiet, grassy area, and third—"

"You don't understand. My foundry stands on the brink of a major innovation in high-pressure steam engines. We're making history here."

"Oh I understand perfectly, Your Grace. You care more for your reputation than your children's happiness."

She pushed open the door of the foundry and swept inside.

"That's not true." He followed her, raising his voice over the sudden noise of clanking hammers and whistling steam.

"It's not?"

"Do you see these men, Miss Perkins? These apprentice founders, journeyman founders, assistant engineers, and pattern makers?"

"I see them." There were men everywhere, some in leather aprons and gloves, feeding coal into chimneys. Some with barrows filled with sand.

"Every single person in this foundry is relying upon me to build the railway so that our engines will have somewhere to roam. They are also relying upon me to win a contract with the fire brigades for a new kind of fire engine. My name, my offspring, my governess, and every last thing associated with my foundry must be upstanding and beyond reproach. Synonymous with strength, power, respectability, and reliability."

She stopped walking abruptly. "You're a *duke*. Isn't the battle already won?"

"My reputation was tarnished by—"

"Your Grace." A good-looking, dark-haired man shrugged into a coat as he approached. He ran a hand through hair damp with sweat. "I didn't know you were bringing a visitor today. I apologize for my appearance, my lady."

"Miss Perkins, this is Mr. Grafton, my chief engineer," said the duke in a clipped voice.

"Delighted, Miss Perkins." Mr. Grafton bowed.

"Miss Perkins is my governess," the duke said.

"Aren't you a bit old to have a governess, Your Grace?" asked Mr. Grafton with an admirably bland expression.

Mari grinned at the engineer. She liked him already.

"My *children's* governess," amended the duke.

She could practically see the steam rising from his ears. Most gratifying.

"Shall I give you the tour, Miss Perkins?" Mr. Grafton held out his arm.

Mari accepted it. "A tour would be delightful, Mr. Grafton. What is your role as chief engineer?"

"I create the initial designs, with the help of the duke, who has been one of the innovators in the area of high-pressure steam engines."

He led her through the open, well-ventilated area. "Here is where the iron is melted and cast, Miss Perkins. We won't walk too close to the cupola furnace, it generates the enormous heat we need."

The men feeding the furnace wore leather aprons and gloves to protect them from the immense heat shimmering from the tall, vertical furnace.

"And here is the assembly room." They moved into another large room, this one with long workbenches and clamps holding the cast metal parts.

"It's a very formidable operation, Mr. Grafton."

"Extremely."

"I'm quite relieved, you know," she said, loud enough for the duke to hear. He was following them and looking quite put out.

"And why is that, Miss Perkins?"

"I had thought the duke meant to get rid of me today."

"Indeed?" Mr. Grafton sent a confused glance in the duke's direction.

"Oh yes, but now I know he won't."

"And why is that?" asked Mr. Grafton, playing into her hands perfectly.

"Because he's obviously trying to impress me, instead."

"TRYING TO IMPRESS—" Edgar fumed, following after Miss Perkins and Grafton, like a carriage's bloody fifth wheel.

Dukes were never fifth wheels.

"You see, Mr. Grafton," Miss Perkins gave his engineer a teasing smile. "I laughed at His Grace's miniature engine the other day, and now he needs to impress upon me the grandeur of his foundry."

"Compensating for something, is he?"

"I've no idea," she laughed.

Edgar saw red. Grafton was going to pay for that one later. He stalked into place beside them. "Don't encourage her."

She sallied forth, hand resting lightly on Grafton's arm.

Miss Perkins in battle mode was a sight to behold.

Her cheeks pink, her eyes blazing like sapphires, her jaw firm and set, her little feet marching along to a military tattoo.

Every single man in the place was stealing glances at her and pounding metal, or pushing carts, that much faster, that much harder.

They were all trying to impress her.

Was that really why he'd brought her here?

Just so he could show her there was nothing small about his ambition . . . or himself?

Some primal display of manhood?

"And this is where the pattern-maker works to create the molds," said Grafton.

Mari lifted one of the beeswax molds from the table. "Is this how you create your miniature engines as well, Your Grace?"

He nodded, showing her how the two halves of the beeswax mold fit together. "I make them first with sand and clay, and then I add metal overlay."

"Grafton," someone shouted from the other room. Grafton bowed over Miss Perkins's hand. "I'm needed elsewhere, I'll let His Grace continue the tour."

"Well? Are you going to show me your fire engine?" Miss Perkins asked Edgar.

He led her to the back room, where they were assembling the new prototype for the engine.

"So many locks," she observed as he unfastened a series of locks to the large open room with windows set high in the walls and carriage doors leading out to the yard.

The noise of the foundry receded when he shut the door behind them.

"We maintain the utmost secrecy here," he said. "We don't want anyone stealing our design."

He caught hold of the edge of a heavy canvas and dragged it away from the new engine.

Her eyes widened. "It's massive."

"Too massive. It's still too heavy and needs more than one horse to pull it. I'm working on a design for a lightweight boiler system."

She studied the engine, her hair catching fire in the sunlight.

"The coal will be fed here." He indicated the copper vat. "And the steam will escape here." He pointed to the black pipe sticking up on the side. "The delivery hose attaches here, and the water will run through the hose, powered by the steam pump, instead of by the parish fire brigade."

"How high will the water go?"

"We will connect the engine to the water main

and quickly raise steam pressure—we hope to shoot water out of the hose up to ninety feet in the air."

"Ninety feet. My goodness."

Finally. He'd impressed her.

"Power. Projection." He lifted his arm and made a fist. Her gaze wandered to his bicep. "Enough water pumping to douse the deadliest blazes."

"I do comprehend the magnitude of what you're trying to accomplish. And I applaud it, and I'll do my part to uphold the standards of your name."

"That's better then."

"But—"

"There's a but. How could there not be?"

"Just hear me out. I had a realization about the twins today. You think of the children's life in France as squalid, dirty, and regretful. When they think of it as freedom. They may have been poor, but they were happy. They were free to be themselves, to explore their talents, they lived with the wide sea and the wide blue sky."

"But they didn't have enough to eat."

"Yes, but they had their nurse, Amina, who let them roam freely. And they had the seashore where they were happy entertaining the holiday-makers."

"England has seashore."

"Your Grace." She laid a hand on his arm. Instinctively, he flexed his bicep again.

"Ever since they arrived here in England, they've been told they're bad. That their very existence is somehow wrong and shameful." She met his gaze, her blue eyes blazing with molten iron. "Please don't box them in with too many rules. Please don't clip their wings."

"If you're suggesting that I should have let them continue reading palms in Hyde Park—"

"No." She squeezed his arm. She was standing very close.

He could smell her delicate floral scent, even here in the foundry, where it always smelled of sweat and coal smoke.

"That's not what I'm suggesting," she said, her eyes earnest. "Only let them be children, Your Grace, instead of symbols of your venerable dukedom. Let them make mistakes. It's how we learn. How we grow."

He placed his hand over hers. So soft, her skin.

So seductive, her scent.

"You must have had a very repressive childhood, Miss Perkins. You speak as one who chafed against a great many rules in her day."

"I had a very pious childhood with stern dictates. I was told that I was inherently sinful. That God was a wrathful God, and he would smite me down if I misbehaved. If I—" she lowered her eyelashes "—indulged my carnal nature."

Sweet Lord. She must be a clergyman's daughter. It was always the vicar's daughters who had the most to rebel against.

Her words saturated his mind with the need to show her that carnality was actually a very good thing.

His hand still covered hers. He wanted to cover her with his whole body, push her up against a wall. Ride with her faster than a speeding steam engine, racing to a shattering release.

"Why did you bring me here, Your Grace?" she asked with a saucy look in her eyes.

"To impress upon you the importance—"

"No, no, that's why you *think* you brought me here. Why did you actually bring me here?"

"I suppose I was somewhat . . . heated."

"Yes. You were irate with me. Why else?"

"I give up, why did I bring you here?"

"You're not going to admit it?"

"Admit what?"

"The real reason why you dragged me here, away from your house, away from your children. Why the door is locked. Why whenever I touch your arm it's bulging and hard as steel."

"Er . . ." Something else was hard as steel. And it wasn't his bicep.

"Just admit it," she insisted.

"I don't know what you're driving at but—"

"You brought me here to kiss me."

"No, I didn't." *Clever woman. Too clever by half.*

They glared at each other.

Steam hissed somewhere. Men shouted.

She was daring him to kiss her.

But he couldn't do that. It was against his code of conduct. Topple one rule and they'd all collapse.

This was a battle for his very soul.

"Oh for Heaven's sake," she said, heaving an exasperated sigh.

And then she twined her hands around his neck, pulled his head down, and sealed her lips to his.

Chapter 13

❧

W HEN MISS MARI PERKINS kissed a man, she went all in.

Her kiss stoked his body into blazing arousal.

Gone was the starched and proverb-spouting governess. In her place, the firebrand he'd sensed when he first met her.

The smell of her, sweet and warm. The oasis of her neck, her little chin jutting against his jaw.

The taste of her mouth, heady and complex as the aged brandy he hadn't tasted in a decade.

Her slight, feminine curves melting against him, like wax pouring into a mold.

Everything he'd denied himself for so long. Comfort, surcease . . . pleasure.

"Oh," she drew back slightly. "Oh that's . . ." She dove back for more.

Her enthusiasm made his blood pump so fast he felt lightheaded.

He couldn't think. Couldn't remember why this was wrong.

He kissed her with the pent-up longing that had built since the moment he met her.

She felt so good. So right. The silk of her skin. The velvet of her tongue. He untied her bonnet and lifted it off her head, never breaking the deep kiss.

This was madness.

She stiffened his cock but she also quickened his heart. Made him long for more than just her body.

The near terror that had swamped him when he stood outside the nursery returned, but this time instead of the blind urge to flee, to run away, he wanted to immolate himself in her fire.

Make this count. Make this last.

He shifted his good knee between her thighs, wanting to touch her with as much of his body as possible. Needing to give her pleasure.

She moaned, opened her legs slightly to give him access.

That soft little moan brought him back to his senses.

They were at the foundry.

There were dozens of men outside the door.

He wrenched his mouth away, hearing his breathing rasp and echo through the chamber.

What in blazes was happening here? His thigh was between her legs.

So his rules and scruples just melted away when a woman kissed him?

"I didn't lift you into my carriage to bring you here to ravish you," he said.

"I know."

"We shouldn't be in here with the door locked," he rasped. "You should have a chaperone at all times."

"I'm not one of your aristocratic ladies, Your Grace. I'm my own chaperone. I kissed you because I wanted to."

"I understand. You're the vicar's daughter. Raised on psalms and proverbs in the countryside." He stroked his knuckles down her cheek.

One more touch.

"You want to be a little bit bad," he said. "A little bit wild."

If this tenderness he felt for her was purely physical, he could blame it on deprivation. Starvation for a woman's soft touch. But their kiss had felt almost spiritual, in a way.

He'd heard church bells ringing.

Heard Handel's *Hallelujah Chorus* with a full choir at Westminster Abbey.

He'd kissed a vicar's daughter, who was also his servant, and an innocent.

He was thrice damned.

So why did the fiery footpath to hell feel like the first glimpse of Heaven he'd ever had?

She wanted to flirt with danger.

HE'D BEEN TALKING about power and pumping water and putting out fires, and some primal part of her mind had simply taken over.

She'd realized that he wanted to kiss her, but his rigid rules were thwarting his desire and that she must be the one to kiss him first.

And so she had.

And now . . . his knee was between her thighs. She was *riding* the hard muscles of his thigh.

He'd been saying something about how they should stop and they should leave. But his knee was still there, belying his words.

She didn't want to leave. Not just yet. And so she kissed him again.

When she'd imagined a gentleman's kiss she'd always imagined a courtly peck on the cheek. Or a chaste kiss on the lips, followed by a pronouncement of devotion.

She'd never imagined . . . this.

Rough and tender at the same time.

Wild yet skillfully controlled.

She'd never imagined a tongue in her mouth, either. The duke's tongue, filling her mouth, pressing inside, making her moan.

It was exhilarating, transporting. Like she was riding one of his engines, flying faster than race-horses. Riding fast and hard away from London, into endless possibilities.

If they'd met when she was sixteen.

If he'd been a farmer.

Or she'd been a debutante dressed in white.

She kissed him wearing the skin of a different Mari, one with infinite possibilities.

His hands were on the back of her neck, angling her into his kiss. Which left her hands free to unhook the front of her pelisse, because she needed more space to breath.

He helped her with the last of the hooks and the garment pooled on the wooden floor, spreading at her feet like water.

One of his hands covered her breast through the fabric of her gown, thumbing her nipple.

Heavens, that felt good.

It wasn't like her to do something so unheed-ing. Behind her was the evidence of his ambition and before her was the man himself, built on just as grand a scale as his steam engine.

He kissed with the same intensity as his conversa-tion, a call to arms.

To his arms.

More, please. More, more, more.

Kiss me forever.

Afternoon sun slanted in the high windows and

striped across their bodies. The engine behind her was hard and solid and the man in front even more so.

His hands caressed the sides of her waist and so she slipped her hands inside his coat.

When she touched him he flinched, tensed, but she soothed her hands over his sides, behind to his back, to the hard ridges of muscle, the dipping valley in the center.

He kissed her neck, the soft brush of his lips under her ear making her shiver.

She gave herself up to the kiss.

She'd been yearning for something to happen.

Around the corner. In the duke's arms.

Something's beginning, the hammers pounded on iron somewhere in the distance.

If you're brave enough to chase it, the steam hissed.

He broke away from her, breathing heavily.

"Mari." He clasped her cheeks in his hands. "We can't."

Can't what?

"We can't kiss," he clarified. "Not in here with the door locked and dozens of men outside."

The moment was gone. Melting like ice shavings on lips. She could feel it slipping away.

The impossibility setting in.

Duke.

Governess.

He set her away from him and bent to retrieve her pelisse. Draping it across her shoulders, he assisted her into the garment.

Mari retied her bonnet. He smoothed his cravat and adjusted his trousers.

"We kissed, Your Grace. And the Lord did not smite us. Hell did not open up to swallow us."

"Not this time. And there will never be a next time."

BESIEGED BY THE devilish duke? Ha! More like mauled by the lascivious lady.

As they walked back through the foundry to the courtyard, the men cast sidelong glances.

Was she marked somehow? Lips swollen. Cheeks flushed.

A dampness between her thighs.

The memory of his kiss like heated metal branded across her mind.

Luckily, they didn't encounter Mr. Grafton again, for then she would have been forced to speak and be polite, and she wasn't sure her social graces had yet returned.

She hadn't thought about it properly through. She hadn't thought about what happened after the kiss.

How awkward it might be to see Banksford at the breakfast table the next day, now that she knew what it felt like to have his tongue stroking inside her mouth, and his hand covering her breast.

He'd said never again, as if he were ashamed of the kiss.

Back in the courtyard, Edgar lifted her into the curricle and waved to a groom. "Please take Miss Perkins to my residence."

The groom nodded. "Very good, Your Grace."

So that was it? No talking about what had happened. Bundle her into the carriage and send her away.

"Don't you think we should talk, Your Grace?" she asked.

"About what, Miss Perkins?" His face was deliberately devoid of emotion.

About what? About that kiss. About the dozens of new emotions jumbled in her heart. "You don't think there's anything to say?"

Moving away, he motioned to the groom and the carriage began to move.

She had been dismissed.

Had it meant nothing to him?

She'd begun thinking of him as somehow, not less than a duke, but perhaps as a man instead of a duke. But here was a very blunt reminder that she mustn't think of him as anything but his rank and his position in society.

He was her employer and her social superior.

She was a plain, ordinary middle C in a city full of aristocratic grace notes.

He waved politely, dismissively, as the carriage left the foundry yard, as if they hadn't just shared a kiss that had burned with the light of a thousand signal flares lit on a mountaintop, warning of an impending battle.

Or perhaps, to the duke, the kiss had been merely ordinary? A spark from the hearth, easily stamped out before it burned a hole in the carpet. Nothing immense, or important, or even meaningful in any serious way.

Whereas for Mari, the kiss had been filled with meaning. It marked a division in her life.

Before the kiss, she'd only read about and imagined such daring acts. After the kiss, she knew that leaping into the fire was not only possible . . . but pleasurable.

All of the secret desires she'd suppressed her whole life had suddenly surfaced, all at once.

Apparently, she had a wanton side.

And not just a side.

A front, back, and everything in between.

This had been a warning. Playing with dukes, a girl was apt to get burned.

No more wild imaginings like the ones she'd experienced in the duke's arms. That she could be someone else. That they could be equals.

None of it was true.

All of it was impossible.

She must bottle up these desires.

Label them *impossible*. Place them on the shelf in her heart next to a host of other impossible things.

Kisses. Love. Children of her own.

All impossibilities.

Her fate had been sealed the moment she'd been left at the door of the orphanage.

And the duke's fate had been sealed from birth as well.

Handsome, wealthy, born to privilege, he must marry well and produce a legitimate heir with the proper bloodlines.

It may be more difficult to avoid the duke than she'd planned, but she must focus on the tasks at hand—educating the children and discovering the truth about her past.

And when she did encounter him, she now understood that she could help him as well.

He didn't believe that he could be a good father, but she sensed that wasn't true.

He already loved his children, he just needed to open his heart enough to be vulnerable with them.

She was certain Michel and Adele could learn to care for him. Her job here was to help them become the joyful, loving family they were meant to be. Create new bonds that would last a lifetime. And then she would leave.

She was a fortress, alone and self-sufficient.

One day she would walk out the duke's iron gate. And never return.

STUPID, LUSTING OAF. Edgar banged his forehead against his desk at the foundry.

She was his servant. Under his protection.

He'd failed her and he'd failed himself.

"That was a very pretty sort of girl. The governess, was she?" asked Grafton, entering Edgar's office.

Edgar straightened. "Yes." He picked up a pencil and pretended to be busily drawing.

The pencil snapped in half. "Damn."

"Your mind's not here," Grafton said. "Maybe it left with the governess?"

"Ungh," Edgar grunted noncommittally.

"Never brought any of the other governesses round to meet me before."

"Confound it, man." Edgar threw down the broken halves of the pencil. "If you've something to say, just say it."

Grafton grinned. "Tsk, tsk. Rather touchy on the subject, are we?"

Edgar scraped his palm over his eyes and then down across his nose and mouth. "You've no idea." He abandoned all pretense of working and settled back in his chair. "I can't stop thinking about her. I'm going mad, I think. She's just so good with the children and she's so . . ."

"Pretty?"

"Lights up every room she enters. She doesn't keep her opinions to herself, either, let me tell you."

Grafton snorted. "So I observed."

"I knew I was going to regret hiring the lady. I knew the second I laid eyes on her that she would drive me mad by inches."

"Wouldn't be the first beautiful governess to turn a nobleman's head, now would she?"

"That's the bloody problem. My father had a nasty habit of ruining servants. Scullery maids, upstairs maids, governesses . . . he tupped anything in skirts. No pretty girl was safe from him. It sickened me. I did what I could to stop it but I was gone at school much of the time . . ."

"I remember," said Grafton. "You spoke of him sometimes. Your voice always held such revulsion. I thought that you were better off, because you had a real father, but then I began to wonder if perhaps my situation was preferable."

Grafton was the illegitimate son of an earl, who had financed Grafton's schooling, but refused any other form of assistance or contact. Edgar had met Grafton during his first year at Cambridge.

"Better to have no father," agreed Edgar.

"I met him once, your father," Grafton said carefully. "You're nothing like him. Nothing at all. For one thing, I know you to be a good man, who would never even look at an unwilling woman."

Edgar grimaced. "No difference, don't you see? Even willing, she's my servant. It's an unequal balance of power. Dallying with her makes me no better than the old duke."

"You're too hard on yourself. The lady was strong-minded and more than capable of fending for herself, from my observation of her."

"It doesn't matter if I have the best of intentions, if I mean to treat her with respect and keep her at a distance. If my actions speak differently than my words, I'm no better than he was."

"Can you trust Miss Perkins to make decisions that are right for her?"

Edgar thought about that for a moment. "She may think they're right for her, but she's so young, Grafton. Remember when we were that young? The idiotic things we did?"

Grafton chuckled. "I remember waving our bare arses at a group of matrons while we were standing up in a donkey cart. Inebriated out of our minds. Utterly sotted."

"Exactly. I made very, very poor decisions. I never touch brandy now. And I'm not about to begin indulging in governesses. The only sensible thing to do is avoid her. I hired a governess to restore peace and order and she's producing the opposite effect. Consuming my thoughts. I need to redirect my attention where it needs to be—here, at the foundry."

"With a bunch of sweaty, unwashed men? I'd rather think about pretty girls, myself."

"You know what I mean," Edgar said impatiently. "We've got to solve the problem of the boiler system. It's still too heavy."

Grafton nodded. "That we do. But sometimes if you try too hard at something, it will elude you, I've found. Maybe what you need is a bit of a holiday from all this." He gestured around the office. "You're wound up too tightly. You're bound to snap, just like that poor pencil."

Edgar glanced down. Another broken pencil in his palm. He added it to the pile of fragmented wood littering his desk.

A holiday. It wasn't the worst idea. But not for Edgar, for Miss Perkins and the children.

She'd told him the twins missed the seaside. And he'd told her there was seashore in England.

His family used to holiday at Southend, less than a day's journey from London.

"Grafton, you're brilliant."

"Clearly," said Grafton. "So you'll be leaving for a spell then?"

"I won't be going anywhere."

"But you just said—"

"I'm not going anywhere. But Miss Perkins and the children will be going to Southend. I'll make all of the arrangements." Edgar leapt up from his desk. "There's no time like the present."

Grafton gave him a skeptical look. "Sending her away won't make your feelings for her disappear."

"Who said anything about feelings? This is mere physical attraction. Out of sight, out of mind."

"Absence makes the heart grow fonder."

Edgar groaned. "Grafton, are we spouting proverbs at each other?"

"It appears that way."

"She leaves, Grafton." Edgar swept a pile of shattered pencils into the bin. "The sooner the better."

Chapter 14

֍

MARI'S HEART HAMMERED as she read the sign.

Arthur Shadwell, Esquire. Engraved on an ordinary plate on an ordinary door on one of the endless rows of brick buildings in Cheapside.

This was her first off day, and she was going to make the most of it. The quest that had begun after Mrs. Crowley made her confession had led her here, to this door, this possibility. The knowledge she craved more than anything. The true reason she was here in London.

The tendrils of connection forming between her and the children were undeniable, and she very much hoped she would have the chance to nurture them into fruition.

But the connection she felt with the duke? An utter impossibility. She mustn't go around thinking that she and Banksford shared anything other than his roof.

Yesterday, he'd made it very clear that he thought of her as an inconvenience.

All of these desires he evoked in her were dangerous in the extreme.

If visiting this lawyer became an opportunity for her, she must take it.

This could change everything. Could she be an heiress? That wasn't likely, but it did happen in novels, sometimes. But if she were an heiress, then the lawyer had been searching for her because someone had died.

She hoped that wasn't the case, because what she longed for most of all was a connection with her past, someone who might be able to tell her the story of her birth, and why she had been left at the orphanage.

Yes, a person would be far preferable to a fortune.

She wouldn't find out anything if she didn't go inside.

Either she would find answers, or she wouldn't. Hope for the best, but prepare for the worst; that way she wouldn't be disappointed.

She adjusted Lady India's blue velvet-lined bonnet so that the brim sat farther back on her head. She needed a full range of vision. Her life may be about to change forever.

A young man with a sloppy cravat and rumpled hair answered her ring. "Yes? May I help you?" he asked.

"Mr. Arthur Shadwell?"

"Yes."

She'd expected someone older, she didn't know why. Probably because the lawyer had visited the orphanage several years past and this fellow looked barely out of university, his face spotted with red blemishes.

"May I come in and speak with you for a moment, Mr. Shadwell?"

He eyed the gold buttons on her pelisse and seemed to make up his mind that she was well worth his time. His manner changed completely. "Miss . . . ?"

"Perkins."

"Miss Perkins, do come in." He bowed unsteadily,

and for one panicked moment Mari thought she might have to catch him and help him regain his feet. But he righted himself and ushered her inside, hastily swiping away stacks of papers from a chair.

His desk was covered in drifts of papers and books lined every surface of the room.

She couldn't help noticing the unwashed stoneware and the heavy smell of rat droppings and cheap gin.

Mr. Shadwell was perhaps not the most respectable of lawyers. Didn't he have a clerk or a maid to assist him?

When she was settled, he took a seat across the desk from her. "I'm afraid I can't offer you tea," he said. "My maid chose a very inconvenient time to run off with my clerk."

Well that answered her question. "Never mind," she said, "I don't want tea. I need information."

"What sort of information? An investigation? I specialize in matters of the heart." He leaned forward and the strong smell of gin intensified. "Is your sweetheart cuckolding you, Miss Perkins? I'll catch him out, never fear."

Mari blinked. "That's not it at all. This is about a past investigation. One you conducted on behalf of a client I should very much like to know more about."

"A past investigation. I see." He steepled his fingers and attempted to place his chin upon them, but missed, catching his nose instead. His head jolted back upright.

That's when Mari realized that Mr. Arthur Shadwell, Esquire, was completely and utterly foxed.

"Do you perhaps need a glass of water, Mr. Shadwell?" *Dashed in your face, perhaps?*

"Could use a little liquid refreshment, at that." He

opened his desk drawer and extracted a flask. Taking several long gulps, he held it out to her. "Care for a nip?"

"Humph," she sniffed. This interview was not going according to plan. Could she trust anything the man said? He was drinking in front of a woman wearing the clothing of a lady, and sitting slumped over as if his head might slam into the desk at any moment.

As much as it pained her, she may have to come back later. When the man was sober. "Should I come back later, Mr. Shadwell? You seem rather indisposed at the moment."

"Indishposed," he slurred. "Not a bit of it. Feeling fit as a fiddle and right as rain. Now tell me about the gentleman in question. Did he take your virtue and you want revenge? You can be frank with me."

"I've no idea what you're talking about, Mr. Shadwell. I'm not here because of some love affair gone wrong. I'm here because you, or I believe it was you, visited the Underwood Orphanage and Charity School near the village of Hathersage, in Derbyshire, less than two years ago. You were inquiring about the whereabouts of a girl who had been left there as a babe, with a wooden toy rabbit and a prayer book."

"Toy rabbit?" he scratched his head. "Can't say as I ever investigated a toy rabbit."

"Not the rabbit, the girl. The girl who was left at the orphanage."

"Never been to an orphanage," he said. "Horrible places, lousy with bedbugs and crying babes."

"How long have you been a lawyer, sir?" Mari asked sternly.

"Long enough," he said belligerently. "Long enough to know that I charge by the minute. And you've been here . . ." He lifted his pocket watch from his waistcoat with unsteady fingers. "Ten minutes, Miss Perkins. Ten minutes of my time. That's—"

"Are you certain you never visited an orphanage in Derbyshire?" she persisted.

"Why would I?" He took another slug from his flask. "Not much action in Derbyshire. No, the love scandals are all in London, Miss Perkins. Your cheating husbands, crimes of passion, courtesans on the side, illegitimate children . . . that's my bread and butter."

"You're the only Arthur Shadwell listed in *Johnstone's London Commercial Guide.*"

"Am I? Sometimes I do see double when I look in the glass." He laughed. Then hiccupped.

The man was impossible. Mari had had enough.

"Well this has been extremely disappointing." She rose. "You do know it's only half ten of the morning. Shameful," she said. "Most shameful."

"Half ten?" He leapt from his desk. "Half ten? Why didn't you say so? I'm late for court. Where's my wig?" He searched the room.

She pointed to the ceiling. There was a white wig dangling from the light fixture.

"How did it get up there? Did you put it there?"

"If you have a sudden memory of visiting the Underwood Orphanage, Mr. Shadwell, you may find me at Number Seventeen, Grosvenor Square. I'm in the employ of the Duke of Banksford. Good day, sir." She stormed out of his office and back to the street.

Mari gulped a breath of air to clear her head and watering eyes after the close confines of Mr. Shadwell's disreputable office. It didn't seem possible that her search could have ended so abruptly and in such drunken ignominy. Arthur Shadwell. That was the name Mrs. Crowley had told her, she was sure of it.

Could it be Shadewell, perhaps? Arturio, or Arlin, instead of Arthur? She would try every variation, because that drunken man inside that squalid office was definitely not the man she was searching for.

Disappointed and a little disheartened, Mari trudged toward High Holborn Street. She would visit Lumley's Toy Shop and ask about P.L. Rabbit.

The duke had said the toy shop was a magical place. And she needed a little magic right now.

Visiting lawyers and kissing dukes were not so dissimilar, she reflected. Both of them made her pulse race with anticipation . . . and both ended in frustration.

EDGAR COULD NEVER kiss Miss Perkins again. Never. And that meant never, ever, not in a thousand years. He could never kiss her again, but he could follow her instructions.

She'd told him to take the twins to Lumley's Toy Shop. Therefore here he was, outside the toy shop, with a child on either side of him.

"Why isn't Miss Perkins with us?" asked Adele, for the third time.

"It's her off day," Edgar said patiently, for the third time.

"What's she doing?" asked Michel.

"She's off . . ." What was she doing? She'd gone out early, Mrs. Fairfield had told him. Did she have friends in London? Family?

"She's off having tea with the bishop, for all I know," he said.

She'd avoided his questions about her family. She'd said her father was a vicar, hadn't she?

He didn't know much about her background, really.

He only knew that Mari Perkins, superior governess, drove him to distraction with her insightful conversation and her passionate kisses. And he was sending her and the children to the seaside. All of the arrangements had been made. He'd rented the entire top floor of the Royal Hotel in Seaside. Today, he would purchase the twins everything they required for a seaside holiday.

His footman, Carl, opened the door for them and a bell tinkled deep inside the shop, setting off a long-buried memory.

Nine years old, entering the doors of paradise, where kind, jolly Mr. Lumley was sure to make him laugh, and give him some boiled sweets from his candy jar.

The shop had been a special place for Edgar. He'd even pretended Mr. Lumley was his father, instead of the cold, bitter man who lived at Edgar's home, but whom he saw only on rare occasions.

And on those rare occasions when the duke was home, they'd walked on eggshells, he and India, and their mother.

They'd never known what might set him off. A wrong word. A toy left in a hallway.

Adele tugged on his hand. "May we have a sweet?"

"I'm sure Mr. Lumley will give you one," he replied.

The candy dish was still there on the oaken counter with the glass top. Everything was exactly the same.

"That's a lot of toys," said Michel in an awed tone of voice, his gaze darting around the shop.

Edgar could tell he was trying to sound unimpressed, but his eyes were lively, jumping over the display shelves filled with toys and games.

"I loved coming here when I was your age," said Edgar.

Two pairs of dark eyes stared up at him.

"It's been open that long?" asked Adele.

Edgar laughed. "I'm not that old, young miss."

"Can I help you find something, sir?" asked a young shop clerk in the same coat of blue and silver the shop clerks had been garbed in when Edgar had visited as a boy.

"Is Mr. Lumley here?" Edgar asked.

"He is, sir. In the back rooms."

"Inform him the Duke of Banksford is here," said Carl, with a self-important shifting of his large shoulders.

The clerk snapped to attention. "Your Grace," he bowed to Edgar. "Yes, sir. Right away, sir," he said to Carl.

"Oh look," cried Adele. "There's P.L. Rabbit!" She pointed to a high shelf over the counter where a row of wooden rabbits, ducks, and dolls sat in a row.

"That's not P.L." Michel studied the rabbit. "He's wearing trousers."

"Well then it's P.L.'s long lost brother, P.S."

"P.S.?" asked Edgar.

"Tim Chin, of course," said Adele.

"Of course," Edgar replied.

"We'll have to tell Miss Perkins that we found P.L.'s brother at a toy shop," said Adele.

Mr. Lumley entered the room, his hair gone silver, but the same kindly smile upon his face. He wore thick spectacles and carried a cane, tapping it in front of him.

"Can it be young Master Edgar?" he asked.

Edgar laughed. "Not so young anymore." He strode to the counter and shook Lumley's hand warmly. "It's good to see you, Lumley."

"Well I don't see so well, these days, Your Grace," said Lumley, "but it's very good to hear your voice. And who are these small shapes?" he asked, turning his milky gaze toward the twins.

"My two children, Adele and Michel."

"We're twins," said Michel.

"We're precocious," said Adele.

"Oh my," said Lumley. "Is that contagious?"

"No." Adele laughed. "It means we're intelligent."

"Then I know exactly what you need." Lumley reached behind him. The shop clerk hovered nearby but the shopkeeper knew the location of everything.

"Here you are, young master." He handed Michel a wooden chess board, and he gave the pieces to Adele. "Have you ever played chess before?"

"Never," said Michel.

"My clerk will explain the rules," said Lumley.

The clerk took the children to a low table by the window, the perfect height for the children.

"I used to love to play chess," said Edgar.

"I remember. You would always tell me how many times you'd won against your friends," said Lumley.

"I see you still have kites."

"Kites will never go out of fashion. Always going to be wind to lift them, you know. Tell me, Your Grace, are you well? How is Lady India? Has she married? Does she have children of her own, now?"

"My sister's not the marrying kind, Lumley. She's always off digging up antiquities."

"She always did like the trowels."

"And the curiosities. Remember when she convinced one of your customers that a small thumb vial contained the actual tears of Cleopatra?"

Lumley laughed. "She was quite good at spinning tales."

"Still is. And she's still placing outrageous wagers. She bet one hundred pounds that I would marry before her."

Lumley frowned. "You never . . . married?"

"I didn't know about the twins until a few months ago, actually," said Edgar. "Or I would have brought them to meet you earlier."

"It's been a very long time. I'm an old man now. Old and alone. Don't end up like me, Your Grace, with no heir or family."

"Can't think about marriage right now. Too busy with my foundry."

"Your foundry?"

"The Vulcan Foundry. We're producing steam engines."

"How wonderful. I always knew you would do something extraordinary."

That was a rare reaction to the news that he was a tradesman. Edgar smiled. "I've missed you, Lumley."

"And I, you, Your Grace."

"I'll go and see how the children are faring," Edgar said. He joined the children at the low table. The clerk was still explaining the game while Adele and Michel listened intently.

Chess was a grand idea. It would keep their nimble minds occupied if it rained in Southend.

The shop bell tinkled again and the store clerk left to answer the door.

Edgar heard the sound of a lilting, cheerful voice answering a question.

He turned and met Mari's blue gaze. She looked startled. Dismayed.

She wasn't happy to see him?

Chapter 15

❧

MARI COULDN'T BELIEVE her eyes. The duke was here with the children. He'd followed her instructions.

He'd ruined her plans.

Now she couldn't make her inquiries.

He was sitting at a low table, his knees drawn up nearly to his ears. Her initial disappointment dissolved. The scene was simply too adorable. The huge duke sitting in a chair three sizes too small for him, playing chess with his children.

It made her want to kiss him. There it was. A plain and proverbial truth.

Two wrongs don't make a right. A penny saved is a penny earned.

And Mari Perkins wanted to kiss the Duke of Banksford every single time she saw him.

"Miss Perkins!" Adele said. "You came."

"Yes, dear, I came." She walked toward the table.

"Who's this, then?" asked the handsome older gentleman who stood at the central counter.

The duke rose. "Mr. Lumley, the children's governess, Miss Perkins."

Mari approached the counter. Mr. Lumley stretched out his hand to touch her hand.

"I'm sorry my dear," he said. "I don't see very well these days. But I can tell that you've a fetching blue bonnet and red hair."

"Pleased to meet you, Mr. Lumley. Your shop is delightful."

"It is," agreed Adele.

"Thank you, Miss Perkins," said Mr. Lumley. "We're one of the oldest toy shops in London."

The children were obviously enchanted, and well they should be.

Kites soared on the walls along with swords, masks, and musical instruments. The shelves were piled high with sailing ships, dolls, tin soldiers, harlequins and other figurines.

Rocking horses, and horses with carts, balls, skipping ropes, and cricket bats were piled along the walls.

There were looking glasses of all sizes, spyglasses, compasses, and all manner of magnifying glasses and other educational tools.

The large oaken shop counter at the center of the room had a glass top. When she looked inside, Mari saw interesting objects and curiosities. Bones, glass phials, and silver ornaments.

It was a children's paradise, filled with magical things.

Mr. Lumley smiled and wrinkles wreathed his cheeks. "His Grace used to be one of my very best customers, Miss Perkins. He liked the tin soldiers the best. Even had a custom armory made. Bloodthirsty, he was. Waged vast campaigns against enemy forces. He'd come and tell me that he needed more cannons."

"Is that true?" Michel cocked his head.

"See?" said the duke. "I wasn't a proper boring milksop."

Adele giggled. "He heard you call him a milksop, Michel."

"I don't think you're boring now, Father," said Michel.

"How magnanimous," said the duke.

It did Mari's heart good to see them laughing and talking together.

"Now the duke makes his own miniatures," she informed the toy maker. "Little toy engines."

The duke gave her a look, but there was residual laughter in his gray eyes.

"I wonder if children will play someday with toy engines, just as they do with horse carts now?" asked Mr. Lumley.

"I shouldn't wonder," said Mari.

"I build small-scale models of my engines," said Banksford. "I'm working on a fire engine right now."

"We had a fire here, several years back," said Mr. Lumley, his hand trembling where it lay on the table. "Nearly lost everything. But I've rebuilt since then. Children always need toys."

"I captured your king. I win, right?" Adele hopped up from the table.

"You did at that," said the duke.

"Then you must have a prize, young lady." Mr. Lumley handed a small wooden box to Adele.

"What is it?" she asked.

"A magic box," said Mr. Lumley.

"Oh no," Banksford groaned. "Still telling the same jokes?"

"Looks ordinary to me." Adele held it up and shook it.

"It's not ordinary at all," said Mr. Lumley, with a twinkle in his cloudy eyes. "It contains all of the modesty of a dandy, the honesty of a lawyer, and the luck of a gambler."

Adele studied the box for a moment. Her eyes lit. "Which is to say it contains nothing at all."

"Clever girl."

"I've got one for you," said Adele. "What kind of dance did the tin soldier take the paper princess to?"

Mr. Lumley thought for a moment. "A cannon ball! I'm right, aren't I?"

He slapped his thigh and roared with laughter. "Ho! Your Grace, I like your children immensely."

"You always did love a good laugh," said the duke. "Shall we go shopping?" he asked the twins. Carl and the shop clerk followed Edgar and the children through the shop as they made their selections.

Now was her opportunity to question Mr. Lumley. Mari gestured toward the wooden rabbits on the shelf behind him, she'd noticed them immediately upon entering. "I was given one of your wooden rabbit figurines as a little girl."

Mr. Lumley reached behind him and placed a wooden rabbit on the counter. "Were you? I've always loved the wooden bunnies. This one's name is Clover." He stroked the green velvet gown the rabbit wore, so much less worn than her rabbit's tattered old gown. "They were very popular decades ago. Now the children only want porcelain figurines, much more lifelike and less roughhewn."

"Did you manufacture many of the rabbits?" she asked.

"Hundreds."

"Might you have a list of the customers who purchased them?"

"I'm sure I do . . . somewhere," he said, with a befuddled expression.

That wasn't very promising. She'd have to come back when she could be alone with him. Perhaps ask to speak with his bookkeeper.

"Why do you ask, Miss Perkins?"

"I never knew where my rabbit came from. I thought perhaps it had a story to tell."

"Most toys do."

Edgar and the children had piled Carl's arms high with toys and games. Among the puzzles and soldiers, spyglasses, and magnifying glasses, Mari noticed little buckets and spades.

"What are these for?" she asked the duke, when he approached.

"You'll find out," he said, with a secretive smile. "I'm planning something for the children, something they'll like very much." He bent down and settled his arm across Michel's shoulders. "Are we forgetting anything?"

"I don't think so," said Michel, his eyes shining and a smile curving his lips.

"What about a book of constellations?" asked Mari. "We can use a telescope and go up on the roof."

"An excellent idea, Miss Perkins," said Mr. Lumley. "I've just the thing."

He opened a drawer and handed her a set of large cards and an accompanying book called *Urania's Mirror*.

"You hold the cards to the light, and it shows the formation of the constellation. They're perforated according to the star's magnitudes."

Mari held one of the gaily-colored cards depicting the constellation Lyra to the lamp. There were pinpricks along the drawing, and light filtered through the small openings. "How wonderful."

"If you could see Miss Perkins right now, Mr. Lumley, you'd see that she has freckles on her cheeks that look like constellations of stars," said the duke, touching her cheek.

He had the ability to liquefy her insides with only a few words and a brief touch, even with gloved hands.

Mr. Lumley smiled. "Then the constellation cards are yours, Miss Perkins. Free of charge."

"Oh no, I couldn't possibly."

"I insist."

The shop clerk wrapped up their purchases and Carl began carrying them to the carriage.

"Will you come back to the house with us, Miss Perkins?" asked duke.

"We can try to see some stars tonight," said Adele.

"You won't see many stars in London these days with all the smoke and smog, more's the pity," said Mr. Lumley.

"Maybe they'll see the stars at the seashore soon," the duke said, enigmatically.

And then she realized what he meant. This was more evidence that he'd taken her advice to heart. He'd hired the French cook, brought the children to the toy shop, and now . . . he was going to take them to the seashore.

"Let's go home," he said.

Home. Was it her home? A temporary one, at best. And one that she could lose at any moment. But that couldn't dim her joy. Banksford was transforming before her eyes, becoming a better father, a thoughtful one.

The twins would be so happy at the seashore.

Excitement brought a spring to her step. She'd never seen the sun sparkling on the sea before.

Or the moon rising over the waves.

"You've a faraway look in your eyes, Miss Perkins," said Banksford as he handed her into his carriage.

"I was picturing the moon rising over the sea. I've only read about it in poems and novels."

"It's a beautiful sight," he said.

There were so many things she'd only read about in poems and books. Too many.

It was time to start experiencing some of them in real life.

She glanced at Banksford. His smile was intimate, his silver eyes filled with the promise of moonlit nights. And moonlit kisses.

Chapter 16

❧

LADY INDIA GAVE the round yellow moon one final adjustment and scrambled down from the ladder. "Where is that brother of mine? He's hosting this event, I hope he remembers."

"I haven't seen him in several days, since we visited Lumley's Toy Shop," replied Mari.

"Edgar went with you to Lumley's?" Lady India's expression was comical in its bewilderment. "That doesn't sound like him at all." She smiled warmly. "You've produced quite a change in him, Miss Perkins."

Mari fixed her gaze on the gauzy blue fabric festooned over the salon ceiling. She didn't want to betray any inappropriate sentiments. Lady India was far too perceptive.

"Didn't we have fun at Lumley's?" Adele handed Mari another gold star.

"We did, indeed," agreed Mari, taking the star and sewing it to the stage curtains.

Lady India had enlisted every available maid and footman in the house for her project of transforming the Silver Salon into an Egyptian nightscape for her antiquities exhibition, which was to include a theatrical enactment of a scene from ancient history.

"I used to love going to Lumley's." Lady India

looked at the twins. "Does he still have that jar of boiled sweets on the counter? And did he give you a magic box?"

Adele nodded. "He's a funny old fellow. I liked him."

Mari had liked Mr. Lumley as well.

The familiar way he'd talked to Edgar, teasing him about his love for tin soldiers.

Mari caught herself. Just because Lady India called her brother Edgar didn't mean Mari could go about doing it, even in her thoughts.

The thought of seeing him made her nervous and excited at the same time.

Butterflies in one's belly sounded like a pleasant sensation—all silky, fluttery wings—but in truth it was nearly a sick feeling. She longed to see him and dreaded it at the same time.

"He'd better come home in the next few hours," said Lady India with a slight frown. "If I were male I would be a member of the Society of Antiquaries, and could host it there, but instead I need Edgar to lend the affair the proper gravitas."

"What's gravitas?" asked Michel.

"Dignity and seriousness," said Mari.

"That doesn't sound very amusing." Adele wrinkled her nose. "We can't have fun tonight?"

"You can have a small amount of fun," said Lady India. "But there will be several important gentlemen in attendance who take themselves very, very seriously. And there's a small, a very small, chance that my mother, the dowager duchess, may decide to attend."

"Our grandmother?" asked Michel.

"I sent her an invitation. But I doubt she'll come," explained Lady India.

Michel jumped up from the floor, running to Lady

India. "How will we know her? What does she look like? Will she like us?"

Lady India laughed and placed her hand on Michel's head. "So many questions."

"We want to make a favorable impression," said Adele with a grave expression.

"She's tall for a female, just as I am." Lady India pointed at her eyes. "And she has the same purple-pansy eyes."

"As for making an impression," said Mari. "If she does appear, you must curtsy and bow in the manner that I taught you, address her as Your Grace, and keep your myriad opinions to yourself for one evening, and all will be well. Mind you, no palm reading," she said sternly.

"Of course not," said Adele with a toss of her head. "Come along, Michel. Let's go practice our curtsying and bowing on Mrs. Fairfield."

She took her brother's hand and they ran away to find the housekeeper, who was supervising the preparation of the balcony where refreshments would be served after the exhibition.

"I hope it was the right thing inviting Mother." Lady India gazed out the window with a worried expression. "I doubt that she will come, but I should have warned Edgar just in case."

"You never told him you invited her?"

"They haven't spoken to each other in years."

"What happened between them?"

"Oh," India laughed, turning back toward Mari. "That's too long of a story."

"That's what Mrs. Fairfield said when I asked about it."

"You'll have to ask Edgar."

All her life she'd longed for a family. Edgar had a mother and yet they never spoke. It was sad.

"You're making great progress with the twins, Miss Perkins," said Lady India.

"Thank you. And won't you call me Mari?"

"And you must call me Indy. All of my friends do."

Were they friends? Mari liked the idea. "I couldn't call you Indy. But perhaps . . . India. I would be honored."

"I'm glad we're friends," said India. "You're not at all like any governess I've ever met. Why must you work for a living? It must be so dreary."

Mari raised her eyebrows. "Michel and Adele *dreary*?"

India laughed. "I suppose that's the wrong adjective. But you seem to me to be made for grander things."

"Your brother accused me of being a spy."

"Did he? I told you not to mind his growling."

What about his kisses . . . should she mind those? And did they have any deeper meaning?

She'd been thinking about their kiss at the foundry. Remembering the play of sinews and muscles beneath his shirt. Wondering what he looked like without his shirt.

You don't have to maul the poor man with your mind every chance you get.

India gave her a little smile. "I'm glad things are going so well . . . with the children."

"They're beginning to trust me, I can feel it."

"Splendid. Now then, are the stars all hung?"

Mari nodded.

"Everything must be perfect," said India, turning in a slow circle to survey the room. "Ravenwood will be here this evening."

"Ah. Edg—His Grace—told us about Ravenwood. Your sworn enemy, I hear?"

"He thinks he's a great antiquities hunter but all he does is lounge about in hotels consorting with the local courtesans, while I'm out actually digging in the dirt, making important discoveries. When he's had his fill of debauchery, he just buys whatever antiquities he wants from unscrupulous thieves. It's beyond provoking."

Mari hid a smile. Sounded like Lady India paid quite a bit of attention to this Ravenwood.

"He'll have nothing to fault you for tonight. It's going to be very impressive."

"You'll make it impressive."

"What do you mean?"

"Oh, didn't I tell you?" She gave Mari an innocent smile. "I have a part for you to play in my tableau."

"I don't know," said Mari doubtfully. "I've never been on stage before."

India drew aside the velvet curtains hanging from the small, enclosed stage the footmen had pieced together from painted wooden panels.

She caught Mari's chin in her hand and turned her head. "Your profile will be illumined by the shining moon. You'll have a crown on your head and a magnificent golden collar necklace at your throat."

"A queen? I'm not sure that I'm queenly enough."

"A Pharaoh, Mari. Not just a queen. Oh, I'm going to ruffle so many feathers tonight. How they will squawk and protest. Especially Ravenwood. I simply can't wait to see his face."

"But shouldn't your Egyptian queen be portrayed by someone more regal? Perhaps *you* could play the role?"

India shook her head. "I'll be narrating the scene.

No . . . I need someone with a powerful presence . . . and a pretty ankle."

"Have you seen my ankles? They're scrawny as chicken bones."

India laughed. "I have seen your ankles, in Edgar's library, remember? And do you seriously believe what you're saying? If you knew the power you could wield over men you'd be dangerous."

"Nonsense."

"I know a regal queen when I see one."

"Have you forgotten that I must care for the children tonight?"

"But they're already in the scene." India placed her hands on Mari's shoulders. "Just stand there, the children will wave their palm fronds, I'll explain your history, and the curtain will drop."

"I don't know. I may become nervous and freeze up with all of those eyes on me." With Edgar's eyes on her.

The butterflies came back with a vengeance. They seemed to think they were elephants.

"That's perfect! It's a frozen tableau. You won't even have to move. What could possibly go wrong?"

"WHERE HAVE YOU been?" India asked, her eyes flashing as she met Edgar at the door. "They're getting restless."

"At The Vulcan. Working on the steam engine." Avoiding certain redheaded temptations.

Robertson divested Edgar of his coat and hat, while India tapped her foot impatiently. "Hurry up, if you please," she said.

"What the devil are you wearing?" He peered at India's garb which was outlandish, even for her. A gown made of thick, gray-green cotton with a pelisse made of thin brown leather over the top, cinched under her bosom with a leather belt.

"It's what I wear when I'm at an archaeological dig."

"Are those hessian boots?" he asked, noting the leather tassels visible beneath the hem of her skirt.

"I had your boot maker design some in my size. What the devil are *you* wearing? I told you to look ducal."

"Don't press your luck. This is as ducal as I get. I'm never dressing in fashionable finery again. Not after what happened when I took Lady Blanche riding. Everyone thinks I'm on the marriage mart now. It was a total disaster."

India smiled. "You are on the marriage mart. Don't you recall our wager? I intend to collect."

"Wasn't that a joke?"

"Don't you know me by now? I take my gambling seriously."

Edgar regarded his traitorous sister. "You didn't put West up to the whole scheme with Blanche and Laxton, did you?"

"That's too complicated, even for me. Now please hurry." She shoved a piece of paper into his hands. "Your introduction."

Leaving him no time to read the paper, she pulled him into the salon.

The room had been transformed in his absence. Blue curtains sprinkled with gold stars draped the ceiling and fell on either side of a small, enclosed wooden stage constructed on one end of the room.

The guests were looking very uncomfortable, reclining on velvet cushions and Persian carpets in front of the makeshift stage.

"You removed all of the furniture?" Edgar whispered. "You're forcing dukes to sit on cushions? Ravenwood looks ominous."

"He always looks ominous. That's his natural expression."

Mari and the children were nowhere to be seen.

Out of the corner of his eye he saw Lady Blanche sitting with an older woman. Why was she here? And no Laxton in sight. Warning bells rang in his mind.

"What exactly is happening here?" he asked.

"Don't think. Just read."

India clapped her hands and Robertson announced Edgar.

"His Grace, the seventh Duke of Banksford, Marquess of Marbrooke, Earl of Glenmorgan, and Viscount Gordon."

India was out to impress if she'd trotted out all of his titles. Maybe he should have gathered a few more details about this undertaking of hers.

All eyes turned to him. He walked to the front of the room before the velvet curtain.

Where were Miss Perkins and the children? He'd given the twins permission to attend.

He cleared his throat, holding up the piece of paper.

Damnably cramped handwriting Indy possessed.

"Esteemed guests. Eminent antiquarians. Ladies. Ravenwood," Edgar nodded at the duke, the next ranking member of the audience. "We are gathered this evening to witness the unveiling of quite possibly the most momentous discovery in the history of archaeology." He coughed slightly.

Not very modest, his sister.

"As you know, I sponsored Lady India's expedition to the Karnak temple complex in Egypt. While she was there she made a startling discovery. An intact solid gold cartouche inscribed with the name of the Pharaoh Hatshepsut."

He had no idea how to pronounce that and had probably just mangled it horribly.

"The same Pharaoh that her esteemed colleagues have named Amenenthe. But they are all wrong, and she will prove it this evening. Using the cartouche and several wall murals, Lady India was able to deduce that Amenenthe was actually Hatshepsut, and that Hatshepsut was . . . well, see for yourselves."

What on earth was that supposed to signify?

There was a parenthetical instruction to make a flourishing motion toward the stage.

Edgar ignored it. This was already silly enough.

India stepped forward out of the shadows.

"See for yourselves," she repeated in a booming voice, throwing her hand out with palm facing the velvet curtains.

That was the cue for the footmen to appear and draw back the curtains of the stage that India must have had constructed in his parlor while he'd been gone the last few days.

What was behind the curtain? Edgar stepped to the side and turned.

A golden moon hung on a velvet sky.

In the distance, a stone pyramid painted on canvas.

Adele and Michel stood at the edge of the small stage, draped in white and waving dried palm fronds at a woman with bowed head.

The woman raised her head.

Edgar's jaw dropped.

India was trying to kill him.

Chapter 17

Edgar stared at the stage.

Mari stood, her face turned in profile, slender neck regal as a queen. A two-tiered crown of gold topped hair that flowed down her back nearly to her slender waist.

She wore a white gown in the Grecian style that bared one of her shoulders, exposing a sprinkling of golden freckles, just as he'd imagined they would be sprinkled.

A wide collar fashioned from strands of gold beads layered one upon the other was clasped round her neck, covering her from the base of her throat to the top of her bosom.

"By gad, that's a pretty gel," Edgar heard the Earl of Haddock say. "Who is she?"

"Artist's model, no doubt," said Baron Rubens, with a lascivious smacking of his lips. "Though I've not seen her before, and I attend all the best salons."

"I'll wager you do, you old goat," said Haddock.

Edgar nearly climbed over the cushions and tackled them both.

That's no artist's model, he wanted to shout. *That's Mari. And she's mine. So eyes off.*

Yes, he was thinking of her as Mari. How could he not? When she had stars shining around her and gold at her throat?

She was causing quite a stir. The few ladies in the room, Lady Blanche included, were eyeing her jealously, while the men were undressing her with their eyes.

Edgar simultaneously wanted to cover her up, and undress her himself.

He should be the only one allowed to ogle her.

No, that wasn't right.

India kept talking but her voice receded to the edges of Edgar's consciousness.

All he could concentrate on was Mari . . . a goddess come to life.

He'd hired her against his better judgment and this was precisely why.

She wasn't merely a governess.

She was a modern incarnation of an ancient goddess-queen.

He was meant to worship at her feet. In fact, he had the urge to kneel at her feet right now. At this very moment. In front of the learned gathering of antiquities experts and archaeologists.

Adele waved her dried palm frond, fanning long, ruby red waves of hair away from Mari's pale, oval face, earning a half smile from Mari that nearly stopped his heart from beating.

In that ancient society he would have been a bricklayer, no doubt. A serf that wasn't fit to touch her hem.

He saw their roles reversed. It didn't matter what dire circumstances her family had fallen upon, or why she was forced to be a governess.

She was a queen. Made to be worshipped.

He'd known it already, seen it in the way she held herself, the way she spoke to him.

The way she put him in his place.

The sharp intelligence she wielded with such grace,

a subtle and charming hammer that shaped everyone around her into something better.

And in the wild fancy of that moment, with the last of the evening sun glancing through the windows and setting her hair ablaze, gold beads glinted and dripped from her throat, ending at the place where he wanted to start.

The pathway from her heart to the tips of her breasts.

Kneel at her hem. Offer his fealty.

Claim her. Make her his own.

Forever.

THE DUKE WAS staring at her with such intensity that the butterflies in Mari's belly had decided to dance themselves to death in a frenzied whirling.

Every gaze in the room was on her. Her hair unbound, coiling down her back, heavy and unfamiliar. She was the center of attention, singled out, but not because she'd done anything wrong, or was being punished.

The trembling in her belly gradually quieted. The reluctance and embarrassment subsided.

Edgar's eyes glowed with admiration and . . . something else. Something that called to her heart, and quickened her pulse, but not with fear.

With power and exhilaration.

He was Edgar. Not a duke, or a monster. Just Edgar.

And she was a queen. Worthy of the worship she saw in his eyes.

"In the year fifteen-hundred before Christ, Hatshepsut, mighty God King of the Pharaohs, ascended to the throne for a two-decade-long reign of prosperity and military campaigns," said India, from her post beside the stage box. "There is only one slight problem with that version of history, my friends."

She paused, allowing the silence to build with anticipation. Then she flung her hand at Mari and, in a loud, booming voice, proclaimed, "Hatshepsut was a *female*."

Excitement rippled through the room.

The man whom India had pointed out as the Duke of Ravenwood recrossed his long legs and folded his arms across his formidable chest.

He looked skeptical, to say the least.

India drew a dagger from the sheath attached to her leather belt and a lady, probably Lady Blanche, whom Mari had recognized earlier, gave a squeak of surprise.

"I pledge my fealty to Hatshepsut. The Mighty God-Queen and first female Pharaoh!" shouted India.

Adele and Michel waved their palm fronds so vigorously that Mari's gauzy white gown lifted at the hem and floated upward.

"Humph," snorted Ravenwood loudly.

India gave him a murderous glance. "In this tableau I present Hatshepsut at her coronation, wearing a replica of the traditional headpiece, and a fine example of an *Usekh* collar necklace. Which I'm sure the ladies in the audience will appreciate for its intricate gold filigree work."

The ladies craned their necks. Perhaps India would start a new fashion.

"When Hatshepsut was barred from ascending to the throne because of her gender, she refused to submit. She claimed that she had been married to the king of the gods and had as much right to sit on a throne as any other Pharaoh."

Mari threw back her shoulders. No man was going to tell her she couldn't be a goddess, if she wanted to be one.

She'd been so set on discovering the truth about her past, needing to know her origins, her history, who she was and how she fit into the world. But what if she already knew?

What if she was the woman standing on this stage. Confident, bold, hair unbound ... slightly scandalous.

The other day, when they'd visited Edgar's foundry, she'd been bold and brave, because she trusted him. He was a good man, with a beautiful dream for a better world. He loved his children, and he never would have dismissed her because she was helping them.

And helping him see how to talk to them, how to be a meaningful part of their lives, not just a provider.

She trusted him.

But maybe it was time to begin trusting herself.

Edgar was still staring, his eyes filled with reverence.

Why should she care if her shoulder was bared? She was naked before him. Her soul bared for him to see.

Not slightly scandalous. Fully. She wanted him. She wanted to know what pleasure was, everything she'd been denied her entire life.

Starved and punished.

Hiding her true emotions, covering over her desires, foregoing her needs and catering to the needs of others. What of her needs? Her desires?

She could have it all. Have him. The thought made her breathless and giddy with longing. It was time to start living her own life, on her own terms. She'd been hiding herself for too long in proverbs, in other people's experiences.

India continued with her story, the audience dividing their attention between what she was saying and the tableau. "In the years after her death her monuments were defaced, her name erased, and she was lost to history. Nevertheless, her story persisted, in the oral traditions, and on the cartouche and wall drawings I discovered."

What an interesting life India led. Mari wanted to hear more about her journeys. Mari had never even considered the idea of traveling outside of England.

"I presented the cartouche to the Egyptian government," India continued, "though I have several excellent charcoal rubbings for your perusal here tonight. And the collar, which the lovely Miss Perkins is wearing—" she swept her hand toward Mari "—will be on display tonight and then at the British Museum. As for my theory on Hatshepsut's gender . . . I'll be publishing my findings. *We* will be publishing my findings."

India nudged Edgar. "Isn't that right?"

"Ah . . . absolutely right. Female Pharaoh . . . long, happy rule. Lady India will prove it to the world."

His eyes never left Mari's face.

Shocked silence.

Scattered applause.

"Claptrap!" Ravenwood exploded, lumbering to his feet. "Utter hogwash! A female could never be Pharaoh."

MARI WATCHED THE argument unfold from her position on the stage. India's sworn enemy was challenging her theory in front of all of the guests. He must be one of those dangerously handsome rakes who thought they could get away with anything.

"Not now, Ravenwood," India said, glaring at the duke.

"But it's utter rubbish. It wasn't possible for a female to ascend to the throne," said Ravenwood, stalking toward the stage. He waved at Mari's necklace and headdress. "This is all nonsense. Fever dreams. You'll never be able to prove any of it."

"Ah . . . refreshments are being served in the Gold Salon, next door," India said desperately. She'd obviously decided to ignore Ravenwood and attempt to distract the guests with food. "Won't you join us?"

Footmen drew the stage curtains, leaving Mari and the twins in darkness.

Adele and Michel set down their palm fronds and rushed to her. "Did you see that?" asked Adele.

"Ravenwood said it was hogwash!"

"I think they're going to fight a duel," said Adele.

"Men can't fight duels with ladies," said Michel.

"They can if it's Lady India," said Adele. "She'll skewer him with her dagger."

"Why don't you two go and see what's happening?" Mari said. "I have to adjust my gown and then I'll join you."

The twins left. Mari searched in the dim light for her pashmina. She couldn't leave the stage box until she'd covered her shoulders and repinned her hair.

India had told her that a maid would come to help her but no one arrived. Probably Ravenwood had created so much chaos everyone had forgotten about her.

She'd have to make do by herself. She twisted, trying to unclasp the necklace.

It appeared to be caught on something.

Drat. It was caught in her hair. Too many tiny gold dangling pieces. They'd become hopelessly tangled.

And her hair wasn't the only thing tangled in the necklace now. The sharp shards of gold had caught the fabric of her dress as she raised her arms.

Mari raised her shoulder experimentally. The fabric of the loose-fitting gown slipped to one side, nearly baring her entire breast. Attempting to restore order to the gown, the necklace caught on her sleeve.

It was a bloody deathtrap of a necklace, and she didn't care if she was learning to swear like a sailor. She was a lady Pharaoh. She could do whatever she bloody well pleased.

But where were all her loyal and doting subjects when she needed them?

Hopefully someone would come to rescue her soon. She certainly couldn't rejoin the party with her hair wild and tangled, and her bosom falling out.

EDGAR STOOD AT the edge of the Gold Salon, trying to pretend that he wasn't holding his breath, waiting for Mari to enter the room.

Footmen carried trays of canapés by the talented Miss Martin. The cook had been worth the exorbitant fee Edgar had paid to steal her away from the Duchess of Attenborough.

It was a warm evening. The wine was flowing. Arguments could be heard breaking out among the learned guests. India had certainly sparked controversy.

Michel and Adele came racing toward him. "Father! Where have you been? We have so much to tell you."

"That was a nice bit of palm waving."

"Thank you," said Adele.

"Wasn't Miss Perkins regal?" asked Michel.

"Very regal, indeed."

"Too regal to keep to yourself, Banksford," said the Earl of Haddock, sliding into Edgar's view. "Where did you find her? Some artist's studio?"

Edgar glared at him. "She's not an artist's model, Haddock."

"She's our governess," Michel said proudly.

"Your governess, sir?" exclaimed Haddock. "Well aren't you the lucky little fellow." He said the words to Michel, but his eyes were on Edgar.

"Excuse us, Haddock." Edgar gave the odious fellow a curt nod.

Haddock slithered away.

"Why did that man say that Lady India's speech was hogwash?" Adele asked, pointing at Ravenwood, who was arguing with India in a corner.

"He's the man I was telling you about the other day, when you met Miss Martin and we had the French bread."

"Well I don't like him," said Adele.

"Shall we go and rescue her?" asked Edgar.

As they approached, Edgar caught fragments of their conversation.

"Balderdash and bilge," said Ravenwood. He towered over India, even though she was tall for a woman. "I always knew you were cracked in the head, Indy."

"And I always knew you were a twenty-four-carat fool with shite for brains, Ravenwood."

"Ahem," said Edgar, breaking into the conversation.

Ravenwood and India turned simultaneously.

"May I borrow Lady India for a moment?" Edgar asked.

"Be my guest," drawled Ravenwood. "And don't bring her back."

"That man," India sputtered as Edgar steered her

away from Ravenwood before someone got hurt. "That man." She grasped the hilt of the dagger by her side. "I hate him with a red-hot passion."

"Sure you do," said Edgar.

"What?" asked India.

"Oh nothing. Nothing at all."

India gave him a warning look. "Where's Miss Perkins?"

"Probably hiding upstairs from all the gentlemen ogling her. Did you have to exhibit her half clothed like that? Didn't you have an artist's model hired?"

"Half clothed? That was nothing! If I'd been true to history, she would have been completely bare-chested."

Adele and Michel snickered.

Edgar choked on his third canapé. "Good God, woman. I'm not sure I should allow you near my governess."

"And I'm not sure you should have been staring at her like that."

"Me and half of London's lords."

Lady Blanche and her ancient companion in the towering feathered headdress were approaching from across the room.

Hellfire and damnation. Edgar swallowed his food hastily.

"Why did you invite Lady Blanche?" he asked India.

"Her great-aunt Hermione sent me a request for an invitation."

"Dash it," Edgar muttered under his breath. "I knew I shouldn't have taken her riding."

"Is that the lady who fainted when she saw Trix?" asked Michel.

"That's the one. And she's headed this way. I've got to go. Distract them. Tell them I had to go to the stables for a moment." Edgar knew that gleam in a woman's eye, the one that said she'd sited her target. Great-Aunt Hermione had that gleam in her eye.

Why did Great-Aunt Hermione have him in her sights?

He backed out the door and into the adjoining salon. He heard India and then Lady Blanche's tinkling tones.

He needed somewhere to hide.

Their voices grew louder. He reached for the velvet curtain, and ducked behind it, into the waiting darkness, retreating until he ran into something warm and solid.

Something warm, solid and . . . wriggling?

His goddess masquerading as a governess.

Chapter 18

⁊

"Is THAT YOU, Your Grace?" Mari groped in the dim light and encountered a solid forearm.

"I'm not here," he whispered.

"Well as long as you're not here, make yourself useful. I removed my crown easily enough, but the dratted neck collar is caught—"

"Shhh."

"Are you hiding from someone?"

"I'm not hiding."

"Then help me. It's hopelessly tangled in my—"

He clapped a large hand over her mouth and pressed her against the wall of the small enclosure with the full weight of his body.

"Oof," she said against his fingers. It was a wonder he hadn't toppled the entire stage box onto its side.

"I swear he came this way," said an imperious female voice. "But I don't see him anywhere."

Another soft female voice said something Mari didn't catch.

"Humph," said the other woman. "Who wants a viscount when there is a duke for the catching? He hasn't shown any interest in a lady in years. You're going to be the next Duchess of Banksford, or my name isn't Hermione Geraldine Harriett Penelope Somerset."

Mari stilled. Who was speaking? And why was she so sure Edgar would be marrying?

Edgar. The man who was currently squashed against her, one large hand over her mouth, the other circling her waist, his arm protecting her from a ridge in the wooden wall behind them.

So considerate. So . . . aroused?

There was another ridge in front of her. Pressing into her belly.

She'd decided to be scandalous, hadn't she? She wriggled closer, relaxing against his solid bulk.

"Great-Aunt, I told you," the soft female voice wailed, "the ride meant nothing. Laxton is the man I love. He'll offer for me, I know he will. He only wants a little more coaxing. He has a very cautious nature."

"Lady Blanche," Mari whispered, only it came out sounding like *lmmblumph* because of the hand over her mouth.

The tips of her breasts tingled where they pressed against his waistcoat buttons. His hand was still cupped over her mouth, bending her neck back. She extended her tongue and tasted his fingers.

Warmth and salt. A memory of ink. A hint of steel from the foundry.

She forgot all about the ladies beyond the curtain.

This was exactly what she'd been picturing when she thought about being scandalous, about taking risks.

Gather ye dukes while ye may.

The thought made her giggle against his fingers. She felt reckless and wild.

And fully awake, for the first time in her life.

"Didn't Lady India say he had an errand in the stables?" said Lady Blanche. "Hadn't we better go and see if he's still there?"

"I saw him come this way, I tell you."

"Perhaps you were mistaken. It could have been

Ravenwood, you know. They are of much the same size and coloring."

"Oh very well. We'll go to the stables."

"And if Banksford's not there, may we leave?"

"My dear, I simply don't understand you. Don't you want to be a duchess? When I was your age, I would have committed anything short of murder for the opportunity to . . ."

Their voices trailed away.

"They're gone," he whispered in her ear. She noticed that he didn't pull away, didn't stop holding her.

He didn't want Lady Blanche.

She threaded her arms around his neck and buried her fingers in his hair.

He held perfectly still for the space of several heartbeats.

And then his hand left her mouth, and his lips replaced it.

His kiss wasn't gentle this time, and she didn't want it to be. She squirmed against his arousal, needing to be closer. *There.* The arm circling her waist clamped tighter, imprisoning her against him in the small, dark space where only the two of them existed.

Edgar kissed her, their tongues tangling. Rough hands stroking her cheek, her shoulder, covering her breast.

She melted into his hands, abandoning control.

Edgar. A name like the edge of a knife, like a scar across her heart.

She leaned back against the wooden walls, something pressed into the tender flesh of her back. Sharp little shards of necklace reminding her of the penitent's shirt, the lash of guilt.

She'd been having thoughts wider than the confines of her life.

Wicked, ungrateful girl. Too proud. Too willful.

Claim his lips to banish the harsh voices, to become new and reborn.

The inside of the stage like a bird's nest, and she the fledgling.

The feelings that beat their new wings in her heart were small, and could be easily crushed, like eggshells.

So powerful. The play of muscles beneath his shirt. His body so different from hers, towering and hard as granite.

A delicious burst of danger, calling her name.

Breathing harsh against her neck as he stilled for a moment. "Mari," he said. "My goddess. What are we doing?"

"I summoned you here, Edgar," she said, shakily.

"We can't stay here."

"I know. But my hair is caught in this collar." And her heart had been captured as well.

She turned away from him, lifting as much of her hair off the back of her neck as possible. "Here."

Tugging gently, he tried to extricate the necklace. It stung her scalp until her eyes watered but she couldn't cry out.

"Blast," he whispered.

"What's the matter?"

"What is this thing made of, needles?"

"It's made of thin gold shards and rubies and if you break off a piece, Lady India will kill you."

"I'm well aware of that. But now one of the buttons on my coat sleeve is caught as well."

"What if I—"

"Don't twist like that!"

Now they were even more entangled.

"What if you shed your coat?" she asked.

SHED HIS COAT. What a brilliant idea.

And while he was at it, why didn't he just strip off her gown as well?

His shirt and trousers.

Her chemise.

Set this stage box a-rocking. Really give the guests a show they'd never forget.

She kept wriggling her luscious arse against his cock.

In the velvety darkness.

With her elbows braced against the wall.

She drove him raving, barking mad.

They'd have to lock him up if she didn't stop wriggling.

He couldn't see her face in the dark. But he knew her eyes were the same color as the velvet curtains.

He knew she made small moaning sounds when he kissed her.

A wave of longing swamped his senses. He'd been a fool to think he could starve it away by throwing himself into his work and staying away from the house.

It didn't matter if she was halfway across London, standing on a stage, or in his arms.

He wanted to lay his heart at her hem.

Offer his fealty.

There was a knocking sound upon the stage wall.

They both froze.

"Edgar? Are you in there?"

Chapter 19

❧

MARI'S HEART STOPPED BEATING.

They'd been caught. There would be a scandal. She would lose her post.

Oh my God, what had she been thinking?

She wasn't a scandalous goddess-queen, she was a governess, who needed her salary and her post.

India stuck her head inside the curtain. "Lady Blanche is gone," she began and then stopped. "Ah . . . should I come back later?"

"Very funny. Help us," said Edgar. "This blasted necklace is tangled in everything."

India laughed, stepping through the curtain. "My, my, this tableau certainly took an unexpected turn."

Mari began to breathe again. Perhaps there didn't have to be a scandal. "I'm so glad you're here."

"Wait a moment, I'll fetch down one of the lamps," said India.

She disappeared.

"Well that was a close call," said Mari with an attempt at a lighthearted laugh.

"Mari, I want you to know that—"

Whatever he'd been about to say was lost, as India slipped back inside, holding a gas lamp. She handed it to Edgar, who held it aloft with his free hand, while India worked on extricating Mari's hair from the necklace.

"There, you're free," she said to Mari, holding up the necklace. "It's probably best if you leave first," she said to Edgar. "We'll follow after a safe amount of time."

Edgar nodded, handed India the lamp and slipped through the curtain.

India held up the lamp. "Now then, do you want to tell me what was happening in here?"

Mari blushed. "I don't know what you mean. He was hiding from Lady Blanche and I was tangled and . . ."

India knew.

"Do you love him?" India asked softly.

"What? I don't love him," Mari said vehemently.

Well she didn't, did she? She wouldn't be that foolish.

"I was only a little carried away," Mari said, wrapping herself in the pashmina. "I got caught up in my role as Pharaoh and I may have . . . he may have . . ."

"You kissed."

"Yes," Mari admitted. "But it didn't mean anything. It was a momentary lapse of reason."

And there are sparks still burning inside me.

"My brother is no heartless seducer. If he kissed you, it means something," said India.

"It means we were both carried away by the moment. It can never happen again."

"Keep telling yourself that, *Mari-rhymes-with-starry*." India's violet eyes sparkled in the gloom. "I have a feeling something's about to begin . . ."

If you are brave enough to chase it.

"Nothing's beginning," said Mari shortly. "Bad beginning, worse end."

"Ah . . . back to the proverbs. Button yourself up. Repin that hair."

"I will, thank you very much. I'm not meant for

gold crowns. I told you it was a bad idea to have me portray your Pharaoh."

"It worked perfectly, from my perspective," said India, with a wide grin.

She held the curtain open for Mari. "Shall we? Your adoring public awaits, my queen."

WHEN MARI AND India entered the Gold Salon, most of the guests were already gone.

India placed the gold collar necklace on a plaster bust of a woman's head sitting on black velvet.

Edgar was talking to the twins, smiling at them in a way that made Mari's heart beat faster.

She was about to make her way toward them when a gentleman with gray whiskers and an avaricious smile appeared at her elbow. "Miss Perkins, is it? Or should I say Hatshepsut?" He clasped her hand and bowed over it. "The Earl of Haddock, your devoted subject."

"My lord." Mari nodded. "I'm not a Pharaoh. Merely a governess. And my charges are just there, so I must go to them."

Haddock followed the direction of her gaze. "Banksford has all the luck," he said smoothly. "I wish I had children in the nursery still so that I might steal you away from him. Would you care for some punch?"

A footman proffered a tray.

"No, thank you," she said. "I must go to the children."

He cocked his head. "You remind me of someone, Miss Perkins. A woman I used to know."

Mari didn't like the insinuating spark in his eyes. "And no gentleman has ever said *that* to a lady before."

He smiled. "I see you've a redheaded temperament. I like that. She had one as well, did Ann."

"Ann?" Mari turned her full attention to him for the first time.

"She was a soprano with the Royal Opera. Had the exact same auburn hair and blue eyes. I've no idea what happened to her. She left the opera. You could be her daughter you look so much alike."

"What was her surname?" asked Mari.

"I'm not sure I recall."

"It wasn't Murray, was it?"

"That's it! The famously beautiful Ann Murray. How did you know?"

Ann Murray. The name written in her Book of Common Prayer. The date that matched the year of her birth.

Could this man actually have known her mother? "Tell me more about her," Mari said.

"I'd be happy to, my dear, but I must leave now. Perhaps you would care to meet me at a tea shop tomorrow for a more extended . . . conversation."

Tomorrow wasn't one of her off days, and meeting strange earls for tea didn't sound very respectable, but she couldn't pass up an opportunity to learn more if the Ann Murray he spoke of could have some connection to her.

She made a quick decision. "I'll meet you at two o'clock at the British Museum, Lord Haddock. I've been wanting to see their collection of Roman and Greek marbles."

His smile was oily as a plate of kippers. He bowed over her hand. "I will count the seconds until tomorrow."

"If you'll excuse me, my lord, I must go to the children."

Before she could leave, Robertson appeared at the

door to make an announcement. "Her Grace, the Dowager Duchess of Banksford," he intoned.

The small number of remaining guests hushed.

"Well," said Haddock. "This is a surprise."

Mari watched Edgar's face as his mother was announced. It was like a window being hastily shuttered against a storm.

Everything shut down. Closed up.

His face. His fists.

Mari wanted to run to him, take his hand, tell him to breathe.

The dowager duchess looked exactly how Mari had pictured her. A grandiose personage, tall of stature, and upright of carriage, swathed in black and topped with white ruffles and feathers.

The lacy turban she wore was so high that it made her the tallest living thing in the room, and underneath it, her silver-streaked hair was dressed in a perfectly round row of ringlets placed at precise intervals along her forehead.

She swirled into the room like a wintry wind, coating everyone's faces with frost.

"The Ice Queen cometh," Haddock chortled. "This ought to be entertaining."

Chapter 20

❧

$\mathcal{E}$DGAR CLENCHED HIS fists as the dowager made her way across the room, guests parting before her like the Red Sea.

Theirs was an infamous estrangement, replete with all of the scandalous ingredients the *ton* craved. Dark family secrets. Betrayal.

Violence and revenge.

She stopped directly in front of him. "Banksford," she said.

"Mother." He bowed.

Mari caught his eye and gave him a nearly imperceptible nod. She stood with the children, one on either side of her. Her steady gaze told him that he could atone for the mistakes of his past. That he could be something better.

He wanted to be worthy of the confidence he saw in her eyes, but at the first glimpse of his mother, the old, tangled wall of thorns had closed over his heart.

Still, he would do his best to be polite.

Everything broken can be mended.

Perhaps this was an opportunity.

He schooled his face to cordiality. "You look well, Mother."

"Not quite one of India's artifacts yet."

She'd softened at the edges, her stern jaw had the

hint of a jowl and her hair had gone light with silver.

Too much to hope that the woman had softened along with her jawline?

"Have you taken up bareknuckle boxing?" A disdainful inventory of his shoulders and arms. "You've a ruffianly look about you."

Too much to hope.

"I work at a foundry. I make steam engines."

Also, too much to hope that he wouldn't answer in kind.

"Most unfortunate." An injured sniff. "I heard you were persisting with your endeavors in *Trade*."

The worst thing a gentleman could sink to. Worse than adultery. Debauchery. Drunkenness.

The eighth deadly sin and the most wicked of all. *Trade.*

He wasn't going to have this conversation again. Not now. Not in front of spectators.

Conversation resumed. Footmen served claret and punch. The fruit arrangement on the sideboard, topped by a towering, spiny pineapple, had been disemboweled.

But he knew that everyone had half an ear on what he and his mother were saying. They were just waiting for the veneer of politeness to slip. For the ugliness to emerge.

"Why did you come, Mother?" he asked, wearily.

"Why did you invite me?" she countered.

I didn't. India did. Where was India, anyway?

Probably arguing with Ravenwood in a corner, again, sparring like pugilists at a boxing match.

"I had hoped you might want to meet your grandchildren." He glanced pointedly at Michel and Adele.

She followed his gaze. Another sniff.

Not good enough.

"Rather too like *that woman*, don't you think?" She took a small sip of claret.

That woman meaning Sophie. "It's not charitable to speak ill of the dead, Mother."

"When have I ever been charitable, Duke?"

It wasn't that his mother was evil, Edgar reminded himself. She was just so entrenched in her viewpoints. And those viewpoints were from the loftiest of ivory towers.

Daughter to a royal duke, she'd made a brilliant match with his father.

And paid the highest price.

She'd suffered, just as much as Edgar had suffered. Ruled by the tyrant. Belittled in public, and in private . . . unspeakable cruelty.

He soothed his voice, battling for control over his temper. "I wanted to come and call on you before now, but I wasn't sure I would be welcome."

She took another small, measured sip. "I had hoped that these rumors of domesticity—children and governesses and the like—meant you were finally ready to fulfill your duty and produce an heir. If, and when, that happy day comes, you will be most welcome in my home. Most welcome, indeed."

Welcome only if he produced an heir. She hadn't changed.

A footman materialized at the dowager's side the moment her glass was empty. Instead of accepting more claret, she sent him away with one twitch of her eyebrow. "Was that too much for an elderly dowager to hope? That you might have decided to do your duty?"

"I'm more occupied with my foundry, at the moment."

"A shame. Then why take Lady Blanche riding? Everyone's saying you're smitten with the girl. You could do worse. Prolific breeding lines."

Edgar was saved from that line of questioning by India's arrival.

"Hello, Mother." She kissed the dowager's cheek.

Their mother stiffened. She'd never been one for physical affection. "Still fond of outlandish attire, I see. What in Heaven's name is that costume? You look like . . . I don't even know what you look like, but you display no aspect of femininity whatsoever."

"It's nice to see you, too, Mother," said India.

She'd always been able to maintain her equanimity when Edgar wanted to explode.

"Have you met Michel and Adele, yet?" asked India with a breezy smile, determined to pretend this was a polite occasion.

Edgar tried to catch her eye, to warn her off, but the ball had been set in motion.

"I have not," said the dowager.

India waved for Mari and the children to approach. Mari's hair was coiled atop her head and she'd wrapped herself in a shawl, but she still looked regal and lovely.

"Mother, allow me to present the children's governess, Miss Perkins," said Edgar.

Mari dropped a polished curtsy.

His mother barely acknowledged her, giving only the slightest of nods. "Perkins."

"And this is Michel." Michel bowed. "And Adele." Adele gave an acceptable curtsy, but kept her gaze boldly fixed on the dowager.

"Come forward child," his mother said to Michel.

Michel approached her, his eyes fearful.

"How old are you?"

"Nine, Your Grace."

Edgar heaved a mental sigh of relief. At least he'd addressed her properly.

"I'm nine as well," Adele piped in.

"I'm not speaking to you, girl," said the dowager, without turning her head. "I detect almost no accent in your voice."

"We had an English tutor, Your Grace," said Michel. "And now we have Miss Perkins. She makes us memorize poetry."

She dismissed Michel with a flick of her wrist and turned to Edgar. "They appear intelligent and well-spoken enough. It's a pity about their birth, though."

"You mean it's a pity we're bastards," Adele said.

The dowager raised her quizzing glass and examined Adele. "Quite."

Mari placed a warning hand on Adele's shoulder. "We mustn't discuss such things in polite company, Adele."

"But you said bastards are filled with potential, promise, and possibilities," said Adele.

A hush descended on the room.

Glasses paused halfway to mouths.

"And so they are," said Mari.

Edgar sensed the change in Mari. The shift from propriety to protectiveness. She would do anything for his children. Defend them, no matter what. From constables or from dowagers.

And so would he.

"Her Grace didn't mean to say you should be pitied," Edgar said, bending close to Adele.

"That's right," said Mari. "It's just that sometimes, through no fault of their own, a person can't see past their own quizzing glass."

"Well," exclaimed the dowager, dropping her quizzing glass. "Who are your people, Miss Perkins?"

"No one of your exalted acquaintance, Your Grace."

India smiled warmly at Mari. "She's from Mrs. Trilby's Agency for Superior Governesses. She's such a treasure."

"Superior governesses. Rather an oxymoron, in my experience," sniffed the dowager.

"Quite," agreed Mari, in a haughty tone of voice. "Such a hysterical, degenerate breed."

The dowager gave her a hard stare. "Are you mocking me?"

"I was merely agreeing with you, Your Grace."

Edgar almost applauded. Mari had put his mother in her place so skillfully that it wasn't even discernible as an insult.

She had a way of doing that. Putting people in their places.

Cutting people down to size.

"It's not right to raise a child beyond their station, Banksford," his mother said, ignoring everyone except Edgar. "You shouldn't parade them about. It's past their bedtime."

"Perhaps it's past your bedtime, Mother." He knew his voice was cold, but he was only matching her tone.

"Well," she huffed. "I knew it was a mistake to come here." She tapped her walking stick on the floor, and a footman scurried toward them.

She stumbled slightly. Edgar reached out a hand. "Let me help you."

"Do. Not. Touch me."

"Are you well, Mother?" he asked, noticing for the first time the lines etched at the edges of her eyes. The slight hunch to her shoulders.

She left without a backward glance.

He watched her leave and suddenly he saw a lonely old woman. Her spine straight because she had set herself against the world.

She had suffered his father's wrath in silence for all of those years.

Wounds that deep couldn't be healed.

They shared the same burden, his mother and he. Shared it and lived with it so differently. He had run away. She had stayed. He'd forged a new life . . . literally.

She'd stayed here, and been the target of society's scorn.

As if her departure was a signal, the remaining guests trailed behind, making their good-byes. Probably disappointed by the lack of shouting. The thin coating of civility they'd been able to maintain.

Michel and Adele stood on either side of Mari, looking stricken, and so very small.

When the last guests were gone, India turned to him. "Well that went splendidly, I think," she said.

"Why did you invite her?"

"I didn't think she'd actually come."

"Did we do something wrong?" asked Adele.

"Not at all," said Edgar. "My mother is extremely difficult to please."

"She's certainly . . . opinionated," said Mari.

"She didn't like us." Adele took Michel's hand. "She didn't even want to meet us."

"That's not true, she'll warm to you eventually," said India. "Let me tell you a story about your grandmother. You see, she was the most beautiful girl in London, once upon a time, and so you know she has a story."

"The most beautiful?" asked Adele.

"When she walked into a room, people wept," said

India. "She inspired hundreds of poems. A famous poet wrote a verse about her eyes, comparing them to amethysts dipped in angel's tears, or some such. Shall I find the poem, and read it to you?"

"I'll take them upstairs," said Mari, quickly.

Too quickly. She didn't want to be alone with him.

She was avoiding his eyes. Was she ashamed of what had happened in the stage box? He never wanted her to feel ashamed.

They needed to talk.

WHAT AN EVENING, Mari reflected, snuggled into her bed after reading to the children and tucking them in.

She'd been kissed by a duke. Propositioned by an earl. She'd stared down a dowager duchess.

Her life was changing. She was changing.

She'd left the gray walls of Underwood far behind. That silent, lonely girl who'd been beaten down by life was thoroughly gone, and in her place was something wholly new . . . and still forming.

Mari stretched her arms over her head, the fine linens stroking her skin.

A lady who navigated the seas of scandal and had wicked thoughts and sometimes even acted upon them. What was she guarding her virtue for, anyway?

She'd never marry. Edgar was an honorable man, but he wanted her, she knew it. She saw it in his eyes, felt it in his touch.

And she wanted him as well.

Kissing Edgar had been like opening the magic box from Lumley's Toy Shop. She'd expected to find all of the restraints, the prohibitions, the guilt of her past. And instead she'd found a heart of velvety darkness that was filled with . . . everything.

Every longing she'd ever suppressed.

Every word she'd ever swallowed.

And every dream she'd never dared to dream.

𝒜 ROUGH, BASS VOICE intruded into Mari's dreams. "Wake up."

"Edgar, you're here." She reached her arms toward him sleepily. "You came to me."

"Wake up," he shook her shoulders gently. "Michel is having a night terror. I need your help."

Not here to seduce her.

He needed her help.

She bolted upright so swiftly that their foreheads nearly bumped.

He helped her down from the bed, his eyes worried and fearful.

"Has he injured himself?" she asked, as she threw a wrapper over her nightgown and slid her feet into her slippers.

"Not yet," said Edgar. "But I can't wake him. And he's making the eeriest moaning sounds. Adele is beside herself. You said you have experience with night terrors."

She laid a hand on his arm. "I do. Edgar, look at me. Everything will be all right. Now take me to him."

𝑀ARI HAD SEEN night terrors before. Michel sat upright in his cot, his eyes open but staring straight ahead. The expression on his face was one of extreme fear, as if he'd turned inward and was seeing a nightmare inside his head.

"It looks like he's awake," Mari said to Adele. "But he's not. He's fast asleep. I've seen this before."

Adele hunched her shoulders. "He'll do this for hours sometimes. I wake up and he's just . . . staring like that. Breathing heavily, like an animal. What is he seeing? Why doesn't he wake up? He never even remembers anything about it in the morning."

"Wake up, Michel," said Edgar, shaking his son.

"Shh," said Mari. "It's best not to try to wake him. We sit with him. And we make sure he doesn't hurt himself thrashing about. These terrors usually only last an hour at most."

"Last time I tried to wake him it didn't go well," Edgar agreed. "He hasn't had one in weeks. Why do you think he's having one tonight?"

"He could be worried about something," Mari replied. She turned to Adele. "Did he say anything to you, sweetheart?"

"He was upset about meeting our grandmother. He wanted her to like him."

"Non. S'il vous plaît," Michel moaned in French, as if he'd heard her. *"Non. Ne partez pas sans nous."*

"Sometimes he . . ." Adele made retching noises.

"Vomits," supplied Mari. "That's rather messy."

"And smelly." Adele made a face. She was trying to be brave, but Mari could see the toll this took on her, not being able to rouse her brother, or ease his terror.

His limbs were all tangled in the bed sheets and his hands gripped the bedclothes so hard his knuckles were white.

Mari eased one of his hands open and chafed it between her hands.

"Sometimes loosening the bedclothes works. He may feel trapped." She spoke in a calm, matter-of-fact voice as she and Edgar loosened the sheets and smoothed them out. "At least he's not a somnambulist."

"What's that?" asked Adele.

"Someone who walks in their sleep. I knew a girl who wandered halfway across a cow pasture in her sleep. And she never remembered a step when she awoke the next day, after we returned her to her bed."

"She's lucky she wasn't injured," Edgar said.

"Sometimes it sounds like someone's trying to kill him," said Adele, gazing at her brother with tears in her eyes.

"It's very frightening, isn't it?" asked Mari.

"Yes," Adele whispered.

"But it will end soon."

Mari attempted to lift his legs out of the cramped seated position.

Without warning, his body twitched into motion, convulsing as if he'd been punched in the belly. *"Non. Non,"* he yelled.

His elbow flew out and caught Mari's lower lip. She stumbled back, the painful sting of the blow momentarily blinding her.

"Mari!" Strong hands gripped her elbows, righting her. "Are you injured?"

Edgar's face coalesced, first a dark brow, then a pale gray eye, finally a handsome, worried face, close to hers.

"It's nothing," she said, wiping her lip with her sleeve.

"Isn't there anything we can do?" Edgar asked in an anguished voice.

Michel was breathing heavily now, twisting his hands in the bedclothes.

Mari felt his pulse. "His heart is beating very quickly."

The moaning began again. Eerie and low, from the back of Michel's throat. As if he were a cornered animal.

"Can you lay him down?" Mari asked.

Edgar tried to guide Michel's legs into a supine position. "No. He won't go."

Michel jumped into the air, landing on his feet on the bed.

Edgar caught him in his arms and held him tight to his chest, speaking in a soothing voice. "Michel, it's Father. You're safe. Breathe now, just breath."

He rocked him back and forth like a small baby.

Michel quieted, relaxing against his father's chest, his head lolling back.

Mari found P.L. Rabbit on the windowsill. "Lay him down now," she told Edgar.

Edgar laid Michel in the bed. Mari nestled P.L. in his arms and Michel curled his body, clutching the rabbit in his hands.

"The worst is over," she said.

"What do you see, my son?" asked Edgar, stroking Michel's cheek. "What terrors lie behind those eyelids? *I had a dream, which was not all a dream. The bright sun was extinguished, and the stars did wander darkly in the eternal space.*"

"Byron," said Mari.

"You're not the only one who memorizes poetry," Edgar said with a faint smile.

Michel sighed, his breathing slow now.

Edgar brushed the hair back from Michel's face and cupped his face with his large hand. "There's nothing to fear." He kissed his brow. "I won't let anything hurt you."

Who knew a brusque terror of a duke could be so sweet?

Mari's heart brimmed with tenderness, and never-to-be-shed tears welled behind her eyes.

There's hope for you yet, Edgar.

When she left this family, she would know that Michel and Adele had a father who was learning to show them that he cared.

Someone to soothe the night terrors. A steady shoulder to lean upon.

A good man to emulate.

She checked on Adele, who was fast asleep, her fierce little face calm in repose. "She's asleep," she whispered.

Edgar nodded, rising from Michel's side.

"He'll sleep through the night now," Mari whispered. "It rarely returns twice in one night."

They left softly, leaving the nursery door ajar.

The corridor was dark and silent.

His hand cupped her cheek, his thumb brushing across her lips. He tilted her face to one of the lamps burning on a hall table. "You're hurt."

Mari touched her lip. Wetness on her fingers. "It's nothing. His elbow caught me."

"It's not nothing. Mari, you're bleeding." The raw emotion on his face caught her by surprise. "Come with me. I'll take care of you."

Chapter 21

&

Mari allowed Edgar to lead her to her chambers. He settled her into a chair and then dipped a cloth into the wash basin and wrung it out, touching it to her lips.

She tensed.

"Does it hurt?" he asked.

"Not too much."

"You're shivering." He slid the counterpane off her bed and tucked it over her knees.

She became acutely aware of the late hour and their state of undress.

He was in a silk robe that had slipped open to reveal one of his powerful thighs. Was he wearing anything underneath?

Her face felt hot and her feet were freezing despite her slippers.

Longing crashed over her, stealing her breath.

He brushed his finger over her lip again and she flinched.

"You'll have a bruise. He clipped you with his elbow and your teeth cut your lip."

His hands ran down her arms. "Any other injuries?"

"Just the lip. I'll look even more of a fright tomorrow."

"What do you mean, even more?" he asked with a puzzled frown.

That had been the old Mari speaking. The one who thought of herself as frightful. Plain and freckled with awful red hair. Too thin and scrawny.

But this evening, on stage, she'd seen something else in his eyes.

"Nothing," she muttered.

"No, I want to know. Do you think of yourself as unattractive?" he asked, tilting her chin up and forcing her to meet his gaze. "Because you're so very wrong. You're beautiful, don't you know that? Didn't you see the way the gentlemen were staring at you this evening? Every man in the room was struck by your beauty. They all wanted to prostrate themselves at your feet."

Her breath caught. "All of them?"

"You truly don't know how stunning you are?"

"I've always thought . . . I was told I was awkward and unpleasing."

"Whoever told you that was a blind fool. If it was a woman, she was jealous. And if it was a man, he wanted you to feel bad about yourself for some unfathomable reason."

"It was a woman."

"Then she was jealous, plain and simple. You have a light shining from you, Mari. It draws everyone's eyes to you. Your smile is incandescent. When you're in a room, everything gravitates toward you, haven't you noticed? The way you were able to charm the children in such short order. The way you charm me. Disarm me."

He was still kneeling at her feet.

"You're the most beautiful woman here."

She smiled. "I'm the only woman here."

"I meant here." He brushed the air as if he held a paintbrush. "In England. On this earth."

That was taking things too far. "You know that's not true," she said.

"I know nothing of the sort." He rose, staggering slightly on his bad knee but quickly righting himself. He held out his hand. "Come, have a look in the glass."

She put her hand in his, mesmerized by the tender light in his eyes. The counterpane slid to the floor as he led her to the tall oval glass in the corner and tilted it forward, toward the lamp.

He stood behind her. "You have golden freckles, more interesting than flawless skin. Lively blue eyes like a sky turning to night. A small straight nose, the slightest bit stern and uncompromising, but the luscious curve of this upper lip, the extravagant swoop."

He touched each place he mentioned, ending with his thumb in the indentation of her upper lip.

She rested her head back against his chest.

"A slender, elegant throat." His hand closed around her throat. She shivered, feeling the immense power he wielded over her.

"A frame that combines delicacy and strength." Both of his hands on her shoulders now, kneading away the tension.

His hands slid down her arms, clasped her hands. "Capable hands, doing hands, hands that teach, and soothe hurt away, and calm terrors."

The rough texture of his fingers reminded her that he had capable hands as well. That despite his privileged status as a duke, he built steam engines . . . shaping his dreams into existence.

He rested his chin in the crook of her shoulder and brought both of her hands round to her belly.

"Slender waist." With his hands over hers, he guided her hands over her waist. "Softly flaring hips."

Her hands, covered by his hands, grasping her hips.

Her hands, his hands, inching slowly up her torso, over her breasts, stopping at her heart's center. "A heart that beats strong and true and brave. Undaunted by the likes of me."

Their reflection in the mirror a study in contrasts.

The strong, uncompromising lines of his jaw sharply delineated in the lamplight.

The soft curve of her cheek.

Beautiful, she thought. And in that moment of discovery she relinquished the entrenched belief that she was plain and unpleasing. Unworthy.

Whatever the future held, she would face it as a new woman.

Bold and free.

She saw herself through his eyes. Slight, small curves, but a symmetry there, a simplicity of line like the curve of a porcelain vase.

A vase that was going to shatter from the tension if he didn't touch her soon, if he didn't calm the butterflies stampeding in her belly.

She turned her head, nestled into his neck. Kissed his warm skin.

She slid her hands, with his still covering them, over her breasts.

She squeezed the tips of her breasts between her fingers, and his fingers tightened over hers.

It felt right. As if the pleasure of his touch was a reward for all of the hardship she'd endured.

He cupped her hands, moving with her, covering her. Lower. Over her belly, beneath the edges of her wrap.

Lower. Between her thighs.

Only thin muslin obstructing his access to the place that ached for his touch.

"You're the most exquisite thing I've ever seen." His eyes were hooded, his breathing shallow. "Do you believe me?"

The surge of elation she'd felt on stage returned, only now there was a difference. She didn't have to wear the costume of a Pharaoh to feel powerful and bold.

She only needed to believe him. Believe in herself.

"Yes," she whispered. "I believe you."

"Then I've achieved my aim." He straightened, dropping his hands from her body.

He would leave her now.

She didn't want him to leave.

She turned toward him. "Why don't you stay for a little while? We can . . . talk."

"That's not a good idea. You've already been hurt tonight." He brushed his finger over her lip. "I don't want to cause more damage. Mark you in any other way."

"Edgar, please stop thinking of me as some fragile female who can't make her own decisions. I'm resilient. Life has thrown slings and arrows at me and I've survived and been the stronger for it."

"I employ you to care for my children. I don't expect or want anything else from you. I respect you, Mari."

He was too honorable to give her what she craved. But the wanton side she'd discovered wouldn't remain silent.

She was through with pretending to be meek; pretending that her needs and wants didn't matter.

"What if I want more from you? You've awakened something in me. I want . . . I want you to satisfy this craving." She pressed her fists against her belly.

"This wanting. I'm the one with expectations." She closed her eyes.

"I expect you to kiss me again," she whispered.

"I CAN NEVER KISS you again," Edgar said, the words echoing dully like a blade struck against stone. "But I can satisfy your craving."

Her eyes flew open, the blue vivid against the copper of her freckles.

She didn't know what he meant. He hardly knew what he meant. All he knew was that if he kissed her he would lose everything.

Every scrap of control and every tenet he'd built his life upon these last ten years.

He couldn't kiss her, but if he only bent the rules slightly . . . if he pleasured her and not himself . . . that would be acceptable.

As long as he didn't take his pleasure, he could give her what she desired.

He trailed his fingers along her inner thigh, over the fabric of her shift.

Her soft moan was musical.

How would she sound when she came? Would she burst into song like a bird?

Grasping her braid in one hand, he worked the ribbon free and began untwining until her hair was free. The fragrant waves of hair slid down her back, slid over his hands.

Slight feminine curves. Warm, floral scent.

Everything he'd denied himself.

He ran a finger down her dressing gown. Slipped inside the sash to loosen the knot.

He opened the dressing gown.

A plain muslin shift like thousands of garments

worn by thousands of virgins and this one set him aflame. Had his cock hard and his balls heavy.

His last mistress, years ago now, had imported the finest silk lingerie from Paris. She knew it had set her off to advantage.

Mari in her plain white shift was far more arousing.

"Do you want me to touch you?" he asked, holding his breath. *Say no. Tell me to leave.*

"More than anything."

He shaped her waist with his hands, marveling at the perfect, scrolling indentation that led to the curvature of her hips. He reached behind her and traced the pronounced valley dipping down her back, taking his time, prolonging the pleasure of discovery.

When he cupped her bottom, squeezing gently, her eyes widened and she made a small noise, half-moan, half-protest.

He jerked his hands away. She was an innocent.

Her eyes narrowed. "Why did you stop? It was just becoming interesting. Touch me again."

He smiled, remembering his thoughts during the tableau. She was a goddess. He was hers to command.

He unbuttoned the top buttons of her shift and slipped his hands inside.

Her breasts were small, yet plump, and fit his palms in a new way. A perfect way.

She gasped, melting into his arms.

She weighed hardly anything but he wasn't going to be able to give her pleasure standing like this. His knee was beginning to go numb.

He lifted her into his arms and brought her to a chair.

No beds. No gazing into her eyes.
No kissing.
Her pleasure, not yours.

Those were the new rules. And he would follow them, clinging to his tenuous grasp on sanity.

MARI FELT HIS caress through her whole body. To her toes. Through the ends of her hair.

She was bewitched by the new sensations.

In the wavering firelight she could see his darker hands covering her pale, freckled breasts.

She shook her head and her hair swished sensuously over the tips of her breasts where he had them surrounded, as if he were making an offering.

He positioned her on his lap, facing away from him.

Like a kettle letting out a little bit of steam, the sighs that escaped her lips told a story to any listener. She was about to boil over.

About to be turned to steam and dissolve into the air.

He was so hard behind her, so strong and commanding.

She tried to slide back against him but his hands trapped her, not letting her move backward.

He pressed his thumb into the depression in her belly.

"You should tell me to stop," he said, low and hot in her ear.

"Don't you dare stop," she commanded breathily.

He laughed. And then she wasn't capable of speech. Because he lifted her shift and slid his fingers between her thighs. She wore no drawers. She was completely naked and exposed to him.

He spread her with his fingers, nudging her thighs open with his legs.

He paused, his fingers opening her, and she waited, needing him to continue.

"Edgar," she said, laying her head back against his shoulder.

"Mari," he whispered in her ear, kissing and biting her earlobe. He slid a finger over the sensitive flesh between her thighs, slick with moisture.

His finger slid inside her body.

The shock of it should have brought her back to her senses, made her stop him, but instead she wanted more. She squirmed against his finger.

He opened her further, two fingers now, inside her.

She could see everything he was doing to her but she couldn't see his face. It was maddening, and arousing at the same time.

She wanted to taste him. She tried to twist in his arms, tried to turn so that she could kiss him, but he wouldn't let her.

He held her trapped, his fingers moving inside her in a soft, steady rhythm. His thumb flicking over the swollen place where all the sensations emanated from.

"I want to kiss you," she protested.

"You can't. Your lip is split, remember?"

"But I don't care," she gasped, as his fingers rocked inside her, faster now. "I want to kiss you."

"You can't."

"Why not?"

"Because you're the one being pleasured, not me."

"Not . . . *I*," she gasped.

"Always the teacher, eh? Well—" he squeezed her nipple with his free hand, while his fingers undulated inside her "—I'm the one giving the lesson now. And you'd better behave."

"Yes, sir."

She stopped talking. He added another finger. There was more of him now, more filling her, moving in a shallow, fluttering movement that started a tremor in her belly.

He settled her more firmly against him. His hard thigh pressing up between her thighs, fingers buried inside her. His lips on her neck, biting her, teasing her. Blowing softly in her ear. His other hand on her breast, gently pinching her nipple.

So many sensations at once.

"That's the way of it," he encouraged, as she relaxed back against him, all thoughts of kissing him flying from her mind.

This was enough for now. Time enough to pleasure him later, to learn how to make him moan.

"I'm not going to stop until you've reached your pleasure," he whispered. "Multiple times."

"M-multiple?" she gasped.

"At least three. Possibly four."

Good lord. The man was overconfident.

"With my fingers." He moved his fingers inside her. "And then with my tongue."

His . . . tongue?

He stroked her softly. "I'll taste you here, I'll lick you until you beg me to stop because you're exhausted from all the pleasure."

She'd never even imagined the depraved things he was whispering.

"I want you to do something for me, Mari."

Anything. I'll do anything for you.

"Breathe. Deep and steady."

She breathed deeply, the breath flowing from her toes to the tingling, throbbing place where his fingers moved softly, ever so softly, over her.

Something shifted into focus. The possibility of pleasure.

"Oh," she breathed. "Yes."

He increased the speed of his fingers, sweeping across the swollen center of her body while his other hand moved from her breast to her sex, spreading her for him, positioning her body in the way he wanted it.

Her head fell back against his shoulder with an audible thud.

He cradled her, swept her along. He whispered something in her ear but she no longer heard the words, only felt the sensation of his fingers inside her, over her.

She moaned, marveling at the music he coaxed from her body . . . her lips.

It was like the chorus of a song she didn't know very well.

Right now she was in the unfamiliar verses, and she didn't know the words.

But the chorus would come soon, and she'd be able to lift her voice with confidence, and abandon, and sing along.

"That's right," he whispered, kissing her neck. "Just let it happen."

The chorus came.

She came.

A tremor. A quake. A moment of gasping pleasure. He stroked her, prolonging the sensation. It was indescribably sweet.

The sweetness spread over her belly, her breasts, into her heart, suffusing her thoughts with tenderness and gratitude.

She knew this song.

And she would remember it for the rest of her life, hoping to hear it again.

He resettled her against him, spreading her thighs. "Sometimes a woman can have another crisis right after the first one. If enough pressure is applied, with a swift and sure hand."

"Impossible. I couldn't possibly . . . I . . ."

She arched against his hand as he worked her hard and quick.

Apparently she was going to hear the song again. *Right now.*

"Ah," she said, her voice high and breathy. "Oh . . . God. Edgar."

Chapter 22

❧

*H*ER SOFT, MUSICAL moans of pleasure gave Edgar a rush of pride and joy.

She came again, gripping his fingers with her inner muscles.

His cock throbbed and jumped beneath her rounded bottom, but he'd achieved his objective. Made her cry his name in passion. Twice.

He knew the logic was flawed, knew that there was a very fine line between pleasuring a girl and ruining her, but he wasn't going to think about that yet.

He would remember her sighs and moans forever.

A memory when he was old and gray and the children had married and produced grandchildren.

"Now do you believe that you're desirable?" he asked her.

"I feel delicious." She stretched and her nipples popped over the edge of her chemise. "Like I slept curled up in the sun. Like I read the best book and I'm still living in that beautiful, imaginary world."

"Never let anyone tell you you're plain again."

"My, so forceful, sir," she teased. "Am I to have another lesson?"

Another lesson might just kill him.

He cared for this woman nestled in his arms. He appreciated her gentle touch. The way she transformed his children.

But he didn't like the way she changed him. The way she made his rules feel unnecessary.

He wanted to soothe her, the way she soothed his children. He wanted to cradle her in his arms and make her life better.

Carry her to his bed, fold her deeper into his arms. Wake with her in the hazy light of dawn.

Wake to the sight of a well-pleasured woman with a smile on her lips.

She turned her head and kissed him, flaunting his rules.

He'd spent seven years pretending to be a commoner, working in a foundry. He knew what it meant to be in service, to receive a wage for that service.

Kissing him was not part of her duties.

This was wrong.

"I must leave," he said hastily.

She raised her head. "Already? But . . . I thought. I thought perhaps you might want some pleasure as well."

"I don't need pleasuring." And that was a damned lie.

"But you said there were multiple kinds of pleasure. I thought you meant . . . I thought you meant *yours*."

"I was speaking of women. The way you can have so many different kinds of climaxes. More than I will show you tonight."

Damn, why had he said that? It sounded like he was promising her more nights.

"Men are simple," he said. "A bout of pumping and we're done."

"I've heard it called a pump handle. So one . . . pumps it?"

"One doesn't do anything with it if one is named Mari. One goes to sleep. Alone."

He'd told himself he'd pleasured her because he

wanted to give her unequivocal proof of her beauty and attractiveness.

Really, it was because he'd wanted to be her first *something*. If he couldn't be her lover, he'd be the first man to bring her to bliss.

A selfish and dangerous urge.

"You're feeling guilty again," she said. "I can sense your thoughts going to that dark place," she said. "You can touch me but I can't touch you? Why?"

"Because it's against my rules."

She narrowed her eyes. "You know, Edgar, we females learn to fit ourselves around the obstacles in our lives. We're expected to adapt and submit whenever anyone is louder or stronger than we are. Well I'm tired of it. I'm tired of pretending to be meek."

"You've been pretending to be meek?" He smiled. "You haven't done a very good job of it."

"You want to kiss me," she said simply. "Why deny it?"

He did want to kiss her. So badly it was rending his heart in two.

"Mari." Edgar lifted her off his lap and onto the floor. "I do want to kiss you."

"See? Now was that so difficult to admit?"

"I want to but I can't. Because you're my servant and I will never abuse my power and position."

"You're just like your gate, Edgar." She crossed her arms over her chest. "Unyielding iron. You don't know how to change, or bend."

He'd already bent quite a few rules tonight. He needed to leave with at least a few shreds of control left.

He could be wrong, but they seemed to be arguing about her virtue. She wanted to throw it away because she was tired of being meek.

Though the idea made his blood sing and his heart pound, it could never happen. "I can't be your rebellion, Mari. There's too much at stake for you . . . and for me."

"Why are you so stubborn?" She crossed her arms tighter over her chest. "Oh silly me. I met your mother this evening. I know exactly why you are the way you are."

And *there* was a topic to lower a man's flag and cool his blood—his mother.

"You don't want to talk about your mother," she accused. "Why?"

Wordlessly, he found her dressing gown on the floor and handed it to her. She wrapped it tightly around her waist, cinching it with a bow.

"How does your lip feel now?" he asked carefully, formally.

"Nothing serious." She smiled. "I'll mend. And so will you."

Anything broken may be mended.

It came to him suddenly that she thought she could mend him. Save him.

This must end.

"You saw the way my mother treated the children," he said harshly. "I was so angry, but then I saw how old she's become. How frail."

"This wasn't the right setting for a reunion. Too many eyes."

"There's no right setting."

"Why don't you visit her in her apartments, where she feels safe and at home? She may be more ready to listen to you there."

"Did you see her face? *Don't touch me*, she said. As if I were a leper."

"I saw an aging woman who doesn't know how

to talk to you, but who was reaching out. She came, didn't she?"

"She came because she thought I might be ready to marry an aristocratic lady. To do my duty. The children only remind her of the reason for our estrangement."

"Do you want to tell me about the reasons for the estrangement? It might be good for you to talk about it." She spoke in a light tone, but her eyes told a different story.

Open your soul. Open your heart.

Break all of the rules.

"Talking about these things, dredging them up from the past, doesn't help anything," he said. "Everyone in that room knew that the meeting between us would end in disaster. I had some stupid, foolish little hope that it might go well."

"It wasn't a foolish hope." She raised her hand toward him. "It was a brave hope. One that could grow into a bridge. A trail of stepping stones across the gap that separates you."

"No man is an island, and all that."

"Proverbs blossom from the seeds of truth."

But he was arid soil. Any optimism blighted long ago.

"You might feel better if you told me what happened between you all those years ago." Her eyes asked him for things he could never give her.

"You evade my questions about your past," he replied, knowing he sounded cruel, but unable to stop. "Why should I talk about mine?"

She turned her face away.

"I was a fool to think she might have softened toward me," he said. "Or show any kindness toward the children."

"I'm not sure," said Mari. "I detected something in

her voice. A falter, so small it could have been easily missed. She didn't look at them with loathing."

"You're imagining things because you want them to be a certain way. You're an optimist. I'm a realist. I see things as they are. And they're bleak. Some rifts can't be mended."

"Was it really so unforgivable, what you did?"

He nodded. "Some stains can never be washed clean. I've made mistakes and I'm paying for them. There are no easy answers for me. You may be able to help my children, but I'm lost. I've rolled too far into the darkness. I can't be retrieved. Or mended."

"Don't say that. When I look at you I see a good man. I see a man who loves his children, who's trying to do the right thing. I see a man who encourages his sister's dreams."

"I've got you fooled then, it seems."

"Edgar . . ." She lifted her hand again, as if she wanted to touch him.

He wanted to retrieve the words before he even said them, but this would be better for both of them. It was better to maintain distance. To be at odds rather than succumb to this treacherous need for connection and comfort.

What he felt for her was nothing like the blind, unheeding passion he'd felt for Sophie. This was eyes-wide-open and agonizingly aware of how beautiful and filled with hope she was . . . and how he could only end up hurting her.

"One spoonful at bedtime and the duke becomes a good man," he said, imitating her lilting voice. "You can't believe hard enough to rescue me, Mari."

He walked to the door.

"There's no cure for what ails me."

Chapter 23

⌒

*E*DGAR'S HEAD POUNDED from a restless night.

His heart ached more.

He'd been surly with Mari last night. He'd pushed her away when she'd only been trying to help.

He wanted to apologize for what he'd said to her. The way he'd said it.

But he couldn't just walk up to her in front of the children and lay his damaged, scarred heart at her feet.

I'm sorry for saying there's no cure for what ails me. It's true, but I'm sorry I said it in such an abrupt manner, because I saw that it wounded you.

I was still smarting from my encounter with my mother. I was lashing out at you because I was angry with her.

These were not appropriate things to say to a governess.

Their acquaintance had taken on a dangerous level of intimacy. And apologies were just as objectionable as caresses . . . perhaps more so.

Because this desire to make her think better of him, to forgive him . . . it stemmed from some deeper place than the desire to bed her.

He wanted her physically, more than anything, but, even more troubling, he wanted her to like him. Because he liked her. Respected her. And was intrigued by her.

Before he left for the foundry today, he would apologize and do something nice for her and the children. Surprise them with the holiday trip to the seashore.

All of the details were in place.

He heard Mari's voice in the breakfast room. His heart raced, anticipating seeing her with the children.

As his mother had said, damn her for being so perceptive, all this domesticity was having an effect on him.

It was giving him longings. And those longings had nothing to do with bedding Mari. Scratch that . . . they had much to do with bedding her, but even more to do with a new desire for closeness. For family.

He stepped into the breakfast room with a smile on his lips. But the children weren't there. Only Mari. And she had on her bonnet and pelisse.

"Good morning," he said.

"Good morning, Your Grace."

The loss of his given name hit him in the gut. And suddenly his entire goal in life was to make her call him Edgar again.

To restore the easy rapport they'd had yesterday. The intimacy.

Before he'd ruined everything.

"What happened to Edgar?" he asked.

"He doesn't need me. I have no cure for what ails him."

"Mari, about last night. I shouldn't have said—"

She met his gaze then, and the hurt he saw in her eyes stopped his heart cold. "No apologies, Your Grace. No guilt. There's nothing to apologize for."

"Yes, there is. I was wrong to speak so harshly. To push you away. My mother drives me a little bit insane."

"Keep your friends close, your enemies closer," she said with a prim purse of her lips.

He'd pushed her back to the proverbs.

"Where are the children?" he asked.

"With Mrs. Fairfield. They've gone out to be fitted for new clothing."

Actually, he'd asked Mrs. Fairfield to outfit the children for Southend with bathing costumes and comfortable clothing fit for the seashore. His house-keeper was privy to the surprise.

"Are you going somewhere?" he asked Mari.

"Out."

"Out where?"

"That's none of your concern."

"But you have no family in London. You're going alone? It's not safe for a woman alone on the streets of London."

"I do have a life that doesn't revolve around you and your children, you know."

"At least take one of my carriages. Take a groom with you. It looks like rain."

Please, let me do something for you. Don't just leave me standing here like a fool.

"And what would I need with a carriage and a groom of my own? I'm *merely* the governess."

Ouch.

She hoisted her umbrella and swept past him, head held high. "Good day, Your Grace."

EDGAR WASN'T FOLLOWING Mari, not really.

He just couldn't let her storm off hating him. He'd think of something, some way to make his apologies, before she'd walked too far.

He'd really made a hash of things this time.

She didn't need him looking out for her. But she was still fresh from the countryside. And there were wolves prowling these streets.

And you're one of them.

He had to follow her because, fool that he was, when he saw her he forgot everything else and just wanted to be as close to her as possible.

MARI HAD A sinking feeling that she shouldn't have met Lord Haddock at the museum.

She'd been grasping at straws. Though Haddock wasn't a straw. More like the proverbial camel.

He led her around the Gallery of Antiquities, elaborating in a booming, self-important tone about the supposed significance of this spear, or that chariot.

He certainly loved hearing himself talk. She hadn't even been able to squeeze in a question yet about Ann Murray.

Her mind was still with Edgar in the morning room.

He'd been genuinely sorry. She'd seen that, but it hadn't made her feel any better. Of course he was sorry they had been intimate. He was an honorable man and he'd made these rules that if he didn't take his own pleasure it would be all right.

This was all so tangled now. She didn't know what to think.

All she knew was that Edgar thought he was bad, just like the children did.

And she didn't know how to save him from that belief.

He refused to trust her, to open himself to her. Perhaps when they went to the seashore and walked by the sparkling blue sea, he'd be able to hear her.

Only . . . he hadn't mentioned the seashore. Perhaps she'd been mistaken about his intentions. Perhaps she'd been imagining things.

Imagining everything. Seeing what she wanted to see. Hearing what she wanted to hear.

Haddock grasped her elbow and she jerked away, irritated by the familiarity of his touch. The earl seemed to think her sole purpose in coming here today was to listen adoringly to a lecture on ancient Greek and Roman marbles.

"And this, my dear Miss Perkins, is a bas-relief representing a nymph resisting the importunities of an old faun, who, as you see, is endeavoring to divest her of her robe. It appears that he's about to uncover his *ultima Thule*."

He leered at her in a thoroughly repugnant manner.

"Rather than realizing his aim, Lord Haddock, it appears to me that the faun is about to encounter the nymph's knee. See here?" She pointed to the nymph's bent knee. "One swift, upward movement and she'd be free of him."

Haddock shuddered. "Pray do not indulge in so fanciful an interpretation of a classic theme. The fauns and satyrs of the woodlands harbored a noble passion for their nymphs."

"Humph." She moved to the bust of a Roman senator.

Haddock followed, draping himself so closely over her shoulder that she could feel his breath on her neck.

She was beginning to have a sinking suspicion about the reasons for his invitation.

All of this talk of wood nymphs and satyrs, and the lascivious twitching of his white whiskers as he attempted to peer down her bodice in the guise of examining the statuary.

She must put an end to this interview.

"Lord Haddock," she said, stepping out of his reach. "You mentioned an opera singer named Ann Murray, whom I resemble. I should like to know more about her."

"Oh that?" Haddock shrugged and the buttons of his waistcoat strained over his belly. "I made her up."

"You what?"

"I invented her. As a way to flatter you. I always tell pretty girls they look like someone famous. It never fails." He touched the brim of his hat. "And you're a very pretty girl, Miss Perkins."

Mari fumed. She never should have come here today. She should have listened to her intuition. It had told her that Lord Haddock was a lecher. But she'd been blinded by the need to learn about her parentage. And she'd rushed away from the duke's house today, refused any assistance, because of her pride. She should have accepted his apology. And accepted his offer of a carriage and footman. Now she was alone with a pestilence of an earl.

"That was a terrible trick to play, Lord Haddock. I'll take my leave now," she said.

"No you won't," he replied, closing the distance between them. "I should like to become . . . better acquainted. In the manner of fauns and nymphs," he said in a truculent whisper.

"You mistake me, my lord. I'm not that sort of girl."

"Are you not? Posing in Egyptian collars with your shoulder bared for all the world to see."

"I only posed as a favor to Lady India. I'll be going now. I don't like your insinuations. Or your taste in art."

"Don't leave so fast, Miss Perkins."

His smile faded. He made a gesture with his hand

and a manservant appeared, seemingly from thin air. Where had the hulking fellow been hiding?

"This is my man, Masterson," said Haddock. "Masterson, Miss Perkins is going to take a ride in my carriage. Please escort her outside."

"I'm not going anywhere with you," protested Mari, truly worried now.

"Don't make a scene, Miss Perkins." Haddock brushed a speck of dirt from his white gloves. "Who would come to your aid? I happen to be a very generous benefactor of this museum."

How stupid could she have been? Earls didn't just invite governesses out for tea. She'd been so focused on finding clues about her past that she'd knowingly walked into a trap.

Yet, they were still in public. Several gentlemen and ladies were perusing the marbles.

Outside, on the busy street, there would be people milling about. Constables at hand.

She had to find a way to quit the earl without arousing undue attention. She was still worried about encountering Mrs. Trilby. And she certainly had no wish to be questioned by any authorities.

Should she make a run for it in here, or on the street?

Masterson gripped her elbow even tighter than Haddock had, and began to half drag her toward the entrance.

She began forming a desperate plan. She'd allow Masterson to lead her outside and then she'd jab him with her umbrella and dart away.

Haddock followed closely behind them down the stone steps and onto the street. "My carriage, Miss Perkins," he said, indicating an enormous coach and four.

"I've already told you. I'm not going anywhere with you." She attempted to pull her elbow out of his servant's grip. "And I'll thank your manservant to release me."

His face darkened. "You're Banksford's mistress, is that it? Believe me, you're meant for better things than being a governess. Why slog away caring for those brats when you could be set up in apartments of your own in Mayfair?"

"You mistake me, sir."

"You're an obscure little governess. You'll do as I say."

"And you're a rude, insinuating lecher."

Masterson dragged her toward the carriage.

"I'll scream," Mari said.

"I don't think you will," said Haddock, dropping all pretense of civility. "I have a suspicion that you don't want attention called to you. That you wouldn't want my word to be held up against yours. You know your place, don't you, Miss Perkins. You'll be a quiet, good girl."

Mari's heart pounded with fear and her palms dampened. Didn't the people on the street see what was happening before their eyes? If he got her into that carriage . . . her stomach lurched.

She couldn't think about that. About the manservant holding her down for his despicable master. How many other meek, defenseless girls had he tried this with?

It made her sick. She would start screaming before she allowed herself to be forced into that carriage. But she wasn't meek and defenseless.

He might think she was, but she wasn't.

She most certainly did *not* know her place.

Not anymore.

She was through with hiding her strength.

The most vulnerable part of the male body was his bollocks, that much she knew from talking to girls at the orphanage. Tightening her grip on her umbrella, she waited for the opportune moment to strike.

Masterson released her arm to open the carriage door.

"I won't be a good, quiet girl," she yelled, darting toward the earl with her umbrella poised to strike.

"Leave her alone or I'll break your bloody nose," a thunderous voice shouted.

Mari stopped mid-stride. "Edgar? What are you doing here?"

Chapter 24

❧

$\mathcal{H}$E WAS RESCUING her. Not that she needed rescuing, at least she didn't think she did, but still, no one had ever rushed to her defense before.

She'd always been alone. Mari versus the world.

Tall and fierce, blocking out the sun, Edgar's face was deadly and his fists looked like stone hammers, ready to rain down justice. "What's happening here?" he growled, and this time his growling touched her heart in a profound way.

The man who hated public spectacles was willing to battle an earl on the street, all for her.

Haddock's face paled. "Miss Perkins and I were having a conversation."

"Looks to me as though you were about to get a parrot's beak to the bollocks," said Edgar.

Haddock eyed Mari's umbrella.

"That's right," she said, waving the umbrella handle. "A very sharp beak."

Edgar gave her a quick, approving look, then turned to glare at Haddock. "You'll never speak to the lady again. And you'll leave like a good, quiet little earl."

"What lady?" asked Haddock, his eyes narrowing. "I don't see any lady. Just a governess disguised in fine clothing, who doesn't know her rightful place."

It happened so quickly, Mari didn't even have time to blink.

Edgar's fist crashed into Haddock's nose, sending the earl staggering back against the carriage.

"I told you I'd break your bloody nose. Now get in the carriage and leave, you craven piece of maggot dropping."

The earl's manservant offered his master a glove to staunch the blood flowing from his nose. Haddock's eyes were wide and glazed. The glove came away from his nose streaked with crimson.

People on the street were staring.

"You broke my nose," Haddock said, stunned.

"Said I would." Edgar stepped forward menacingly. "Care to have your kneecaps broken as well?"

"And your bollocks beaked?" added Mari, brandishing her parrot's head umbrella.

"Gentlemen settle these matters with pistols," Haddock said, blood streaming down his face.

"Is that a challenge?" Edgar asked with a disdainful curl of his lip.

The earl's face blanched. "I'll see that your railway never gets built, Banksford."

"And I'll see you in hell, Haddock." Edgar's face was impassive, his eyes steely.

"Oh for Heaven's sake," said Mari. "It's not worth fighting a duel over. Go home, Lord Haddock. And don't ever try that again. I would have defended myself. I would have screamed. Don't think females won't fight back or make a scene. We're not all meek and easily overpowered."

Haddock sneered at Mari. "You're not worth any of this. I don't know what I was thinking."

"Insult her one more time and you die." Edgar shook with rage and the tips of his ears had gone red.

Mari could see that he meant it, and so could the

earl. He scuttled into his carriage, leaving without another word.

Luckily, no constables had become involved. The curious onlookers dispersed.

"Edgar," Mari said, laying her hand on his arm.

His eyes were still hard as steel, and his body rigid.

"Edgar," she said again. "It's over now."

She saw him return to his body from whatever dark place he'd been inhabiting.

He took a quick breath and swiped a hand through his hair.

It was over. She hadn't been forced into a carriage. Edgar had rescued her.

She hadn't needed rescuing . . . probably. Though she was grateful for not having to find out.

"You were magnificent," she said to Edgar. "Thank you." Her shoulders shook, her knees suddenly weak.

Edgar laid his arm around her shoulders. "Can you walk?"

"I just . . . need a moment." She steadied herself against his solid, comforting bulk.

"Can he block your railway?" she asked.

"It was an empty threat," Edgar said, but a muscle twitched in his jaw, telling her that perhaps it hadn't been entirely empty. "The threat to you, on the other hand, was real. He was trying to force you into his carriage. I saw everything."

"I've been forced into carriages before and emerged to tell the tale," she said flippantly, but she was still shaking inside from the panicked thoughts of what might have occurred.

"This was different, and you know it. Why were you talking to him?"

"I met him at the antiquities exhibition. He seemed

a nice enough fellow, and I've been wanting to see the bronzes at the museum."

It sounded unconvincing, she knew.

He searched her face. "Never mind, it doesn't matter why you were talking to him. What matters is that you are safe, and that you didn't end up in his carriage."

His kind words made her feel slightly teary-eyed.

She'd never lied to him, not outright. Not with any kind of bad intent. She'd told half-truths. Diverted the conversation away from dangerous subjects.

How tired she was of evading his questions. She wanted to tell him everything.

Yes, Edgar. I'm everything Haddock thought I was. I'm not superior. I'm not a gentleman's daughter. I've sinned by omission.

She couldn't tell him out here on the street. Couldn't bear to have him walk away in anger.

She glanced at him, a thought occurring to her. "Were you . . . following me?"

He avoided her eyes. "Might have been."

"Why would you follow me?"

"Because I have an apology to make, and you wouldn't let me give it to you earlier. And . . . I have a surprise for you and the children."

The seashore. The thought cheered her. Even though it meant she couldn't pursue her quest to discover the truth of her birth, going to the seashore with Edgar and the children would accomplish other goals. It would bring him and the children closer together.

And Mari wouldn't have to be so wary and careful when she was away from London.

Mrs. Trilby couldn't find her there.

"Come," he offered his arm. "Let's go home."

That was the second time he'd said those words to her.

It was beginning to make her feel as though he believed she belonged in his house.

And she was beginning to believe that she belonged in his arms.

Despite all of his rules, was he beginning to feel the same way?

One of his long arms was still draped across her shoulders, supporting her as they walked.

Mari smiled.

She'd take that as a fairly reliable indication that he felt the same way.

"ARE WE TRULY going to the seashore?" asked Adele.

"Truly," replied Edgar.

When he'd surprised the children with the news yesterday, they'd been so happy.

This morning, they were dancing with anticipation, darting back and forth to the windows, watching for the traveling coach out of the library windows.

"Calm down, please," said Mari. "We are not whirling dervishes."

Edgar laughed. "There'll be a long carriage ride ahead, best to allow them to run off some steam."

He wished he could go with them, but he and Grafton were testing their new engine today. They'd built the boiler as small and light as possible, but he wasn't at all sure that it would hold up under pressure.

"Where is Southend on the map, Father?" asked Michel.

Edgar spun the globe. "Here."

"Not too far from London." Michel perused the globe. "Have you been there before?"

"I went there often as a child because we had a

house there. It's less than a day's journey by coach. Of course, if there were a railway to Southend, people from London could be there within the hour, gazing at the sea, awash in the setting sun."

"Wouldn't that be wonderful?" asked Mari. "To be able to travel so easily."

"Someday," Edgar said. "Someday it will happen. I'm sure of it."

Mrs. Fairfield entered the library. "Were you speaking of Southend? I remember it well. I was so sad when the house burned to the ground."

"What happened?" asked Mari.

"There was a fire. We almost burned to death in our beds. The house was utterly destroyed."

"How dreadful," Mari said. "And so now you are doing something about that memory. Finding better methods to fight fires."

He nodded. "Our new fire engine is nearly finished."

"May we see it?" asked Michel.

"Someday," said Edgar. "Today you're going to the sea. Is that the sound of the carriage?"

The children ran to the window. "It's here!" they cried. "Hurry, Miss Perkins. No dawdling."

She laughed as they tugged her out the door. "No dawdling, Your Grace," she called back at him.

Wait. Did she think . . . ? Had he told her he wasn't going with them? His heart sank. He honestly couldn't remember.

He followed Mari and the children outside. Mrs. Fairfield began supervising the loading of the carriage. Was that one of his trunks?

After he helped the children, and then Mari, into the carriage, she looked at him expectantly.

He hadn't told her.

"Off you go then. Have so much fun," he said, hoping he was mistaken and they knew he wasn't accompanying them. "Bring me back some shells."

"You're . . . you're not coming with us?" Mari asked, the light leeching from her eyes.

The children stared at him. "You're not coming, Father?"

"I can't." He straightened his cravat. "I thought I'd told you. We're testing the new engine design at The Vulcan today."

"Oh," said Mari.

Such a short little word with such vast meaning.

He'd disappointed everyone. Again.

He backed away from the carriage. Nodded at the coachman.

Waved as the carriage left.

It was the right thing to do. For everyone's sake. He needed to work. The children wanted to see the seashore.

Mari needed to get away from London, after her harrowing experience with Haddock and . . . he wanted to saddle a horse and chase after them.

If it was the right thing to do . . . why did it feel so wrong?

Mrs. Fairfield gave him an accusatory look.

"What?" he asked.

"You know what. Those children thought you were going with them. And so did Miss Perkins. I even thought you were going. I had your trunks packed. They're with the other trunks."

He hadn't told anyone he was staying here? "I thought I told everyone about testing the engine today."

"Apparently you did not." She shook her head. "You can lead a horse to water, but you can't make him drink."

"Now you're the one spouting proverbs?"

"Miss Perkins has vastly improved the household, and she's gained the twins' trust. It's just a shame that she can't trust you."

And what in the devil was that supposed to mean? Mrs. Fairfield had never spoken in that tone to him before.

He trailed her back into the house, where even Robertson gave him a disappointed look, and that was saying a lot, because Robertson's facial expressions usually ranged from impassive to glacial.

"You as well, Robertson?" Edgar asked. "Has my entire household turned on me?"

"I like Miss Perkins, Your Grace," the butler said. "And . . ." He drew himself up. "And . . . she deserves better."

Robertson marched out of the entrance hall.

Wait a moment, wasn't his butler supposed to stay in the entrance hall?

It was clearly mutiny. And all because he'd sent his children and their governess on a delightful seaside holiday.

All you've done, a voice whispered in his mind, *is turn your back on everything you care about.*

This. He gripped the rolled-up engine plans he'd retrieved from the hall table. *This is what I care about. This is why I'm alive.*

Keep telling yourself that, you fool.

He grabbed his greatcoat, because Robertson wasn't there to garb him, and left the house at a trot.

You can run but you can't hide.

He needed to be at his foundry.

He'd find peace and clarity there.

ᎬDGAR DID NOT find peace and clarity at The Vulcan.

He found billowing clouds of acrid smoke. He broke into a run.

Grafton and the engine were standing in the middle of the courtyard. The smoke was coming from the engine. That was normal.

But . . . the boiler was overheating. Edgar could see it from here. It shouldn't be that glowing orange color. That color signaled . . . catastrophic boiler failure.

"Grafton," he shouted. "Get back."

His friend looked up, saw the color of the boiler, and began to run.

The explosion shook the walls, and threw Edgar to the ground, the deafening sound echoing in his eardrums.

Metal shrapnel flew everywhere. Grafton had reached safety, thank God, ducking behind a brick wall.

They always tested the engines in the middle of the courtyard for just this reason.

So much for lightweight boilers, thought Edgar bitterly.

He'd been so sure this one would hold up.

They'd cast the boiler themselves, melting the iron in the blast furnace, and he'd had them add a strengthening compound while stretching the metal as thin as it would go.

Too thin, apparently.

It hadn't been able to withstand the pressure. They'd never convince the fire brigades to use their engines if the boiler exploded in the fire fighters' faces.

Edgar picked himself up. "You alive, Grafton?"

Grafton appeared, coughing and shaking his head. "Bit dazed, that's all."

When the dust and smoke settled, men poured out of the foundry doors with buckets, dousing the still-smoking engine.

The engine was supposed to be the thing doing the dousing. Not the source of the fire.

Another failure.

"Damn it. Why didn't it work?" Edgar asked Grafton. "Why can't the boiler withstand the pressure? We built it stronger this time."

"You're the one who's wound so tightly you're going to explode. That's why the designs aren't working. You want it too much. You're forcing it. We have to give up, old friend. We have to tell the fire commissioner that we're not ready to demonstrate our engine yet."

"I'll never give up," Edgar said. "We'll find a way to make the boiler work."

"We have to forge a heavier boiler, that's the only solution."

"No. There's got to be a way for it to stay light-weight."

"You realize that we could have both been killed just now, don't you? I'm not really trusting your ideas right now. I think you need . . . how can I put this delicately . . ."

"I know I'm wound tightly. Damn it, man. You think I don't know it?"

"Is it the governess?"

Edgar didn't answer. If he didn't say anything, he wouldn't say anything incriminating.

"Out." Grafton pointed at the exit. "You need to

leave now or something bad is going to happen. Your designs aren't working because your mind is else-where. Go to your governess. Forget about engines for a day or two."

"I can't."

"Can't? Or won't."

"She and the children left for Southend an hour ago."

"You're an idiot." Grafton shook his head and a scrap of metal fell to the ground. "You should have gone with them."

"So everyone seems to think." He'd wanted so badly to go with them. But he had to be here.

"Trust me on this one, friend." Grafton clapped him on the shoulder. "You need a holiday in the worst way."

"I'm not going to abandon this project. Abandon you. When we're so close."

"Life's short." Grafton flicked his hair out of his eyes. "Go spend time with your family. Take a holi-day. The work will be here when you get back."

Go spend time with your family. Take the children to Lumley's. Go visit Mother.

Everyone was giving him the same message. The foundry had swallowed him, subsuming human in-teractions.

"And after you marry that governess," said Graf-ton, "you two can name your firstborn son after me."

"Pardon?" Edgar choked on the word.

"Don't pretend you haven't thought about it."

"What, marrying her? Or naming my heir Am-brose?"

"I can tell you from experience, that being named Ambrose is the quickest way to ensure your son will be strong, manly, and fearless." Grafton preened, flexing his sturdy arms. "If you don't like Ambrose, there's always my middle name. Percival."

"I'm not naming my heir Ambrose. Or Percival. In fact, I'm not siring an heir at all. Now would you please drop the subject?"

"Not until you chase after that governess of yours and don't stop until you're holding her hand as you run along the sparkling sands of Southend. And splashing about in the surf. And rolling—"

Edgar groaned, cutting Grafton's speech short. "I can't go frolic at the seaside. Not when there's work to be done here."

"Then I'll just have to keep suggesting names for your heir until you leave. How about Ethelbert? Or Pearl?"

"Pearl?" choked Edgar.

"I knew a boy named Pearl once, poor fellow. Ambrose will make a man tougher. Pearl will crush his spirit from the start." Grafton shook his head. "What about Gruffyd? A good, strong Welsh name. Or there's Archibald . . . though one wouldn't want to curse the poor thing's pate. Or—"

"I'm leaving, I'm leaving." Edgar headed toward the exit.

Maybe the answers he sought would arrive more easily when he was walking along the seashore with two playful, chaotic, exuberant children. Seeing life through their eyes. The newness, the wonder and the endless possibilities.

Maybe the answers would come to him more readily when he was right where he wanted to be. With Mari.

Envying the wind for ruffling her hair and the sun for kissing her freckles.

WHEN EDGAR ARRIVED back home, he informed Robertson that he was riding to Southend, since Mrs. Fairfield had already sent his trunk ahead of him.

Robertson merely nodded, his mask of implacability restored, but Edgar thought he detected a sparkle in his eyes.

"Very good, Your Grace. You may deliver this letter to Miss Perkins. It could be important, as it's from a lawyer in Cheapside."

Edgar accepted the letter. "Now I'm the postman?"

Robertson wisely refrained from commenting.

"Please say hello to Miss Perkins and the children for us," said Mrs. Fairfield, bustling into the room.

"Would you like to come as well?" Edgar asked, thinking that his housekeeper could probably could use a holiday as well.

"Oh no, Your Grace. I'll use the opportunity to inventory the silver. Do have a splendid time. I'm sure the Royal Hotel will be quite comfortable. Though it won't be the same as the old house."

Edgar hadn't been back to Southend since the fire. The thought of seeing all the familiar sights filled his heart with longing, and a conflicting sense of dread.

He'd only been a little older than the twins when his father had attempted to burn the house down, with Edgar and India still inside.

Blinking away the memory, Edgar walked to the window. "It looks like rain. I'd better leave."

"Does it?" asked Mrs. Fairfield, joining him at the window. "And here I thought that the sun was trying to pierce through the clouds."

Chapter 25

✺

"MISS PERKINS, WE'VE been expecting you." The porter in his smart black livery bowed low, for all the world as if she were a duchess. "Master Michel, is it? And Miss Adele?"

The children nodded, too exhausted after the day-long journey in Edgar's traveling coach for their usual chatter.

"Right this way please," said the porter. "You've the entire uppermost floor of the hotel. I believe His Grace won't be joining you?"

Mari shook her head. "He will not." She tried to keep the disappointment from her voice, though she must have been unsuccessful because the porter glanced at her sharply.

He ushered them down a hall to an open-well stair with a wreathed handrail. As they climbed, their way was lit by the last rays of the setting sun, shimmering through a glazed, domed roof lantern.

During the journey the children had forgotten their disappointment in the general excitement of new sights and new roads. They'd talked the entire way, playing word games and singing songs.

She'd joined in the singing, but her heart hadn't been present.

It wasn't only Edgar's occupation that kept him in

London. It was a reluctance to allow their—whatever this was between them—to deepen, to evolve.

The sea had opened before her eyes, spreading its blue-green mantle across the horizon, and her heart had opened as well, letting her know in no uncertain terms that she longed for Edgar to be there with her and the children, witnessing her first glimpse of the sea.

Even inside the hotel the air smelled salty and there was a breeze from the sea in the very voices of the staff.

"Would you like to see the Assembly Room?" the porter asked when they arrived at the first floor. "There's a very fine Venetian window."

"We'll explore tomorrow, I think," said Mari. The twins plodded next to her, their movements wooden with fatigue.

He led them to the upper floor and into a handsome sitting room with mullioned windows that would no doubt have a splendid view of the sea in the morning.

"Oh la la la la." Adele rubbed her eyes. "This will do, I'd say."

The porter took his leave and a maid and two footmen arrived with a hot supper for them. The children were almost too tired to eat, their little chins nodding toward their chests.

Michel yawned.

"Bedtime for tired children," said Mari, when the asparagus soup and roast pheasant had been devoured.

The maid, who told Mari that her name was Harriet, assisted Mari with putting the children to bed in a high, enormous bed with heavy purple velvet curtains festooned with gold tassels.

"It's the royal apartments, miss," she said to Mari, almost apologetically. "We're not used to having small children."

"Well they certainly won't be hurt if they fall out of bed. This carpet is thick as my ankle."

She wasn't supposed to mention the richness of carpets, probably, but she was so tired of maintaining her ruse of superiority.

"Thank you, Harriet." She could even thank the servants.

The children were asleep before she even left their room, which adjoined her grand suite of rooms.

Such extravagance.

An entire floor of a hotel for one charity school governess and two illegitimate children.

It was a stark reminder that she and Edgar belonged in separate worlds. The intimacies they had shared could never mean as much to him as they had to her.

He was wealthy, titled, and experienced in the ways of the world.

Probably this time apart was for the best. Maybe she would regain her senses and refocus her attention on the children, and her true purpose for seeking employment as their governess.

When they returned to London she would redouble her efforts. Visit every Ann Murray she could find and make inquiries about Mr. Shadwell.

Temporary, fleeting pleasures could never provide the answers she sought.

A cold, solitary bed might be lonely, but it was all she'd ever known.

"No DAWDLING, MISS PERKINS!" The next morning, the children flew ahead of her, tripping merrily down the pathway to the beach.

A manservant and maid followed with blankets, and baskets containing all of the children's toys and books.

The day was fine, the sun shining through the clouds.

Michel sniffed the air. "It doesn't smell precisely right, but it will do."

Adele hugged herself. "It will more than do, Michel. I didn't know England could be so sparkling."

Mari found the specimen boxes from Lumley's and set the twins to the task of finding and identifying all of the minerals and rocks listed.

The sun sparkling on the water filled her mind with golden light.

The colors were muted here. Grays and tans, browns and golds. Speckled over rocks and painting sand and charred pieces of wood from fires past. The delineations between the clouds and the sea. Strong lines sketched in gray, white, and cobalt.

In the distance, a rock that looked like a spiny, barnacled sea monster, its head beneath the waves, stood ready to rise and devour them all.

"Is this malachite?" Adele brought her a greenish stone.

"I don't believe so. That would occur perhaps in Cornwall." Mari opened the book of minerals and they pored over the colored plates.

"It could be olivine," said Adele.

"We'll make a notation for further study, shall we?"

Adele placed the small rock in a box and Mari added a scrap of red silk ribbon, to indicate that they weren't sure if it was olivine.

The children were so happy here, so open and trusting. She was glad to have this opportunity to help guide them during this difficult transition in their lives.

She'd fought for this escape from the narrow confines of the orphanage. The sea surrounded her, the widest vista she'd ever seen.

The sand was soft beneath her fingers. She stretched her arms over her head, leaning back against a cushion, and the sun warmed her, penetrating her skin and finding her heart.

The sea roared in the background, murmuring that Edgar was compassionate and caring. That he would learn how to spend time with the twins, how to give them love, instead of just possessions. Her feelings were layered like the gray and white clouds overhead. Blue sky was attempting to break through the clouds and doubt.

Adele stretched out next to Mari, kicking her toes in the sand. "Are you happy, Miss Perkins?"

"Very happy. The sea is more spectacular than I ever imagined."

"Isn't it?" Adele picked up a speckled gray rock, smoothing it with her finger. "But there's one thing missing, isn't there?" She avoided Mari's eyes, staring at the rock instead.

Mari shaded her eyes with her hand and looked over the horizon, where the sea met the sky.

"Yes," she said, "I wish your father were here as well but he's very busy right now with his steam engines. He's going to build an engine that will fight even the worst fires and save many lives."

He hadn't been back to Southend since the fire that claimed his house, and nearly claimed his life.

The painful memory had kept him away for so many years. She couldn't help thinking that if he had come with them it might have helped bury the dark memories for good.

"You smile more when Father is near," said Adele, throwing the rock toward the sea.

"Do I?" Mari replied, flustered.

Adele nodded. "What's Father's real name?"

"Edgar," Mari said, her voice catching.

Adele hopped up and grabbed a sharp stick of driftwood.

"*E-D-G-A-R* . . ." she wrote with the stick, etching his name into the damp sand.

She surveyed her handiwork. "Edgar," she spoke. "Yes, it sounds like him. Hard around the edges but with a promising *ahhh* in the middle."

Adele was definitely going to be a poetess.

"What's your first name?" Adele asked Mari.

"Mari. Like Mary, but with an *i*."

Adele spelled out *Mari* in the sand next to *Edgar*.

Michel approached and took the stick from Adele. He gave Mari a devilish grin and drew a heart around both of their names.

"Why did you do that?" Mari asked.

"Because you belong together," shouted Michel, already running away.

Adele chased after him and they both disappeared behind a jagged outcropping of rocks.

Edgar and Mari, written in crooked, childish script and bordered by a lopsided heart.

Mari rose, intending to sweep the names away, but something stopped her. The words danced in her vision and a sharp-edged thought scratched at her mind.

If Edgar was learning to care for his children . . . could he learn to care for her?

Because she didn't just love these intelligent, inquisitive children. She cared for their father as well.

She reached down and lifted a conch shell to her ear. She had a secret to whisper into the shell's dark interior. "I'm falling in love with Edgar," she announced.

She lifted the shell to her ear. No answer except the roaring of her own blood pounding in her ears.

"I know it's a thoroughly impractical thing to do," she told the shell. "I know it will end badly and I'll be hurt. But do I really even have a choice?"

Of course the lonely governess tumbled madly in love with the handsome duke. It happened all the time in the novels she read.

It was happening to her right now.

She was plunging headlong and heedless, like Michel and Adele rolling down sand dunes.

She didn't know where her fall would end. Where did she want it to end? Somewhere with Edgar's arms around her, warm as sunshine. The twins' carefree laughter in her ears.

We belong together.

Surely she was permitted to dream a little on a sunny day at the seashore.

The twins raced back into view, leaping over tide pools on their way back toward her. They'd found something to show her. She readied a specimen container.

She had quite a collection of shells and dried, withered things.

They swooped down on her like seagulls on a limpet, capturing her hands.

"Come and see what we've found!" cried Adele.

"Another sea urchin?" asked Mari.

"It's over there," Michel said, tugging on her arm and drawing her across the sand.

"A sea star?" she asked.

"More like a sea monster," said Adele.

They laughed merrily, pulling her along.

They rounded the bend and Mari lurched to a halt.

Her eyes must be playing tricks on her, because she thought she saw a devilish duke, rising from the sand like some mythical monster, dark and commanding against the sun.

Until a smile touched his lips and lit his eyes, like sunshine sparkling over the gray sea.

And then, he was merely Edgar.

And she merely loved him. With all of her newly widened heart. She didn't know what that meant in the grand scheme of things.

She only knew it was true.

Chapter 26

ℰDGAR CLOSED THE gap between them, his gait uneven on the shifting sand. All he could see was Mari's sparkling blue eyes and wide smile.

His heart lifted and flew into the sky like a seabird.

She wore a loosely flowing gown of lavender muslin with a soft gray shawl wrapped around her shoulders and her bonnet dangled down her back.

"You're being kissed by the sun." He touched Adele's nose, his eyes still on Mari's face.

Mari lifted a hand to her cheek. "More freckles."

"I like your freckles," he said.

"Why are you here?" Mari asked. "I thought you were testing your new engine."

"We tested it. It exploded."

Her face paled beneath her golden freckles. "Was anyone hurt?"

"Was there a loud boom?" asked Michel.

"Very loud," said Edgar, "but no one was hurt. My engineer thought I needed a holiday, so I jumped in a carriage, stayed overnight at the inn in Wickford, and here I am." He grinned at the children. "Are you having fun?"

Adele bounced on her heels. "We're glad you came, Father. We have so much to show you. Just today we've already found sea urchins, and sea stars and semi-precious stones—"

"And we built sand castles and rolled in the sand and Miss Perkins said we could eat oysters tonight," said Michel in a rush.

"They have sand in their ears, I'm afraid," said Mari.

"We have sand *everywhere,*" answered Michel proudly, shaking one of his legs and watching the sand pour out of the leg of his trousers.

Edgar laughed to see them so happy and excited. He mussed Michel's hair. "I brought you something."

"What is it?" asked Michel.

Edgar walked back to the rock outcropping and retrieved the kite he'd brought. "This is the same kind of kite that I used to fly here, on this very beach, when I was your age." He held up the green kite he'd purchased from Lumley's on his way out of London.

"It's a beauty," said Michel, touching the green silk stretched across the lightweight wood frame.

"What shape is a kite, children?" asked Mari.

Adele frowned. "It's not a diamond. Which means it's not a rhombus."

"Very good," said Edgar, impressed.

"It looks like the same shape as the scales on Trix's back," observed Michel.

"Quite right." Mari nodded. "It's a quadrilateral but the equal-length sides are adjacent. When we return to London we'll take the kite's measurements."

"For now, why don't we just go fly it?" suggested Edgar, with a grin.

Mari smiled. "A splendid idea."

"Now then." Edgar handed the spool of twine to Michel. "Stand with your back to the wind." He positioned his shoulders. "Hold it by the bridle point." He demonstrated and Michel followed. "Now let out the line!"

The kite caught in the wind, lifting easily, and Edgar showed Michel how to pull on the line to make the kite climb higher.

They all walked along the beach, the kite soaring and dipping ahead of them.

A strange feeling soared inside Edgar. Something simple and effortless.

He was happy, he realized.

He hadn't been happy in a very long time.

He walked ahead, with Michel and the kite, but he was as connected to Mari as if they stood hand in hand, breathing in the same rhythmic cycle. "What's this?" he asked, glancing down at the crooked letters scrawled across the damp sand. "Edgar and Mari." With a wavering heart drawn around the whole thing.

Mari caught up, wiping at the letters with the toe of her boot. "It's nothing. The children wanted to know our names."

"I drew the heart," called Michel over his shoulder as he tripped along the beach behind the kite.

Edgar caught up with him. "Why did you draw the heart?"

Mari and Adele fell behind, examining something in a tide pool.

Michel gave him a sidelong glance. "Dunno. Just felt like drawing one."

They walked side by side, father and son, on the same beach he'd walked as a boy, with the same green kite leading the way.

"When I go to Eton, will I be able to come home on holidays?" asked Michel.

"I thought you didn't want to go to Eton."

"We've been talking, Adele and I, and we know that we have to grow up." He puffed out his chest.

"We'll grow up. And we'll have our own lives. It's the way of the world."

He sounded so much older than his nine years. Edgar almost regretted being the one to give him such a worldly outlook. "If you don't want to go to Eton, you don't have to go."

"I think I do want to go. What's it like?"

"Some of the boys will be bullies and some will be friends. But you don't seem to have a problem defending yourself. They might make fun of your French name, though. You could change it to Michael."

"No," scoffed Michel. "If they laugh at my name I'll teach them a lesson."

"I'm sure you will." Edgar took the kite string, manipulating the line to make the kite dance in figure eights. "I suffered my share of knocks at Eton. I was teased for being a namby-pamby ducal heir, but then I blinked and suddenly school was over."

Time moved so swiftly.

He looked back at Mari. She and Adele were walking hand in hand.

In such a brief time she'd transformed his life. Everything she touched blossomed. His children, half wild when they'd arrived, wary and closed, now laughing and open.

His own heart, shuttered and frozen. Now cracked open.

She was the sun breaking through the clouds.

The patch of blue sky opening in his heart.

"They're talking about Eton," Adele reported. "I heard Michel mention the school."

"Perhaps we can convince your father not to separate you."

Adele shrugged. "Michel and I have been talking and we've decided it's good for him to go. I'll stay with you." She placed her hand in Mari's. "We'll have lots of adventures, won't we?"

"We most certainly will. And perhaps you'll go to a private academy for girls. You're just as clever as your brother, perhaps even more clever."

"We're both good at art and music but I'm much better at sums."

"So you are. Perhaps you'll be a mathematician and discover a new theory or two."

"Or a poetess, like our mother."

"Have you read any of her poetry?" asked Mari, softly.

"Yes." Adele nodded, staring out over the sea. "She visited us several times and she always brought a book of her poems. She told us to memorize poetry, just as you have done."

Mari's throat clenched. The poor thing. So much sorrow for a young child to bear. Did she know how her mother had died? That she'd taken her own life?

Mari hoped she didn't know.

"She made me memorize a poem she'd written," said Adele. "She said it was a poem for me . . . for us. It was called 'The Bells of Mary-le-Bow,' and it began: *When you hear the bells of Mary-le-Bow, this my child you will know, that I am watching over you, my heart ringing always, soft and low . . .*"

Mari placed an arm around her shoulders.

"Do you think she loved us?" Adele squinted at the sea, blinking away tears. "Or were we like a ship's anchor, weighing her down when she wanted to be free?"

"I'm sure she loved you." Mari squeezed her shoulders. "You're very lovable."

"Do you think so?"

"Absolutely. You're precocious and opinionated. You learn quickly and you feel things deeply. But you don't make a very structurally sound sand castle." They stopped at the two sand castles the children had fashioned earlier.

Adele's had mostly crumbled away, but Michel's stood tall.

"Michel's is better," agreed Adele.

"He's better at putting up walls. Just like his father."

She watched Edgar show Michel how to make the kite dance merrily.

"Do you think Father loves us now?" asked Adele.

"What do you think?"

"He's here with us when he could be in London. He defended us when *Grand-Mère* was rude. He hired Miss Martin."

She made her list as though she were adding up sums. Her face brightened. "He loves us."

"What did I tell you? You're lovable." Mari squeezed her shoulders. *I love you as well.*

The children would grow too old for a governess. And Edgar would marry . . . and then where would she be? Wind tangled her hair and sand stung her eyes.

Edgar and Michel reeled in the kite.

"Come on," shouted Michel, motioning for Adele to follow him. They chose long pieces of brown kelp and waged an epic battle, shrieking and running along the beach.

She and Edgar returned to the blanket and the umbrella.

"The children are so carefree here," she observed.

"The sea gives you wider thoughts. Maybe I'll solve the engine problem here."

Was that the only reason he'd come?

"That's not the only reason I came," he said, as if he'd read her mind. "I'm sorry I forgot to tell you I wouldn't be traveling with you and the children. I thought I had. Sometimes I'm so intent on my work that I forget everything else."

"I understand," said Mari.

"I haven't been back to Southend since the fire." The subject brought clouds to his eyes.

"Our estate was there." He pointed at a distant bluff. "There's nothing but a burnt husk left."

"What happened?"

He was silent for a moment, his eyes hooded. "I can still smell the smoke. Feel it choking my throat. The memory never leaves you."

"You were inside the house while it was burning?"

He crossed his ankles, leaning back on his elbows. "India and I were inside. My father started the fire."

"What do you mean he started it? On purpose?"

He nodded tersely, his face closed and wary again.

She waited for him to say more. He remained silent, staring up at the sky.

"This place has so many joyful memories for me, and so many painful ones. But I'm glad to be here." He stared into her eyes. "With you and the children."

"Today, Adele told me she either wanted to be a mathematician or a poetess."

He laughed. "Or both. Words like sums. Equations like poems. A passionate nature balanced by pragmatism. I don't fear for Adele. She's very strong-minded."

"She said she thinks she won't mind if Michel goes to Eton."

"He told me the same thing. If he can overcome his night terrors, he'll be ready."

"Give him time. Stay to the schedule. Explain any

changes to him thoroughly, before they happen, if possible."

"It's all because of you, Mari."

"It not all me. They respond to you as well."

"I thought the children were frightened of me. I didn't know how to interact with them, but now they seem to . . . like me."

"Yes, they do."

He laid his hand over hers on the blanket for a moment.

A brief touch, but her entire body responded, igniting with desire.

Oh Heavens. She was definitely in trouble. She'd given her heart to a devilish duke. Relinquished it completely.

This would end badly. But for now, with the sea stretching beyond their toes, she was determined to pretend that life could be simple.

"I wish . . ." he said, staring at the gray horizon. "I wish I could have held them as babes. Seen them grow week by week. Year by year. Helped them take their first steps. Collected their baby teeth in a jar."

"You're here with them now. You're collecting new memories."

He gazed at her. "So I am."

Just over those hills the road stretched back to London, back to the danger of discovery and the buried secrets of her past. Even if Edgar could accept her being a charity-school girl, would he ever be able to forgive her for deceiving him?

All she wanted to do was stay here forever, the four of them, in this land of make-believe.

Chapter 27

◈

"TELL US A story about P.L. Rabbit, Miss Perkins," Adele said later that evening, after Mari had tucked the twins into bed.

Mari perched on the edge of the bed. "Aren't you too tired?"

"We're not a bit tired," said Michel, suppressing a yawn.

"Miss Perkins isn't the only one who has stories to tell." Edgar strode into the room. "How about I tell you one tonight?"

Garbed in black trousers and a black coat over white linen, he was so handsome it stole Mari's breath away.

The twins made room for Edgar in the middle of the bed and Mari settled in a chair by the window. The light was beginning to fade from the sky.

Soon the sun would be gone and the moon would rise.

And she would be alone with Edgar. The thought shimmered in her mind like moonlight over ocean waves.

"Are you ready?" Edgar asked the children.

"Ready," said Adele.

"Once there was a rocking horse named Sir Peter Teazle," he began.

"That's a silly name," Adele said.

"He was a silly horse, because he had an impossible dream. He wanted to win the Derby."

"A rocking horse can't win the Derby." Michel yawned.

"As I said, it was an impossible dream until one day, P.L. Rabbit appeared in his nursery. 'Why so glum, Sir Peter Teazle?' she asked, twitching her adorable little nose."

"She's not adorable, Father. She's fearsome," said Adele.

"She can be a pirate and still have an adorable nose," he replied. "Now, are you going to keep interrupting me or can I tell the story?" he asked with mock sternness.

"Continue," said Adele.

"'Why so glum?' P.L. asked. 'I want to race in the Derby,' said Sir Peter Teazle. 'Well then why don't you?' asked P.L. Sir Peter gave her an incredulous look. 'Because, can't you see? I'm stuck on these wooden tracks and I can't go anywhere at all.' 'Oh that's easily solved,' P.L. said in her confident, lilting voice. 'All you have to do is believe, and anything is possible.'"

"Excuse me, Father," interrupted Michel. "Is there going to be any bloodshed in this story?"

Edgar shook his head. "Afraid not. It's a . . . romance, in a way."

"Ew," said Michel. "Romance."

"Let him finish, children," said Mari. Her heart had started racing at the word *romance*, and was attempting to gallop out of her chest.

"'Have you ever tried moving your hooves?' P.L. asked Sir Peter."

Edgar shifted his long legs on the bed, to accommodate the fact that Michel had collapsed against his shoulder and his eyelids were beginning to close.

"'Of course I have,' replied Sir Peter. 'Try it again,' commanded P.L. The rocking horse tried with all his might. 'It's no use,' he said, dejectedly. 'Oh for Heaven's sake,' said P.L. 'Just move your legs, you stubborn plow horse.' And she gave him a mighty push. And do you know what happened . . . ?"

The sound of gentle snoring met his question.

Mari laughed quietly. "I think they're asleep."

Edgar caught her eye. "I don't think they liked my story."

"They're exhausted," she said. "I like your story. I'd like to know the ending."

Holding her gaze, Edgar finished the story. "Sir Peter leapt off the tracks. 'Well,' he cried to P.L. 'What are you waiting for? We've got a race to win!' So P.L. hopped right onto his back."

Adele lifted her head from Edgar's shoulder. "And they won the race," she mumbled. "Didn't they."

Edgar smiled. "They did, indeed. Though there were a great many perplexed gentlemen who had bet on proper horses, and studied all the odds, only to find that Sir Peter Teazle, a wooden rocking horse with a rabbit jockey on his back, went flying by everyone else and claimed the prize."

Emotion welled in Mari's chest.

She could be reading more into the story than Edgar wanted her to, but it seemed to be about an obdurate man who was stuck in his tracks, treading the same path, and someone urging him to break free, to forget about his rules, to believe in himself.

Seeing him with the children here at the beach was satisfying some deep need in her. To see them become a family. To know that even though he was gruff and huge and intimidating, he had a heart wider than his shoulders, big enough to love these children, and gentle enough to protect them from life's disappointments.

She knew that when she left, he would always be there for them.

"They're fast asleep," he whispered. He eased his way off the bed, tucking the counterpane around the children.

They left the room on tiptoes. Harriet, the maid the hotel had provided, was sitting outside the door.

"They're sleeping," Mari told her. "I've no doubt they'll slumber the night away. They're stuffed full of oysters and sunshine."

They'd shared a simple meal at a seaside restaurant where the proprietor had recognized Edgar.

"Very good, madam," said Harriet.

Mari and Edgar walked down the corridor toward the sitting area with its glass doors overlooking the sea.

"A walk on the beach, perhaps?" Mari asked. She didn't want the evening to end. "To watch the sun set and see the moon and the stars come out?"

"I can see the stars right now." He lifted her hand and kissed her knuckles. "And we can watch the sun set from this window."

Mari shivered from the touch of his lips brushing her flesh and the promise in his eyes. "I'll just be a moment. I need to . . . wash up."

The children weren't the only ones with sand stuck everywhere. She needed to at least splash herself with water. And brush her hair, which was tangled from the wind and salt spray.

"I'll only be a moment," she told Edgar.

How had everything become so mixed-up and tangled?

Edgar paced the length of the room and back again.

He should leave Mari a note telling her that he'd gone to bed. And while he was at it, he could leave her the damned letter that he'd somehow completely forgotten to give her during the lazy, sun-soaked day.

He could leave the letter from the lawyer, and the note, and be gone in the morning.

It was all too much, this togetherness and tenderness. Where did he think it would lead?

You know exactly where it's going to lead. And you've been guiding it there, pushing your acquaintance, your friendship, down intimate paths. Telling her secrets. Telling the children stories while she listened with stars in her eyes.

Yes, that's what he should do. Write her a note and leave. That was the right and gentlemanly thing to do. It had been a mistake to come here.

No, it hadn't been a mistake. The day had been perfect.

His mind veered one direction, and then the other, until the door opened and Mari reappeared.

She'd changed into a glowing ivory-colored gown and the moment he saw her flushed cheeks and freshly-brushed auburn ringlets pinned atop her head, he knew: he could no more leave her tonight, than the stars could leave the sky.

"You look beautiful," he said simply. "That gown suits you."

"One of Lady India's cast-offs." She performed a curtsy, holding the sides of the filmy white dress and swishing the frothy hem over her ankles.

She wore dainty white kid slippers with red rosettes at the toes.

"You look utterly delectable," said Edgar.

"It's the shoes," she replied. "They appear to be made of frosting and rose petals. I think this gown must have been meant for a grand ball and a blushing debutante." The words were light. Teasing. But he heard the ache beneath her words.

She'd never had a season. Never been a debutante dressed in white.

"I never attend balls," he said. "They're highly overrated. But I would attend one if you were there, dressed in this flimsy bit of sea foam. I'd take your dance card and I'd write my name on every line."

She swatted his arm with an imaginary fan. "Your Grace. Such scandalous talk. You're making me feel quite wicked."

Mine, his brain asserted. *Mine to claim for every dance.*

They stood side by side in front of the windows, watching the light fade.

The gray sea shimmered with the last rays of the setting sun, like the final words of a poem.

Pale mauve and dainty shell-pink faded into the gloaming.

The sun slid under the dark water.

Sounds of the sea still roaring in his mind. Desire for Mari eddying through his body. Desire and something else. A nameless emotion, welling like water under sand, eroding his defenses.

She slipped her hand into his and the simple gesture completely undid him.

All of his fine resolutions imploded. Codes of conduct?

Highly overrated.

If he were a controlled, regimented gentleman with a precise, perfectly ordered life, he might escort her back to her chamber. But he wasn't controlled or perfect. He was riddled with flaws.

Flung into pieces like an exploded engine.

Not even caring if the servants saw, he clasped his

arms around her slender body, pulling her so close he could feel her heart beating through thin, gauzy muslin.

Her lips opened to him, her tongue meeting his.

She stood on tiptoes and locked her soft arms around his neck. Without breaking the kiss, he lifted her, one arm crooked under her knees, the other around her back, and carried her down the hallway, not stopping until they reached his chambers.

He kicked open the door, then kicked it closed again when they were inside.

Her tongue danced inside his mouth, quick and nimble, composing frenzied poetry. Need pounding through him like surf.

Claim her. Make her yours.

Up against the wall now. Next to the balcony door, which stood ajar. A breeze ruffled her skirts, cooling the sweat from his face.

Shift her body around him. Her thighs around his hips. His lips leaving her mouth but only to find her breast.

Feeling for her bodice, dragging it down.

Small, upturned breasts with ruddy nipples, straining over the boning of her corset.

He dipped his head and traced the contours of her breast with his tongue, spiraling closer and closer to the nipple until she moaned and her head fell back.

His lips closed around her nipple, suckling the taut peak.

Her fingers fumbled with his coat buttons. He lifted her arms, wrapping them more firmly around his neck, bracing her against the wall, and then he shrugged out of his coat and flung it aside.

He groaned, burying his head in her neck, cupping her round bottom through the fabric of her gown.

She framed his face with her hands, sought his eyes. "I need you," she said fiercely. "I want you." She lifted her hips, seeking his cock.

The friction was pure bliss and pure torture.

"Mari," he groaned. "You want this? You want this as much I do?" He had to ask one more time.

"You're thickheaded, aren't you? Yes. That's what I've been trying to tell you. Listen to me, Edgar." She caught his head between her palms. "All my life I've hid my true feelings and desires beneath a stifling cloak of obedience and silence. I'm through with it. Do you hear me? I want you to make love to me."

Her words soaked through his mind until he was saturated with the need to believe that nothing mattered beyond this night, that being with her was inevitable, and he'd known this moment would happen from the first moment he laid eyes on her.

She wanted this. He wanted this.

The sea had washed into his mind, swept away years of denial and suffering. They would find so much pleasure tonight. It was waiting for them, around the corner. Only a few buttons and one scarlet bow away.

Outside, beyond the door, stars gathered to watch.

"Edgar?"

He lifted his head from her breast. "Yes?" He stilled. She was going to tell him to stop.

He prepared to release her.

"Put me down," she said.

He nodded. Gritted his teeth. Slid her to the floor. It was better this way. He'd lost control.

It had been madness.

"That's better," she said. "Now I can do *this*." Her fingers closed around the flap of his breeches, cupping his cock.

"A duke in the hand is worth two in the bush," she said, with a wicked grin.

Edgar appeared to be choking to death.

Mari relinquished her grip on his tool, and thumped him on the back instead.

"In the b-bush," he sputtered. "Mari." He rumpled her hair with his hand. "You're going to be the death of me." His grin slipped away.

"All good things in all good time," he said gently. "We should wait."

"Yes, but, what's well begun, is half done," she replied with an arch smile.

"Oh?" His smile returned, tilting his sensual lips upward. "And fortune favors the bold, does it not?"

"Precisely. And . . . and the early bird catches the worm."

"The worm?" His eyebrows shot upward.

"Did I say worm? I meant the python."

"That's better," he growled. "Now, right and forward, Perkins. No dawdling." He made a spinning motion with his finger.

He wanted her to . . . turn around?

She turned her back to him.

"I've been wanting to untie one of your bows since I saw you bending over to read the titles of the books in my library."

She sucked in her breath. He wanted her to bend.

She walked to the bed and bent forward, offering her backside to him. "If you wish a thing to be done, you'd better do it yourself, Your Grace."

She glanced back over her shoulder, loving the fierceness of the desire in his eyes.

Within seconds, he was behind her, and the scarlet sash was a heap on the floor.

He unbuttoned her white gown and slid it down her body, helping her step out of it, until it lay in a froth of white at their feet.

The over-chemise. Then her stays. Until all she wore was a thin cotton shift.

He shaped his palms over her buttocks. "A thing of beauty is a joy forever."

He lifted her hips and the hard, pressing length of him slid against her core, nudging her thighs apart. His fingers closed around her waist.

Her breathing came faster. She wanted to see him as well. Feel him.

"Are you still clothed?" she asked, attempting to twist around to see him. "That's hardly fair." He loosened his grip on her waist and she turned around, rising to stand before him.

She tugged his shirt from the waist of his breeches impatiently. He raised his arms, shimmying free of his shirt.

Greedily, she drank in the sight of his naked body.

Her reaction was instantaneous, a melting between her thighs, a recognition that this was what she wanted.

His frame of steel, stretched over with taut skin and ridged muscles. Dark hair dusting his chest, leading her eyes down his taut stomach, ridged with muscles, into the fall of his breeches.

She'd said she wanted to touch him and it was true. All of him.

"Now your breeches," she commanded.

He slid his breeches off, kicking free of them. He wore nothing beneath.

He was naked. Gloriously naked, his sex standing tall above a patch of dark hair.

He stood with his legs apart and hands at his

sides. He let her look her fill, a smile playing across his lips. "Do you like what you see?" he asked, ringing his sex with his fist, offering it to her.

She nodded, dry-mouthed. He was stiff with desire. Hard for her.

"Share and share alike," he said, glancing pointedly at her shift.

Bravely, with the last of her courage, she pulled her shift over her head and stood before him, naked as the day she was born.

The chill in the room gave her gooseflesh and tightened the peaks of her breasts.

She resisted the urge to cover her mound with her hands.

He swallowed, his Adam's apple working visibly. "So beautiful."

The raw emotion on his face told her that he spoke the truth.

When he closed the distance between them, his sex led the way, bobbing eagerly. She almost smiled from nervousness, almost, but then the hot, hard length of him slid against her belly as he took her lips in a searing kiss.

He laid her gently onto his bed, working his fingers into her hair, removing the last of her hairpins, the gentle prickling sensation on her scalp tingling through her whole body.

Madness in her thoughts, in her heart.

Joy as well—strange joy bubbling up from her heart. This body she'd thought of as an island, never to be touched by another, never to know love. This body had surprised her.

And his body was a revelation. She ran her hand down his firm, ridged belly, closing her fingers around his staff, testing the weight of him in her hand.

"Mari," he groaned, bucking against her palm.

"*You're* beautiful," she whispered. "Your body was forged by hammer and steel."

His hands cupped her breasts. "And you're a goddess, with soft, supple breasts like . . ."

"Yes?" she prompted.

"I'm trying to think of a good fruit analogy but your hand is . . . curled around my . . . cock."

Such a naughty word, *cock.*

"Smaller than melons and bigger than grapes," she said. "I'm thinking oranges? Maybe peaches?"

"I'm . . . not thinking at all. Damn," he groaned. "Yes. Like that. Squeeze it harder as you get to the base."

"Like that?"

"Just like that."

She could become addicted to having this much power over him.

"I want you to do something for me, Edgar," she said. "Breathe. Deep and steady."

He smiled, realizing she was repeating his own words, and then the smile fell away and his stomach muscles visibly clenched, rippling with effort.

His fingers clutched her shoulders.

"Mari," he groaned, pulsing in her hand.

He lifted himself over her, supported by his strong arms, positioning himself between her thighs. Instinctively, she lifted her leg and wrapped her thigh around his waist.

He moaned into her lips as he kissed her, his cock jutting between them, the head of him pressing her belly button, the base of him sliding against her sensitive flesh.

No sound except the meeting of their bodies.

The sea still roaring in her ears.

A mindless need building. She knew enough to understand that he was holding back from entering her. That he wanted to be inside her, that everything in his nature must be begging him to take her, to slide inside, but he was holding back.

It pleased her, this holding back. This iron control of his.

It made her feel safe, and cared for.

Because, if she were being honest, this was all a bit frightening. She'd turned to her proverbs because she thought they made her sound worldly and experienced.

When really, she'd never felt anything like this before. Never even could have imagined anything as elemental as this.

In the novels she'd read, this . . . rawness . . . was only delicately hinted at. The duke always had a rigid jawline, and the lady always had melting eyes, but there'd certainly been no discussion of *this*.

This wetness between her thighs, and the slickness of sweat between her breasts.

His sweat and her sweat mingling.

The grimace—half pleasure and half pain—on his dear, handsome face.

The control cording his neck, clenching his jaw. He kissed her neck. Her shoulders. Her breasts. "I'm going to map each one of your freckles, Mari."

"That could take years," she gasped.

He slid lower and kissed the freckles on her belly. Then he licked her.

"What are you doing?" she asked.

"I like these freckles on your belly, they're delicious." He licked her again. "I love how you have freckles everywhere. Do you perhaps have some . . . *here*?" He kissed her inner thigh.

"I don't know!"

"You don't know? Let me examine. I think there's another one just . . . here."

Tasting more. Her inner thighs. Higher, until she tensed and tried to evade his kiss. He was kissing her *there*. Delving into her with his tongue.

Good gracious. She tensed her muscles. Should she stop him? What did it taste like? Was this . . . *done*?

He lifted his head. "Stop thinking, Mari." He dove back to his task, spreading her thighs wider.

She stopped thinking. Just rode the sensation building in her belly. Allowed herself to feel and to be. When her crisis arrived it rose swiftly, without warning, breaking inside her like a wave.

She buried her fingers in his hair, holding his head in place, riding his tongue. Riding the sensation that spiraled outward into her belly, her thighs, her mind . . . and her heart.

A tidal pool of emotion, seeping through her mind. She loved him. She wanted to join with him.

"Take me," she said. "I need you."

He used his knee to part her legs, to position them wide.

The hard, hot feeling of his cock parting her flesh, notching home between her thighs.

"I'll go slowly. Mari, breathe please. You're so tense."

She inhaled and he entered her, slowly, stretching a passage, finding his way in the dark, into her.

"Edgar." A whisper. A prayer.

A kiss in answer, full and satisfying.

*H*ER SALTWATER AND honey on his tongue.

Her voice in his ears, asking him to take her.

The need drove him forward, guided his cock.

Best to enter her now, after her orgasm, while pleasure still flowed through her body.

Make it good for her, even though it was her first time.

Her first time. A sliver of guilt wedged in his mind.

"Stop thinking, Edgar," she said, pulling his lips down and kissing him.

He pushed inside, halfway now, nearly there. Using every scrap of control he could muster.

"Does it hurt?" he asked.

"Yes."

"I'll stop."

"No." Fists on his shoulders, fingers in his hair, pulling him back. "No, don't stop now. Please move another inch, Your Grace."

He did. And then another, until he was entirely buried in her tight, wet heat.

He stilled, listening to her breathing. Feeling her inner muscles pulsing around him. The most beautiful feeling in the world. He could explode right now. Just from the feeling of being inside her.

"Edgar?" Her voice held a question. "It might be . . . too much. I want it, I do. It's wonderful, but like this, you're so heavy . . ."

He tensed. It was too much. He was hurting her. He pulled away from her.

"No, don't leave me," she cried, holding his shoulders. "Is there another way?"

Ah, he understood now. He rolled over, staying inside her, until she was on top.

He set her knees on either side of his hips. "You move, Mari. When you're ready. Find the rhythm that you like the best. I'll stay right here, inside you."

He wanted to stay there forever.

She nodded. Bit her lip, her eyes shadowed.

"You set the pace," he said. "You're in control. I'm at your pleasure, Mari. I'm yours."

Long waves of hair brushed against his chest as she began to move, tentatively at first, easing herself back and forth.

It was torture. Pure and simple torture not to move. Not to thrust.

He gritted his teeth. "Yes, that's the way of it," he gasped. "Take your time."

What he wanted to say was, *ride me. Ride me like a racehorse.*

Instead, he let her experiment, only moving with her gently, following her movements.

"Oh," she said, a note of discovery. "That's . . . nice." She rocked back and forth, finding her pleasure.

He rubbed his thumb across her sensitive core. "How about now?"

"I think . . ." She braced her palms on his chest. "I think it's going to . . . work."

Praise be, she began to move again.

He moved with her, thrusting gently, inside her liquid warmth, the heat of her gripping him.

He wasn't going to last much longer.

Not when he could see her breasts bouncing jauntily above him.

Her hair brushing against his nipples. Her face, focused in concentration, as she discovered lovemaking for the first time.

He was her first lover. The thought sank into his mind like a setting sun, suffusing his body with wonder as his orgasm built, ready to burst.

She rode him harder, faster.

He stilled her by holding her hips. Lifting her, he reversed their position, laying her on her back and bracing himself over her on his forearms.

He pushed inside again.

She moaned, low and guttural.

"Wrap your legs around me," he said.

She followed his instructions, her thighs clos-ing around his hips, heels on his lower back. They moved together, her hips rising to meet his thrusts.

He didn't know if she could come again but he couldn't last any longer. One more deep, ecstatic thrust and he slid out of her, pumping himself with his fist, spilling his seed over her belly.

"Mari," he groaned into her hair, sinking on top of her. "So. Good."

Her hands soothed his back.

She kissed his neck. He lay, mindless, on top of her. He was crushing her.

He rolled away and gathered her into his arms, placing her head against his chest.

She nestled into him.

Outside the sea still swept against the shore.

Here, in this room, he'd just experienced the best lovemaking of his life. He felt grateful, satiated, and something new, something he'd never felt before.

Not some giddy, heedless, selfish emotion.

A steady, abiding, rock-solid feeling of caring. For this woman. For everything she'd given him. Shown him.

What did it mean? Now that he'd broken all of his rules, what had he become?

What would they become . . . together?

Chapter 28

❧

SHE AWOKE FROM a dream of having his arms around her, to find that his arms were around her, blanketing her, keeping her warm from the night air.

They'd left the balcony door open.

She rolled out from under his heavy arm. Shivering, she walked across the room on bare feet and closed the door. She went to the washroom and relieved herself. Washed away the soreness between her legs.

She tried not to disturb him as she lifted his arm and nestled back into his chest, but he started awake, his heart beating beneath her ear.

"Are you awake?" he asked.

"Yes."

Moonlight slanted across the bed. They hadn't pulled the curtains because there was nothing but the wide sea beyond the balcony doors.

He tucked her head into the hollow of his shoulder, stroking her hair. "How do you feel? Not too sore?"

"A bit."

Her heart hurt a little bit as well. Because reality was beginning to intrude again. She'd given her body to him, and he'd stolen her heart in the bargain.

This wasn't going to end well.

"I can feel your thoughts going to a dark place," he said. "What's the matter?"

"Nothing." She smiled up at him.

"Would you like me to tell you a story?" he asked.

"That would be nice."

She expected him to say something funny, a story about P.L. rabbit. Something to make her smile. She gathered her strength to oblige him. To laugh and make a joke and pretend everything was wonderful and there would be no tomorrow.

No reckoning.

"My father was a drunkard," he began. "And by that I mean he drank nearly a half bottle of whiskey or brandy every single day. He was a pleasant enough man during the daytime, until the poison saturated his gut. Every night he transformed into a monster."

This wasn't the story she'd expected. Mari held still in his arms, hardly daring to breathe.

He kept stroking her hair, his voice growing deeper, rougher, more jagged with emotion.

"When he was deep in his cups, he hit my mother. He hit me. He never hit India, thank God."

"Oh Edgar," she whispered against his neck. "Why do people do such terrible things?"

"It was the drink . . . and this great sadness and emptiness inside of him, that he couldn't escape, no matter how much whiskey he drank."

She listened to his heart beating, to the words he wasn't saying. *I was scared. I was scarred.*

"We lived in fear, by his whims, his great rollicking highs and his evil, mean lows. That's why it hurt so much when you accused me of being the same way. That everyone in my household lived by my whims."

"That's not what I meant, you know that. I was teasing you. I wasn't accusing you of being a monster. I was only trying to cut you down to size."

"It cut me. Made me think. Made me wonder if despite all of my rules, I'd become him, after all." He sighed. Kissed the top of her head. "You couldn't have known the demons I was battling. The ones I'm still battling."

Yes, she could sense that his demons were noisy, clamoring in his head, telling him he was bad, that he was wrong.

She traced the whorl of hair on his chest with her finger. *Keep talking, Edgar. If you keep talking, you drown out the demons.*

"When he had the drink in him, he chased after the servants. And when he wasn't at home, he was whoring and purchasing mistress after mistress. Again, trying to escape his sadness, his anger, in a frenzy of meaningless sexual congress."

She held perfectly still, willing him to keep talking. She sensed that this was the first time he'd shaped these thoughts into something he could tell another soul.

"When I was young, I couldn't do anything about his reign of terror. I couldn't defend the serving maids, or stop him from hitting our mother. He tried to kill us all. Here, at Southend. He was drunk and he set fire to the curtains. He wanted to die. He wanted us to die."

Mari soothed the hair back from his brow. "That's too much for a young child to bear, Edgar." And she'd thought her childhood had been hard.

"When I grew older," he continued, "I learned boxing. Fencing. Anything that honed my body to be a brick wall that he could batter, but never break. A wall that would deflect his fury from others."

A tear slid down her cheek. She ached for him. For the young man he'd been, trying to absorb all of that anger. Protect everyone else.

"There's something about you, Mari." He lifted her chin. "Something that makes me trust you. Even that first night, in my library, I told you things I'd never told anyone else."

"Sometimes we need to speak of the bad things in order to silence them forever."

"I think you're right. That's why I'm telling you this story."

"Keep going, Edgar. I want to hear. I need to know."

"When Sophie left me, I was so furious with my father. More furious then I'd ever been."

His chest rose and fell more rapidly now. She deliberately slowed her own breathing, showing him how to be calm.

"I came home one evening, and my father had . . . my father had . . ."

THE WORDS TWISTED inside Edgar's mouth, blocking his tongue, choking his throat.

Her small hands framed his face. Rubbing his temples, soothing him with the scent of her. Warm and good and wholesome.

He took a deep breath. "He'd tried to choke my mother. There were marks around her neck. She was sobbing in her chambers when I came home. Something snapped inside me. The rage swelled up, obliterating anything good. Anything human."

She didn't betray any shock. Didn't draw away in disgust.

"I saddled my horse and I found him at his club, drinking brandy and laughing with his friends. I walked into that club and I spat upon his boots. I challenged him to a duel, in front of dozens of witnesses. He laughed at first. And then he saw I was deadly serious."

Noonday sun on his face.

Raising the heavy pistol. Correcting the tremble in his fingers.

His father's mocking smile.

The crowd that had gathered despite the privacy surrounding the duel.

Grafton had been his second. He'd attempted to talk him out of his folly.

Too much like a Greek tragedy, old boy, he'd said. *Nothing good can come of it.*

"I wanted to murder my own father," he said. "Actually imagined the bullet ripping through his heart, taking his life. In the end, I found I couldn't do it. I fired at nothing, several feet away from him."

Mari inhaled. Let her breath out again.

"The old duke experienced no such qualms. His bullet caught me above my kneecap. 'I was merciful,' he told me later. 'Could have been your heart,' he said."

Merciful.

Edgar screwed his eyes shut.

"But something came of my challenge. After that day he changed. Left us alone. He would leave for weeks on end and we had no idea where he was. Drinking himself to death in a squalid gin house, but harming no one but himself. My mother grieved. And she was angry with me for airing our filthy secrets before the eyes of the *ton*. She never forgave me for challenging him to that duel."

"You had to. You had no other choice."

"She didn't see it that way. Mother is made of strong, aristocratic fiber. Bear everything in silence, is her motto."

"You had to speak out. So that he wouldn't ruin other lives. You changed him."

"He changed me as well. After my wound healed, I left London. Renounced my heritage. Even changed my name. I became a foundry worker in Birmingham. I learned a trade. I was never going to return. And then . . . when my father died, I had to come back because he'd nearly ruined the family, and I wasn't going to let my sister and mother suffer any more. My mother never forgave me, though."

"People grow apart," Mari said, "but they also grow together as well. Like you and the children. There they were, minding their own lives, in their own little patch of sun, seeking roots and hoping for rain, when fate bent them toward you, another seeker, another thirsty soul. And together you form a whole."

"They're still growing. My mother and I . . . it's too late for us. So that's my story. Not a pretty one and it doesn't have a happy ending."

She lifted his hand and planted a kiss in the center of his palm. "I believe you can mend the rift with your mother. You're a good man, Edgar."

She made him feel that he could be good.

That he'd never truly made love with anyone before, that this experience was something so wholly new he didn't even have words for it.

She kissed the center of his palm again, her lips cool and gentle against his skin. "I wish we could stay here forever," she whispered. "London feels so far away. Life is simpler here."

She kissed him again, this time using her tongue, drawing circles on his palm. Which didn't seem like it should be so erotic, but was making his cock swell and his heart race.

Letting her touch him, caress him, made him so vulnerable, but somehow he didn't mind.

God help him, he was hers.

Hers to torture. In any manner she might devise.

SHE PLACED HER palm over his heart, spread her fingers wide. *I love you.* Could he hear it?

She hoped he could feel, hear, what she couldn't say.

She was thanking him for telling her the story, so that she understood why he'd fought so hard against kissing her. Because he didn't want to become his father. Because he was a good, honorable man who had risked everything to protect his family.

She thought: We're attracted to someone for their strength, their beauty, their perfections . . . but we fall in love because of imperfections.

Because of the pain they've overcome.

He kissed her, and she surrendered to the pleasure, loving how right it felt to be held by him. To have his tongue inside her mouth and then . . .

He was inside her again. It stung but it felt right.

Pushing inside her with his whole body, propped up on his strong forearms, his hands, palms spread wide, on either side of her, anchoring her to the bed.

Then sinking down on top of her, knotting his arms around her, the hard bulwark of his chest meeting her chest.

Heart to heart.

He rubbed his foot against the arch of her foot. Kissed her neck with soft little nips of his teeth.

"God, Mari. Damn."

His movements increased, his deep, low moans of pleasure igniting her own pleasure.

A few more deep, strong thrusts and his body tensed, and he pulled away from her, spilling into the bedclothes instead of her. He collapsed beside her.

Reached for her and nestled her against his chest.

His breathing slowed to a rhythmic sighing, like the noise of the sea, a soothing lullaby.

"I want you to know it's never been like this with another, Mari," he said.

"I'm glad," she murmured.

"I've told you so much about my past. What of your childhood?" he asked. "You said it was repressive. Your father was a clergyman?"

The mellow warmth in her heart began to cool. She longed to confess everything. Tell him about the beatings and the harshness she'd endured at the orphanage. But how could she tell him about her past without fabricating more falsehoods?

"I'm so tired, Edgar," she whispered, keeping her face hidden against his chest. "Can we talk in the morning?"

"Of course." He kissed the top of her head. "Whenever you are ready."

He drifted to sleep but Mari stayed awake. She didn't want this night to end.

His heart beat in the steady rhythm of waves breaking against cliffs.

He'd told her his dark secrets. It was time to tell him hers.

No matter what happened, no matter if she lost everything. She could no longer live with this barrier between them.

Tonight she could dream in his arms.

Tomorrow she must tell him the truth.

Chapter 29

❧

AN IDEA PULLED Edgar out of sleep; a thought tethered by a dream.

Something trying to rise in his mind, like the sun would rise soon outside their window.

Mari asleep in his arms. His children sleeping nearby.

A heap of beach rocks and shells on the bedside table. He picked up one of the purple sea urchins the children had collected, turning it in his hand, feeling the hard little bumps and the long ribboned ridges that formed its structure. So simple. So elegant. So . . .

"That's it!" He bolted to a seated position.

"What? What is it?" Mari rose on one elbow, hair the color of sunrise tumbling around her shoulders.

He held up his treasure. "A sea urchin."

"Yes," Mari soothed. "A nice sea urchin. Now go back to sleep." She burrowed back into the pillows.

"No. Mari." He tilted her chin toward him. Her eyes drifted open. "Look at it. What do you see?"

"Ah . . ." She rubbed her eyes. "A little onion-dome for an underwater church?"

"Ribs," Edgar said.

"Ribs?"

"Yes, ribs." He lifted the delicate purple dome. "See here—how exquisitely thin this shell is, and yet it's unbroken with no trace of the living creature that once inhabited it. How has it survived the vicissitudes of pounding waves and churning currents? Ribs!"

Mari smiled at him indulgently. "All right then. Ribs." She poked him in the ribs. "We all have ribs."

She wasn't understanding him. He needed to slow down.

"See here, and here." Edgar pointed out the ribs that ran up the spherical shell-like lines of longitude. "We just need to add ribbing to the engine boiler to increase its strength. It's so simple! Why didn't I think of it before?"

He kissed her on the lips and jumped out of bed. He must return to London while the idea was still fresh in his mind.

"This is what I've been searching for. I'll take the sea urchin to Grafton. We'll model the boiler on it." As he spoke he ran around the room, shrugging into his shirt and coat and flinging his cravat over his neck.

"Um . . . Edgar. Aren't you forgetting something?" asked Mari.

Edgar looked down at his bare legs.

Mari burst out laughing.

"I think Grafton would prefer it if you wore trousers." Her gaze flicked across his thighs. A slow grin spread across her face. "Though I wouldn't mind if you decided to go bare."

"Oh you like the trouser-less look, do you?" He walked to the bed and knelt down, wrapping his arms around her. "Impudent minx." He kissed his way from her neck to her lips, reveling in the way she returned his kiss so enthusiastically.

"Mari," he groaned, stroking his cheek. "I don't want to leave you."

Her hair was even more tumbled now, her cheeks flushed, and her eyes bright with desire.

"Go." She gave his chest a little push. "Go and build your engine. We'll be home before you know it."

Home. It was truly a home now with Mari and the children living there. He gave her one last lingering kiss and reluctantly broke away.

First, find his trousers. Second, build his engine. And third . . . kisses. Definitely more kisses.

THIS WASN'T QUITE how Mari had pictured the morning progressing.

Edgar was throwing on his clothing, covering up all those sleek muscles. All she wanted to do was rip his clothes off and tumble him back into bed.

He'd had some sort of engineering breakthrough and she was glad for him. But she'd thought they might share a sleepy morning tumble. And afterward, as they lay satiated, she'd planned to tell him the truth about how she'd come to work in his home.

Now he was dressed and ready to leave, his face all angles and excitement in the new morning light.

He tilted her chin up and kissed her lips. She closed her eyes, remembering what his firm, demanding lips had done to her last night.

"I'm leaving now, Mari. But we definitely need to talk. About last night. About . . . everything."

His hand smoothed over her hair. "I want to know absolutely everything about you. I'll need the name of your uncle, or whomever you were living with in Derbyshire."

Mari froze. Did that mean what she thought it meant? Was he planning to . . . propose?

Of course he was. He was an honorable man, re-member?

Oh God. It was all too complicated now. She'd leapt into the fire so willingly.

"Say something, Mari."

"Good-bye, Edgar," she said stiffly. What else could she say? Her mind was reeling.

Reality intruding so quickly, it felt like quicksand sucking her down into a darkness of her own creation.

Duke. Governess. Not even a superior governess.

She'd wanted this pleasure in his arms, but she hadn't thought it all the way through.

"I know this design will work," he said with a delighted smile. "It's all because of you, Mari."

"Good luck."

"I don't need luck. I have you. Oh I almost forgot." He paused at the door, and came back, drawing something from his inner coat pocket. "I was supposed to deliver this letter. What a fool I am. I can only say my head was addled."

"A letter for me?"

"From a lawyer in Cheapside."

He handed her the letter.

She sat, stunned, as he kissed her one more time and left.

A letter from Mr. Shadwell.

She hardly dared open it. She left the bed and put her clothing back on.

It was still dawn. If she hurried, she could be down the hallway and back in her own room with none the wiser.

She ran swiftly and made it to her chambers, collapsing on the bed, breathing heavily.

She slit the letter open with trembling fingers.

Dear Miss Perkins,

My son informs me that you visited our offices and that he may have neglected to mention my existence. If you are, indeed, the child whom I sought at the Underwood Orphanage and Charity School, I would very much like to meet you. I will await you next Thursday at one o'clock at my offices. Please do bring any proof you may have of your claim.

    Sincerely,
    Mr. Arthur Shadwell (the Elder. And the Sober),
    Lawyer

Mari reread the letter for the third time. On the fourth reading, hope began to trickle. On the fifth, a rush of joy flooded her heart and she leapt out of her chair, dancing with the letter around the room.

Proof of her claim. Her claim to be wanted, to be searched for, to be *someone*.

This could change everything. If she and the children left Southend a few days early, she would be back in London in time to keep the appointment.

Her birth no longer a mystery. The possibility of . . . well, there were endless possibilities. She could have family in London.

Ann Murray. She could have a mother.

Edgar had said he wanted to know everything about her and it had made her so sad to think that there was nothing she could tell him. Nothing but lies.

And now . . . the possibility of a truth to tell. Whatever it was, it would be the truth.

At last.

There was a knock at her door. The twins burst

into the room, followed by Harriet. "Where's Father?" asked Adele.

"We've already had breakfast," said Michel. "We want to go fly our kite. It's a windy day. No sun at all. Perfect for kite flying."

"Your father had to leave early," Mari said. "He had a brilliant idea for his engine."

"He's gone?" Michel's eyes clouded over. "But he said we would fly the kite again today."

"Why are you still wearing the same dress?" asked Adele.

"Ah . . ." There was no putting anything over the precocious Adele. "I fell asleep in it, silly me. And then I awoke early and your father told me he was leaving and I haven't had a chance to change into something new."

The maid gave her a knowing look.

Mari shooed the children out of the room. "Why don't you go and make some chalk drawings on the flagstones while I dress."

"It might rain later," said Michel. "Our drawings would be washed away."

"Then you can paint water colors. Harriet will find easels and paints."

"My pleasure, miss," said Harriet.

"I want to see charming seascapes," Mari told the children. "So charming that your father will want to hang them in his salon. Quickly now, before it rains."

The children made no more objections, trailing after the maid.

Adele turned back. "When we return to London, do you think we'll have a letter from Amina?"

"I wouldn't be at all surprised. She should have had time to return your letter by now."

Adele's shoulders lifted. "I do hope so," she said, as she followed Michel and the maid down the corridor.

MARI AND THE children arrived back in London three days later. They'd been delayed on the roads by heavy rains, so they arrived in the morning, instead of late the night before.

Today was the day she would meet with Mr. Shadwell. She only had a few hours to prepare.

The gate at Number Seventeen, Grosvenor Square, still said that it scorned to change. Mari didn't know why she thought it should have changed. She was the one who had changed.

She was different now. She had a new awareness of her body. Head to toes and all the places in between that Edgar had kissed, caressed, and coaxed to song. Though it wasn't only a physical change. She was not the same woman who had walked through this gate after her disastrous meeting with Mrs. Trilby.

Instead of having to don confidence and courage like a mask, she understood that strength already lived inside her. It had always been there, but she'd been afraid to own it, or to utilize it, for fear of retribution.

Whatever was revealed at the meeting with the lawyer today, and whatever happened with Edgar, nothing could take away that strength now.

"Good morning, Miss Perkins. Good morning, children. How was the seashore?" asked Mrs. Fairfield, meeting them in the entrance hall.

"It was wonderful!" said Adele. "We ate oysters and rolled down sand dunes."

"Not at the same time, I hope," said the housekeeper.

"We flew a kite, and we still have sand between our toes," said Michel proudly. "And we made sand castles. Mine was the best."

Mrs. Fairfield laughed. "My, my, my. What a jolly holiday. I'll have to go with you next time. I do love sand between my toes."

"You do?" asked Michel with an incredulous expression, as if he'd never thought about housekeepers leaving their houses.

"Indeed I do. And my sand castles are award winning. They even have china closets."

"Bof," exclaimed Michel. "China closets."

"Now then, children," said Mrs. Fairfield, bending toward them. "You'll never guess who's here to see you!"

"Father?" asked Adele. "But this is his house."

"Not your father, he's at his foundry, no, it's someone you've been longing to see. You sent a letter to her and instead of writing back she came in person."

Adele and Michel stared at each other, eyes wide. "Amina!" they cried in unison.

"Take us to her, Mrs. Fairfield," urged Adele.

Mrs. Fairfield chuckled indulgently. "She's in the parlor. Come along and we'll go to her."

How wonderful for the children to see their old nurse. They were so excited they could barely contain themselves.

Mari followed Mrs. Fairfield and the children to the parlor where a woman and man sat on the sofa, reading an almanac together.

When the twins saw their nurse they started running, greeting her with arms thrown around her waist, burying their heads under her arms.

"Amina, *ç'est toi! Tu es venu nous trouver!*"

Amina hugged them. "In English please. I've been practicing my English," she said in a thick French accent. "And it's not Amina anymore, I'm Mrs. Shriver."

She gently detached the children from around her waist.

"You're married?" asked Adele.

"This is my husband, Mr. Shriver."

"Pleased to meet you," said Mr. Shriver. He was a distinguished-looking gentleman with dark hair and a noble nose.

"And this is Miss Perkins," said Mrs. Fairfield. "The children's governess."

Mrs. Shriver smiled glowingly. "I've heard wonderful things about you from Mrs. Fairfield. I'm so glad the children are in good hands."

"I've heard wonderful things about you as well," Mari said warmly.

"We didn't know you had a sweetheart," said Adele to her former nurse.

"Mr. Shriver and I have known each other for a very long time." Mrs. Shriver blushed prettily. "But it wasn't until after you left that he asked me to marry him."

Mr. Shriver clasped her hands in his. "My love, my one true love."

The two of them gazed into each other's eyes, seeming to forget there was anyone else in the room.

"Ew," said Michel. "Romance. I'll never fall in love."

"Never say never," said Mari.

"Isn't that true," said Mrs. Shriver. "Look at me, I didn't get married until fifty years of age. Have you ever heard of such a thing?"

"Are you fifty, my dear?" Mr. Shriver stared at her adoringly. "And here I thought you were thirty-five."

"Oh you." She swatted his arm playfully. "Mr.

Shriver is a horse breeder. We're here in London on our *lune de miel*, er . . ."

"Honeymoon," supplied Adele.

"Yes, our honeymoon. That's what he told me. But really, I think we're here to watch the Derby."

"What kind of horses do you breed?" asked Mari.

"Arabians. Would you like to see my race horses someday?" Mr. Shriver asked the twins.

"Would we," said Michel enthusiastically.

The children were obviously in good hands, and this was Mari's off day. She slipped out of the room quietly. She loved those children dearly, but they were exhausting sometimes. The long carriage ride filled with questions and conversation had tired her out and she needed to prepare for her meeting with Mr. Shadwell.

He'd said to bring anything she might have to support her claim. That meant P.L., and the prayer book, and perhaps she should compose a timeline to present him of everything Mrs. Crowley had told her about the circumstances of her arrival at the orphanage when she was only a babe.

She'd just gathered everything and was beginning to compose the timeline when there was a knock at her chamber door.

"Yes?" she called.

Carl opened the door. "Someone to see you, Miss Perkins."

"Thank you, Carl. Who is it?"

"A Mrs. Trilby, miss."

Mari's body went numb. "Please tell her I'll be down in a moment," she said, her voice coming from somewhere far away.

"Yes, miss."

Mari gathered the prayer book and P.L. Rabbit and placed them in her cloth bag. Whatever happened, she had to keep her appointment with Mr. Shadwell.

She donned her coat and bonnet and descended the stairs to meet her doom.

Chapter 30

❧

When Edgar arrived home that afternoon, his house was in a state of chaos but he supposed that was to be expected. Mari and the children were home now. The house wouldn't echo with silence when he walked through the halls.

It would echo with laughter.

He couldn't wait to find Mari and tell her the fantastic news. Finally, *finally* the engine was lightweight enough. The new boiler design they had forged was working perfectly, the ribbing giving it the strength and resiliency it needed to withstand the high steam pressure.

And then there was the other matter.

The matter of the engagement band burning a hole in the pocket of his waistcoat.

An ostentatious band of diamonds that the jeweler had assured him was fit for a duchess . . . but probably not fit for Mari. She was simply too unique. Too utterly herself to follow the dictates of fashion.

He'd have another ring commissioned later—a simple setting would be best. Perhaps a twist of gold with one ruby to match her hair.

He'd been searching for this meaning, this feeling, throwing himself into his work, groping blindly, and then Mari had happened.

Their night at the seashore hadn't been a mindless coupling.

It had been strong, true, honest . . . and it had changed him.

He'd opened his heart to her, told her his sordid history and she'd accepted him for the flawed, bitter man he was. And her acceptance . . . her love . . . was everything he'd ever wanted.

He'd never be able to put those walls back up.

His heart twisted. But what if she didn't love him? Or, worse, what if she only thought she loved him, but it was a mere infatuation and would fade quickly?

She might wake up one day and find herself married to stubborn old him, with two half-grown children, and feel trapped.

These were the thoughts chasing each other around his head like a hound chasing its tail as he entered the house, only to find everything in an uproar.

"What's happening, Robertson?" he asked.

"I'll let Mrs. Fairfield tell you, Your Grace. I don't understand it at all."

"Your Grace," Mrs. Fairfield wailed, appearing in the doorway. "They've taken her."

Michel and Adele came running down the stairs. "Bring her back, Father!" cried Adele.

"They can't just take our governess," said Michel, his face stormy and fists by his side.

"Slow down, please," said Edgar. "You're not making sense, any of you. Taken her where? Someone please tell me what has happened."

Mrs. Fairfield stared at him, splotches of color on her cheeks. "That horrible Mrs. Trilby from the governess agency came to the house today with a constable. The same one who brought the children home that day. They escorted Miss Perkins away. She went willingly. I've no idea why."

"That mean old constable. He's just sore because I popped him with my slingshot. I would have had another go at him, if it had been in my pocket," said Michel fiercely.

"We shouldn't have let her go," said Adele.

"It must all be a terrible misunderstanding," said Mrs. Fairfield.

"That's exactly what this is," Edgar said, his mind immediately rejecting any other possibility. "A terrible misunderstanding."

"Father?" Adele pulled on his hand.

"Yes, love?"

"She took her cloth bag, and her umbrella, and P.L. Rabbit. That means . . ." Her lip wobbled. "That means she's never coming back."

"Hush." He tilted up Adele's chin. "Of course she's coming back."

He reached out his hand and Robertson handed him his hat.

"Go and fetch her back, Your Grace," said Robertson. "We're all relying on you."

"There's nothing to worry about," said Edgar. "I promise you I'll bring her back."

"THIS PERSON MISREPRESENTED herself to a duke," said Mrs. Trilby. "She claimed to be from my agency. It's libel and slander and she ought to be locked away. Surely there's a law against it, sir."

Mari had followed Mrs. Trilby and the constable to a nearby police station. It was better to have everything out in the open, though she hoped Edgar didn't find any of this out until she had a chance to tell him herself.

She'd been going to tell him the truth, directly after her meeting with Mr. Shadwell today.

"There's no law against lying, madam," said the chief constable. "If it harms no one."

"His Grace will vouch for my service being exemplary," Mari said.

"Oh I'm sure he will, you wicked, wanton creature." Mrs. Trilby rounded on the constable, her shoulders shaking with outrage. "When the Earl of Haddock informed me that one of my governesses had . . . had *seduced* a duke and was living with him in flagrant sin, in front of his children. Well! It's my reputation that suffers, sir. And she isn't one of my governesses. I took one look at her and knew the truth. She's soiled and . . . and not superior in the least."

Haddock. She should have known. He'd found a way to hurt her after all.

"No law against tupping a duke, madam," the constable said in an exasperated tone. "Now, I do have other, more pressing matters to attend to." He turned to Mari. "Miss Perkins, you're free to leave now. Apologies for your trouble."

"This is an outrage!" said Mrs. Trilby. "The good name of my agency sullied in such a manner. Of course the duke won't prosecute her. She has ensorcelled him with her favors."

She'd been branded a scarlet woman now, in front of a constable, and she hadn't even been able to muster the will to deny it, because it was true.

"Mrs. Trilby, I do apologize for misrepresenting myself to the duke, but you did promise me a position, and I was desperate. I had nowhere else to go, no one else to turn to, and no money. You threw me out onto the street."

"Do not speak to me, you shameless girl. Mrs.

Crowley must be turning over in her grave. To think a pupil from her school, one of her girls, behaved in such a manner. It's unthinkable."

"Mrs. Crowley hated me and would no doubt feel vindicated by this turn of events."

"There, you see?" said Mrs. Trilby to the constable. "She doesn't even dispute that she's living in sin with that devil of a duke."

The constable sighed. "Mrs. Trilby, it seems to me that the only way anyone will know if one of your governesses might be, shall we say, intimate with her employer, will be if you tell them. So I suggest you keep your mouth closed, and all will be well."

Mari was beginning to like this constable.

"I came here willingly," Mari said, "so that you might hear my side of the story. But I really must be going now. I have an appointment with a lawyer."

"You can't just let her leave, sir!" insisted Mrs. Trilby. "I demand that you charge her with defamation and fraudulent misrepresentation."

There was the sound of raised voices from the outer room. The constable perked up instantly. "Do you hear that, ladies? I've got to go. Important goings-on. Come along now, both of you, Mrs. Trilby. Miss Perkins."

Mrs. Trilby was forced to follow after the constable.

Mari walked behind them. The shouting grew louder as they walked down the hallway.

A furious male voice, deep and unmistakable.

"What have you done with my governess?" Edgar roared.

He stood in the center of the room, an immense, glowering monstrosity of a knight in shining armor. But would he defend her honor when he knew the truth? That she was in his house under false pretenses. That she'd deceived him.

The clerk at the desk clapped his hands together. "Here she is, Your Grace. You see? We're returning her to you."

"Mari." He strode toward her, eyes steely and handsome face worried. "Did anyone touch you? Look at you the wrong way? Because if they did, I'll have this entire station shut down."

"I'm unharmed," said Mari.

"She came willingly, Your Grace," said the now anxious-looking constable. "She was treated with respect."

Mrs. Trilby made a disgusted noise in the back of her throat. "Respect? She's unfit to be serving in your household, Your Grace. She's an orphan. A charity girl of unknown origins. She lied to you. She's not from my agency at all. She's . . ."

"Mrs. Trilby, I presume?" Edgar gave her the exact same look of dismissive, aristocratic disdain that his mother had used on Mari.

Mrs. Trilby swallowed. "Yes, Your Grace."

"Please know one thing, Mrs. Trilby. I don't care where she came from, or what she's done. She could be the leader of the most notorious gang of cutthroats in this city and I would defend her honor, do I make myself understood?"

The butterflies returned to Mari's stomach in droves. His conviction took her breath away. "Thank you," she said, wanting to touch him but holding herself in check.

Mrs. Trilby pursed her lips. "You can't honestly mean to say that you don't care about the qualifications of your servants. She misrepresented herself.

It's a slanderous outrage on the sterling reputation of my agency and I will—"

"You will be quiet, you awful woman." Edgar stood at his full height, every inch the commanding, arrogant duke his gate would have society believe him to be. "You're the one slandering my future duchess."

Wait. His *what*?

"Your what?" Mari asked.

Mrs. Trilby's jaw flapped open. "You can't be serious."

"Oh I'm deadly serious," he said. "I have a ring in my waistcoat pocket."

He did? Their eyes met, and Mari saw the truth there.

"But, but . . ." sputtered Mrs. Trilby. "Dukes don't marry governesses."

"No buts, Mrs. Trilby," said Mari in grand, trilling tones. She walked imperiously to Edgar and slid her arm through his. "Good day to you, Mrs. Trilby."

And she stuck her nose in the air, as any future duchess might, and sailed out of the room on the duke's arm.

And she didn't stop sailing grandly until they reached his carriage. Then her shoulders deflated, as if she'd been a hot air balloon descending from the sky.

"That was a very nice thing to do, Edgar. But I know you don't really want to marry me."

"Yes, I do."

She sighed. "You just think you do, because you're so honorable and you'll do the right thing by me, as you did by your children. Not because it fits with your life, but because it's the right thing to do. And that's no reason to be married."

His face closed up, just as it had when his mother walked in the room during Lady India's antiquities exhibition. She'd wounded him, which was all for the best.

She'd been hiding too much from him.

This love was a double-sided coin, forged by sadness.

One side of the coin, love, longing, and hope. The other side, the keen edge of loss and the bitter taste of tears.

Oh she would shed tears. So many tears. When this ended. When she could never see Michel and Adele again. When she was banned from their sight. When he wed another.

She laid a hand on his arm. "I release you from any obligation. Now if you'll just convey me to Cheapside, I'm late for an appointment with a lawyer."

"I don't want to be released from any obligations," Edgar protested.

"I know what you're thinking," Mari said. "You're wondering if everything Mrs. Trilby said about me is true. Well, it's all true."

ACTUALLY, EDGAR HAD been thinking about how beautiful she was. About the way her skin glowed from within with a light that was all her own.

"I . . . deceived you," said Mari. "I was going to tell you today, after my meeting with the lawyer. There are unknown circumstances about me and my life and I was hoping to find some answers before I had the conversation with you."

The easy rapport they'd shared at the seashore was gone.

Forever? No, he refused to believe that.

"What are the unknown circumstances?" he asked.

"I never wanted to lie to you. Everything I've told you was as close to the truth as possible. I said that I never knew my mother and that my father was a distant figure. I'm an orphan, Edgar. Raised in a charity school."

"Why didn't you just tell me? Did you honestly think that I would have turned you out for being educated at a charity school?"

"The man I met in your library on that first day was looking for any excuse to throw me out."

"Mari, I didn't know you then. So much has happened. I've changed. You've changed me—"

"I lack the requirements for governess to a duke," she interrupted, her tone formal and wooden. "I wasn't educated in an elite school. I'm not of good family, I don't even know my parentage."

"But I don't understand. How did you find out about the position if you didn't possess the qualifications for it?"

"I came to London because I'd been promised a position as governess to a tradesperson with a large brood of children. My trunk was stolen at the coaching inn and I was fifteen minutes late for my appointment with Mrs. Trilby. She threw me out into the street and refused to offer any assistance. I was desperate. Alone and friendless in an unfamiliar city."

"I'll close down her agency," Edgar promised. "She can't get away with treating people like that."

Mari placed a hand on his arm. "I'm the one who acted wrongly. I overheard Miss Dunkirk telling Mrs. Trilby that she'd left your household. I saw my opportunity and I seized it."

He took a deep breath. "So you blustered your way into my house and you're of uncertain parentage. As I've said before, you're not a typical governess. Just as I'm not an ordinary duke. Don't forget that I left the aristocracy for seven years and lived as a foundry worker."

"I know, Edgar, I know. You're nothing like I thought you would be. You're not unyielding or arrogant. But right now, can you please take me to Cheapside? I'm already late for my appointment with the lawyer. I may learn the truth about my origins today. This could change everything. For better . . . or for worse."

He'd take her anywhere she wanted to go. He'd take her to the Archbishop for a special license, if she'd let him. But the urgency in her voice made him realize that this appointment with the lawyer was extremely important to her.

He gave the instructions to the coachman and climbed into the carriage. They would sort everything out. This couldn't be the way things ended.

As they neared the lawyer's offices, Mari's shoulders tensed.

"Are you anxious?" he asked.

"Terrified. I've thought about this moment for so many years. Imagined so many possibilities."

He clasped her hand. "I'm here with you. We'll face this together, whatever it turns out to be."

MARI STARED AT the carpet. She hadn't noticed it when she'd been here before, but now she stared at the pattern in a daze. Gold ornamental urns strung together with garlands of red and blue roses. *Blue* roses?

"What did you just say, Mr. Shadwell?" she asked.

"Mr. Lumley of Lumley's Toy Shop is your father, Miss Perkins. Or, should I say, Miss Lumley."

Edgar leaned forward in his chair. "Are you quite sure, Mr. Shadwell?"

Mr. Shadwell raised his thick white eyebrows. "Do I appear to be a jesting sort of fellow? Does anything about my demeanor give you the least indication that I might play pranks? I know my son is—there's no delicate way of putting it—a sot. But I can assure you that the apple fell far, far from the tree."

Edgar glanced at Mari. She was happy to have him there. He was such a strong, steadying presence.

She gathered her wits and took a deep breath. "Am I of legitimate birth?" Mari asked the lawyer.

"You are."

"And my mother?"

"Deceased. I can tell you no more than that. You must ask your father, Mr. Lumley, for more particulars. I am permitted to tell you, however, that you are his sole heir. Which means," Mr. Shadwell cleared his throat, "you are an heiress of considerable fortune."

Blue roses danced before her eyes. Legitimate and an heiress. She raised her head. Edgar was gazing at her with a tender smile on his lips.

He rose from his seat and offered her his arm. "Shall we go to the toy shop, Miss Lumley? I believe you have a fortune to claim."

Her head swimming, Mari said her goodbyes.

"Can it be true?" she asked Edgar as he helped her into the waiting carriage.

"We'll soon find out."

"A fortune," she whispered.

A fortune . . . and a family.

"That's right." Mr. Shadwell nodded. "And you, Miss Perkins, are an heiress."

Chapter 31

THE BELL TINKLED as Mari and Edgar entered Lumley's Toy Shop.

The shop clerk met them at the door and bowed. "Your Grace. Miss Perkins."

"Are you back so soon, Your Grace?" Mr. Lumley called from the counter. "How was the seashore? Have you brought the children for another game of chess?"

Mari hesitated, holding back from entering the shop.

"Go to him," Edgar whispered in her ear, taking her hand.

"What if . . . what if he doesn't know me? What if I'm not his daughter? What if Mr. Shadwell has everything wrong." *She couldn't bear it. This sudden, all-consuming hope ripped away.*

"Go to him," he urged. "You can do this." He squeezed her hand and his touch gave her strength.

She walked toward the counter. "It's just me and the duke, Mr. Lumley. We've just been to see a lawyer named Mr. Arthur Shadwell and he told us the most extraordinary news."

"Mr. Shadwell, you say? The lawyer in Cheapside?" Mr. Lumley turned his face toward Mari.

Could he be her father? He must have been much older than her mother.

Edgar handed her the cloth bag and she laid it on the shop counter and extracted P.L. Rabbit. "When I was a babe, I was left at the Underwood Orphanage and Charity School in Derbyshire. This rabbit was left with me."

Mr. Lumley's fingers moved over the rabbit. "She's wearing a green velvet dress."

The tremor in his hands increased as he slid them across the counter toward Mari.

He touched her hand. "You were left at Underwood, Miss Perkins?"

"I was."

"You have red hair." His hand lifted to her hair. "You said she has freckles, Your Grace?"

"She does," Edgar replied, moving closer to them. "Scattered like golden stars across her nose and cheeks."

Mr. Lumley removed his spectacles. "Your mother had freckles and auburn hair."

"Was her name Ann Murray?" asked Mari.

"Ann?" Mr. Lumley frowned. "No, her name was Pauline."

"How strange," said Mari. "There was a prayer book left with me at the orphanage inscribed with the name Ann Murray."

"You were born at a nunnery," said Mr. Lumley. "The prayer book must have belonged to another woman. Your mother's name was Pauline, but I called her Clover, because of the color of her eyes. Do you have green eyes, my dear?"

"My eyes are blue," she said. "Like yours."

Tears streamed down Mr. Lumley's face. Mari's cheeks were wet as well.

"I didn't know about you until three years ago," he said. "Or I would have searched for you sooner. Why did the headmistress at the school tell Mr. Shadwell that you had died of a fever?"

"She hated me. It was only on her deathbed that she repented of her falsehood and called me to her side to tell me the truth."

"And then you came here to London."

"To find you."

"I learned of your birth from your grandmother. It's a very sad tale. Pauline and I ran off to Gretna Green to marry because her parents opposed the match. She was younger than I, but we were very much in love. She was highborn, and I was only a toy maker."

Mari took his hand. "That's a good reason for running away."

"Her parents pursued us. They wanted to stop the wedding but they were too late. We were married and we consummated our marriage that night. They abducted their own daughter the very next day."

"I don't understand," Mari said. "Why would they do that?"

"To keep the marriage secret. I thought they'd hidden Pauline away in Scotland somewhere. I searched and searched for my bride with no success. By the time I returned to London, they told me that she had died in a carriage accident."

He broke down then, sobs wracking his body. Edgar gave him his handkerchief.

"I only found out recently that when they learned Pauline was with child, they sent her to a nunnery. She died in childbirth. And you were given to Underwood, with one of my wooden rabbits. The one I had given to Pauline as a wedding gift."

Her mother had died giving birth to her. So many conflicting emotions churned in her chest. Sadness for the mother she'd never known; astonishment at discovering she had a father.

Mr. Lumley patted her hand. "I only wish I'd found

out sooner. I gather from Mr. Shadwell that Underwood was a very somber sort of place. No place for a daughter of mine. I would have filled your childhood with laughter and with love."

"I know," said Mari. "I know you would have."

Edgar smiled. "I had very similar feelings, Lumley, when the twins arrived on my doorstep. I would have given them everything if I'd known about them."

"I've no other children," said Mari's father. "I never remarried. You have some distant cousins, though, my dear."

"And I have grandparents in London?" she asked.

"I can't tell you their names. It's better if you think of them as being dead."

"I understand," said Mari. "You're all I need. You are more than I ever thought I'd have."

"Isn't it extraordinary?" She turned to Edgar. "I've finally found my family."

EDGAR NODDED, BECAUSE that's what she wanted him to do. Because that's what he should do.

He should be happy for her. This *was* extraordinary and miraculous.

She'd found the truth about her past. Except he had a bad, ungrateful feeling in his chest. A hard knot of doubt and hurt.

I thought you'd already found a family, he wanted to say. *I thought you belonged with me and with the twins.*

You're all I need, she'd said. To her father.

Not to Edgar.

"How good of you to bring her here, Your Grace," said Lumley. "She's your governess. And you'll be losing her."

"Losing her," he repeated, the hollow feeling in his chest growing stronger by the second.

Mari didn't correct him. Didn't tell Lumley that she was more than just his governess. She was his lover. He'd hoped she might want to become his bride.

Maybe she didn't need him now. Didn't want him.

Lumley and Mari were still talking. Something about how much money she would inherit and how she could live in luxury from this day forth. The toy business must be going well. His shop was one of the oldest in London.

"Why, you're an heiress now, my dear," said Lumley with a wide smile. "I hear heiresses are much in demand on the marriage mart these days, with all of these titled gentlemen falling on lean times. We should be able to find you a perfectly respectable husband."

Mari laughed. "Now you're getting ahead of yourself. I don't want a respectable husband."

She didn't want a husband.

He'd never even considered it. Had he just assumed that she would want to marry him because he was a duke and she was a governess?

Edgar was disgusted by his own selfishness. He'd assumed things he shouldn't have.

Maybe he shouldn't even be here. This was a private family moment between Mari and her father.

"Close the shop, Tom," called Lumley to the clerk.

"Sir?" Tom approached.

"Tom, I want you to meet my daughter . . . what's your Christian name, my dear? I never asked you."

"It's Mari."

"It rhymes with starry," said Edgar, too softly for them to hear.

"It's a very nice name," said Lumley. "And my name is John."

"Your daughter? I didn't know you had a daughter," said Tom, gaping at Mari.

"Neither did I." Lumley smiled. "Isn't it wonderful?"

Mari's eyes brimmed with tears and happiness.

"I should be going back home," said Edgar.

"Oh of course," Mari said. "Well I'll be back tonight to see the children and tell them the news in person."

He nodded and drifted away quietly. Mari didn't stop him from leaving. She'd already forgotten about him, it seemed.

She didn't want a husband and, even if she did, why would she want one like him? Someone as starry-eyed and filled with hope and conviction as she could never be happy with someone like him.

One night hadn't made the darkness recede forever.

Outside on the street, Edgar lifted his face to the fine drizzle of rain that had begun while they were inside the shop.

He'd promised the children he would bring her back. He'd lied.

He couldn't go home, couldn't face them just yet.

He gave the coachman instructions to a house he'd never visited before.

The dowager duchess's apartments in Mayfair.

"BANKSFORD? TO WHAT do I owe this dubious honor?"

"Hello Mother."

"Why are you here?"

Mari had suggested that he visit his mother in her own home. She wasn't happy to see him, that much was obvious. "May I sit?" he asked.

His mother narrowed her eyes. "You may sit, but I will stand."

Edgar sighed. It had been a mistake to come here. "I didn't come to fight with you, Mother."

"Then why come at all? After what happened at India's antiquities exhibition I didn't think I'd see you for another decade, or so."

Edgar closed his eyes. "I came to apologize. You probably don't believe that, but it's the truth. I understand that I caused you great anguish by my actions. When I challenged Father, and then when I disappeared. I'm sorry."

She was silent. He opened his eyes.

"Are you well?" she asked. "Because you don't sound like my son."

"I don't feel like him. I'm weary of this enmity, these dark, sad memories. I want to make things right. I want to make amends."

The dowager sank into a chair. "I never thought I'd hear you say such words."

"I never thought I'd say them."

"What has changed? Or, perhaps I should ask, who has changed you? Wait." She held up her hand. "I know. It's that Miss Perkins. I saw the way you gazed at her. You're besotted with the governess."

There was rancor in her voice, not gentleness. She must be thinking of the times her husband had become infatuated with their servants.

"This is different, Mother. I love her with all my heart. I mean to marry her, if she'll have me."

His mother's face remained impassive. "I see. And you've come to seek my blessing."

"No, I came to apologize. I realize now that I should have found a less public way to confront Father. Challenging him to a duel was reckless and wrong and cost you so much pain."

For the very first time, his mother's careful mask of aristocratic composure slipped away.

Was she going to cry? Edgar reached for his handkerchief and realized he'd left it with Lumley. There was no precedent for this moment.

He'd never seen his mother's face twisted with emotion. Not even when his father had hit her.

She lifted her eyes to the ceiling, obviously fighting back tears. "I've had many years to think this through, Edgar. And I've come to the conclusion that you did what you had to do."

"It was wrong to challenge him so publicly."

"Perhaps, but someone needed to make him pay for what he'd done. I didn't like it, Edgar. I hated the scandal. But the things he did . . . I should have fought harder. I should have been strong enough to protect my children. Sometimes I think I should have . . . I should have been the one to challenge him." Her hands tightened into fists. "I fantasized so many times about putting a bullet through his heart. But I never did anything."

Now Edgar was the one struggling not to cry. "It wasn't your fault. He was stronger than you."

"I should have taken you and India and left. But I stayed."

Edgar sank to his knees in front of her chair and caught her thin blue-veined hand in his. "I don't blame you. And I don't blame myself anymore. I've decided to stop wallowing in the past. I'm moving forward. I'm seeking the light. And there is light to find, I know it. I've seen it."

His mother laid her hand on top of his. "Miss Perkins, I presume?"

Edgar smiled. "Her name is Mari. It rhymes with starry."

The dowager gave a small snort. "I can see there's nothing to be done. You'd better marry the girl."

Edgar gaped at his mother. Those were the last words he'd ever expected her to say. "What did you say?"

"Marry that girl. She's got more spirit in her little finger than all the debutantes in London put together."

"She does, doesn't she?"

"Then what are you talking to me for? Go win your fiery Miss Perkins."

"That's just it. She's not Miss Perkins."

"What do you mean?"

"She was raised in an orphanage, and she just found out that she's the legitimate offspring of Mr. Lumley, of Lumley's Toy Shop."

"Legitimate, you say?"

"And an heiress with a considerable fortune. Also, her mother was highborn, though Lumley won't divulge the family name."

"Well." The dowager nodded. "That does change things. She may even pass muster."

Edgar bristled. "She's far superior to any other woman."

His mother patted his arm. "Of course she is."

"The only question is whether she'll have me. Maybe she doesn't need me anymore. She's independent now, an heiress. It's not too late for her to make some sort of debut in society. She's only twenty. She would attract suitors, Lord knows."

"Are you trying to tell me that my son, the Duke of Banksford, might lose out to some minor baronet or the like? Pure twaddle!"

"Mother, I have to let her make up her own mind, I can't pressure her."

"Have you been intimate with the girl?"

"Yes," he admitted. It wasn't exactly a topic one expected to discuss with one's mother.

They'd consummated their relationship, but he didn't want to trap her into marriage by using that, if she didn't want to marry him.

He'd been careful. There was no reason to think she could be with child.

"Then it's a special license," his mother announced. "You'll be married within the month. I'll see to everything. Go now."

"Mother, I can't simply assume that she wants to marry me."

"You'll never know whether she wants to marry you or not unless you ask her. You're a fool, Edgar. As stubborn as an ox."

That sounded more like the mother he knew. "What if she only thinks she loves me? She's so young. She has her whole life ahead of her. I might be a millstone around her neck."

"Edgar. Listen to yourself. You're talking about what happened with you and that Sophie woman. This is completely different."

Maybe that was true. Mari kept telling him to trust that she knew her own mind. If he asked her to marry him, and she said yes . . . he would believe that she meant it.

"You're right, Mother."

"I generally am."

"I have a ring." He pulled the diamond band from his pocket.

"Oh that won't do," said his mother. "Too vulgar. Wait here a moment."

She left the room but then returned almost immediately. "Take this instead." She held something that glinted gold in the lamplight. "My wedding ring. I removed it the very same evening that he . . . that he shot you." Her jaw clenched. "I never wore it again.

I loved that ring when he gave it to me. I know you might find this difficult to believe but there was a time, a long, long time ago, when we were happy together."

Edgar had never heard her say anything like that. All he'd seen was the conflict. The drinking. The silent suffering.

"He changed so swiftly," she said. "The devil took him. Here." She shoved the ring forward. "I want you to have this."

He accepted the ring. It was a simple gold band with a brilliant red ruby in the center, ringed by small diamonds.

It was perfect. The ruby would match Mari's hair.

"She said she would return to the house tonight, to tell the news to the children in person," said Edgar.

"Then home you go. And Banksford?"

"Yes, Mother."

She drew herself up. "Don't you dare come back until I have a wedding to plan."

Anything broken may be mended. While we breathe there is yet hope.

He and his mother had actually talked to one another as people, not as symbols of past hatred, past fear.

Mari had been right about everything.

He climbed into his carriage with hope soaring through his heart.

He had a goddess to propose to tonight.

The only problem was that he was merely a duke.

Chapter 32

❧

"**W**HAT'S WRONG?" MARI asked when Robertson answered the door at Number Seventeen later that evening. The butler's face was even more somber than usual.

"The children are missing again, Miss Perkins. And they're not hiding in any of their usual haunts."

"We've searched everywhere." Edgar strode toward her, his face lined with worry.

"It's my fault," wailed Mrs. Fairfield, following at his heels. "I shouldn't have brought their former nurse here. They think she abandoned them yet again."

"No, it's my doing," said Edgar, his eyes bleak. "I came home and I told them your news, and then I was called back to the foundry, and—"

"What did you tell them?" Mari asked urgently. "Edgar, what did you tell them?"

"I told them that Lumley was your father and that you were an heiress and that you wouldn't be their governess any longer."

Mrs. Fairfield gaped at him. "What's that you said?"

Mari staggered. "Edgar. I was going to tell them the news of my birth in my own way."

"Miss Perkins? What's this?" asked Mrs. Fairfield. "You're an heiress?"

"I'll tell you the whole story later, after we find the children," she said.

"They're not in the park," said Edgar. "Nor any of the nearby parks. I even went to the church of St. Mary-le-Bow, because Sophie had written a poem about it. No one has seen them." His eyes glittered with tears. "Where are they? Mari, we have to find them."

She nodded reassuringly. "We'll find them. Don't worry. Have you searched the nursery?"

"Of course, dear," said Mrs. Fairfield. "That's the first place we looked."

"Not for the twins," Mari explained. "I mean for a note. I don't think they would just leave without telling anyone. Not anymore." She trusted them not to do that. Even if they were hurt by her news.

"You're right," said Edgar.

They climbed the stairs together.

"I should have let you tell them, only it was weighing on me so, and I thought . . ." Edgar cast his gaze away from her. "I thought if I told them early, they might persuade you to stay, for a time."

"I never told you I was going anywhere, did I?"

He looked taken aback. "But . . . you have a new family now. You don't need us."

"What are you talking about?" asked Mari.

"You said you'd found your family. That you didn't want a husband."

There he went again, making her heart skip a beat. "I said I didn't want a *respectable* husband, if you'll recall. Now stop talking foolishness. We have to find the children."

They searched the nursery, turning over toys, and thumbing through books.

"Edgar." She pointed at the blackboard. "Look. Hidden in plain sight."

The message was scrawled across the blackboard in Adele's girlish handwriting.

We're going to Lumley's Toy Shop. We need Miss Perkins more than he needs her. Signed, Adele and Michel Rochester.

"I need you, too," she whispered. The twins loved her and she loved them. She had so much love to give. And now she realized that she deserved affection in return. "Right, then," she said, sniffing back her tears. "Best foot forward. No time to waste. Back to my father's shop."

"But didn't you just leave there?" asked Edgar.

"We dined in a restaurant several streets away from the shop. We must have missed the children's arrival."

In the carriage, Edgar slipped his arm around her and Mari rested her head on his shoulder.

It was enough right now to be back in his arms.

To know that the children loved her. Whatever happened, she wanted to be in their lives in some way.

The ride was brief to High Holborn Street, but the carriage rolled to a halt before they reached the shop.

Edgar alighted. "What's happening?" Mari heard him ask the coachman.

"Blockade," the coachman replied.

Mari stepped down from the carriage. The air was crisp and cold and there was a smell of smoke on the air.

"What's the matter?" she asked Edgar.

The coachman pointed at smoke billowing in the distance. Mari noticed, for the first time, that there was a snarl of carriages and carts, all barred from making their way farther on Holborn.

"Go back," a man shouted at them. "It's a fire."

At the words, a sinking fear gripped Mari. "A fire?" "Where?" Edgar shouted back.

"Lumley's Toy Shop, I think," called the man, shaking his head. "Would be a shame for all those toys to be lost."

Mari's heart stopped.

Edgar raced to the constable who was blocking the way. "Let us pass," he cried. "My children are in Lumley's Toy Shop."

"No one's getting through, sir. The street's blocked except to the fire brigades, when they ever decide to arrive."

"The fire brigades," Edgar muttered. "I don't trust those bumblers to fill my bathwater."

He addressed Mari. "Stay in the carriage where you'll be safe. I'm going to the foundry to fetch my fire engine. It's the quickest way to put out the blaze. Grafton will still be there. He'll help. We'll be back before you know it."

"Go," she said. "Hurry, please."

"It's a stone building, Mari. There's time."

The coachman helped him unhitch one of the horses from the carriage. He leapt onto the horse and galloped away into the night.

Mari shivered with cold and fear. She couldn't just sit there, waiting for him.

The carriage might not be able to pass through, but she could, if she made herself less visible.

She removed her velvet bonnet with the blue plumage and stepped down from the carriage.

"I need your cloak," she said to the coachman.

He surrendered it without a protest.

She shrugged into the long blue greatcoat, pulling the collar up over her cheeks.

And then she darted into the shadows.

She must reach the toy shop. She must save the children.

Chapter 33

ᔕ

THE TOY SHOP wasn't burning.

But it would be soon, if the fire at the bookseller's next door wasn't brought under control.

The sound of the flames crackled and popped in Mari's ears.

A window shattered. She could see books burning inside the stone building.

She didn't think the children were in any immediate danger. Surely her father had been able to remove them to safety when the fire broke out next door. Unless he hadn't found the children in the shop.

What if they'd fallen asleep in the shop and he hadn't noticed them? The thought chilled her, despite the heat emanating from the fire.

Edgar had better hurry.

She searched the length of the street. The fire brigade was just arriving with its engine drawn by three horses. Onlookers were gathered in knots outside of the houses across the street from Lumley's. She walked among them, searching for the children.

"Do something," Mari yelled at the men of the fire brigade, who were milling about purposelessly.

"Not our building, miss," one of them replied.

"What did you mean, not your building?" she asked.

"Our company didn't insure the bookshop. We'll

wait and make sure the flames don't spread to one of our buildings."

"They're going to spread if you don't put them out."

The man shrugged. "Another brigade will be here soon."

Mari stalked down the street, so furious she could barely see straight. Edgar was right. The fire brigade system needed to change.

"Miss Perkins," a thin little voice called.

She stopped walking and spun around.

Adele flung herself into Mari's arms. Mari wrapped her arms around her, crooning softly. "Sweetheart, you're safe."

Michel and her father came next, hand in hand.

"We were so worried," said Mari. "So worried. Don't ever leave again, do you understand?"

"I thought you were the one who was leaving," said Adele.

"I'm not going anywhere."

"Where's the duke?" asked her father.

"He'll be here any moment. He thought your shop was burning and he's bringing his fire engine from the foundry. He's right, you know. These fire brigades are hopeless."

They watched from a safe distance as the fire brigade formed a line on either side of their decrepit old engine and the men on one side pulled down on their levers, while the men on the other side pushed up. But no water came out the end of the hose.

To Mari's dismay, the battered old hand pump engine shuddered, emitted a groaning, scraping noise, and stopped working altogether.

Next, the men formed a bucket line and began passing buckets of water but it was maddeningly slow, and wasn't doing anything to stop the fire's progress.

The scene was chaotic and confusing, with some men advocating for calling a different fire brigade, and others calling for more buckets.

Her father watched the blaze with worried eyes. "That's Mr. Brookfield's bookshop. I feel terrible for him."

"Why is that other fire brigade simply standing around watching?" she asked.

"They're from another insurance company," said her father. "See? The foreman has blue livery with the gold sun on it. They won't lift a finger until the fire threatens to spread to the buildings insured by their company."

Mari shook her head, disgusted by the whole thing.

The children watched, wide-eyed as the flames burned inside the tall stone building, licking through the ground floor. The fire could easily spread next door.

"Should we take the children away?" Mari asked her father.

"No." Michel shook his head. "I want to stay and watch Father fight the fire."

"He'd better hurry," said Mari's father.

Finally, Mari glimpsed Edgar's gleaming engine, pulled by one sleek chestnut horse, barreling down the road toward them. Grafton rode beside the engine on another horse.

"There he is," cried Mari.

THE FIRE BRIGADE tried to form a blockade to prevent Edgar from dismounting, but everything was too chaotic. There was too much shouting, and smoke and flames and men running everywhere.

"It's not Lumley's," said Grafton.

Thank Heaven. He was right. It was the bookstore

next door. But he'd seen no sign of Lumley or the children. He had to be certain that they were safe.

He tied a handkerchief firmly around his face. "Is anyone inside that bookstore?" he asked one of the brigade men.

"No, the bookseller left in time."

The flames were starting to spread into the second story, licking out the windows. He and Grafton had ridden as close to the water main as possible, while still being able to reach the fire with their hose.

"Let's go," Edgar said to Grafton. "They're not making any headway with those buckets. Not when it's reached the second story."

He leapt down and located the foreman of the Hand in Hand fire brigade.

Grafton stayed behind to unhitch the horses and remove them a safe distance, locking the forecarriage of the engine in place with a pin to prevent it moving.

It was Edgar's job to convince the fire brigade foreman to give him the socket to connect to the water main, because each parish had different ones.

"Give me the socket. You're not making much progress with those buckets," said Edgar.

"You can't fight this fire with no license, no company," said the man, glowering at Edgar.

"I don't have time for your politics. My children could be inside that toy shop. I'm not going to let the fire spread." Edgar grabbed the man's collar. "Now give me that socket or I'll take it by force."

The foreman reluctantly handed over the socket and Edgar sprinted back to help Grafton connect to the main, set up the hoses, and quickly raise steam pressure.

When everything was ready, Edgar handed the

gunmetal nozzle to Grafton. "You direct the stream. I'm going to find the children and make sure they're safe."

Grafton nodded. "Good luck."

Suddenly, Mari appeared from behind them, dressed improbably in the coachman's greatcoat, which hung down past her ankles and scraped on the ground.

Edgar caught her by the shoulders. "Mari, I told you to stay in the carriage."

"As if I would stay in a carriage when the twins were in danger."

"Have you seen them? Are they safe?"

"Quite safe." Mari gestured over her shoulder, and he saw Lumley and the children watching them.

He ran to them. Gathering the children into his arms, he kissed their cheeks.

"Father," Adele cried, clinging to him.

Michel shuffled his feet manfully.

"I was so worried about you," said Edgar. "I love you both so much. Never, ever run away again. Promise me."

"We promise," said Michel.

"They came to me," said Lumley, coughing slightly. "To tell me that they needed my Mari." He smiled at Mari. "I told them we could share her."

"Is that your engine?" asked Michel, pointing at Grafton where he was wrestling with the copper branch pipe.

"Yes, it is." Edgar rose. He caught Mari's eye, trying to communicate everything he hadn't had the chance to say yet.

That he loved her, as well. And he hoped she loved him.

"I'll be back soon," he said. "I've got a fire to fight."

He left the children with Mari and Lumley and ran back to Grafton. "Here," he shouted over the noise of falling debris and shouting men. "I'll man the boiler, you take the hose."

The flames were climbing higher now.

There was still time to save Lumley's shop but they must hurry.

"WHAT'S HAPPENING?" ASKED Mari's father, his face turned toward the blaze that was still smoldering, but greatly reduced now.

"Father is shoveling coal into the boiler," said Michel.

"And Mr. Grafton has hold of a copper hose nozzle and the water is shooting so high in the air," said Mari. "You wouldn't believe it."

The two men and their new kind of fire engine were the subject of much intense curiosity. Some in the crowd cheered them on, while others stood on the sidelines, arms crossed and faces grim.

Edgar worked tirelessly, sweat pouring from his brow. His shirt clung to his chest, displaying powerful muscles, as Grafton aimed the heavy stream of water at the still-smoldering bookshop.

"The fire's contained now," she told her father. "It won't spread to your shop."

His shoulders sagged. "That's very good news. Though I do feel sorry for poor Brookfield. I'll have to help him build his book collection again. Such rare volumes he had. What a tragedy."

"It could have been so much worse. I'm so glad you and the children are unharmed. You'll have to come home with us tonight to the duke's house in Grosvenor Square."

"Do come back with us, Mr. Lumley," said Adele. "We can read you some of our stories about P.L. Rabbit."

"Does she have many adventures?" he asked.

"Does she!" Adele glanced at Michel and the two of them grinned. "She's a pirate rabbit."

"She's an Arctic explorer," said Michel. "She speaks ten languages."

"And she and Sir Peter Teazle won the Derby," explained Adele. "We write new adventures for P.L. every day in our journals."

"Did you now?" Her father laughed. "That's not a bad idea, you know."

"What's that?" Mari asked.

"A series of stories about my wooden rabbit. We already have books that come with little toys, like tops and jacks, but we don't have a little book that comes with a big toy."

"It's brilliant," pronounced Mari.

"We'll write the stories," said Adele.

Grafton finally threw down the hose and Edgar joined him beside the engine. Mari could see them talking with the fire brigade foreman. The flames were almost completely doused.

The bucket line began again, to subdue the last of the fire.

Grafton dismantled the hoses while Edgar walked back to them.

"You did it, Father," said Michel, running to meet him.

The two of them walked back together.

"There's going to be quite a fight over our illegal use of a fire engine with no insurance company to back it. Luckily, I'm a duke," said Edgar. "And also, luckily, the engine works. And it beats the devil out of buckets."

"Your fire engines will save so many buildings, and so many lives. I'm so proud of you," said Mari, her heart swelling with joy. Now he just had to build that railway.

"Are you?" he asked, his eyes soft in the near darkness.

Soot was streaked across the strong lines of his face, and his hair fell into his eyes. He brushed it back with his hand.

A look of panic crossed his face. "Do I still have it?" He felt about his waistcoat. "Don't tell me I've lost it."

"What are you talking about?" Mari asked.

He drew something out of his pocket. "This."

He dropped to his knees in the streaming water and soot, holding something out toward her.

Something that glinted with gold and glowed like fire.

"I'm an obstinate fool who can't see past his own nose," he said. "But I know one thing."

"Edgar, your poor knees. Get up off the paving stones."

Mari's heart thudded and her vision narrowed. Not too narrow, because it had to be wide enough for Edgar's broad, broad shoulders.

"*Mari-rhymes-with-starry*, you walked through my door and you broke all of my rules. You put me in my place. And then you made me love you. Wait." He closed his eyes for a moment. "This is coming out all wrong."

"Edgar . . ." Tears filled in her eyes.

"I love you, Mari. You give me hope. Hope that my life has meaning. That I'm not only living in opposition to some painful memory. You hang the stars in my sky. Without you, I won't be able to see my way in the dark."

"Ew," said Michel. "Romance."

"Hush," Adele told him. "Can't you see he's trying to ask her something?"

"You'd better ask her what you're going to ask her, Your Grace," called her father. "Because I'd like a nice hot glass of whiskey and honey."

"I'm trying to," said Edgar. "Now then, where was I?"

She wanted to hear him say the words again. "You were saying that you loved me," she prompted.

"You toppled my wrought iron walls like so much crumbling plaster. Thirty years from now, I'll feel the exact same way. I love you. Plain and simple. But can you love me?"

Mari smiled. "Edgar," she said, and she wondered at how steady her voice remained. "I'm a thoroughly practical person and I told myself I would never allow sentiment to muddle my thinking. But I'm thoroughly, impractically, impossibly in love with you. Now do please get up."

"Then you'll have me?" His eyes sparked with pleasure. "You'll have me, Mari?"

"Oh for Heaven's sake," she replied. "Of course I will."

"Hoorah!" cheered the children.

Edgar leapt to his feet and gathered Mari into his arms, sweeping her into a long, blissful kiss.

When he slipped the ring on her finger she saw that it was a ruby in a simple gold setting.

"My mother's ring," he whispered in her ear. "She wanted you to have it."

"You visited her?"

"Yes, and she told me not to come back until there was a wedding to plan."

"What's going on here?" asked Mr. Grafton, joining them and wiping grime and ashes from his face with a handkerchief.

"She'll have me," Edgar said, wonderingly.

Mr. Grafton chuckled. He clapped Edgar on the back. "Ambrose, it is, then."

Whatever that meant. Mari would have to ask him later.

"I'll finish with the engine," Mr. Grafton said. "You go home."

They all walked back together to the waiting carriage. Mari holding the twins' hands, and Edgar helping her father find his way in the dark.

This was her family.

Five lost souls who had found each other at last.

It was all she'd ever wanted.

Epilogue

Two months later

THE BELLS OF St. Mary-le-Bow rang out lustily on the wedding day of the Duke of Banksford and Miss Mari Lumley.

When the happy couple descended the stairs, the gathered crowd was treated to the sight of a duke who was everything a duke should be, but rarely ever was.

Tall, handsome, and utterly besotted with his new bride.

The way he gazed at her made the assembled ladies sigh with envy, and hope for a groom who might gaze at them like that one day.

The bride had unfashionable freckles and fiery auburn hair, but she was radiant in a gown from Madame Clotilde's of palest cerulean silk dotted with tiny pearls like stars strewn across a night sky. She had a very unconventional wedding bouquet, however.

It appeared to be some sort of tattered old wooden figurine of a . . . rabbit? At least it had very rabbitlike ears.

Some whispered that she was the duke's former governess. Others whispered that she had been born out of a long-buried scandal.

The bride and groom paid no attention to any of it, laughing and chatting with their families, the duke's two illegitimate children weaving joyfully in and out of the assemblage as everyone made their way to the waiting carriages.

"Let's go home, Mari," Edgar said, holding out his hand.

She placed her hand in his. "Yes, let's go home."

MARI'S HEART WAS so light and buoyant that the only thing tethering her to the earth was Edgar's hand on her knee, hidden by the tablecloth.

Their gathered friends and family were eating wedding cake, and arguing loudly about who had played the greatest role in bringing the two of them together.

"You owe me one hundred pounds," India said to Edgar. She held out her palm. "Pay up."

"What does she mean?" Mari asked Edgar.

"I placed a wager that he would be the first to marry," said India. "And when he would have thrown you out on your ear, I told him you were precisely what this household required."

"And then you brought me a lovely new wardrobe," said Mari. "Very clever."

"She did?" asked Edgar.

"It was all part of my grand plan," said India, smugly. "I knew that dusty old black gown had to go."

"On the contrary, it was my plan," said Mrs. Fairfield. She smiled at Mari. "I knew the moment I laid eyes on your rosy cheeks and bright smile that you would be the perfect mother for the children."

"You can't claim credit, either one of you," said the dowager sternly. "When Edgar came to visit me, I told him he was a fool, gave him my ring, and made him promise not to return until I had a wedding to plan."

"She did tell me I was a fool," said Edgar. He squeezed Mari's knee. "And I was. A big, stubborn fool."

She kissed his cheek. "You're my big, stubborn fool."

"Ew," said Michel.

"You'll have to get used to it, Michel, my boy," said Edgar. "Your mother and I will be kissing quite frequently."

True. They only stopped kissing to eat and sleep. Oh, and to be wedded, but that had included quite a long and thrilling kiss at the end.

"The kissing is all your fault," Adele told her brother. "Remember when I wrote their names together in the sand? You're the one who drew a heart around it."

Michel looked embarrassed. "I might have done."

"A secret romantic," teased Mari's father. "But it wasn't because of any heart drawn in the sand. I'm the one who orchestrated this union. I sent the lawyer searching for Mari and gave her a reason to come to London, setting the whole thing in motion."

"That you did," said Edgar. "And I thank you heartily."

"But I should still receive my one hundred pounds," insisted India, jokingly.

"Piffle," said the dowager. "Mr. Lumley and I should split the prize. Everything traces back to us, wouldn't you say so, Mr. Lumley?"

Mari's father turned his face toward the dowager. "Well said, Your Grace. You know, I remember meeting you many years ago, before my eyesight faded. I still remember the unusual amethyst of your eyes."

The hint of a smile crossed the dowager's face. "I remember meeting you, Mr. Lumley. I believe my son wished you were his father instead of . . ." Her voice trailed into silence.

"And now I have you for a father-in-law, Lumley," Edgar said. "I couldn't be happier."

Mr. Grafton stopped eating cake for a moment and lifted his fork in Edgar's direction. "I predicted you'd marry her, didn't I? You'll have to name your first-born Ambrose after me."

"Pardon?" Mari asked. "Ambrose?"

"Ambrose Percival," said Mr. Grafton.

"Edgar," remonstrated Mari.

Her husband looked sheepish. "Between India's extortion and your ridiculous name, Grafton, I'll be lucky to escape this meal with the shirt on my back."

Mari silently agreed. She'd been dying to rip off his shirt all day.

"Aren't you going to claim credit, Ravenwood?" asked India, glaring at the darkly handsome duke, whom Edgar had invited over his sister's strident protests. "I've never known you to miss a chance to soak up all of the attention in a room."

"For shame, Lady India," said Ravenwood. "You know this day belongs to your brother and his beautiful bride." He lifted his glass and drank a toast, giving Mari a rakish wink.

"I must admit, we did have something to do with it," Mari laughed.

Edgar's hand inched higher on her thigh. "Oh," she squeaked. "Ah . . . have you tried the grapes, Your Grace?" She thrust a platter of grapes at Ravenwood.

The conversation resumed around them, rising like a wave, swept along by playfulness and love.

"Do you think all families argue so vociferously?" Edgar whispered in her ear.

"I'm not sure. This is the only family I've ever known," she whispered back.

And it was the best family in the whole world.

"I have something to show you, my love." His wicked fingers traced a circle along her inner thigh. He tilted his head toward the door.

"Edgar," she whispered. "Stop that. We can't leave our own wedding breakfast."

"They won't even notice. Come."

Sure enough, everyone was too busy arguing and laughing to notice when Mari and Edgar slipped away. Or, if they did notice, they pretended not to.

"Where are you taking me?" asked Mari as Edgar led her away. "To your bed?"

"Impudent minx. Not my bed."

"Oh." Unexpected. "*Oh*. I understand. Not your bed. Perhaps . . . the library carpet? But we don't want to scandalize any footmen."

"Mari," said Edgar sternly. "Please take your mind out of the gutter for one moment."

Where were they going?

Through the entrance hall, down the gleaming marble stairs and out the front gate.

The street was peaceful. Delicate blossoms drifted down from the trees. A breeze ruffled the hem of her skirts.

Something had begun today. Their brave new life together.

Edgar made a spinning motion with his finger. He wanted her to . . . turn around?

"Really, Edgar? The front gate. With our entire family inside eating wedding cake. Wouldn't that be, well, illegal? There might be constables about, you know."

He rolled his eyes. Then he cupped her chin with his hand and lifted her head toward his gate.

"Oh," she exclaimed. "You changed the motto. *Amor Vincit Omnia*."

"Love conquers all." Edgar kissed her cheek. "It conquered me and I was a heavily armed fortress."

"I saw the cracks in your armor immediately."

"And you administered the tongue-lashing I deserved. Speaking of which, I think I might deserve another. I'm having very bad thoughts about a certain redheaded governess."

She stood on her tiptoes and placed her palm over his heart. "And I'm having very bad thoughts about a certain devilish duke. Very bad, indeed."

He kissed her then. Really kissed her. Until she was flushed and breathless with longing.

She loved him with all of her heart.

A love designed by trust, forged by desire, and tempered with respect.

A love built to last forever.

Continue reading for a sneak peek
at the next book in *LENORA BELL'S*
School for Dukes series

For the Duke's
Eyes Only

Coming October 2018!

"**D**O YOU EVEN know how to use a blade?" India curved her palm over the smooth hilt of the dagger she always carried by her side.

"This is all the weapon I've ever needed." Gold-brown eyes beneath thick dark brows lit with a wicked promise. His smoldering gaze nearly incinerated the gown from her body.

She drew a shaky breath. "Be serious, Ravenwood. Bedchamber eyes aren't going to defend you from a cutpurse in a foreign alleyway."

He shrugged. "You'll have to save me then. We're a team now. At least for the next fortnight."

"We're not a team." She shook her head vehemently. "We're a provisional partnership. A distrustful duo. You'll have to save yourself."

"I'll swagger around and carry a big knife. No one will challenge me."

"If you carry a knife and don't know how to use it, you'll end up facing its blade."

"Then teach me."

"What, here? In the middle of St. James's?"

"No." He grabbed her wrist and pulled her down a narrow side street between two buildings. "Here."

His gargantuan shadow loomed against the brick wall, dwarfing hers. He might have the advantage of size but she was quicker.

She'd always been quicker, even when they were children racing through the park that divided their family estates, discovering Roman ruins and making plans to travel the world together in search of adventure.

Plans that he had abandoned.

India gripped the hilt of her knife.

"Very well," she said. "You sense I'm a threat. You raise your knife."

He lifted an imaginary blade.

She lunged, letting instinct take control.

He parried, a split second too late. Her fist slashed across his forearm and then slid home against his flat abdomen.

"If this were a knife you'd be dead." She slid a finger along the taut flesh beneath his ribcage. "Never parry with your unprotected hand. Always stay behind your blade."

She lifted his giant hand, wrapping his fingers around a pretend dagger, positioning his wrist. "Maintain a firm grip on the hilt. Keep the knife edge up and out, pointed toward the threat."

His eyes glinted in the dim light. "You've always wanted to touch me, haven't you, Indy?" he said in a husky whisper.

She dropped his hand as if it were a pile of hot coals and stepped away from him. "In your dreams, Ravenwood."

In her dreams.

Sweat-soaked, sheet-twisting dreams. Forbidden dreams.

Dreams she'd been having since he'd been a reckless boy with a disarming grin, daring her to jump her horse over the highest fence.

Now he was even more reckless, breaking hearts

across three continents with his legendary charm. He'd broken her heart, once upon a time.

He was her enemy. Her rival.

And she did want to touch him.

Desperately.

A secret she would take to her grave.

"Shall we call a truce?" he asked. "I can be pleasant."

She didn't want him to be pleasant. She relied on him to be infuriatingly arrogant.

Pleasant was dangerous.

Change three letters and pleasant was pleasure.

"We don't have to be pleasant to one another," she said. "We follow the plan. Complete our mission. And return to our separate lives."

She sheathed her dagger and headed back to the crowded street.

He followed.

Why was she so aware of him, even when she couldn't see him?

She must hide her desires more carefully.

Build her walls higher.

She could never let him see how he disarmed her.

She would find the strength to ignore him. That's what she'd do. She'd completely ignore six feet of overly confident, sinfully good-looking duke. On board a ship. In close quarters. Overnight.

India groaned.

This was going to be her most dangerous adventure yet.

At Avon Books, we know your passion for romance—once you finish one of our novels, you find yourself wanting more.

May we tempt you with . . .

- **Excerpts** from our upcoming releases.

- Entertaining **extras**, including authors' personal photo albums and book lists.

- Behind-the-scenes **scoop** on your favorite characters and series.

- **Sweepstakes** for the chance to win free books, romantic getaways, and other fun prizes.

- Writing **tips** from our authors and editors.

- **Blog** with our authors and find out why they love to write romance.

- **Exclusive content** that's not contained within the pages of our novels.

Join us at
www.avonbooks.com

An Imprint of HarperCollins*Publishers*
www.avonromance.com

Give in to your Impulses!

These unforgettable stories only take a second to buy and give you hours of reading pleasure!

Go to *www.AvonImpulse.com* and see what we have to offer.

Available wherever e-books are sold.

AVONIMPULSE

IMP 0811